Dibt

10 Fr

Brigh

CW01066973

This edition 2000

Set in Times New Roman

Printed and bound in Great Britain

Cover by David O'Connor

A DEAL WITH GOD
By
JUDE REDMOND

(The man who sold his soul to God but didn't read the small print!)

This book is about communication and the lack of it in today's society. It has a pace that burns from the page and is constantly unpredictable, amusing and contentious. This is a book to make YOU *think*!

Jude Redmond is a man fighting with life. His youth would best be described as playing Poker with Fate and he has just lost the penultimate hand and his mobility. Despite this he manages to console, advise and entertain a succession of friends and the lovely Magdalene with whom you *will* fall in love. Meanwhile he is slowly killing himself and pondering a quicker method. Life is not easy for a bankrupt, dipsomaniac cripple.

This is an nine day roller-coaster through the secret world of quasi-intellectual pubs and the inner thoughts of the dispossessed.

Suddenly a solution to all of his problems presents itself to the hapless Jude. A deal with God? Is this the last hand with Fate?

To Uncle Bill, the Nightingale and anyone who cares enough to keep reading.

If you are not, how on earth could you know?

Saturday 5th June: **PRIDE**

I hate hangovers. To wake up at five in the morning, people who say 5 a.m. simply trivialise the horror - they know nothing of insomnia - with every single part of my body screaming in pain is no way to start a feasibly enjoyable day. But as they say: 'Self inflicted - *no-ho-ho* sympathy'. And it is my fault. For some reason that is inextricably linked with beer-fuelled quasi-logic I occasionally think that brandy, or whisky, or vodka or whatever over 40% will be as good a painkiller as cannabis. It is fine on the night but rather unbearable the next day. As Confucius say: 'Best thing for hangover - bottle of whisky night before!'

The worst element of waking at that ungodly hour is the complete lack of any chance of getting back to sleep so I took the only sensible course of action and rolled a sleeping draught. Heaven!

Seven-fifteen did not seem quite so bad relatively speaking. If space and time are relative why didn't they come to my birthday party? Saturday, Saturday, Saturday. What does one do until opening? Choices are the worthy and informative Open University or the mindless kiddies offerings? I settled on the 'whoop, hey, don't ya know on a self-absorbed tip' option and a bottle of something rouge to ease the pain. Opening eventually crawled into existence at a lamentable rate. Thank God I do not wear a watch anymore.

Got to the Carpenter's Rest at ten minutes past desperation hour to discover Peter was suffering a similar fate to my five in the morning state. Only he can make monosyllables sound utterly disinterested.

Matthew turned up for a drink and chat or rather a moan, at least he has a foreseeable end to his worries. Bart also dropped in to the emotional surgery showing all the signs of impatience innate to the hyperactive. People with boundless energy can be really annoying at times.

Peter kindly sorted out a taxi back to the Hunting Lodge where I was just lighting-up the first of the evening's knockout drops when Mags rang. Her life is such a roller-coaster but at least she seems happier now. Sleep and nightmares came eventually.

* * *

- Hello Peter. How's you?
- Oh bugger off!
- As good as that? Lots of fun last night?
- How on *earth* would I know?
- Serves you right. Would you like a silly joke to cheer you up?
- Do I have the slightest choice? Oh go on then don't pout.
- What is the difference between Ofsted and plastic surgeons?
- I'm quivering with anticipation.
- Plastic surgeons tuck your features up!
- Oh God it's going to be one of those days I can feel it in me water. I suppose you want serving? What can I get you?
- Pissed please.

1

- Oh so *droll* at such a painful hour. I do wish you wouldn't attempt humour when I'm walking wounded.
- It is the best time to score untold petty points.
- Which that reminds me how are the crochet classes going?
- Steadily down the drain like most things.
- Oh dear, how sad, never mind.
- Where would I be without you to cheer me up Peter?
- Another pub darling. Now if you'll excuse me I have reputable customers to attend to so cough up two quid and stop whittering so.

* * *

- Hello mate.
- Matthew dear heart how *are* you?
- I do wish you wouldn't use camp humour.
- Sorry mate. Do you want a pint? Guinness please Peter. Anyhow how are things?
- Bloody awful! What's that on your neck, a spot?
- No it is the foundations for a new nose. The old one was severely damaged through cocaine abuse so I have traded it in for a new one. Granted the location leaves a lot to be desired but it should be pleasantly aquiline. Do you want a joke to cheer you up? There is no need to look like that. There are no such things as problems there are only situations and situations have solutions.
- Oh yeah? Where did that bollocks come from?
- Some sales training manual from my dim and distant past. But seriously there is no correlation at all between the size and complexity of a problem and the difficulty of a solution I promise you. Have you ever heard of the N.A.S.A. pen?
- No?
- In the eighties when the Space Shuttle first started doing major experiments with ants and doughnuts to help with world peace and so on but they had all sorts of trouble finding a pen that would work in zero gravity since there was nothing to get the ink moving don't you know. So like Americans do they spent about five million quid or dollars or whatever developing a pen that would work in those floaty conditions because it had a little pump that made the ink move.
- Yeah right.
- Honestly my friend you can buy them for an extortionate amount, they are made in Newhaven by Lady Penelope or whatever they are called but anyway N.A.S.A. spent all this money on a pen with a pump and the Russians faced with the same problem used pencils!
- No!
- Absolutely true. Anyway my friend what is up as they say?
- Well bloody Jess is being an absolute nightmare. She just won't accept it's over and she's found out about Sally.
- Oops a buttercup.
- To put it mildly. She's sending us both vicious letters and e-mails not to mention the 'phone calls it's just pure spite, malice and wounded pride. How on earth did I marry that, *bitch*?
- You both said: 'I do' at an inappropriate moment! But how is Sally taking all of this?
- I don't know really but she seems all right. I just don't know how I got into this mess.
- Easy mate you were lied to. Thanks Peter. A toast Matthew, here's to Ollie God rest his soul.

2

- To Ollie?
- The late and great Oliver Reed.
- Oh right yeah, to Ollie. What do you mean lied to?
- Well when we first met Jess she seemed absolutely delightful. Not the most beautiful specimen of the female form but looks certainly are not everything by any means. She seemed charming, funny, intelligent and above all caring and she stayed that way for the two years or so you were together before the wedding, yes?
- Well yeah.
- And then as soon as we were on her home turf in California she completely changed and has stayed that way since, instant cow just add matrimony. She *lied* to you. I remember the way she treated you and me just before the ceremony which is why I offered you that ticket to Paris.
- We had a good time in that bar didn't we?
- Oh yes! What did that wonderful barmaid say when you told her you were getting married in three hours?
- 'First time honey?'
- They were funny. But when those clouds came roaring over the garden as you two were exchanging vows my stomach was churning. It just does not rain in California in May! I felt like Gregory Peck in the Omen. And what's happened since? She has just made your life impossible. I have seen it mate and I know the person that you are Matthew, Jess has nothing to offer but misery. You have nothing to feel guilty about because she was inherently dishonest about her own personality. Lying to people you claim to love is simply inexcusable. Sally on the other hand is wonderful and loves you. Yes technically it is adultery but actually you have been faithful to both have you not?
- Slight overlap.
- So shock me sideways, you are human.
- But everyone was taken in by her?
- We all were but that is the thing with Americans. They are not the most popular breed in the world due to their understanding and caring foreign policy, in fact if you go travelling around the world it's the worst nationality to have because so many people hate Americans. It is normally all right to be English thank God but do you know the best nationality to be around the world?
- No?
- New Zealand. Why? Because they have never been nasty to anyone. No-one in the world has a grudge against New Zealanders because they are all lovely and you can pretend to be one because no-one is absolutely sure what the accent is supposed to sound like.
- What about Australians?
- No because they supported Indonesia with the atrocities in East Timor plus they can get violent without too much provocation. But back to Americans. They are generally despised but when you find an intelligent and educated one they are highly pleasant and great company and that is what we all thought Jess was like. You cannot blame yourself for being taken in like that.
- You reckon that Americans are despised do you? Why's that exactly?
- An unsubtle combination of ignorance and pride unfortunately for the rest of the world.
- What do you mean?
- Well you must have heard at least eleventy-three different stories of archetypal American ignorance?
- Like?

3

- Well something that actually happened to me. Years ago I was working in a shop which sold Union Flags that were about four foot long by two foot across in genuine, highest-quality polyester. One day an American couple came in wearing his and her Hawaiian shirts, Nikons round necks, stupid shorts and socks all covering shiveringly obese bodies. The chap said 'Hey son, we love your flags!' 'Thank you guv'nor.' said I, 'That's eight nikker to you squire.' The owners wanted us to talk like the Artful Dodger for some reason. The American replied: 'What colours do they come in?'
- No!
- Absolutely.
- What did you say?
- I was tempted to say: 'Go somewhere highly unpleasant and suffer an eternity of misery you disgustingly ignorant Johnny Foreigner!' but I merely retorted: 'We have some round the back in cerise, vermilion and magnolia but they are not popular and rather expensive being made from Guatemalan yak's whiskers!'
- What did he say?
- 'No thanks son we'll stick with the regular one.'
- He wasn't embarrassed?
- Not a hint I am afraid to say. One can only assume it is true that Americans have no sense of irony. Another classic was overheard on an aeroplane by a friend of mine who used to be a stewardess. They were flying over Windsor on a lovely clear day when Ester heard a brash and unmistakable voice saying: 'Isn't it clever of them to build the Castle by the freeway!'
- You are joking?
- Sadly no.
- Any more?
- Oh loads, positively tower blocks full. But my favourite was apparently a radio conversation at sea. Imagine if you will a proud American voice and an English counterpart sounding not unlike Charles Hawtrey: 'This is the U.S.S Intrepid. We are currently on a collision course. Strongly advise you alter your course twenty degrees east. Over.' 'Oh hello Intrepid that's a lovely name, I'll bet you *are* brave. We suggest you alter your course twenty degrees west. *Lovely* chatting with you. Over.' 'You obviously do not understand. This is the U.S.S Intrepid, a battleship of the United States Navy. We are telling you to alter *your* course twenty degrees east. Over.' 'Oh hello again Intrepid. This is Easter Island Lighthouse, your call!'
- Classic.
- Honestly mate there are so many stories along those lines it is ridiculous. It really makes me wonder why Americans are so proud of themselves as they do not have the slightest reason. The good ol' U.S. of A. is the home of meaningless pride, ignorance, intolerance, prejudice, ill manners, sloth, gratuitous violence, outrageous sexism, obesity, atrocious television that infects the world and almost a complete lack of anything of value culturally. Can you think of anything good that has come from the States as they are appropriately named?
- Um...
- Peter? Can you think of anything even vaguely forgivable that originated in America?
- James Dean was very dishy.
- Why do I bother trying to wrestle a modicum of sense from you?
- No-one wants you to.
- Thank you for your input.
- Pleasure. Ciao.
- Why are you so angry at Americans Jude? You were charming when we were over there.

4

- Well I am English am I not? I cannot sink to their level. I don't know it's just that everything that I despise about our modern world as we plough into the next alleged millennium seems to originate in the U.S.
- You're not going to get all socialist on me again are you?
- Not right now, no but it does intrigue me why they are all so proud of themselves. Take one of the most insidious scandals of the modern world, prejudice or pre judging.
- Obviously.
- Take a subsection like the odious practice of racism, this ridiculous idea that if you have two people of different skin colours one will be inferior in some way to the other. World champions and gold medallists every time are the Americans. At the time of the American Civil War there was a world-wide slave trade including Britain but as public support for human rights increased the majority of the world said: 'Oh all right then!' and stopped the practice. In America they had a war over the issue because thousands of God-fearing southern Christians wanted to keep their right to have slaves: 'Cos they're niggers'. And the U.S. is arguably still the most racist country in the world. Different races are still ghettoised and subjugated all the time and otherwise vaguely sentient human beings still honestly think that if you are anything other than Caucasian you must be a threat to democracy and 'the American way'.
- How do you know that?
- At the last count there were *five thousand* web sites in the U.S. dedicated to racist propaganda and the Ku Klux Klan have recently appointed a publicity expert to increase enrolment and exposure going into the next century. In a recent poll of young Americans in other words those that have been brought up since the Sixties, over fifty per cent agreed with racial segregation. How on *earth* can anyone be proud of living in a country where that level of gratuitous hatred is indirectly endorsed by a democratic government? Who *are* these people? It is quite disgusting!
- Sure but we have the B.N.P. over here and they're just as bad.
- Absolutely but where do that particular group of inadequates look for inspiration? Racists are the wasps of humanity since they do nothing for society or the environment they just occasionally indulge in acts of gratuitous violence, plus they both annoy the hell out of you in beer gardens. Funnily enough there was an article recently about some foul-minded member of the B.N.P. who is over the pond raising money for his lamentable party and they had a photograph of him looking 'hard' in front of a Union Flag. The only problem was the flag was upside down!
- Really?
- Yes pathetic is it not? It just shows how worrying proud and ignorant these people are. Funnily enough Jamie told me a great story just t'other day.
- How's he doing?
- Surviving and smiling as ever.
- Oh good, I'll have to give him a call at some point.
- Do that. Anyway he got a call from a fellow broker along the lines of: 'I've got this job but I simply cannot place it.' 'Tell me more' said Jamie, never one to miss an opportunity. 'Well it's five million A5 flyers, full colour, two sides and glossy'.
- Five million?
- Oh yes. So Jamie said: 'Keep talking.' 'There's just one problem, it's for the B.N.P.' 'Forget it!' he replied and quite rightly I feel.
- Good of him.

- Absolutely! A lot of people put him down but I have never known Jamie to be anything other than decent and honest. Back to the story. He turned the job down not surprising his mate in the slightest and about a week later his mate called again but sounding a good deal more chipper: 'I've managed to place that job.' he said, 'Who with?' enquired Jamie. 'A Pakistani firm near Farringdon!'
- No!
- Indeed. Marvellous is it not. Take their money that's what I say. Yes racism exists to some extent everywhere but its spiritual home as it were is America. They harp on about 'white supremacy', 'white pride' and 'white purity' but what is so pure, admirable or supreme about whites? Let us have a look at the twentieth century Caucasian hall of fame. There is Hitler, Stalin and other political extremists, every serial-killer and the majority of mass-murderers, all the exploitative corporations, football hooligans and of course paedophiles. Whites have given to the world; concentration camps, ethnic cleansing, Third World debt, exploitative capitalism, terrorising communism, global warming, ozone depletion, conspicuous consumption, eating disorders...
- I get the point.
- But who do these pure white types actually hate? Negroes who have given us gospel music, soul music, rhythm and blues and so on plus being the world's greatest athletes, the Jews who have a wonderful family-orientated culture, beautiful soulful music of their own, are a lesson in bravery in the face of aggression and of course Jesus...
- Where is this going?
- The point I am clumsily making is that the objects of hatred for these fascist groups are peoples that have given us all sorts of enormous cultural benefits for some time. For example all modern popular music has its roots in black, gay or Jewish culture. What do white people do to other cultures? We steal their land and resources, tell them that they are poor because they do not have any dollars and then subjugate and abuse them as an ongoing commercial venture. All of which does not even touch upon the abuse of children by western perverts that is rife in many developing countries. If that is purity, supremacy and something to be proud of I shall walk on water.
- You can't even walk.
- My point entirely Watson.
- Come on they're not that bad, in fact you're being pretty bigoted yourself.
- I know, ironic is it not? However what is the difference between stereotyping and prejudice? As you pointed out I was perfectly civil when we were in California and James' Texan wife is quite lovely. Stereotyping is having pre-formed opinions about groups of individuals but bigots are people that are not open-minded enough to give others a chance and alter their opinions when proven wrong. Stereotyping is based on experience and bigotry is based on uncompromising ignorance. I foolishly pander to stereotypes like most even though there is no psychological evidence to support the notion. Racists just hate for the sake of it normally due to misplaced pride and ignorance.
- That's a cop-out and you know it!
- Quite possibly but it makes sense to me. When I was in Spain a couple of years ago, you remember when I disappeared for a couple of weeks.
- When the husband found out?
- They were separated but that is a separate story. While I was over there I was introduced to this couple in a boozer. They were both in their forties and seemed very pleasant, he was a bluff rugby-player type called Jacob and she was a very attractive blonde lady called Sam. I

was just about to shake hands when whoever it was introducing us said they were from South Africa and you know how white South Africans were perceived circa 1993?
- Not the world's most popular race! So what did you do?
- I dropped my prejudices, talked to them for a while and got on very well for the simple reason that they were terrific people. That is my whole big thing point, if you treat everyone with an open mind then more often than not you will be pleasantly surprised. I have been lucky enough to meet people from all over the world including some very interesting Russians and it always seems to me that people are never as one would expect them to be. Humanity always seems to be in a state of grace under pressure no matter what politicians or the media say.
-You sanctimonious muppet, you're saying 'be tolerant' and then slagging off millions of Americans that you've never even met!
- Quite possibly but I do not *like* hating people, in fact I am talking more about American culture than individuals. We did meet some lovely people over there even those rednecks that we drank under the table were great fun. What were there names? Bobby-Mutt and Billy-Spike or something wasn't it?
- Something like that. And the barmaid's face when we walked back in that evening was quite a picture.
- I have never seen a chin hit a bar before. No it is not so much the people as the pervading attitudes which are spoon-fed to them through their politicians and media. That is the thrust of angst with them. If their dodgy attitudes were restricted to their own country that would be one thing but their films, television, computer games, fast alleged food and so on pervade the whole world in such an insidious manner. There are two words that are understood everywhere in the world.
- Which are?
- Coca-Cola which as we all know is *so* good for you. Their dubious influence is everywhere like a global rash. Because of America we think that Communism is evil do we not?
- Well isn't it?
- I do not know enough about it but I do think that Russia's actions in the Cold War have only been interpreted from America's perspective. The Russians fought and lost millions in the First World War before having a rather nasty revolution just as the Americans finally turned up in Europe to take all of the glory. Russia then tried to build a new political system based on equality which is very laudable. Unfortunately Stalin was a complete hatechild and killed millions himself which was not so good. At the start of the Second World War the Russians were allied to Hitler even though they were politically poles apart, if you'll excuse the pun, mainly to keep out of trouble whilst they were trying to bring order to their enormous country. Then Hitler showed what a hatechild he was and invaded the U.S.S.R. coming within spitting distance of Moscow. Do not forget that something like twenty-seven million Russians died in the Second World War as opposed to two million Americans, probably of fright, two and a half million Britons and so on. By the end of the war the Russians had arguably suffered more than any other country and what was the situation at that point?
- Go on?
- America, a country with a completely different ideology was all over Europe and acting aggressively with atomic weapons to back them up. Remember Russian troops have never been anywhere near America except Siberia which does not really count but American troops have been on Russia's doorstep since 1945. And they still are. Is it so surprising that Russia created a buffer-zone to try and protect themselves when they could not cope with more conflict from aggressors?
- Well yes, but come on.

- I am not saying that they are perfect but there are two sides to a cliché. Take the situation in Kosovo. You know as soon as you hear the words 'humanitarian crisis' and 'urgent intervention' someone in Washington has either been caught with his pants down, having economic problems or both and innocent people are going to be bombed from a safe distance. There was a highly pertinent comment the other day from what is he called, Pally Flirting or whatever but he pointed out that it was somewhat ironic that the Americans are bringing in their Apache helicopters named of course after the race that *they* ethnically cleansed a couple of hundred years ago.
- Fair point.
- Honestly who is the more trustworthy, Russia or America? Anyway what *are* the those helicopters there for?
- The war effort?
- God's whiskers no! The thing is you see that although the Apaches are the most fearsome gun and rocket ships in the world as each one could destroy a decent sized village in seconds, they are not going to use them. Why? Because their precious pilots might be shot down and we simply *cannot* have that! It is similar to an American wrestler refusing to baby-sit in case he gets beaten-up! So to ensure that none of those oh-so lovely seals and walruses or whatever they call themselves gets a scratch, they will continue bombing hospitals, bridges, media centres, embassies and innocent people generally. Quite frankly they will kill any number of foreigners to stop one American dying. The irony is that when these useless sea lions or whatever get home I would wager that they all receive medals for their 'conspicuous bravery'.
- You're just becoming a cynical old git.
- Au contraire my good sir, I am not cynical merely observant.
- At least the Americans were involved in Kosovo.
- Oh indeed, their being there was an absolute boon. You know that there was that debacle at Pristina Airport when the Russians nipped in sharpish?
- Yeah?
- Well that was because the U.S. troops were not ready and Washington was insisting that their soldiers were the first ones in so that they could have nice propaganda pictures for their glossy magazines back home to 'oh and ah' over whilst eating 'mama's apple pie'. A comment at the time was: 'Will the Americans ever be on time for anything in Europe?' Then when the Russians got there first Washington ordered British and French troops to raid the place.
- You're joking? So what happened?
- The British commander said: 'No!' I think his exact words were: 'I'm not starting World War Three for you.' and thank God he did refuse. The whole situation was outrageous but absolutely typical of America. There was a story that in 1917 some American troops were in a cafe in London and one of them complained his coffee was cold. 'Well it's been waiting for you for three years!' quipped the waitress.
- They're good at quipping, waitresses aren't they?
- Better than we are at tipping at any rate.
- Oh very good. But what I haven't heard is why the Americans were a day late in the first place.
- I don't actually know. Quite possibly because they were not allowed anywhere near the place until it was safe. They are cowardly people, walking around with their guns claiming to be: 'The land of the free unless we don't like you then we'll kill you'. How can anyone be proud of being allowed to walk the streets armed when thousands die every year because it is such a *stupid* law. Apparently their highly-flawed constitution is far more important than the

hundreds of thousands of families and friends who have loved ones meaninglessly slaughtered every year. But of course you are not allowed to smoke in public because it is dangerous! The fact is that not only are their gung-ho attitudes messing up their own country but also they are trying to ruin the rest of the world as well. Is it just me or is this out and out madness?
- It's probably just you.
- You might be right. Too many poisons floating around my brain cells but I shall tell you a funny story about the last time I was visiting James out there.
- Where's he based?
- Dallas, Texas, in a suburb called Denton.
- How does he cope?
- Apparently it took him two years to become inured to it although all his friends are academics and armchair revolutionaries, quoting Karouac and being vaguely amusing so that it is not too bad for him. I do worry though because I was there for only ten days and there were *three* shootings, one in the car park of a boozer that we drank in every day, one in a restaurant that we were going to eat in that evening and a drive-by jobbie just down the road. It is incredible that we can become complacent and unshocked by something so horrific as a person pulling up somewhere in their car and killing complete strangers indiscriminently is it not? When I say there were three shootings seven people actually died.
- Really?
- Honestly it is horrendous over there my friend. Anyway I had meet this glorious creature called Martha who was one of James' students. We were in the boozer one night when she saw this chap she knew who was a clerk in the Marines and an absolute spooning muffin! He was about five feet six, had on the silly uniform with the tie tucked into his underwear or whatever, the *really silly* haircut and he was chuntering on about how magnificent the Marines had been in the Gulf War, this was just after. He was getting right up our noses so I decided it was high time for something of a wind-up. You know that I am most partial to a spot of fool-baiting?
- I can remember a couple of occasions.
- It is a very popular spectator sport. I quietly said to Martha: 'Next time he mentions the Gulf War tell him to ask me about it.' and she agreed to do so. Lo and behold within about two minutes he was on the topic again: 'Brave marines, risking life and sandwiches blah, blah blah.' and Martha said: 'Well if you want to know about the Gulf ask Jude.' So this excus for an action man looks at me goggle-eyed and asks: 'Were you in the Gulf sir?' with respect dawning in his beady littles.
- What did you say?
- 'Martha I told you that I do not like to talk about it!'
- No?
- Oh yes it was a classic wind-up.
- So what happened?
- Well you know those scars on my leg could look like bullet holes?
- Yeah?
- I convinced this bloke that I was in the British Forces in the Gulf and was the only survivor, though wounded, of a 'friendly fire' incident in which I lost all my friends. By the end of my tirade I had him by the throat and was yelling: 'The only reason I'm in your junkyard of a country is because my sister-in-law wanted to show me that not all Americans are trigger-happy f***-ups who don't know their arses from their elbows!'
- Oh lovely. What did he say?
- Well other than apologising for everything American including Mickey Mouse and the Waltons for some reason, it transpired that his brother ran a bar and restaurant and I did not

pay for a drink or meal for the remainder of my stay. I suppose I should feel a modicum of guilt but as I recall it was that evening that the lovely Mary invited me into her black silk-sheeted, four poster bed.

- Worth it then?
- Oh yes she was a glorious lady. I wanted to bring her back: 'Let me take you away from all of this?' I pleaded. 'Bugger off, I've got a career!' she replied.
- What did she do?
- She was on the ladder in a record company. Fair enough really.
- Easy come easy go, huh?
- Excuse me but I refuse to be tarred with your 'women are objects' brush thank you very much. I respect birds me!
- You do have a very female attitude towards relationships actually. It's probably why you get hurt all the time you muppet.
- Ah well it is all part of life's rich tapestry. Who was it that said: 'If life is a tapestry we are standing on the wrong side'?
- I don't know. Where do you get these quotes from?
- Cynic's Weekly! This last edition came with a Nostrodamus end-of-the-world countdown calendar.
- You're joking?
- Yes.
- Anyway you were slagging off Americans. You must have something to say about the Gulf War?
- Where do you start? Ironically it was Apache helicopters that were responsible for the 'friendly fire' incidents there.
- How many were killed, I know they killed more British than Iraqis?
- Officially sixteen actually over eighty. I was lucky enough to meet a journalist who was out there and he had some interesting stories to tell but the thing that stuck in my mind was the difference between the American and British camps. According to him the atmosphere amongst the Britons was one of quiet   professionalism with the troops cleaning their weapons and practising drills whilst in the American camp everyone was highly nervous and writing letters to 'mom'. He reckoned that 'friendly fire' was down to inexperience and panic essentially.
- Good God!
- Calling those helicopters Apaches is actually rather sick when one thinks about it. It was a genuine holocaust that was perpetrated against the Indians or Indigenous Americans or whatever patronising phrase is applied to them these days. Did you know that they only comprise one per cent of the population of their own lands now? The tragedy is that they were a beautiful culture. Did you know that many of the tribes had four sexualities?
- Four?
- Indeed. There were men who were hunter-gathers, women who cooked and reared the kids, women who were hunter-gatherers and men who cooked and reared the kids with all of them enjoying equal respect within the tribe. Their culture of equality and sharing was the complete antithesis of the God-fearing, invading greedy settlers and that is why they were all but wiped out. The North American Indians were the first to find out how American culture works, through dishonesty and violence. It is still the American way today. What is his name? When Clint Clingon gets into trouble what does he do? He lies and bombs somewhere! It is that attitude and example that everyone else follows like sheep. I cannot believe they are still making films glorifying that disgusting period in their developing history. They have even got

10

a western now where a Negro is pretending to be a cowboy and 'shootin' up the town'. It is no wonder that inner-city minorities are arming themselves and acting like 'good 'ol gunslingers' since that is all the culture that is available to them. 'If in doubt be violent with the biggest weapon you can find, 'cos that's what grandpappy did!' If this world is destroyed by bombs you can be sure that directly or indirectly America will be to blame. God bless America, proud of the proud. There was me trying to cheer you up and you are looking all depressed again, I am sorry my friend.
- That's O.K. I'm feeling much calmer actually although I do think you're talking a load of bollocks. How's the leg?
- Don't ask but may I give you one last thought?
- Go on then.
- In my diatribe against the U.S. I did not even need to mention Vietnam, the Mafia and modern gangs, assassinations or Watergate. How many gates are there now? The really sad thing is that this is a modern phenomena. Have you ever seen a film called Twelve o' Clock High?
- No.
- If you get a chance to watch it do so because it is how young Americans used to be.
- Yeah, yeah very thought provoking, but still a load of bollocks. I'd better be going. Thanks for the drink.
- My pleasure. Don't worry about Jess because it will stop when the divorce comes through and don't neglect Sally because she is suffering just as much as you.
- You think so?
- Absolutely. You are both getting dodgy calls are you not? Get through it together, that is what love is all about. See you soon my friend.
- See you Jude.

* * *

- I see you've chased off another of your disciples with your ranting and raving. Honestly Jude you should stick to telling jokes and get off the soapbox once in a while.
- Yes Peter I know I talk too much, you do not need to tell me.
- Personally I think you need telling every day and it should be your personal mantra in front of the mirror every morning: 'My name is Jude and should talk less.'
- I hate mirrors.
- I'm not surprised. Now let *me* tell *you* a joke.
- Any danger of it being amusing or even funny?
- More chance or danger if you must than the majority of yours dear heart.
- How exciting, please do tell.
- Three nuns go to the zoo one day just for the hell of it.
- In jokeland.
- Oh do shut up for once. So they are wandering around and eventually come to the gorilla's cage where they were looking admiringly at the vision of brute strength when suddenly a thick, hairy arm reaches through the bars, grabs one of the nuns, pulls her into the cage, throws her over one broad, hirsute shoulder and repairs to his little hut at the back of the cage. The other two nuns look on helplessly as their sister's distressed cries echo from the hut: 'Oh you beast, you brute, you could have shaved!' et cetera. After a few minutes the nun comes staggering from the hut, torn, bloodied and generally dishevelled and falls into the other two's arms. They immediately rush her to the nearest hospital. In hospital she's recovering in bed and the other

11

two are at her bedside holding her hand and so on like you do. Suddenly she says: 'Sisters you have to promise one thing.' 'Of course sister' they reply. 'You must promise never to mention this, incident, ever again. Not to me nor anyone else.' 'Of course sister.' they agree at once. Anyway she makes a full recovery and the years roll past, time moves on. Years later the gorilla nun, as it were, is on her death bed and what a coincidence the two other nuns are at her bedside comforting her when one of them says: 'I know we promised never to mention the gorilla again sister but could we ask you just one question?' The dying nun looks at them through tired eyes and says: 'Very well, one question.' 'Did it hurt?' they ask. 'Hurt? Hurt?' she says, 'He never wrote! He never rang!'
- Very good. I like that.
- Oh I'm so pleased. I suppose you want another pint?
- Yes please and one yourself.
- I would imagine that I'm now sufficiently recovered thank you. Yes, yes I'll be right with you. Honestly anyone would think this was a service industry!

* * *

- Hello Jude you old lush, I thought I'd find you in here. What's happened to your mobile and where's the paper been? What have you done to your leg?
- Ah 'tis young Bartholomew minus due respect for elders and betters. I do not use the mobile any more, the paper has folded, if you'll pardon the pun and I have not done anything to my leg! The blame for that rests squarely on a grey Sierra and a small and rather hard area of London Road.
- Oh shit! Do you want a pint?
- Do one-legged ducks swim in circles?
- I don't know, probably not. What would you care for?
- Lots of things, wounded squirrels for example. Don't look at me like that, a Harveys please dear chap.
- And I'll have a Stella thanks. What's that on your neck, a spot?
- No it is the foundations for a new Adam's apple. The old one was becoming worn out through excessive drinking so I have traded it in for a new one.
- Sure. It's a bloody great spot. Cheers mate.
- A toast I feel, to Jeff.
- Jeff who?
- The late and great Jeffrey Bernard.
- Yeah whatever. So what's happened to the paper?
- I though it was going well until Thaddeo let me in on the little secret that we are two grand in the red and could not afford to print the issue that was due out about a month ago now. So I started brokering a deal with Broadside Publishing to take over the financial side of things as they have the infrastructure and we would keep editorial control.
- That's what's his name, Sam Jones isn't it?
- The very same and he was going for it too, bending over backwards with chequebook he was. Then half way through sorting it all out my leg gave up and I cannot be chasing around dealing with everything. The other three are just moping around and saying they don't trust him.
- You're joking!
- No. It's all been very frustrating but there you go. I would have got away with it if it wasn't for those pesky kids!

- So what's wrong with the leg?
- You know I had that accident nine years ago?
- Well yeah but you were fine a couple of months ago.
- I know. I have a degenerative condition from the accident which is now a lot more obvious than it used to be. Anyway I am starting to bore myself so I must ask you to think of a more interesting topic of conversation.
- O.K. That's an interesting lighter, where did you get it?
- A delightful bistro the last time I went to France on a shopping mission. This delightful chap owns a small cafe on the waterfront in Dieppe but always stocks large numbers of cigarettes at very reasonable prices. Whilst one sips a Stella or similar he is happy to fill a bag with my rather large nicotine shopping list whilst throwing in lighters, matches and anything else he feels might be appropriate. He has a sort of shovelling motion that is obviously difficult to stop once in operation.
- Sounds great.
- It's marvellous. Cafes that sell cheap cigarettes when one has spent hours fruitlessly searching for a hypermarche with a tabac are something of a boon.
- He just gives away lighters?
- He gives away boxes of lighters! Actually Grasshopper now you are part of the heady world of media that lighter is an interesting lesson in marketing.
- What?
- Absolutely it is how one markets British goods abroad. Firstly take that look of incredulity from your face you cheeky jumping insect type thing. To start with it is bright yellow which stands out and a good basic colour. Other colours are red, excellent as red and yellow are perfect marketing colours, just ask any clown and a hint of black to finish it off. Superb colour scheme. Now what is it promoting? British cigarettes so you have your various B and H letters floating artistically around with, wait for it, a London taxi in the middle! Fantastic! But the masterstroke that *must* have had the creative department fretting for weeks; what does B and H stand for? Of course, British and Humour. Isn't that lovely! I would be quite happy with that for an epithet. 'I shall have eleventy-three cartons monsieur.'
- All this from one lighter.
- Do not underestimate the power of advertising and marketing because it does work. But that is not all. On t'other side we have the name of the cafe-tabac, 'Les Voyageurs'. Wonderful is it not? It just rolls of the tongue like duty-free scotch when one has overdone it somewhat.
- Lovely thought!
- Not an image to dwell upon is it, sorry. But anyway 'Les Voyageurs' sounds great even though it is only the French for 'The Travellers' which would be pretty lame would it not? Being France of course there would be a small crowd gathered round as he changed the sign saying: 'Rene, I am so glad zat he is changeing the nom of his petite cafe. 'The Travellers' was just trop englaise for ze tourists tu sais? En suite, petite pois, encore encore! 'Les Voyageurs' is much, ow you say, better for ze trade.' Then he would go into the cafe, order a coffee and cognac and lean against the bar stroking his moustache. The French know how to live in a civilised fashion. But I am bibbelling disastrously. How is the new job my friend?
- It's all right. Very parochial as you said it would be but what are *you* going to do now?
- Retire gracelessly dear heart.
- You're not going to be a journo any more? You are an ex-gumshoe?
- How could I carry on? To write features you need to interview people and to interview people you need to be able to move around. I cannot move anymore so no more journalism for me. Sorry mate but I will not be able to help you out as promised

- Don't worry about it.
- Oh but I do, I do I do. I am racked with remorse and stricken with grief. Je suis desole!
- Oh shut up! But what are you going to do?
- I think I shall become an alcoholic.
- What do you mean become?
- Thank you *so* much, I shall rush to you for a character reference. I shall need one because I have seen a niche in the market for after dinner parties games if that makes sense.
- What?
- You must have been to a poncey dinner party where everyone is being very proud of not much and the conversation flags somewhat? Of course you have. I am compiling a list of games to play in these circumstances. For example, prequels.
- Prequels?
- Prequels. You think up the name of the film before the *sequel* that became famous. Par example, the Vaguely Competent Seven became?
- The Magnificent Seven.
- Easy is it not? All right then try this, The Italian Interview?
- The Italian Job.
- You've got it! It is great fun. Dr. Maybe is another favourite as is The Eagle Has Taken Off and The Self Assemble Kits of Navarone.
- Oh God! Are you playing prequels again Jude?
- Yes Peter, very astute of you.
- You know my favourite? Anonymity? Go on guess.
- I don't know.
- Honestly Grasshopper, free your mind. Go on Peter put him out of his misery.
- Fame of course. Go on Jude it is your turn to baffle.
- All right. Did You Let the Dog Out? Which film came after that one?
- Let the dog out! I haven't a clue.
- Ah young Jude, you baffle indeed. Go on I've got customers.
- Lassie Come Home!
- Oh God!
- You can see there *is* a gap in the market. I have only to start thinking of how to do the marketing so I might need a reference from you dear news hound in the making.
- Any time but honestly Jude don't worry about it. Your help would have been great but I'll just have to work harder and find all my own stories.
- How's it been so far?
- Like you said cat up a tree stuff.
- Ah but you can have great fun with those stories. 'The terror of the cat mewing plaintively, audible above the nervous whispers of the gathering crowd. The small cheer as the fire brigade arrive, reassuringly competent and burly. The first trepidous steps up the ladder as the cat's eyes widen, is this rescue or more danger?' You can really go for it.
- I can't write as well as you.
- You can do whatever you want. Let me give you a quote. In 1903 the Wright brothers flew Kittyhawk and changed history but this quote comes from 1902: 'Flight in heavier than air craft is an extreme challenge. It will not happen in my lifetime and I doubt it will happen in my children's lifetime'. Who said that?
- I don't know but they must've looked pretty stupid in a year's time.

- Wilbur Wright! Underestimation is as foolish as arrogance and pride Grasshopper, your ability develops with age. With any luck you will get a story like the classic cat one from the seventies during the firemen strike.
- What was that one? I'm not as old as you.
- Delicately put. Do you not worry that you might be slightly too subtle to be a reporter?
- It's only the truth.
- Which often hurts Grasshopper. You have yet to walk on the rice paper. What happened was that the army stepped in when the fire brigade were fighting for better pay and so on and they had these trucks known as Green Goddesses. One of the first calls was a cat up a tree which they duly rescued to the delight of the little old lady who owned *darling* little tiddles and she invited the soldiers in for tea and cakes. After half an hour or so the soldiers started to head back to barracks waving goodbye to the hospitable lady and promptly ran the cat over!
- No! Really?
- Oh yes it is a veritable classic that one, documented everywhere.
- How often does something like that happen round here?
- But this is a 'thriving city with a rich and diverse culture' according to our lords and masters. There must be fascinating stories everywhere.
- Oh sure but there's not much in the way of scoops is there?
- But Grasshopper scoops do not just fall into laps, one must seek them out.
- Like where? Do give me the benefit of your wisdom oh master.
- So sarcastic for one so young! Well one thing you could do is have a look at our glorious council and particularly Lord Bishop. People think that sleaze only occurs in national politics but they do not seem to realise just how much dodginess occurs on their own doorsteps. For example our wonderful integrated traffic system that is quoted by the deputy Prime Minister as being a roaring success. If gridlock every morning from eight until ten, every evening from four until six, every weekend that the sun pops out to show us a new hat and every bank holiday whatever the weather is a success I dread to think what a system that does not work looks like.
- London every day I'd've thought. Just because it doesn't work does not point to a story. Everyone in the town knows it doesn't work. Every single person that has been in a taxi over the last few years knows it doesn't work so we're hardly talking an exclusive here.
- No, no, no. We are not talking about the fact that it is about as useful and aesthetic as a talking Tele-Tubbie with no batteries, the story is why it happened in the first place? There was no referendum or consultation with the public, they just decided to do it and we have had to struggle with the results since. You need to find out who the planner was in case he or she turns out to be a mad professor from Milton Keynes who does not even drive! That would be a story in itself. Look into the firms that were awarded the contracts, the work just seemed to go on and on and definitely went over budget. I have heard tell that there was distinct cronyism involved with those contracts.
- How so?
- The firms that ended up doing the work had links within the council. They were told how much other firms were bidding and they were able to undercut them. When the work started it quickly went over time and budget thus making a mockery of the original price which ended up being a fraction of the final costs. That could be interesting. Find out which firms were involved at the start and have a word with them. You could also find out who is really pally with the council's top knobs in case the M.D. of your paper is in there with the owners of the new shopping centre and all the other firms that seem to benefit from this council's exclusive generosity. Another thing that will intrigue would be to get yourself an interview with

15

someone in those offices opposite the Town Hall because you simply will not believe it. I have been to some flash places in my time but those offices are positively *opulent*. Carpet you could sleep *in*, smoked glass and marble everywhere and the most glamorous women you have ever seen. They are very happy to spend our council tax on their own comfort.
- That's a lot of work especially as most of that I'll have to do in my spare time.
- Of course it is. Investigative journalism is very hard work. Did you know how long Woodward and Bernstein worked on Watergate?
- Who? Oh you mean the two reporters
- Yes the two reporters. People seem to think that it took them about a week and it was easy but it was over two years that they worked virtually non-stop before Nixon resigned. You obviously have not read All the President's Men? It is a must-read for every aspiring journalist.
- Yeah?
- Oh yes and I shall lend you my copy if you want. It is amazing how disgusting politicians can be.
- Disgusting's a bit strong isn't it?
- No. I would have said it is a very fitting and appropriate adjective to sum up people that are lying, cheating, stealing, self-serving, nepotistic, fraudulent, perverted, prolix and generally useless to anyone other than themselves. These are the people that accuse single mothers and the disabled of being lazy and greedy and then take away a large chunk of our government expenses that we did actually find useful to eat and generally stay alive while *they* get tens of thousands of pounds at least for sitting on their arses having puerile rows. It is the same the world over. Take the latest 'gate'. It is amazing that with the speed and efficiency of modern journalism someone can be arrogant enough to think he can get away with doing what exactly he wants. It is not what he did so much as the fact that he lied about it and still is.
- Still is?
- Sure. The official line is that: 'Their friendship blossomed over a few weeks before developing into something inappropriate'. The fact is that they had sex within two hours of meeting and two weeks later he could not remember her name. I think the poor woman has been treated abysmally by everyone including the press.
- It is a shame that the tabloids ruin the name of decent journalism isn't it.
- They are the Dark Side of the Force young Bart, ruled by the evil Darth Burdoch and Dandelion, Lord of the Wapping Lie. Do not give in to the Dark Side. Actually it would be great to have a light sabre and I do not mean an emaciated tiger.
- You would like a light sabre? You're supposed to be a pacifist.
- Killing politicians mercifully would not affect my conscience in the slightest. The proud of the proud, rotten bounders, charlatans and cads to a man.
- I thought that was Americans?
- No they just think they can be proud because their politicians tell them so. They are actually the most ignorant and miserable race in the developed world but that's another diatribe. You see propaganda never went away it only became more sophisticated, now it is called 'spin'. From the earliest recorded histories politicians have taken our money, made us believe it was for our own good and then exploited us in as many new and interesting ways as their devious and selfish minds can think up behind their closed doors. Now they use the media to distract us from what they are really up to. The conversations that ordinary people have about society originate in misleading articles in papers and on television that take away our attention long enough for politicians to pull off a fait accompli. For people that do not follow the news there

are soap operas and series that portray different areas of life and living in a completely inaccurate manner.
- Oh come on this is conspiracy theory stuff.
- Not at all. You remember the recent story about a new vaccine for meningitis that will be given out sometime in the Autumn and 'Hussar for the government'?
- Yeah sure, it's a great idea.
- Ah-ha! The day that story broke with everyone, strangely, straight on it there was another, less reassuring story. This government has been relying for cost cutting purposes on only two firms to produce the standard inoculations that should be given virtually automatically to young children. Unfortunately both companies have been having problems and the most basic of jabs are in short supply. The shot given to new borns is currently being delayed for seven months and the one that should be given at around six months is a year behind leaving thousands of children unprotected.
- Against what?
- Whooping cough, rubella, mumps and so on. The government is saying that no-one is at risk and will continue in that line until some poor pawn's baby dies and then the risk will be 'minimal'.
- But that *is* a scandal!
- Hence the announcement about meningitis but it gets worse. The new vaccine itself only protects against fifty per cent of cases so it is not actually that good but to whom are they giving it first? *Babies* because everyone likes *babies* so it is good P.R. Politicians used to just 'air kiss' babies but now they slap a needle in them as well, a sort of 'kiss and yell'. Then when the second batch is available it will be given to those most at risk, *students* because they are not so popular with the great British public. Spin, spin, spin, spin...
- Who carried the story?
- Channel 4 News and nobody else. I was disappointed with The Gardener on that one.
- You mean The Guardian?
- No he has a new job description now. Apparently we do not need quite as much guarding any more so some new duties have been added to his remit, mainly in horticulture. A very similar thing has happened at Buckingham Palace where you can now see guardsman, bearskins under arm, picking up litter and doing a spot of weeding in the grounds.
- You're mad Jude!
- Not at all.
- Anyway that's one story. At least we're being informed about I don't know, G.M. crops for example.
- And what good pray, does *that* do us? None! Whatever we say they will take not the slightest bit of notice of us, they will just push occasional stories about 'no evidence of harm' to keep us unsure because we have never been given the true story. While they plant these foul unnatural things all across our green and pleasant land the truth about the actual affects will be *very* secret. Even Chassy Prince was ignored when he wanted answers.
- That was odd wasn't it? The hereditary heir to the throne standing up for the population against the democratically elected government!
- I know. Actually I am something of a fan but that is another story. The point is we do not want genetically modified food and would you people stop messing about with nature just to make a fast buck! Have these people no memories? Does B.S.E. not ring any bells? That particular disaster started when they gave cows sheeps' brains to eat that had been infected with scrapie. What the *hell* were they doing feeding *herbivores* any part of another animal's anatomy? Oh yes it is cheaper and no-one will know. Nature is very finely balanced and the

minute you start messing about with it the repercussions can be enormous. When will they learn that short cuts are not cheaper in the long run?
- It cost the farmers rather dearly.
- Not to mention the families and friends of the forty odd people who have died of C.J.D. which is a very unpleasant way to go. Actually that would make an interesting feature.
- What would?
- There was a very high percentage of vegetarians amongst the C.J.D. victims. They have tried to explain it away by saying they must have had a 'bad burger' before they stopped eating meat but quite frankly if having a macslime burger is that dangerous we would be seeing a *very* large drop in our population by now.
- How many were veggies?
- I am not sure but certainly the last three reported cases were.
- Really?
- Absolutely but the point is G.M. foods are almost certainly going to damage a fair part of the ecosystem even if they do not lead to fatalities in humans which in itself is very likely.
- Oh come on that's scaremongering.
- No it is not. They are messing around with D.N.A.! When you consider that Down's Syndrome is merely one half of one pair of chromosomes missing it becomes very scary what they are doing to these plants. That is the problem, we do not know enough and it is so obvious that this whole scenario is about a few mega-corporations making money. That is the *only* reason for all of this! The people trying to tell us these Frankenstein foods are all right are the people making money from them and their political mates. These crops have already shown that they damage Monarch butterflies so what else will they kill? Do not forget that not so long ago a large drugs company was telling us that their new wonder drug called Thalidomide was perfectly safe. We do not want apologies and farcical levels of compensation in twenty years time we do not want G.M. crops *now*!
- It does make you wonder.
- Although you know there is humour in everything. The best quote from last week was Laura Farmer-Pathos-Blenkinshop or whatever her name is. It went something like: 'When I was asked to be against G.M. foods I immediately thought: "I didn't know General Motors had gone into catering!"'
- God she's stupid!
- Do not go leaping cannons Grasshopper. With any luck she was being ironic. When you earn as much money for writing so little you will have made it as a journo my friend. I shall never be in a Sunday Broadsheet.
- Fair point. So what do you think will happen with G.M. foods then.
- Oh it will carry on going because these companies have too much 'political clout', meaning they have bribed the right people, for anyone to stop them. Plus of course our politicians are far too proud to ever admit they might have made a mistake. Unlike the rest of humanity they simply are not fallible you know and never make enormous cock ups. When they do foul up they merely have endless and powerless inquiries to find scapegoats and hope the whole thing will go away.
- Cynic!
- I am not a cynic. I merely read a newspaper that is not anyone's propaganda sheet and watch the only news program that has any of what is now called 'attitude' I believe. Unlike the majority of the country I have some notion of what is *really* going on. Par example mon brave, within the first week of coming to power this government abolished tax relief on private medical insurance which was another story that did not make the headlines.

- I didn't hear about it.
- Probably not. Then everyone is shocked and surprised when hospital waiting lists go through the roof especially for things like hip replacements and so on. You would have thought someone would have seen the link but oh no. So to take away our attention from the fact that the beleaguered N.H.S. is effectively on its knees we get pictures of shiny new hospitals paid for by the private sector to give us debts in years to come but look lovely now. These people are too proud to ever admit to being wrong.
- I must admit to being confused about those hospitals. No private sector company would give money away. How will they recoup their dosh?
- I do not know but it is rather worrying don't you think? But we will be the ones to suffer you can bet your bottom Euro on it. We always have to pay for their mistakes. What for example is the Millennium Dome all about with its bizarre zones? Do we want this thing? Er, no thank you. It might have been a good idea at the beginning but it is now a veritable albino pachyderm. How much money is being squandered on something that is not going to be ready on time and sounds as interesting as Margate Pier on a rainy Tuesday. 'The what zone, sorry?' The latest news is that the Jubilee line will not be ready despite the workers being paid a thousand pounds a millimetre but do not worry, there will be buses to take us there! What *is* going on? It has even just been struck by lightening! Most buildings have to have been around for ages *and* have a lightening conductor before being treated to a bolt or two but not our Millennium Moan. It is not even going to be permanent! It will be there long enough for the exorbitant entrance fees to cover some of the costs of the whole ridiculous project and then it will close. Genius I call it!
- It is a touch expensive and I've got no intention of going anywhere near the place.
- I do not blame you at all. They just will not back down even though it is becoming more farcical every day. But you can say the same for teacher's pay, the railways, reforming the House of Lords, the tube, computer systems all over the place, the so-called ethical foreign policy that is actually arming and flooding the Third World, so-called freedom of information, the D.S.S., Northern Ireland...
- Northern Ireland?
- Sure. The number of people there that actually want violence are so few that they are statistically insignificant but the politicians have to show the world how *very* important they are and drag the whole thing on and on and on generally arguing about semantics. If it were not so sad it would be laughable. It was politicians that started it and it is politicians that are keeping it going to fuel their pride and self importance. As for all this hoo-ha about fox hunting...
- You don't support it do you?
- I do not know enough about it to have a valid opinion. Opinions based in ignorance are worthless Grasshopper. But I do know that tradition and frenzied anthropomorphism have no place in reasoned arguments. I shall tell you one thing though, it does not strike me as a particularly serious issue in the context of right now with the enormous human suffering throughout the world. When human suffering ceases to exist I shall start worrying about animals, pompous as that sounds.
- What are your politics anyway?
- Well I used to be a lavatorial anarchist as I wanted to smash the cistern. Then I was a nihilistic hedonist citing Charles Bulowski and Hunter S. Thompson as inspirations: 'My only regret is that I didn't take enough cocaine!' and so on. Now I am a middle class socialist and believe that everyone has the right to sound pompous and pretentious.
- Like you?

- Exactly! But to sound pompous and pretentious you need to have a decent education and that is an important issue. Education is our future and not to be neglected in any way. So many of the world's problems are down to ignorance and it *can* be changed. It is not what is taught but how it is taught in order that at some point every child discovers the joy of learning and that most wonderful discovery can be enjoyed for the rest of his or her life. But I digest, we were lambasting politicians. You know something that I do not understand?
- Women?
- Well obviously but I meant about politicians.
- What's that mate?
- How do they always manage to get away with being exposed? Take two public figures recently disgraced, the footballer and the slime ball. What were their names?
- Who?
- You are *so* sharp. Cliff Toddle and Sandy Meddlesome. Now Cliff says something foolish about disabled people and everyone is up in arms shouting for his resignation including dear *Tony* on national television. Excuse me a second but I am disabled and I was not even slightly peeved in fact I resent able-bodied people telling me when I should feel insulted.
- You don't think he should have been sacked?
- Of course not! It has not done the slightest bit of good for anyone. Amidst the clamour for his resignation someone actually pointed out that there was no-one to replace him! The whole thing was ridiculous! The man is a *footballer* not a philosopher. It does not matter one jot what he thinks about anything other than football and quite frankly it was wholly unprofessional of the interviewer that the conversation cropped up at all. If anyone had had the slightest bit of nous they would have put him in charge of making all football stadia wheelchair-friendly by 2002 or whatever and then some good would have come from the situation. But no let us ruin someone else's career because of a vicious newspaper.
- So where does the slime ball fit in.
- Well around the same time he was in trouble for some very dodgy dealings that did whiff more than a little of fraud. Eventually he goes although keeping his main job but everyone knows that it is only a matter of time before this highly dubious individual is back to run the country again. There does seem to be a hint of double standards on the go. Plus of course he was 'grassed up' by another M.P. who did not like him. They really are the cesspit of humanity. Who was it that said that anyone wanting to be a politician should by definition not be allowed to be one?
- I don't know.
- Someone terribly clever. I think the only reason they go into politics is as a backdoor to getting laid! They are all so ugly that power is the only way they will ever get to sleep with beautiful women. Go on name a good-looking politician?
- Um...
- Peter? Can you name a handsome politician?
- J.F.K. was very dashing in sepia I always thought.
- Bang up to date as they say. Thank you Peter I think you are wanted.
- Yes, yes, coming. No work for the vaguely naughty round here.
- But politicians are the perfect example of why pride is the godfather of sin my dear Bart. They harm they do to the world everyday is immeasurable mainly because they keep most of the details secret. Then of course we get the blame. As a smoker I seem to be blamed for most of what is wrong with the world. Any time that there is a fire it is blamed on a cigarette or a chip pan. Have you ever tried setting fire to something with a cigarette? You need a lot of patience, I always give up after ten minutes but it is not *my* smoke that is increasing asthma,

breathing problems, strokes and everything else it is the carbon monoxide, carcinogens and other noxious bits and bobs that churn into the atmosphere from cars and industry every day of every year. Twenty-four-seven I believe is the modern parlance.
- What about passive smoking?
- That has been invented. For decades politicians have been bribed by the 'we want to make more money' lobbies not to do anything about the damage they are doing to our environment so they think up a way of shifting the blame. If it were not for these people we would have had electric, wind-powered or solar-powered cars years ago. As for passive smoking it does not make sense! Smokers are damaged in two ways, the heat of the smoke burns the little hairs in the trachea, cilia I believe, which causes your smokers' cough and the smoke in the lungs reaching a density of about one in five that can trigger cancer. With passive smoking the heat has gone from the smoke so no damage there then and the density of smoke in the lungs is about one in two hundred. I do not understand why it is supposed to be so dangerous.
- What about Roy Castle?
- God rest his talented soul. He is an extreme example. Playing the trumpet in a smoke-filled room would obviously lead to problems but merely jogging in an inner-city for five minutes is equivalent to smoking twenty cigarettes! Stop giving me a hard time for the sins of others.
- But it is bad for you.
- So is everything. Living shortens your life. As my father says: 'Anything in large quantities is bad for you especially if it falls on you!'
- Very funny!
- But the worst thing about politicians my friend is how they latch on to good P.R. during tragedies. As soon as there is an earthquake or natural disaster anywhere they are straight on our television screens being selfless. They are not the ones risking their lives and leaving their families in fear whilst travelling to God knows what. But they imply that they are. Do you remember Mrs. Butcher in Downing Street being *so proud* of her efforts in the Falklands? As the song goes: 'Who takes all the glory and none of the shame?'
- Oh shit that's my pager. I'd better go.
- Wonderful to see you my friend. Good luck with the job. I am sure that you will find your scoop and I shall give you a call in the nearish.
- Cheers Jude. Is the leg going to get better?
- Not without divine intervention.
- Sorry mate. See you soon.
- I hope so. Peter dear heart would you call me a taxi please?
- You utter, utter taxi.
- Thank you. Now that that attempt at humour is out of the way would you order a taxi to take me home please?
- I'll consider it an honour.

* * *

- JUDE!
- MAGS!
- JUDE!
- WHAT?
- Are you stoned?
- Working on it but currently sentient.
- WHAT?

- When trying not to sound half-cut and rag-and-boned it is always advisable to use words like 'sentient' and 'coherent' in a vain attempt not to sound hog-whimperingly trashed. But do not fear, I shall probably make sense for another hour or so and I shall definitely remember the conversation tomorrow. Anyway you sound all of a dither are you all right?
- Yes I'm fine, just a bit shocked. JUDE!
- What is it Sweetie?
- I've been asked out on a date!
- *Wonderful!*
- What am I going to do?
- At a guess, go on the date and have a great time because it is definitely your turn.
- BUT IT'S A DATE!
- I know that but it has been a while and it is about time some bloke plucked up the courage. I did say 'plucked' didn't I?
- But I'm so nervous! He's even made a joke about my name already.
- What is wrong with your name, it is a beautiful name.
- Magdalene! She was a prostitute wasn't she?
- I think you are taking a very tabloid attitude towards your namesake. She was and always will be a female icon.
- How? She was a prostitute?
- Only to begin with. You must remember those were very different times and she was probably from a poor family and forced into the profession by her father. They were rough times when women did not have careers. The thing with dear Mary Magdalene is that when the indecisive men were saying things to Jesus like: 'Go on then, show us a miracle and we'll believe. Oh! A miracle. No we're still not convinced!' she did not need any convincing because she just believed. And then there was the beautifully touching scene when she poured perfume on His head and washed His feet with her tears, drying them with her hair. I suppose the modern equivalent would be running in for an impromptu massage with some aromatherapy. Anyway the men standing around tried to kick her out but Jesus insisted that she stay and essentially said: 'Don't do that for a living any more. Come on tour with me and my mates!' and she did.
- Really?
- What were you doing on Sunday mornings in your formative years?
- Probably in a succession of pubs. That is a lovely story.
- It gets better. Because she was obviously a favourite of His she was the first person to see Him after the resurrection and she did not doubt a thing. Jesus was an early egalitarian and Mary Magdalene an early emancipated woman so whoever this bloke is he has no right to take the mickey out of your name. Anyway what is *he* called?
- Magnus Farquar!
- *No!* A hint of pots, kettles and being dark of hue on the go I feel.
- I know! I couldn't keep a straight face.
- Who is he anyway?
- Remember when I was temping at that firm of accountants?
- He's an *accountant*? God's hearing aid are you mad woman?
- No listen. There were a couple of the guys that worked there that I got on quite well with, this older chap called John and Magnus. Anyway when my contract expired Magnus was on holiday so I didn't get a chance to say goodbye to him. I mean he's not all that but he seemed quite nice, you know, had a sense of humour and so on. So he came back from holiday and

found my number from somewhere and has just rung up TO ASK ME FOR A DRINK. WHAT AM I GOING TO DO?

- First of all calm down you lunatic. Have you got a bottle of something rouge and relaxing by your side?

- 'Course.

- Plenty of cigarettes?

- Yep.

- Spliff?

- Unfortunately not. Bloody typical isn't it! I could really do with one just now.

- Just breathe deeply. 'Good thoughts in, bad thoughts out; good thoughts in, bad thoughts out.' The best thing to do is to go out for a drink or a meal, make him pay and enjoy yourself. Borrow Mike's mobile or something in case he turns out to be creepy and pre-book a taxi for half ten or something so that you know you will get home all right and *enjoy yourself!* How did you leave the offer?

- I said I was watching am important program and would ring him back but I rang you instead. I'm really nervous Jude, it's been such a long time.

- I know Honey but you are over all the shyte now. You have managed to survive all of the horror that those b*****ds gave you and now is the time to really get back into life. This Magnus might not be all that but at least it is a chance to get back out there. The world has missed your beauty and charm. I know it takes a bit of courage but you have been *so* brave these past five years and you are *such* a survivor. Now it is time to do a bit of living. Yes?

- You think so?

- Absolutely. But more to the point what does this muffin look like?

- Muffin? Honestly Jude you make me die. Well he's quite tall, short dark hair, slim, not bad face..

- Is he rich?

- He makes out that he is, you know, dropping his horse into conversations...

- Did it crush anyone?

- What? You lunatic just listen!

- Sorry.

- Where was I?

- Lemming horses.

- Oh yeah. He's got a flash car too, always quite well dressed, looks like an extra from thingee... Carrie Mebeagle and he's got one of those designer handbags that men carry these days. Are you choking or something?

- Are you *joking* or something? I am all for equality and all that but did you say: 'Male handbag'?

- Yes. Haven't you seen one yet? They're all the rage with the poseurs up here.

- God's duvet what will they think of next? Anyway if he's rich let him take you to the swankiest restaurant near you and make sure he spends a fortune because you *are* worth it Honey. That's what Winnie the Pooh says when he gets home you know.

- What is?

- Hi Hunny I'm home!

- You're mad! But what should I do now? Ring him back and, what?

- Give him another twenty minutes or so, ring back sounding very nonchalant and say you have a window for Monday or Tuesday next week when you will be free for dinner and make sure it's not macslimes he has in mind.

- But what if he's boring?

23

- Then refuse to see him again. You are not working together anymore yes? So if you do not want to see him again you do not have to. Remember just take it one step at a time and get used to dating again if that is what you want.
- Well I have been happily single for five years now. Do I really want all of this? I'm feeling so nervous.
- Is it anticipation or dread?
- A bit of both.
- Completely normal so do not worry. I know you have survived through some horrible times and you are used to being single but relationships can be fun too. What we all have to do is make sure you do not end up with another hatechild and you know that Dave, Eve and I will protect you from the hooded claw et cetera do you not? That is because we love you and you mean too much to risk your happiness in any way. You can tell this Magnus Faraway or whatever that unless he treats you like the absolute lady that you are he will feel the wrath of Moses!
- Moses?
- My walking stick.
- Oh! How is the leg Honey? There's me rabbiting on. Is it any better?
- No I am afraid not. It just hurts all the bloody time. Anyway I am having to sell the Hunting Lodge.
- Oh no, not your lovely flat! I'll have to come and see it again.
- Yes do. I think we are completing next week sometime so make it before then.
- But why sell it? Can't you rent it out or something?
- That would not be a hassle free retirement would it? No Honey it is like a relationship that is well and truly over. I would not like to think of someone trashing the my flat. I cannot handle the stairs anymore and I cannot even clean the place which is getting me down.
- You were always so house-proud.
- This is it. So I am having dinner with the folks this week with polished begging bowl to see if I can return to Redmond Grange in an ignominious fashion.
- Will it be O.K.?
- Oh yes. We get on very well these days. Actually dad told me a great story the other day. Apparently there was the wine critic from the Daily Torygraph out to dinner one evening with a friend in a restaurant that had a conservatory behind the main bit, the ceiling of which was covered in grapes and vines and so on. Towards the end of the meal the manager, owner or whatever came up to this wine critic and begged a favour. 'Of course.' he graciously replied and the owner asked him to try some white wine and produced a glass as if by magic. The critic did his routine, though swallowing rather than dampening the floor and said: 'Hmm. Interesting. Where pray, does it come from?' 'Actually.' said the owner, 'From the grapes we grow on the ceiling that you can see.' 'Ah.' replied the critic, 'It doesn't travel well!'
- The rotten bastard!
- I thought it was highly amusing actually.
- Yes it is. I just don't like critics being nasty to people. But how are you feeling Jude? Are you O.K.?
- Actually I am horribly depressed. I have a big spot on my neck. It is like the foundations for a new nose or something equally horrible. I mean Mags I am going bald, grey and my face was recently described by an ex-friend as having been 'squatted in' and I am still getting spots! The world is a hideously unfair place.
- I still love you.

- That is all that keeps me going in the long hours of insomnia. Have you heard that one? The one about the insomniac, agnostic, dyslexic who lies awake in bed pondering the existence of Dog!
- You're getting stoned that was terrible. But answer my question damn you! ARE YOU ALL RIGHT?
- Yes I am fine. Considering they were going to amputate my leg nine years ago I have had seven great years of two workable legs so I have been quite lucky really. I have had plenty of time to get used to the idea of ending up disabled so there is no need for sympathy. I think that I am going to enjoy my retirement at Redmond Grange so do not be worrying about me. You had better ring your new beau before he starts fretting had you not?
- Actually it's a bit late now. I'll wait until tomorrow.
- You see you are straight back into the swing of things. Treat 'em mean like Mr. Bean, or summint? Actually while you are here could I ask you for some advice?
- Of *course*.
- I am thinking of getting another tattoo done.
- Not another one?
- The others are getting lonely.
- What are you thinking of?
- A bar-code.
- Why?
- It came out of a conversation I had at a press party where I was talking about the current nanny state with a very interesting lady from the local radio station. She said something like we are all numbers and I replied that I had always considered myself to be more of a bar-code! The idea stuck.
- A bar-code. For goodness sake. Where are you going to have it done?
- At the tattooist near the Carpenter's Rest.
- No you fool, where on your body?
- Left hand.
- Are you mad? You'll never get a job with a tattoo on your hand. You know how bigoted people are.
- Honey I am never going to be able work again anyway so what does it matter? It is a protest in my own small and insignificant way against materialism, commercialism, consumerism and the general mercenary attitude of modern society. You cannot have a protest on your shoulder or somewhere.
- Jude if you want a silly tattoo done get a silly tattoo done. Knowing you it'll look quite cool. Now go to bed and I'll call you tomorrow.
- All right Sweetie. Thank you for calling and sleep well.
- And you. Love you.
- Love you too.

Sunday June 6th : ENVY

As usual waking was a matter of pain realisation. From nightmare drenched sleep to the nightmare of existence with a small: 'Ow!' Dean Martin once said: 'I feel sorry for people that don't drink, when they wake up in the morning that's as good as they're going to feel *all day*!'. If you extrapolate that a little it would answer all of those people that say I drink too much. Mind you the late and great Dean also said: 'I am not drunk if I can lie on the floor without holding on!' which is probably more appropriate.

Even though the days are just rolling into one at the moment Sundays still have a dread about them. The very name is synonymous with boredom probably due to memories of dresses, incense and tedium in large, cold buildings. That and no meaningless but enjoyable daytime television. It is all too worthy on a Sunday. Bloody religion!

So far I am sticking to the promise I made to myself and my liver that I would not start drinking until I had eaten something. So at half past nine after a Mars bar and half a pint of milk it was the perfect moment for a drop of something rouge to ease the burden of waiting until opening time.

I know that everyone is exhorting us mere mortals to use public transport if only for the sake of the environment but I cannot see the deputy prime minister hanging around of a Sunday morning waiting for a number 7! I eventually got to The Carpenter's Rest just after opening where Peter was being his usual self, a subtle mixture of hangover and Kenneth Williams.

Simon the Cerise Pimpernel turned up for a pint. I do wish he would just stay in touch like normal people. It is funny that I seem to be the only person that likes him, I know he is pedantic and occasionally rude but no-one seems to realise how much pain and horror he has been through. Still he seems a little more human every time he does appear from the ether although his problems seem a long way from being over.

Philip appeared later on and brought a ray of sunshine to an otherwise cloudy Sunday. It is amazing how stable and genuinely happy he is. As ever he listened to my rantings with a sardonic smile which was as infectious as the plague.

Peter gave me a pep talk and got me a cab. He really is a very decent man and friend.

* * *

- Peter, well met by cloud light on this dubious Summer's day.
- Oh shut up with your cheerfulness. Honestly the way you twitter on anyone would think that you had no concept of the misery of hangovers.
- Another Saturday night? How much do you remember of this one?
- Mercifully little although my lodger took great delight this morning when I asked about the broken lampshade in the hall. Apparently my robust frame would have broken a concrete one with the momentum I acquire in a downward spiral!
- Were there many pieces?
- A veritable 3-D jigsaw.

- Any mention of super glue would be...
- Treated with derision.
- Was it valuable?
- Only third dynasty Ming, a piece of junk but I really must stop diving through my front door. I have started to dream that I'm Evel Knieval which is scary. Those outfits were just horrendous! It brings me out in hives merely to contemplate.
- Is this a regular occurrence, the diving rather than the dreams?
- Oh yes. The trouble being that I am so impressed with myself for not only remembering the keys, finding the right one and then getting it into the tiny hole that I completely forgot to move my feet at the required moment. A crash of *enormous* proportions is inevitable.
- I know the feeling only too well.
- Last week I landed on the cat apparently. The poor thing was traumatised for days, right off his Kanga Chunks he was. Eyes like saucers but don't grass me up to the R.S.P.C.A. will you Jude? They'd lock me up for sure and I simply wouldn't be able to look Kafka in the furry face on visiting days.
- Kafka?
- Yes. A mix up on the birth certificate so they tell me.
- What was he supposed to be called then?
- I dread to think, Katfa or something.
- Do you get people moaning about how much you drink?
- Not as many as you I'd wager but yes it does crop up from time to time. It's not so much the concern as the look of concern in their faces that has me reaching or is it retching, for the barth bag. Mother is the worst of course. She has a terrible habit of ringing me every morning and noting down in her impressionists' diary whenever I am sounding a little less than perky.
- Or pinky?
- Oh very amusing. First pint doing its stuff? I know it's an impressionists' diary because she gives me the same one every Christmas. It's always Monet and his bloody garden for January. He wasn't an impressionist he was just terribly myopic. Give me some gouache and a pad, I'll take off my bins and the result would be indistinguishable.
- Possibly you should take night classes.
- Love to darling but I'm simply *too* busy drinking at that time. Ah I see the more temperate customers are flocking to our shores. Would you like another before I am inundated by the 'May I have a look at the menu' crowd?
- Does the Pope wear a silly hat and kiss airport runways?
- Not as regularly as you drink dear heart. There you go if you'll excuse me the Duchess looks absolutely parched.

* * *

- Mr. Redmond! How are you sir?
- Simon the veritable Cerise Pimpernel. I am not so bad, how are you?
- Straining up under the bear as they say.
- In all the right places.
- That's a very pleasant looking pint of something or other you seem to be quaffing but do they have some more on the premises?
- It would not hurt to ask.
- Peter my dear friend?
- Oh it's you.

27

- May I have two pints of your finest Harveys please?
- No! You'll have to make do with the second-rate stuff we inflict on everyone else.
- That's a compromise we'll have to live with. Is that a rather large spot on your neck?
- Good lord no it is the very latest in espionage technology. Hidden in what rather cunningly appears to be a spot is a camera and microphone as used by the C.I.A. in their most dangerous missions. Anyway Simon how are you?
- Better than you by the looks of it. You know what it's like, same shit different day.
- Not Delilah again?
- 'Fraid so. She wouldn't let me see Alex again this weekend after last week's debacle.
- Oh God! What happened?
- It was so stupid I mean it wasn't *me* that locked her out. I'd dropped Alex back off to her last Sunday as per the arrangements. She had decided to give me a hard time and was shouting abuse at me, you know if she wants to hate me that is her prerogative but to be swearing and shouting in front of the boy, it's not on really. I decided to say nothing and left but she followed me down the path screaming abuse at me and her door swung shut thus locking her out and Alex in!
- You do not really need a two year old rampaging round the house unattended do you?
- Not with Alex's unusual love of electricity no. So it was all my fault that she locked herself out and I had to find a ladder and break in. Fortunately Alex had only discovered some chocolate and he was merely in need of a cleaning up job. I went to leave again and Delilah was still in torrent of abuse mode and I must admit I lost my rag and shouted back. She has refused to speak to me since and when I went to pick Alex up today no-one was home. I don't know where they are and the solicitor is uncontactable until tomorrow so I decided there was only one thing to do, seek out my best drinking partner and get pissed. After all you do have a Ph.D. in cheering people up.
- From the Open University I presume. Is this silly joke time?
- That's where I'm at.
- What did the slug say to the snail?
- Go on?
- 'Big Issue!'
- Yes that's rather subtle. Try this one, a bishop, a politician and a headmaster are walking through Hyde Park. They pass by a bench on which are sitting three ladies of the night. The Bishop says: 'Would you call that a jam of tarts?' 'No' says the politician, 'That is a hoard of whores.' 'Surely not.' rejoins the headmaster, 'It is an anthology of English pros!'
- Fantastic I like that, I shall have to tell Peter that one later. So what will happen with Delilah and Alex?
- Oh her solicitor will argue with my solicitor and I'll probably have him on Tuesday night as normal. It's not the first time she's pulled this stunt.
- When is the final hearing?
- In a couple of months. When did you become so knowledgeable on custodial law?
- I did a feature a couple of months ago. Of course you would not have seen a copy so I shall stick one in the post for you. Essentially I spent two hours interviewing this lovely woman who has been practising family law for twenty years. I now know that at the final hearing, visiting and parental rights will almost certainly be set in stone and you have to be a vicious, twisted, violent piece of excrement of a father not to get your visiting rights. If Delilah then continues to flout the rules she can be imprisoned which is decidedly to be avoided but is a decent deterrent.
- I certainly hope so. This past year has been a nightmare.

- I know mate which is why I worry every time you disappear.
- I always show up again though don't I?
- The proverbial dodgy small coin. The other interesting thing that cropped up with this solicitor was that she stressed that mediation is the key in these situations. The trouble is that it all gets too fraught and many unscrupulous solicitors, of which there are a couple, will goad one party into being unreasonable and it all gets bogged down in petty jealousies. You end up in a tug-of-war of envy. When you get that situation of no communication between parents only the solicitors benefit the slimy hatechildren.
- Tell me about it. I am earning great money at the moment but after tax, C.S.A. payments, solicitors and then my own bills there isn't much left.
- The problem is that Delilah is a little emotional is she not? But put yourself in her position, you did disappear on the beer did you not?
- Yeah with you!
- I do feel guilty mate I can assure you but anyway you could have treated her a little better. I know that life has been tough but you are supposed to handle these things together not develop silence and drinking problems. At this moment Delilah absolutely hates you with, as far as she is concerned good reason. It is against every instinct in her body and mind to hand her only child over to someone she hates. It is very difficult for women in these scenarios. Is she working at the moment?
- No she just takes half of my wage packet.
- Which is fair enough. So she has little to do during the day except dwell on the past and feed her hatred no doubt with a bevy of friends to assist. Not very helpful. Unfortunately that means the onus is on you to cool the temperature and start building a new relationship with your ex-wife.
- That's not fair.
- Life isn't you muffin! I know it seems unreasonable but you have got to do something otherwise there is a real possibility that Alex will be damaged psychologically.
- How?
- As you can imagine there have been numerous studies done but it has been shown that a child will try to support whichever parent it is with at the time. This is why Alex will cry when you are returning him but then run up the path joyously shouting: 'Mummy!' Children get very confused in these situations which can lead to terrible insecurity and more serious problems later on. So you have got to calm Delilah down.
- That is easier said than done. All she ever does is shout and scream at me.
- Then send her a letter emphasising the point and keep making the point until it gets through. She is not a remorseless alien she is a hurt and defensive woman that does not trust you anymore.
- Nothing is ever easy is it?
- Nothing worthwhile it would seem. Just do not give up my friend and things will improve. I am a firm believer in the power of positive thought.
- You sound like a salesman.
- Well with positive thought I have come from a dangerously shy and insecure teenage angst machine to a local publicity and marketing guru. Sure it is medium fish in a small pond stuff but I shock my old school friends.
- What do you mean: 'I have come from'?
- It did sound just like that Bozo-Dog Doo Daa Band track did it not?
- That's easy for you to say.

- You know the one about body building: 'Before I was a four stone apology, now I am two separate gorillas!' No by positive thought I am not referring to those companies where it is like a religion although I have never met an unhappy born again dietician. If you have a situation the best thing to do is imagine it working out really well. Worrying does not affect anything in this world but if you think positively all the time you are more relaxed and actually more capable dealing with the situation. With positive thought you become confident and happy and envy is just a bad memory. That is the theory anyway.
- But you have to plan for things going wrong.
- I doubt it. I have always found that spontaneous but thought out action was always best. You get the news, you think about it, you ring up whichever friend will give the best advice and you go for a pint and think about it. Then you do something. If you have more time think about it straight, drunk, stoned and then straight again.
- Then be spontaneous?
- Absolutely! The other benefit is that if you have been thinking all these positive and happy thoughts but it still goes marrow-shaped at least you have had the happy thoughts which is better than nothing. It will work out my friend just give it a little more time and patience.
- I hope so I really do. Anyway what's happened to your leg? Is it permanent like you were talking about?
- I am afraid so. It is only downhill from here.
- I never got you that critical illness cover sorted did I?
- Do not worry kind sir you have had enough worries of your own. The timing was bad that is all. I am having dinner with the folks tomorrow night to see if I can go back to Redmond Grange and I am selling the flat.
- For a reasonable profit I hope. Will it be all right to move back with your parents?
- I would imagine so since we are getting on famously at the moment like an Indonesian forest fire. To be honest I am looking forward to it. I am very lucky my folks are wonderful. A couple of months ago I was swimming with Dad, he is a member of a sports club down the road and he likes the occasional swim to keep in shape and he likes me to go with him. I generally make it two times in three, as you can imagine at nine o' clock of a Sunday morning I am not at my peak.
- Swimming will be good for you now I would imagine?
- It is wonderful Simon. It is the only environment where I do not need a bloody stick. Sorry Moses.
- Moses?
- The name of my stick, this is Moses. Have you seen those range of cards with Old testament cartoons? No? They are wonderful. There is one that has a man praying in the bottom right corner and these light rays coming from the top left. The caption is: 'Hi this is God. Sorry I'm not in at the moment but please leave your prayer after the tone! Beeeeep'. But in the same series there is a cartoon of Moses by the Red Sea which is doing its a la fountain bit and the Israelites are amassed on the shore. Moses is looking distinctly narked and the caption is: 'What do you mean *muddy*?'
- I like it! That's very good.
- But I was telling you about Dad. We were at the pool and I had got out and was in the changing room with Dad following. He was stopped by this chap who is the father of a guy I went to school with called James Tudor. Mr. Tudor said: 'Mr. Redmond isn't it?' and Dad agreed. 'And isn't that..?' he went on but Dad said: 'Yes that's Simon.' So this chap came marching into the changing room with big smile and outstretched hand and said: 'Simon it is

good to see you.' I shook his hand and said: 'Hello Mr. Tudor, it is Jude actually!', meanwhile Dad was in the corner sniggering!

- That's a great one. Snatching an opportunity like that is most admirable.
- The thing is he's seventy-five this year! You simply would not believe it and Mum is just as bad. Have you meet Samuel who I used to do the merchandising with?
- Sure. Has he paid you back yet?
- No of course not but it is only money. Anyhow one day we bumped into Mum down the road from the office. We were almost certainly going to the pub which I did not mention to her of course The previous week Samuel and the infamous Percy Percy had borrowed the recital room at the music school to put up a stand that they were taking to an exhibition in Manchester as they needed to make sure it all went together and I had helped sort them out with a suitably sized room. As one would I introduced them: 'Samuel this is my mother Mary, Mum this is Samuel'.
- As one would.
- Then my mother said in her regal voice, she could teach the Queen elocution you know: 'Oh so it was *your* erection in my front room was it?' and Samuel replied: 'Yes I was very proud of it!'. I was standing there saying: 'Mother! Samuel!' sounding like a complete prude!
- Fantastic. How old is she this year?
- I could not possibly tell you her age as I would almost certainly be struck by lightning or something. She is known as The Dragon you know, last birthday she blew on the cake and lit the candles! Let us just say she will be enjoying the fifteenth year of being in her 'prime'. I must admit I am so lucky with my folks. Sorry mate I am being very tactless going on about them.
- That's all right. I don't think about Mum much these days, only when I'm down.
- I am sorry Simon. It does not say much about modern society when most of the time I am embarrassed to have two parents that are still together and wonderful people but there you go. Anyway it is good to see you. How about a toast? To the late and great Little Ern possibly the greatest straight man ever.
- To Ernie and of course Eric.
- Oh yes! Hopefully they are on a cloud somewhere doing the dance. So what are you up to?
- Still working for the insurance crooks and I've moved to a flat in Eastbourne.
- Eastbourne! I suppose they have opened it for the season.
- It's not that bad. It's cheaper than here and there is a perfectly reasonable pub up the road where I have been skinning the locals with tricks and so on.
- Like what?
- O.K.. See this twenty pound note?
- Yes.
- If you can burn a hole in it it's yours.
- All right.
- But I'm going to hold it here, tightly over your forearm. I wouldn't try it. Some bloke did the other night and I had to stop him as there is no chance.
- Very clever. What else?
- Give me two pound coins. Thank you. Now I'm going to represent three football teams with these two coins. 'Old 'em. Alterin' 'em. Just like that. And, Dun dee. Ha ha!
- Very good now give me the coins back. Thank you. Do you actually take any money from these people?
- No. They're all a bit aggressive looking and my nose hasn't recovered yet.
- You always were more Conan the Librarian were you not?

31

- You being Attila the Pun I presume?
- In a former life according to my football coach! It is quite ironic you doing that trick with the coins.
- What do you mean?
- Well you work in insurance and that was a microcosm of the way insurance companies work. They take your money and laugh at you.
- Look I know you had a rather unpleasant time with an insurance company but that is a bit too simplistic.
- I thought it was rather a good analogy myself. I do not want to sound unpleasant Simon but I do not understand how you can work for these despicable people. Over the years insurance companies have worked hand in glove with capitalism to create a world based on fear and envy where no-one is happy just constantly striving to be seen as more important than others. It is part of the language now when someone sees a large house or an expensive car one of their first thoughts is: 'I wonder what the insurance is on *that*?' Insurance is essentially a hidden fun tax.
- A what? Hidden fun tax? You're not making any sense.
- That is how the world is seen is it not? With any commodity the more fun it is going to be the more expensive it is and the greater the insurance. What your company and others have done is create a tiered system of envy and fear. Society deems that the more 'successful' one is the more money one has but it has to be spent ostentatiously otherwise no-one would realise just how *important* you are. But because others are now envious they want your showy toys and you have to protect yourself by bolting your doors and for goodness sake insure everything.
- You cannot blame us for everything.
- No but you do go to amazing lengths to ensure that the system continues to make your shareholders happy whilst society itself is dissolving through the envy of the mass of 'have littles' against the few 'have everythings'. Envy is such a destructive and all-consuming emotion just look at what happened to Salieri because of Mozart. Envy is evil and insurance companies are nurturing it.
- That's a little over the top Jude.
- Not really. If you did a poll of ordinary people in the street asking what items they would like to be able to afford everyone would have quite a comprehensive list. If you took away the insurance costs a lot more of what these people desire would be affordable to them. Because of the disgusting level of consumerism we now have everyone wants more and more of the inanimate objects that they believe will make them happy. Then along comes the insurance man with his tales of horror about people who lost everything and were not insured. The poor loves, if only they had signed here, and here, oh and here and given away enormous amounts every month for very little. With the scare stories we are told peace of mind is now a rare commodity.
- That isn't what insurance is all about. It is there to protect people against their losses.
- Oh sure! When was the last time *you* tried to claim anything on the insurance? Quite frankly insurance companies should all be called: 'Spiel, Sloth and Loophole.' It has been a long time since insurance companies were anything other than fear-stoking leeches. 'What the large print giveth, the small print taketh away.' Take my parents. They have been burgled three times in twenty-two years. Property taken; about two grand's worth, damage done; the same. In other words a fraction of what they have spent in bolts, locks, alarms and happiness through over-hyped fear.

32

- Like any business insurance and assurance for that matter sees human weakness and takes advantage of it.
- You see that is what I mean even the terms are confusing. What is assurance and what is insurance? With one you take our money by scaring us and the other by bribing us. 'You can be just like the person you envy in twenty years time if you give us all your money *now*!' and the advertising is so good that people fall for it: 'Look at the lovely little squirrels!'
- I agree with you they're complete bastards but that is the way of the world. There is nothing you can do to change it.
- The world is always changeable and that has been demonstrated numerous times through history if they still teach any. But it is not just taking advantage of a human weakness, in this case fear of the unknown, it is also about breeding an unpleasant human emotion namely envy. Through the various forms of media we constantly have images of beautiful and wealthy people thrust upon us. They swan about and everyone is jealous of them which is why the tabloids do such a roaring trade in the falls of the mighty. Because we are essentially envious of these characters we take the mickey out of them and when they do the slightest wrong or have a small tragedy we say: 'Serves them right!'.
- It does happen a lot. I suppose that's why all these pop groups 'want to be taken seriously'.
- Absolutely. The ridiculous thing about the whole system is that the rich and beautiful types that are paraded for us to be jealous of are in fact envious of and reliant upon us. They crave our acceptance and a lot of them our money even though they are richer than we shall ever be. When what's her name cannot handle her party lifestyle anymore she runs into de-tox but when she comes out she feels that she has to justify her actions to the general public and all she gets is contempt.
- Well she's a stupid, ignorant, dilettante.
- She speaks very highly of you. How do you know what she is like? I do not and I would not judge. Tell me this who is the worse off between an 'it person' socialite who develops a dangerous and costly drink and drugs habit and has to go to de-tox in America or a council tenement heroin addict who gets sent to de-tox in the local hospital?
- Well they're both pretty sad cases.
- Indeed.
- I don't know. It's decidedly bloody for both of them.
- The 'it person' would get a lot less sympathy and the whole exercise would be carried out in public with widespread derision but he or she would probably have the better chance of survival. Essentially there is very little difference you would not agree?
- Yeah, sure.
- So why is everyone jealous of everyone else? You know the expression: 'The grass is always greener over there'? Well yes but it is generally Astroturf! I know what you are saying that insurance companies do not start the cycle of envy and that is true enough. Envy starts forming in childhood at school where my pet hate consumerism has recently invaded.
- You don't like consumerism do you?
- I *hate* it! In fact I am going to have a new tattoo done, a bar-code on my hand.
- I await with anticipation. Only you Jude.
- Anyway do you remember your school days? I was in hand-me-downs until I was fifteen and I had a lot of female cousins! There was the system in place of each year looking down on the year below but within each year there was generally cohesion and little jealousy.
- Sure the good old days. Nostalgia just ain't what it used to be!
- And it was all fields round here but when we were at school there was very little in the way of fashion in fact I was fifteen before I heard the word 'trendy'. Now however every child has

to have the latest football strip, trainers, pocket games machine and so on but the children that do not have all of these things are envious of those that do. How many have everything? Virtually none because the consumer machine will churn out this rubbish faster than the vast majority can afford it. This is what sets the cycle off. For some people there will be no way out and for the rest of their lives they will wish they were someone else and somewhere else with different people. It is *everywhere* and that is what office politics is all about.

- We've had plenty of that haven't we? Remember when Nick tried to tape our 'phone calls and I got my mate from C.I.D. to give him a call?

- His face! 'Yes Chief Inspector, I didn't realise I was breaking the law and there is a sentence attached to this crime!' I do not think he ever forgave you for that. You see he was jealous of us. Even though the muffin was a manager we were far better at the job than him, more popular in the office and we could make him look stupid merely by using a word of more than three syllables. That is why he kept on accusing us of not being 'team players' because we could not be bothered going to ten pin bowling evenings.

- What did you say to him before I started working there? I know you said something to him.

- Who, little old me, being a touch acerbic to a fatuous fool? What upset him was that I refused to be impressed by the fact that he drove a B.M.W. As far as I am concerned the cars are very aesthetic but the people that drive them vary somewhat and it is no indication of anything other than a good income. One day he was going on about how he cleans it every Sunday using special wax for the chrome-spoked wheels and I merely asked: 'How small is your penis?' For some reason he took offence. Of course what used to really wind him up was he knew we had been drinking.

- I don't quite know what their problem was. Just because we drove their precious company cars after three pints, it was nothing to worry about.

- Of course. Three pints is not a problem but the day you fell over in the office was a touch worrisome.

- I had overdone it that day.

- But again it was pure envy. Some of the classified people were determined to get us into trouble and the: 'They smell of alcohol!' routine is a tried and tested one. The fact that I smelled of Lockets and you of Gold Spot and chewing gum never came into it. They knew we had been enjoying ourselves while they munched a cheese sandwich at their desks and they *hated* us! It was very sad.

- I never knew what I had done to upset them.

- Just be happy probably. Envious people are unhappy and unhappy people are envious but that place was nothing compared to the college.

- Really?

- Oh God yes. It was unbelievable the utter shyte that went on there. I was foolish enough to think that by doing my job well and I was very capable, that would be enough and I refused to get involved with the gossips. Within six months their envy and hatred had built up enough for them to launch an attack on me which nearly got me fired. The classic: 'He smells of alcohol!' routine again. The ridiculous thing was that there were no cars involved this time and in the pub there were also the Head of Art and Design, the Head of I.T., some people from Student Services and so on.

- It wasn't against the rules to have a pint at lunch?

- Of course not. It was *madness!* Then it became obvious to the board that my boss who had been claiming my successes and blaming me for her cock-ups had been doing just that. In her envy of my ability she then forced me out. The fact remains that I was the most successful person to ever do the job.

- It's a load of bollocks isn't it.
- Bags full! It is so depressing sometimes to see just how unhappy and envious people are. What for example are these so called designer labels all about? Not so long ago a designer suit would mean that it was well designed, made from wonderful material and would fit like the proverbial. Now these companies just shove a label on anything made in an Indonesian sweat shop and up the price tenfold. People actually fall for this and a bit of fancy stitching apparently puts you above the rest who are also wearing second-rate clothes with a little label on them. Is it just me?
- No. I decided to go to a bespoke tailor for my new suits. Five suits, two different styles and three different materials. The total cost was one grand.
- That makes sense but of course you will be envied for being so sensible. The trouble is that this ridiculous jealousy is everywhere, even politicians are at it. Everyone is suspicious and envious of everyone else to keep in *Tony's* good books. That is why this government is too busy messing about with politics instead of actually governing the country. Why on earth is the whole farce of fox-hunting come up again?
- It bores me shitless. As an issue it affects so few people so why is it important?
- Search me although did you hear the story of the lovely black M.P. what's his name? Pally Boating. He was on a hunt one time and a nearby protester shouted: 'A hundred years ago they would have been hunting you!' Pally smoothly replied: 'One hundred years ago I would have been *eating* you!'
- Love it. He is one bright guy isn't he? What's happened to him?
- I do not know. Possibly he actually is a socialist and therefore out of favour. There was another lovely line form a politician just t'other day. Do not laugh but I was listening to Wireless 4, I said don't laugh. Thank you. Actually it was Gardeners' Question Time.
- Oh give in Jude!
- Honestly! Merely because I am maturing and my tastes are changing there is no need for abuse. Let me get to the story. Someone in the audience asked a very detailed question about leeks, something to do with trimming last years roots or something and one immediately thought: 'That man *knows* about his leeks!' It transpired that the questioner used to be the Chairman of the T.U.C. and one of the panellists said: ' I always wondered how you could look so calm and even tempered in your former job, it was obviously your gardening keeping you sane.' 'No.' replied the chap, 'I just didn't know what was going on!'
- That's quite scary really. I do not envy politicians.
- I do. They get paid extremely well to sit on their collective behinds in meetings which as we all know are an excuse not to do any real work. 'A committee is a group of the unwilling, chosen by the incompetent to do the unnecessary!' as they say.
- And what's the definition of a camel?
- A strong cigarette?
- No a horse designed by a committee!
- Very good.
- So the world is consumed by envy is it?
- It is all around us. Men are envious of heartthrobs and know which Hollywood actors they are taller than. Women are envious of models and film stars and gloat over paparazzi pictures of cellulite. You know one of the best statistics ever?
- Other than 82.7% of all statistics are made up on the spot?
- That is funny isn't it. Vic Reeves? No the statistic I was thinking of is Marilyn Monroe, arguably the sexiest woman of the century was five feet six and a size fourteen.
- Really?

- Why not? The thing that gets to me though is why do so many people hate the Royal Family? That has got to be pure envy. What have they ever done except have more money than the rest of us?
- That is the only reason anyone ever gives for hating them. I like them, the amount of 'invisible exports' they create is enormous.
- Plus it is the most respected and known Royal Family in the world. When Edward VIII abdicated he was courted throughout the world as they even love our cast-offs. Why is it that people dislike the Royals but love The Simpsons?
- What?
- They are directly comparable. Homer says things like 'Doh!' and Prince Philip says things like: 'That fuse-box looks like it was put in by an Indian, or do I mean cowboy?' Both Marge and the Queen respond with: 'Heeummpgh.' Both Bart and Andy Prince were a bit annoying a few years ago but are now garnering some respect. Lisa and Charles have always been a bit sensible and starchy and we all wish that Edward spoke as much as Maggie in fact he would look quite sweet with a dummy! I am convinced that the Queen Mum and Grandpa Simpson would get on like a castle on fire!
- What about Princess Margaret?
- Either of Marge's sisters. Would you like a great story about Prince Philip?
- Go on?
- You know I used to do a lot of sailing?
- Huff and Saemus O' Hooligan?
- Well yes but this story involved Jamie the print broker, you have met him.
- Oh yeah.
- In sailing circles Prince Philip is known as Phil the Greek and he has a beautiful Sigma 38 based at Cowes. One year during Cowes week a race started and about three fleets went off on the same course including Yeoman, Phil's boat and Dodgy Lady, the boat Jamie was on. They were approaching and just rounding a mark when the wind dropped and all these boats started to pontoon together. As often happens at these moments a hush descended on the boats until suddenly Jamie shouted out: 'Oi! Phil? We'll have five donna and ten shish over here please!'
- No! What happened?
- Well Phil was at the back of the boat in a straw hat drinking what looked suspiciously like a gin and tonic. In the silence he raised his head, gave a beatific smile and raised his glass. All the other sailors burst into laughter and applause.
- Brilliant!
- There is also a great story about the Queen Mum. Apparently all of her staff are gay and one day she rang down from her apartments and said: 'One does not know about you old queens but this old Queen would like a gin and tonic!'
- Bless her! But that is another thing against the Royals isn't it, she's German and he's Greek.
- Oh for goodness sake! That might have been their origins, as mine are Irish but they have been British for some time now! If people are willing to believe that Greg Rudetski is English and cheer him on it would be a hint of hypocrisy not to support the Windsors.
- At least they sound British. You're right the only reason people ever give for disliking the Royals is the boring fiscal one.
- What really annoys me is the reaction to the Royal Family in the wake of Diana's death. My father is seventy-five this year and is part of the same generation as Elizabeth and Margaret. During the Second World War they all lost a myriad of friends and family. My father is a year older than The Queen and he lost untold people. The types that criticise the Royal Family for their reaction to Diana's death know *nothing* of what that generation went through. In the

Second World War my Father fought in the R.A.F., one of my uncles, John, fought in the Army and my father's other brother, Ken, fought in the Navy. All of them have medals that you would not believe. Do they talk about it? No! Unfortunately Ken died two years ago.
- I'm sorry mate.
- These things happen but just before the funeral I saw Uncle John. Do you know what he had to say about his brother's death?
- No?
- 'He was far too young.' and that was it! What people do not realise is that the Queen's generation had a large amount of their friends die very young and they had to deal with it in a stoic fashion. When Diana died they dealt with it as they always have done: 'It's a real shame but life goes on'. All the people shouting for flags at half mast and all the tabloid-inspired public hysteria only shows how this population have forgotten about the amazing things that the Queen, Princess Margaret, the Queen Mother and all of them did during the War. They did far more than Diana could *dream* of but everyone forgets that conveniently do they not?
- But the world has changed.
- Not to the extent that we should forget the bravery of our elders. But as far as the current world is concerned there are rich people and poor people and I would rather live in a world that has over-priviledge and under-priviledge than one where everyone is in the shyte. I cannot believe that people still think that money buys happiness. How many sob stories are there in glossy magazines about how miserable multimillionaires are? These poor rich types lock themselves away in their gilded cages and will never again know the simple pleasure of throwing on some clothes and wandering down the pub. I feel sorry for them.
- Do you?
- Of course. They will never know about sauntering around town on a Sunday afternoon watching couples hold on to the last vestiges of the weekend, going to actually very entertaining barbecues where you meet lots of new people, going to pubs by rivers in the summer and somehow getting wet or even going for country walks and investigating graveyards. It is amazing how happily unimportant one feels in a graveyard. Rich people have lost all of this and they have to catharsise on chat shows as well as at their expensive shrinks. My Dad told me a good one the other day.
- A good what?
- Well he used to love going round churches and he quoted his favourite epitaph: 'Tears will not bring him back; so I weep.' Wonderful is it not?
- That's very good but people will still buy their lottery tickets and hope.
- Hope of having an unhappy and rich life just like the people they are envious of? Did you hear the one about the priest who wanted to win the lottery so that he could fix the church roof?
- No?
- Well every night he prayed and Saturday came round but he did not win. So he prayed again and Wednesday came round but again nothing. By this point he was becoming impatient and his prayers became a little bolshy. Suddenly a voice came from Heaven and boomed across the church: 'Meet me half way, buy a bloody ticket will you!'
- I've just about got time for another. Similar? Yes please Peter.
- Oh God! If you must.
- So do you do the lottery Jude?
- No of course not. The folks do though.
- Of course soon to be back at Redmond Grange. So what are you going to do with your creative mind?

- I do not know. I tell people that I shall become an alcoholic but they always say: 'What do you mean become?' That joke just is not getting the mileage it should. But I am thinking of writing a compendium of party games.
- Party games.
- Indeed. You know when you are at a boring dinner party that needs rescuing from terminal dullness and you would like to say: 'Hey! Has anyone played Oddefs before?'
- Oddefs?
- Yes. This is quite an intellectual one this, you give me a word and I have to think up an *odd definition* of it.
- Oh right. Um. Aquiess?
- That is a female Aqui otherwise known as a Mermaid.
- Oh dear. How about bathos?
- Um. That is the Greek God of soap.
- Yes I suppose so. Try persiflage?
- That is one of my favourite words. It means gentle irony does it not. 'Do not overreact dear Bishop it was merely a hint of persiflage!' Wonderful word.
- Yes, yes but what's the oddef?
- Persiflage? He was the Blue Peter gardener!
- One more and then I'm going. Anecdotal.
- Ah now that is a northern term used by parents as an admonition to do something.
- Yes?
- It came originally from a mother exhorting her son to assist the authorities. She said: 'Our Nick, do tell!'
- I'd better catch my train.
- Have you got your big glove?
- You fool. Look I promise to stay in touch this time. Good luck with the leg.
- Indeed. Let me know how it goes with Alex and I hope to see you soon my friend.

* * *

- Hello little one.
- Philip! Or should I say: 'Uncle Puffin!' How are you?
- I'm all right. I hoped to find you naked.
- I could strip off now?
- No. It wouldn't be the same without the element of surprise. Are you ripping off the state again by pretending to be a war veteran or something?
- Absolutely. I grew tired of the office routine and have devised an ingenious plan to be on government expenses for the rest of my days. As they say: 'Working hours should be from two 'till two fifteen every other Wednesday, although I might be late!'
- It does sound a bit energetic. Did the spot come as part of the package?
- Actually I'm modelling myself on Darth Maul.
- Oh really?
- Yes. This is my first lump as part of the process of becoming a feared Lord of the Sith. Soon I shall be covered in them, striking fear into every heart. This may look like a walking stick but it is in fact my training light sabre.
- Have you seen it yet?
- No.

38

- Let's sit outside and I'll tell you it's not worth seeing. Let's go this way as it'll be harder for you.
- No thank you. I shall go the no steps route.
- Race you!

- Beat you!
- I refuse to indulge in spontaneous and degrading competitive sports Uncle Puffin.
- Jude's a bad loser, Jude's a bad loser.
- Quite possibly, I am English. So who shall we toast?
- Benny Hill.
- Benny Hill? Why not! Cheers. Anyway you were going to tell me about the Ghost of Dennis the Menace or whatever it is called.
- That's right. Well the plot is non-existent and the characterisation shallow but don't let me put you off.
- Oh no.
- The special effects you have seen before and quickly become tiresome but don't let me put you off.
- No, no.
- There are some really annoying characters that ruin the little that there is in the way of dialogue. Oh. There's something in my eye.
- Your finger.
- Oh yes but don't let me put you off.
- I am trying not to be.
- All in all it was very puerile and a waste of money really but don't let me put you off.
- I shall wait for it to come out on video.
- Oh I've got you all miserable now haven't I? Bad Uncle Puffin. You looked so happy when I walked in too. You poor thing. Would you like a laughable joke to cheer you up little one?
- Yes please Uncle Puffin.
- This chap's wife is pregnant, and early one evening she gets a craving for live snails.
- Live snails?
- This is in Joke Land.
- Sorry.
- That's all right, one interruption is forgivable but two is becoming rude. So he goes to the supermarket to get some live snails. On the way home he decides to nip in for a quick pint and he's just leaving when a mate walks in and insists he has another. One thing leads to a something and he eventually staggers home at midnight. After fumbling around for his keys, dropping the snails in the process, he realises he hasn't got them so he rings the bell and his wife appears at a window none too pleased. He eventually persuades her to let him in and as she opens the door he shouts: 'Right chaps come on we're almost there!'
- Wonderful. Consider me cheered up.
- I like that one. What did the snail on the back of a tortoise say?
- I dread to think?
- 'Wheeeeeeeee!'
- You are utterly insane my dear Phil. Actually your joke reminds me of a true story about a mate of mine Huff.
- Huff?
- Sure it is a sailing nickname. Huff got me into sailing a few years ago and has been sailing for most of his life. Anyway one day his long-suffering wife asked him to get some bread. He

39

went down the road and decided to have a pint first. In the pub he bumped into David who owns a lovely X Boat and they decided to go for a spin and sailed to Jersey.
- To Jersey?
- Apparently. They spend the next fortnight sailing around the Channel Islands, drinking too much and having fun before eventually returning home. Walking back to his flat Huff bought a loaf of bread which he dropped nonchalantly on the kitchen table. His amazed wife could only say: 'But I wanted brown!'
- Oh no! What did he do?
- He offered to go out again but she would not let him, quite understandably in the circumstances.
- Bit of a character Huff is he?
- Oh no. Very quite and retiring. A bit like myself really.
- So what is wrong with your leg?
- You know I had a crash nine years ago?
- No I didn't actually.
- Really? We must have always had more interesting things to talk about.
- Like now you mean?
- Very similar.
- I'm sorry. What's the story? You can tell your Uncle Puffin.
- Well. Nine years ago I worked as a hod carrier and I had my little bike, a 175 motor cross jobbie called Boozy. One night, July 23rd 1150 hours, a car pulled out in front of me, I somersaulted over the bonnet landing on my right leg which essentially shattered. They were going to amputate but saved it at the last minute using a technique developed in Russia in the Twenties to help mine victims so I was told. I had two years of intensive surgery and about a year in plaster. Then I had seven years of two workable legs and had a great time exploring the hidden depths of hedonism: 'My only regret is that I did not have enough sex!' In March the leg packed up. Essentially it is on strike because so much damage was done in the accident that it was like super-glueing a glass back together. Now it just does not work anymore.
- Will it be amputated?
- I do not know. It is a possibility because most of it is cold to the touch.
- It is isn't it. That's quite creepy.
- I am seeing someone soon. Plus my spine is twisted round due to nine year old, never diagnosed whiplash.
- So you could sue someone?
- I would not put myself through litigation again. I just have to accept it and carry on. At least I had seven good years and now I can retire.
- Is that what you are going to do now, retire? If you're going to retire you must have a highlight.
- A highlight of my life? That is an interesting thought. I would have to say seeing the Boomtown Rats ripping up posters of John Travolta and Olivia Newton John on Top of the Pops. It was the most anarchic thing I had ever seen and it really affected me artistically. How about you?
- I was going to say when my daughter was born but that seems a bit pedestrian now. Actually would you like to come to a party?
- Do dolphins actually *know* what to do with a beach-ball? Yes I would love to.
- It's my daughter's engagement party on Saturday at my place and I'm inviting everyone I know to have more friends there than she does. I'm like that you know, fiercely envious!

40

- It is Anne is it not it? I would be honoured sir.
- It's fancy dress though.
- Oh no! I cannot do my normal fancy dress thing any more. I used to wear my D.J. and have a water pistol but you cannot have Jimmy Bond with a limp can you?
- Well you have to be a film character and you have five days to think of something.
- Who's the lucky fella?
- A chap called Cain would you believe. He's very nice though a bit wild. He reminds me of you though without the hump and the bolts. I should have him killed really but I can't be bothered as I'd rather have the party. So yes come along Jude. I know your costume will be you all over, cheap but a lot of effort.
- I shall rush to you for a character reference.
- But you're retiring.
- Well it is a more positive way of saying: 'I'm giving up on everything' which would be a better description quite frankly.
- No more paper?
- No. I am fed up with media anyway. Everyone seems to think it is very sexy and exciting but all of those bright young things that used to do work experience with me were very keen not to do much. 'Never work with students and animals!' That is what I say. I just feel hugely disappointed with the modern media. Increasingly it is just a forum for the people that run papers and so on to peddle their views and prejudices.
- You think so. Personally I steer clear of television and papers these days as they only depress me.
- Good move! Switch off the fools' lantern! How people can let the flood of insidious propaganda just pour into their homes is beyond me, it is the very Devil's Magnifying Glass. It just provides them with stereotypes to envy or look down upon and it means that most people never actually think for themselves, they just digest the low fat, hypoallergenic ignorance that spews from their screens. They try to make out that violence and other unpleasant activities that producers insist are a fact of modern life infect our children with envy and hatred not to mention the videos and violence-ridden computer games. If advertising works which it does, then how much more are people affected by the stuff they concentrate on?
- Not a fan then?
- No. We are told that the tales of envy, bitterness, betrayal and revenge known as soap operas are 'real life'. No they are not! Real life is ordinary people getting home from a lousy job, not mixing with their neighbours and watching soap operas. It is all part of the continuing breakdown of a once friendly and decent community. Now everyone is scared and envious.
- I like watching the news though.
- So do I most evenings. Do you know how people should use television properly?
- Go on this should be interesting?
- Let us compare and contrast. First 'how not to'. Take copy of today's T.V. guide, 'That might be interesting. There is bound to be something good on this morning's one, as long as you like babies, fashion, cooking and minor health complaints. Oh that could be amusing. I can have lunch then. If I catch the end of that it leads into that and I like Australian propaganda. My friends say that's quite good. They're talking about Viagra tonight so I can feel smug. Another fly-on-the-wall documentary, I like those. I must see what's happening with thingie and whatsit. The film has a lousy review but I quite fancy her and I'll probably fall asleep.' That is what they call a wasted day.
- It happens all too often.

- Scenario two, 'How to do it properly', do di di do do How! Again with T.V. guide, 'No, no, no, no, oh a black and white with Jimmy Stewart. I shall tape it. No, no, no, no, Simpsons *yeah*! News. No, no, no. Interesting documentary, I shall tape it. I must start watching some of those tapes. No, no, no, absolutely not. Right that is that sorted out. Now to do something constructive until opening time.' A pleasant and potential-laden day I would wager good sir.
- I would agree except you need more cartoons in there. It amazes me I must say that not only is television just a stream of lack of consciousness but these idiots actually watch the junk they are fed.
- The papers are just as bad. Why do people buy tabloids? They are just a waste of trees. Take that poor rugby player what was his name? Barry De Bacleo. What on *earth* was that all about? That week had a big news story every day the first evidence of G.M. crops being detrimental to the environment, the Home Secretary admitted to changing his mind over Trial by Jury and I do not mean Gilbert and Sullivan, there was a war on in Kosovo and the Chinese Embassy had just been bombed, transport and health were under fire again...
- An interesting week then?
- It was a veritable news-fest but what was on the cover of Screws of the World? England captain took drugs! What was it all about? They had been trying to catch him out for three months! *Three months*! Eventually they tricked him into saying something stupid which is hardly a capital offence and by the Monday he was tried, convicted and sacked. Are we at the point where a man's career is worth less than a cheap headline in a sleazy newspaper?
- It didn't make any sense at all.
- Oh but it does! Run through this with me. The various newspapers owned by Darth Burdoch and Dandelion had been rubbishing the England rugby team for a while and with some of their reviews you wondered if they had been watching the same game. Then the England captain was assassinated in print. Ask yourself these questions, what is about to happen in the world of rugby union?
- The World Cup.
- Which is the best Northern Hemisphere team?
- England.
- What nationality does the Lord of the Wapping Lie purport to be?
- Australian. Ah ha!
- It is fairly obvious to me but then I do not watch television or read the tabloids so I am open minded.
- They must be very twisted and envy-ridden these reporters and editors.
- They are not reporters, certainly not according to the dictates of C.P. Scott. They work very hard to ruin other peoples' lives and the only motivation has to be jealousy of some sort but the blame does not rest there.
- No?
- No the buck stops with the utter *fools* that buy the damn things! If the population of this formerly great country stopped buying tabloids, read a decent broadsheet and watched a news program that was a little more than surface we might get some sort of turnout at elections as people would actually be informed for once. What is the point of having history when no-one knows what is going on around them? Quite frankly there are about fifteen million people in this country who are directly responsible for the tragic death of Princess Diana.
- That's a bit extreme.
- No it is extremely logical. If no-one bought tabloids there would be no paparazzi and she would still be alive. If only people realised that they hold the power. They proved it in

Liverpool so why not the rest of the country? You know there is a great truth out there that no-one seems able to see.
- Except you? You are the only one marching in step?
- I do not know but it strikes me that propaganda never went away. It is still with is but a lot more subtle and used by a wide variety of people for a huge range of purposes. It is not just the government and the war effort anymore. You can tell how happy a society is by the extent of criticism that goes on in all areas of life. Happy people do not criticise for no particular reason. At the moment in our country there are daggers drawn everywhere and everyone is full of envy. Everyone wants to be something else. The tabloid branch of our media is turning us into people that we are not. I would say two things about our media, there are a few people that have enormous influence in our lives because they control information and the list of non-Germans that did and still do support Nazism is quite a distinguished one.
- Oh, that's deep! Your trouble my friend is that you are an idealist. What you say might make sense to you but people like to have their petty jealousies. They like to have people in the spotlight to, as you said, either envy or despise. It is amazing when you hear people talking about celebrities and they say: 'I hate him!' How would they *ever* know?
- I do not know but I do know that without envy life is so much more enjoyable. Modern life is very comfortable in many ways compared to even fifty years ago so why do people insist upon making it unpleasant?
- Fifty years ago there was still rationing.
- Well exactly. Years ago I was a God-botherer and there was a little anecdote that I thought was quite deep in its own little way. Life is like a mountaineer who sets off looking at the peak with ambition and determination. Like most people he got a to a point where he realised he could go no further and so had two choices.
- Does this involve having a flask of hot beefy Bovril with Sherpa Tensing?
- It could do. His two choices were whether to look up enviously at the summit and those above him or just turn around and enjoy the view. It is the same for all of us. No-one seems to realise that in the same way that love and hate are very close and the opposite of both is indifference, envy and pride are very close but the opposite of both is?
- Marmite?
- No keep up with the conversation Philip. The opposite of pride/envy is equality. When you actually believe that all humanity is interestingly different and individual but we are all absolutely equal life becomes the wonderful experience it should be. No-one to be envious of and no-one to look down upon just help if you can.
- You really believe in equality don't you?
- Sure do. It works for me on an individual level so why should it not work in communities and societies? No-one has really given socialism a try. Let me give you a definition of equality in action.
- Must you?
- No but you will enjoy it.
- I doubt it. It's been your turn to make me miserable now. I'd rather talk about something nice like runny babbits or flutterbys.
- I beg your pardon?
- Granted. Oh go on then.
- If you are sure? Last Christmas Day I was in here with a crowd I had not met before but we were getting on very well, telling jokes and so on.
- You must have felt out of place.

43

- Like a fish in a frying pan, mixing my metaphors like the plague. I told a terrible joke but it fitted in with the situation.
- What joke?
- The one I am trying, quite hard I feel, to tell you. Thank you. A chap went into a brothel and said to the madam: 'I need the biggest, blackest woman you have please.' She took his money and steered him towards room twenty-seven or whatever. Sure enough there was an exceedingly large coloured lady there and your man asked her to strip naked and lie on her back with her legs parted as widely as possible. She did as asked whilst he proceeded to walk around the room chin in hand staring at her. After a few minutes she started tiring and wanted to know what he was doing. 'Don't worry.' he explained, 'It is just that we have a new leather sofa and I wanted to see what it would look like with pink cushions!'
- Not only is that a terrible joke but it has nothing to do with equality.
- Possibly not but the audience did. Out of the six people I told that joke to three of them were black. Did they laugh? Oh yes! In fact by the time I left I had been invited to a party and had four new 'phone numbers in my pocket. That joke, as you said, is in very poor taste but who is it actually offending? Equality is not about being polite under duress to people you do not know anything about, it is realising that we are all different and we are all equal. One should treat everyone with openness and respect.
- Right. Everyone the same hmm? Buy me a pint then.
- Here's the money, you get them.

- So what are you going to do to keep that razor mind of yours active Jude?
- I do not know.
- Are you still at your flat?
- For the moment yes but I am selling it and will probably move back to the folks in a couple of weeks.
- Oh are they nice your parents?
- They are great and wonderful company, I am very lucky. The last time I saw Dad a couple of weeks ago, he told me this great story. You see he was in the R.A.F. during the war and at one stage was billeted to Amman.
- I thought he was a scientist?
- That was after the war when he became a molecular chemist.
- Is he very small then?
- Oh for goodness sake! I am trying to tell you a story. When they arrived in Amman they were given the local commander's book of rules, 'third paragraph inst. of the above' and so on but one of these rules, 22c or whatever, just had the word: 'Cancelled' next to it.
- Cancelled? Really?
- Yes. The story goes that one night the C.O. was woken from his sleep by the sound of a woman screaming. He went to his door just in time to see a scantily-clad young woman laughing and squealing as she ran down the corridor with a naked Flight Lieutenant in hot pursuit. The C.O. had the chap arrested in the morning and swiftly arranged a Court Martial.
- Shame!
- At the Court Martial he was represented by a very clever fellow officer who quoted rule 22c which stated: 'An officer must be suitably dressed for the sport in which he is engaged.' so the chap got off!
- Wonderful. Does he tell stories like that all the time.
- Oh yes. In a dreadful American sitcom he would be the old guy that always talks about the war and everyone groans as he starts. What these producers do not realise is that these stories

and especially my Dad's are fascinating and far more entertaining than children being obnoxious.

- So you don't mind going home?
- Thank God I can. I would be dead by now if it were not for my parents. My mother is just as bad. She is wonderful. Like many Irish mothers she insists she is the most hospitable host in town and if you mention you are hungry within five minutes you are being ushered to a table set for a five course dinner! I am looking forward to it.
- It's a bit dangerous going back to live with your parents.
- Really?
- Oh yes. A friend of mine had a terrible experience. He'd had a bust up with his wife and with nowhere else to go he returned to the family home. The first morning he wakes up at about six and decides: 'I think I'll have a wank!'
- Like you would.
- Well yes. He puts his stereo headphones on, AC/DC or something appropriate I wouldn't know of course.
- Of course.
- So he gives himself a right seeing to, a real back-archer you know. When he opens his eyes with a sigh there is a cup of steaming coffee next to him!
- No! Oh my God! You would have to kill yourself immediately.
- But don't let me put you off! Is it nice your parents' house?
- Redmond Grange?
- Is that it's name?
- No it is number 18 but I like to be pretentious. It is lovely, opposite the clock tower in Enshemgate Park.
- Oh it's nice up there, very posh.
- I know. They have all these strange parties with white wine and canapés.
- They ought to have one of those out here. The sun's a bit strong.
- Would a prawn vol-au-vent do?
- It would have to be a big one but talking of going home if my wife thinks I'm happy she won't be.
- The joys of domestic bliss. How is she now?
- Much better thank you.
- Give her my best won't you?
- Of course. I'll give you a tinkle and we can sort out a smoke in the park or a drink or something but I'll see you Saturday anyway?
- Oh yes! I would not miss one of your parties for the moon. Cheers Uncle Puffin.
- 'Bye little one.

* * *

- Jude?
- Yes Peter?
- I think you're a little bit pissed now.
- Yes Peter.
- It's definitely time you went home.
- Yes Peter.
- Shall I call you a cab?
- Yes Peter.

45

- Are you all right?
- No Peter.
- I don't suppose you are really.
- Lets just say that Jude United is at the top of the Depressive League and in contention for the Suicide Cup. This week's Suicide Cup.
- Come on Jude, you're strong enough to deal with this.
- Am I really? That is good news.
- Look you fool you'll find a way of dealing with it and survive. It's what you're best at. Meanwhile if you get to the semi-finals give me a call. Any time.
- Thanks mate. I appreciate that.
- Now piss of out of my pub.
- Yes Peter.

Monday 8th June: **GLUTTONY**

I woke up at two fifteen on the sofa with a mouth like a camel's sandal, an empty bottle of brandy on my chest and a cigarette butt between two heavily blistered fingers. Movement was dreaded but inevitable. Every single part of my body was screaming: 'You bastard!' I have really got to stop doing this to myself. There was only one thing to do, make one of my renowned Bloody Marys. It is the celery salt that does it don't you know!

As soon as I saw myself in the bathroom mirror I knew that I *really* must stop doing this to myself. What a mess! I thought about shaving as two day's growth is not particularly flattering but upon noticing my shaking hands the thought lapsed. I have no intention of holding a sharp object to my face using those vibrating digits. I hobbled to bed, I cannot honestly use the word 'back' and eventually drifted off but unfortunately it was to an old and feared nightmare. They say that most people only dream in black and white with no sound so why is it that I get glorious Technicolor with quadraphonic sound? It makes bad dreams *really* scary.

The morning proper sauntered in eventually and I decided it was high time I had some real solids. One microwave lasagne later the rouge flowed and an Elvis Costello moment seemed appropriate. Everyone on the wireless was sounding far too happy for my state of mind.

Tom arrived with his mate Jonathan to dismantle my bed and then proceeded to dismantle the rest of the flat as well. I hope the folks do take me back otherwise I am truly buggered. I do wish Tom would pull himself together, I always have to give him pep talks. He needs to get off his personal slippery slope very soon.

Mags rang from work all excited now that she has fixed up a date with the accountant. Am I being prejudiced about accountants? As soon as anyone says that word I yawn instinctively, still Mags seems happy enough and that will do for now.

This afternoon I did my bit for society in general and gave some blood. For some reason they can always find a vein easily and it flows out very pleasantly. Calling me a 'good little bleeder' is the standard joke. They held it in the happy-clappy church near the station rather than the Corn Exchange which is the usual location. I must admit the atmosphere was more convivial than normal probably due all of the pictures of happy-clappy people that proliferated the place. It was my tenth time and they gave me a tie-pin which was very sweet but it is as quaint as it is useless. I intend to never wear a tie again.

I had dinner with the folks, chicken something or other tasty. I am lucky to have them but I have to be drunk or stoned to tell them which always diminishes the message somewhat. I really should stop being such an alcohol glutton.

* * *

- Hello?
- Jude it's Tom.
- Come on up.

47

- Hello mate. How are you. You look a little tight may I say.
- I'm O.K. Jude. Have you meet Jonathan?
- I think so. How are you Jonathan?
- Fine, fine.
- Can I get you kind labourers some liquid refreshment?
- I think Tom needs a coffee. I certainly wouldn't mind one.
- Tom? Coffee?
- I doubt it have you got any vodka?
- Sure. What with it?
- More vodka.
- A man after my own liver! All right chaps get to work and I shall put the kettle and the distillery on.
- They won't suit you!
- Very good, very good!

- A toast gentlemen, the late and great Ken.
- Ken who?
- The late and great Kenneth Williams of course! Cheers. So what is happening to make you drink neat vodka at eleven in the morning Tom?
- Don't even fucking ask Jude. Anyway you're on the red wine.
- Well that would appear to be the end of that illuminating conversation. There is a difference between drinking and being sozzled at this hour Tom. Jonathan did I ever tell you about my favourite bed story?
- I don't think so Jude. Is that a spot on your neck?
- No this is the latest in drinking technology. It works on the same principle as a camel's humps by drip-feeding me beer when I am not in a pub. It is absolutely *wonderful* and every home should have one!
- It's a bloody great spot.
- Thank you so much for noticing. May I continue with the story now? Thank you. I was on holiday by myself in Spain, sunny Espania, as I needed to get away for some reason. I was staying in a hostel and just wandering around drinking and reading the sort of books one never normally gets a chance to read.
- Like what?
- Oh *hello* Tom. Books like Far from the Madding Crowd, The Monk, Wuthering Heights and so on.
- Very nice.
- So Jonathan, I was sitting outside an English bar one night reading Keats ostentatiously when I could not help overhearing a conversation between a Yorkshire couple in their fifties. It went something like: 'So what's up with Bill and Joan then?' 'I don't know, everything was going fine for them. The kids had left home, his pension had come through, they had the new extension done, bought a new car, and they even had a water bed but they just seemed to drift apart!'
- Really? How marvellous.
- The thing was that I could not help laughing out loud and the woman came over to my table. 'Oh hello.' she said, 'We've noticed you sitting here by yourself, would you like to come and join us?' Trying very hard to keep a straight face I replied: 'It is all right thank you. I am quite happy here with my book.'
- Very polite.

48

- Of course but she carried on: 'Oh you like being by yourself do you?' 'That is right.' 'You'd get on ever so well with my niece as she likes being by herself as well!'
- Oh no! Did she realise?
- Oh yes she was definitely a 'mouth in motion before brain in gear' sort of person and she blushed, said goodnight and I wished her well. I was giggling for the rest of the evening imagining myself and some young woman sitting at opposite ends of a pub reading and occasionally waving to one another over the crowd of sociable people! It was *quite* hysterical. Well Thomas are you feeling a little more communicative? What is on your mind my friend.
- Just life really. It's just one nightmare after another. Tell us a joke and I might relax a bit.
- Sure. You will like this one Jonathan or is it wrong of me to assume you prefer male company in your own bed?
- Oh no accurate enough.
- How do you know when you have been burgled by gays?
- I don't know I haven't heard this one?
- Your furniture is rearranged and there is a quiche in the oven!
- That is funny!
- You can always make me smile, Jude.
- It is a veritable gift. Do not stop working gentlemen get that bed dismantled! How is my darling Judy?
- Not very happy.
- Why Tom?
- I got pissed last night and we had a row.
- About?
- Money as normal. I hit her.
- Not again you BLOODY FOOL!
- I couldn't help it she just wouldn't stop going on.
- She was 'going on' to try and get some sense out of you! How do you think she feels working all night in that grotty pub with drunken men leering at her and then coming home to find you drunk in charge of the kids? I am not surprised she was 'going on'.
- Yeah I know.
- Then put your knowledge into action. It is one thing to get drunk, silly and lose the battle against gravity as is my wont of an evening but if you become violent when drunk you only have one option, *stop drinking*!
- It's not that easy.
- Try harder. If you continue like this and Judy decides to leave you I shall back *her* up, not you and if she needs someone to stand up in court and say that you were violent I shall do that too.
- I suppose you would call that being a friend?
- If it stopped you drinking and wrecking your own marriage it would be the best thing anyone has ever done for you, you spooning muffin.
- I doubt it.
- What are these money problems exactly?
- We just never seem to have enough. The forge is picking up and I'm also working part-time, Judy's been promoted and will probably be able to leave the pub soon, she really wants to but I don't know it just never seems to go anywhere and God knows when we'll be able to go on holiday.
- And that is what is making you drink and hit your lovely wife?
- Look it's hell O.K. How long do I have to graft before we're comfortable?

- Well it took my folks over forty years. That is cheering news is it not? Look mate you are simply a victim of media inspired gluttony. You want a holiday? Why? Why on earth does anyone need to go to a foreign country to relax? You might get some sun if you are lucky but does anyone actually explore the local culture? No you could be anywhere. For you with three kids going anywhere is a nightmare, you would spend far too much money and come back exhausted having lost count of the number of rows would you not? And do not say: 'I doubt it'.
- I suppose so.
- You, like everyone else, watch these programs that insist you *have* to go on holiday, you *have* to have a new kitchen, bathroom, conservatory, you simply *must* have a new car, you *have* to follow this seasons fashions and so on. It is *rubbish* my friend. They are merely inciting people to gluttony.
- What's all that got to do with eating too much?
- Gluttony, dear Tom is quite simply wanting more than you need. Yes it applies to people who eat too much which is everyone in the developed world but it also relates to consumerism. Look at it from the other point of view you have a delightful wife who *does* love you, you have three great kids who would be happier in a more relaxed home-atmosphere, you have a big enough house for all of you with a garden, you have a new and growing business that you love, you have A to B transport and you have a lot of friends who will help you when you need it. Was any of that untrue?
- No.
- Then what more do you or anyone else for that matter need? Does this make sense to you Jonathan?
- Veritable words of wisdom Jude.
- You see my friend we are all victims of an immense confidence trick. We are constantly bombarded with all sorts of information about things and they are only things, that we do not actually need. The more we buy the wealthier the producers of these things become and the more useless junk they turn out. The result is a world where 80% of the wealth is owned by 10% of the people. There is enough to provide for everyone's needs but instead a world has been created where people can say without guilt: 'I would like to give to charity but I am saving for my holiday/new washing machine/car/whatever.' It is *sick*!
- The old: 'Money can't buy you happiness' routine?
- To re-mint a cliché. But of course it cannot. Happiness comes from within and is based in an acceptance and reconciliation of oneself. Things are just things. But there is a very clever system of propaganda in place whereby the people that can afford these things are paraded in front of us smiling happily and we want to have what they have. Gluttony is very instinctive probably as a method of survival but it is no longer necessary within this society. You do not need this stuff. How can anyone justify couture fashion? It is overpriced and virtually useless as they wear it once and throw it away. Gluttons!
- They do look beautiful though.
- Jonathan these models would look beautiful in my old jumpers and that is why they use them.
- I suppose so.
- The government should put an extra V.A.T. on designer goods, slap another ten per cent or something and the money could go to charities for the homeless. Those lovely, lovely darlings can easily afford it. When you start to think about things with a free mind not much about modern society makes any sense at all.
- Only when you're pissed.

- I do not think that was a sensible contribution to the subject young Thomas. Ah got you smiling! Do you want a coffee now?
- Yeah please Jude. That would be a good idea.
- Jonathan?
- Oh yes please.
- Keep dismantling.

- Take this for an example, in twenty years time how many blades do you think there will be on a man's razor? The one I use occasionally has two, they have just brought one out with three so at this rate by the year 2010 your average razor will have seventeen blades for a 'closer shave'. What an absolute waste of time, resources and money. My Dad shaves every day with his safety razor and his face is as smooth as a rather wrinkled baby's bottom! We do not *need* this stuff and we *definitely* do not need most of the beauty business.
- The beauty business?
- Absolutely. There are enough shampoos, conditioners, make-up ranges, soaps, spot treatments and so on now. We do not need any more! It is total overkill and gluttony. If these bloody companies used their clever scientists for something useful like cures for cancer instead of a thicker mascara the world might get a little better.
- How much do they spend on developing new products?
- A few third world economies. It cannot be justified and what about cars? Why do we need them to be developed any further? Excuse me but cars are helping to destroy our environment and are a reason for the huge increase in asthma and respiratory problems apart from the huge number of people they kill every day. What *are* they doing? Would it not be a better idea to spend some time and money on making the bloody things more environmentally safe and I mean *safe*, not the meaningless 'friendly', rather than how to put a bloody *drinks-cooler* in one?
- What will they think of next?
- The fact is that we are being conned into buying more and more of this rubbish that actually does not benefit us in the slightest. Television, videos and computer games stop family conversation that used to be an important part of the learning process. Instead of learning to communicate our children now learn how to swear and be violent.
- There is no link between videos and violence.
- Bovine manure my friend! Advertising works so what we watch and hear does influence everyone you *cannot* have it both ways. Everyone was shocked when James Bulger was killed but quite frankly I am amazed it does not happen every day. In America it nearly does of course and who led the communication revolution? It is very ironic how the communication revolution actually decreases real, meaningful communication. Everything that emanates from cathode-ray tubes affects us all.
- Q.E.D. I suppose?
- Damn right. Cars stop people from exercising and again restrict conversation. We are constantly told that there are more exciting places than where we live so no-one knows about their home towns because they have never walked around them simply exploring. They drive to the hypermarket instead. A cultural palace each and every one!
- Computers?
- Are fantastic things and an excellent educational tool but should not be used for mind-numbing games and the explosion of exploitative pornography. Quite frankly it is a crime that they are so expensive because it is creating a cultural divide. The gap between the I.T. rich and I.T. poor is a scandal but take something else, fashion. What the *hell* is that all

about? We are told to spend large amounts of money to all look the same. You know when you are fashionable because you look just like someone else. I am terribly sorry but I happen to be an individual human being not a sheep called Dolly! I shall wear what keeps me warm and comfortable whether it is this season's or from the Eighties.
- You can't say that me or Jonathan are fashionable.
- You are just conforming to non-conformality like so many young people do. You still all look the same and then become infuriated for being 'labelled'. People of the world wake up! The point is, dear Tom do not let yourself be taken in by consumerism which just leads you into a vicious circle of gluttony that will never make you happy. Enjoy what you have and make the most of it. Remember the happiest family on T.V. were the Waltons!
- Are you saying we should all live on a mountain to achieve happiness?
- No I am saying that that specific program was about people that had enough and were happy because there was no television and they talked to each other and so on. They are a prime example of enjoying what you have. The stupid thing is that the people that one sees splayed across the glossies saying how lucky they must be are the same people that turn up a few months later in a different glossy saying how miserable they are! It is *all* a confidence trick.
- Okay Jude I have tried not to butt into your conversation with Tom but what you are suggesting is a conspiracy theory that makes Paul McCartney's alleged death look like chicken feed.
- As long as it is vegetarian and organic no doubt? Absolutely Jonathan. Propaganda has never gone away it has just become more subtle. What would happen to our economy if everyone realised that they were buying shyte by the bucket load because they believe advertising? It is not worth contemplating.
- So what are you saying?
- Just because everyone else falls for the trick it does not mean you have to. Be aware of what is going on and remember that there is a system of envy and gluttony in place that is actually inspiring millions of people to become wasteful, vacant, lazy, uninformed, fickle, indifferent, uncaring, gluttonous and miserable. All of this is in place to make you think that you do not have enough to be happy. We are all manipulated by the few rich people keeping the rest of us poor and wanting. What I am saying Jonathan is do not fall into the trap.
- I told you he had a brain on him didn't I Jonathan?
- You said a brain not a limping revolution. He's has enough hot air to send Dicky Pickle around the world three times in his balloon.
- That was one of the most individual compliments I have ever been given. Thank you Jonathan.
- My pleasure.
- You always make sense Jude but, I don't know you always remind me of Columbus. No-one believed him until he proved it but you can't prove any of what you are saying.
- True on a global level but I can help *you*.
- How?
- Let me give you another story. Have you finished now chaps? That bed is looking very dismantled.
- Yeah we've finished.
- You are welcome to my hospitality until you want to go but as I was saying Tom and I am sorry to bring this up because of your own family situation, what you have to realise is that your children are currently forming an impression of you which is drunk and argumentative. At this rate you will not see much of them in the distant future.
- What are you saying Jude?

- I am talking about the deep and complicated relationship between a father and his children. My own father I love and respect and he is an inspiration to me. If I achieve half of my Father's decency then I really have achieved something. Let me illustrate that. My brother, James is a high-ranking scientist in the States and if you happen to be into the world of X-ray crystallography then Professor James Redmond is your guru. Just to fill you in Jonathan my father is a scientist. James has been travelling all over the world to conferences and so on and every time he meets someone who has been to the university here they always mention the story of Uncle Joe.
- Uncle Joe?
- Yes. Every chemist that has visited the university and then meets James talks of Uncle Joe: 'Sure I was doing some research into these miserable polymers and getting nowhere when someone suggested that I ask Uncle Joe. He's this old guy that wanders around the labs in a brown lab coat so I asked Uncle Joe for some help and he virtually solved all of my problems. A great man and chemist.' James has lost count of the number of times he has had that conversation.
- So what's your point?
- That is the story I tell to show people how incredible my Father is. Tom what are your children going to say about you?
- I don't know.
- You are the only person that can give them an opinion. Stop wasting your life because it is not just yours anymore. Anyway to lighten the situation somewhat I want to ask your opinion on something.
- After all that pontificating you want our opinion on something?
- Not yours obviously Jonathan, you quite clearly have no innate sense of style!
- You're more bitchy than most of the queens I know.
- It is a talent. Seriously chaps I am thinking about having another tattoo done.
- How many do you have if you don't mind my asking?
- Eight.
- Where?
- Arms and back. But I have no intention of showing you Jonathan I merely wish the opinion of my old friend and possibly yours if I can be bothered.
- What of mate?
- A bar-code on my left hand.
- Why?
- It all came from a conversation I had a while ago when I was trying to get the paper going.
- What did happen to that?
- Do not ask it was a disaster. I was at some do in the Corn Exchange and I got into conversation with a lovely woman about civil liberties, the Nanny State, and so on. She said that we are all just numbers and I retorted that I had always seen my self as more of a bar-code. Merely a bit of wit but it started me thinking. The current train of thought is to have a bar-code tattooed on my left hand as a protest against consumerism, commercialism and the general mercenary attitudes that exist. I might have mentioned them earlier on.
- They did crop up I believe.
- So what do you think?
- Why the left hand?
- Purely logistics. Because of Moses here a tattoo on the right hand would be problematic when it scabbed up as the pressure on the hand would damage the tattoo.
- What numbers would you have?

- I am not sure yet. I have been thinking about 'Jubilee 2000' but that is very transitory no matter how worthy.
- You'll have to be careful in supermarkets. You'll either double your shopping bill or be charged with shoplifting your own hand!
- I wonder what it would come up as Jude? You'd want a crate of beer or a case of vodka.
- Knowing my luck it would be a bumper pack of nappies.
- It's not a brilliant idea having a tattoo on your hand.
- Why not?
- Well it won't do you any favours at job interviews.
- Tom I am never going to be able to work again. Interviews are not an issue.
- In that case I'd say go for it. What do you think Jonathan?
- Oh absolutely. I would like to see your others though.
- Maybe another time.
- So what are you going to do now Jude?
- Finish this bottle of rouge.
- You know what I mean. Where are you going to live?
- I am having dinner with the folks tonight to see if I can move back there. It will become Redmond Grange Hospice for the Virtually Useless.
- You get on with them?
- Sure Jonathan, they are great.
- What will you do with your time?
- I have not a clue. Survive I suppose I am not quite ready to swing from a tree as yet.
- You'll survive Jude, you always have. Why are you smoking roll-ups?
- It is a false economy drive. Smoking is just so expensive these days that I cannot afford two packs of Marlboro a day so I supplement one pack with roll-ups. Money is tight for everyone my friend but I do not let it get me down. I would say it is time you went home with a big bunch of flowers and apologised to your lovely wife.
- I think he's right Tom.
- I doubt it.
- Oh, ha, ha. Thank you for taking the bed apart. Would you be able to re-mantle it in a week or so?
- Yeah of course mate. No problem.
- Actually I am not going to need a lot of this stuff at the folks so is there anything you want?
- Do you mean anything?
- Just ask and I shall give you a yea or nay.
- The television? The sofa? The microwave? This table? The video?
- No that is not mine to give but you can have all the other stuff. There are also some clothes that might do for slaving over a hot forge.
- Thanks Jude that's great. We'll just go and get the van.

- Right Tom now that you have emptied my flat you may depart. Actually can you give me a lift to the station. It is my day for bloodletting.
- No problem.
- Let us depart then.

* * *

- Hello?

- JUDE!
- Mags?
- JUDE!
- Yes?
- I'VE DONE IT!
- What? The four minute mile, scaled the Matterhorn with only a toothpick, learned to play the flute? What have you done Honey?
- I have a date with Magnus.
- Congratulations, hussar and who would have thought that the world would end on a Monday?
- You muffin! I'm ringing from work so I'd better be quick.
- Nonsense it is your right to make 'phone calls from work. Actually the E.U. or one of those useless and corrupt bodies are bringing in decent law for a change saying that employees are allowed to make personal calls. Damn right too! But anyhow Mags, love of my life and light of my heart I am bursting with joy and wonder that you have achieved so much, so soon. When is the date then?
- Wednesday night.
- Come on what did he say?
- Well he was being very cool. I left a message on his voice-mail saying that if he wanted a drink or whatever he'd better call me soon.
- Nice one.
- So he called this morning sounding all nonchalant and saying that Wednesday night he wouldn't be busy so I said: 'If I'm too much of an inconvenience don't bother!'
- Excellent. Does he have the faintest idea what he is in for?
- What do you mean?
- I mean my dearest Magdalene that you are far too wonderful for most men to even talk to.
- What about Magnus?
- I do not know as yet but carry on.
- Well that lost his cool a bit and he asked if I would like a drink or dinner so I said: 'If you think I'm coming out just to feel hungry you'd be wrong. It's dinner of course!'
- You are dynamite! What did he say?
- Well he asked if he could pick me up but I don't want him knowing where I live.
- Good move.
- So I told him to meet me in the pub next door. Of course he doesn't know it's the pub next door and at least I'll have my friends around me.
- Do you know where he's taking you?
- I've forgotten the name but it's somewhere really posh in Richmond.
- Hark at her and good for you! How are you feeling?
- Nervous.
- Do not be Honey. Remember that he is chasing you. Make sure he is worth your company because quite frankly, I have never meet a vaguely interesting accountant but you never know.
- What should I do then?
- At dinner? Order the most expensive thing on the menu and pick at it to make sure he is not lacking in generosity. If he moans about wasting money then drop him! But also order a really good wine, not necessarily the most expensive just one that you will enjoy. After all you will be too nervous to eat much so make sure you have something decent to drink. Also insist on pudding. It is *vital* you have some pudd!
- Why?

- Why not? In the words of oh what is his name the broadcaster? Fanny Faker, that's the fella! In the words of Fanny: 'Live for the moment, there were people on the Titanic who *waved* away the sweet trolley!'
- You're mad. I was a bit put off by him pretending to be cool.
- Do not be harsh, we all do it. It shows that he is really keen if he is trying to be suave. A few years ago I met this lovely girl in a boozer. Now what was her name? I really ought to remember the names of my lovers. Liz! That was it but I was chatting away with her, getting ever so well and I thought that I would try and be flash to impress her. I had had a few pints by this point.
- Surprise me.
- BOO! Will that do?
- Get on with the story you lunatic.
- So I produced a pack of Marlboro and offered her one which she took. I then brought out the Zippo and tried to do the showy lighting trick, you know the one?
- When you flick it alight you mean?
- That's the fella but I succeeded, it actually worked and I felt *blessed*! Unfortunately I had cut my finger on the damn thing and was dripping blood all over her clean white jeans as I lit her cigarette!
- Oh no! You never quite manage do you?
- It depends on the situation.
- Did you pull her then?
- She stayed with me for a while yes.
- But that one didn't last either? I suppose you consider yourself a stud?
- Mags you know what my life has been like. I am no 'stud' I have just always been a caring man with nothing going for me. Women love the first and hate the second so my relationships last about six weeks but we were talking about *you*. If he is trying to be a la Jimmy Bond it shows you are in, if you will pardon the expression. Take your time and decide if he is worth it.
- You think so?
- Honestly Mags he is the one thinking that he is into you so take your time and remember the old and dreadful musical gag.
- Which is?
- Sometimes B sharp, never B flat but always B natural.
- Thank you Jude. I'd better get some work done.
- Of course Honey but ring whenever you want, the machine is off. Be happy Sweetie, it is *definitely* your turn.
- 'Bye Jude. Love you.
- Love you too.

* * *

- Good evening dear Mother of mine. You are looking resplendent in lilac may I say.
- You can say as much as you like along those lines.
- But the shoes clash! Honestly Mother red shoes with lilac what *were* you thinking?
- Get in you dreadful man. How a son of mine could be so rude to his long-suffering mother.
- What do you mean 'long-suffering'? You have a great time. I might have to go into Basil Fawlty mode: 'Stuck underneath the hairdryer again dear? Nail file a little sharp this morning was it my little nest of vipers? Wrist a touch tired from holding heavy Maeve Baenchy novels

for too long? There, there you *poor* thing. Just lie down in this iron maiden and it will soon be all over!'
- You lunatic. Go and talk to your father while I finish the dinner.
- Have you not got it trained to leap into the oven of its own volition as yet?
- No it's been very intransigent. No amount of whipping will budge it.
- I shall buy you a Barbara Woodhouse book for Crimble.
- What would you like with your Chicken Marengo? Rice or spaghetti?
- Spag please Mum and don't just stand there woman! Give me a bottle of something rouge if you would and I shall seek my father in the jungle that is your patio.
- Cheeky blighter! It's a beautifully maintained patio and there's an open bottle out there.
- You know me so well.

- Hiya Pops. How's you?
- Ah number 1. Still on the stick?
- God's larder I told you to stay at home! Sorry Dad but Moses is so insecure being scared of the dark or something that he just keeps following me around. I trust you will not treat him like a gatecrasher. What is this? Cotes de Rhone? It smells more like Cotes de Grimsby, still needs must when the Devil's your chauffeur.
- Actually that would be quite fun. We never get the excitement of gatecrashers at your mother's dos and I sometimes dream of someone, looking not dissimilar to yourself a few years ago storming in, throwing canapés against the wall and being generally rude to the terminally dull people your mother insists upon inviting round here. Variety is the spice and all that.
- Avoiding clichés like the plague?
- Like the bubonic plague.
- Why is it that you both always offload each other onto me?
- How do you mean?
- Well it is always: 'Your father!' or: 'your mother!' so why do you never admit to each other?
- You've heard of the 'Seven year itch'? Well this is known as the 'Forty year glitch' but you're too young to know about that yet.
- Welcome back to: 'Patronising is us!'. Anyway the garden is looking good.
- It's a mess. When you consider the amount of work that has gone into twenty square yards of garden over twenty-two years it is quite pathetic! We wouldn't get it into the Chelsea Polytechnic Flower Show.
- Firstly that would be due to being in the wrong location and secondly it is now a university.
- Hah! They'll never be universities.
- But as I was trying to say or compliment rather, the garden does look very pleasant. Those roses in particular are spectacular.
- Until your mother cuts their heads off and sticks them on top of her piano.
- There is a horticultural French revolution on the go at Redmond Grange is there? With Mum being the chief Tricoteuse?
- I don't know why I bother sometimes.
- Just 'sometimes' now is it? That is an improvement as it used to be 'at all'.
- I'm mellowing in my middle age.
- Of course you are Pops. How are the tomatoes coming on?
- Bloody waste of time as normal. Fifteen years I've been trying to raise tomatoes and there's been a total of three vaguely edible ones so far although your mother was rather ill after eating hers last year.

- Stop grinning! She was ill for days.
- The peace and quiet was heavenly. This year I am trying a new variety which are supposed to be foolproof so it is bound to be a bigger disaster than normal. They are called: 'Gardener's Delight' which strikes me as being the height of foolish optimism. Still we shall see.
- I am sure that they will be a great success.
- They'll probably develop the Millennium Bug early leaving me with a greenhouse full of rotting vegetation as per normal. There was rather an amusing letter in the Times the other day that reminded me of an old joke. Have I told you the Barbie doll joke?
- The 'Barbie doll joke'? How can that be an old one?
- It's all relative you fool now listen!
- Yes Dad.
- This chap rushes into a toy shop and says: 'It's my daughter's birthday tomorrow. What Barbie dolls do you have and how much are they?' The rather bored salesgirl recites: 'There's Malibu Beach Barbie, she's £19.99. There's Pony Trekking Barbie, she's £19.99. There's Moped in Milan Barbie, she's £19.99. There's Alpen Skiing Barbie, she's £19.99.'
- Is that her whizzing down a hill of muesli?
- Oh very good. May I continue? Thank so much. Where was I? Oh yes: 'There's Water-skiing in St. Tropez Barbie, she's £19.99. There's Moon Buggy Barbie she's £19.99 and there is Divorced Barbie who is two thousand, seven hundred and fifty-two pounds!' The man chokes slightly and inquires: 'Why is divorced Barbie so expensive?' 'Well.' the young lady retorts, 'She comes with Ken's car, Ken's house, Ken's horses...'
- Like it! That is very good but I hope you are not making a young man cynical about marriage?
- You were born cynical, from your Mother of course.
- I am not cynical! What did Oscar Wilde say? 'A cynic is a man who knows the price of everything and the value of nothing.' or something.
- That's about right. Funnily enough I bought a book recently entitled: 'The Bumper Book of Insults' which I shall lend you. As you would imagine Oscar features rather strongly and my favourite so far is: 'Oh Oscar I passed by your house the other day.' 'Thank you!'
- Pithy. You are not going to get a more succinct insult than that are you? Shall we have a toast to the late and great Oscar?
- I don't know what he'd think of me toasting him with mineral water but why not! To Oscar.
- To Oscar. My favourite of his was the story of him doing a Greek oral exam where they gave him a scene from The Passion. Which university was he at?
- Magdalen College Oxford.
- Well an oral exam there then. Anyway he was translating the Greek story of the crucifixion into perfect idiomatic English and the examiners were very impressed. After a time one of them asked him to stop but he continued. A minute or so later he was asked to stop again but blithely carried on translating. Eventually one of the examiners said: 'Really Mr. Wilde that is quite enough!' but Oscar replied: 'Oh do let me carry on, I want to see how it ends!'
- Very good. I have always wondered why he was singled out for punishment when homosexuality was so rife in his circles at the time?
- Well he got greedy did he not. He wanted it all, not only to be a recognised writer and wit but a renowned gay as well. He was gluttonous with his own fame.
- As opposed to glutinous?
- Not an image I want to dwell upon thank you Dad.

- There was another of his but it has escaped my mind for the moment I'm becoming so absent-minded. Did I ever tell you the story of old Prof. Jenkins? He was terribly absent-minded.
- Did I ever meet him?
- Possibly. His best trick was to wander around the place with his specs on his forehead asking: 'Has anyone seen my glasses?' Lovely chap. One time he was at a Town and Gown do and was sitting next to a very attractive woman in her late thirties. 'But Professor Jenkins you must remember me?' she cries. 'Ummm?' responds the beleaguered don. 'Bristol 1978.' she continues, 'You asked me to marry you.' 'Ah!' says the Prof. coming to life. 'Ah yes. Ah. And um, did you?'
- Wonderful. Yes I think I do remember him. He always called me Eric for some reason.
- That was one of his sons' names but it is very hard for *me* to remember yours most of the time although I can remember all of the names of my fellow squadron members. There was Terry 'Knobby' Fletcher...
- Not now Dad thank you. Just stick to No. 1 and we shall be all right. Do you remember when I was studying Psychology?
- Hah! Of course I do and a bloody waste of time that was! What was your quote?
- 'If psychology is a science it is the science of sweeping generalisations, vague hypotheses and the occasional intelligent guess to provide a sketchy mind-map for the middle-class, Caucasian quasi-intellectual.'
- Bloody marvellous that was.
- I hope you're not swearing in front of our son Joseph?
- No dear. This bloody house has too many windows to eavesdrop from but yes I remember it was about seven years ago?
- That's the one. A friend had lent me a textbook that was far more interesting than the one we were supposed to use which was a boring tome of a thing. One of the features of this book was that it had cartoons all the way through and one of them was an elderly couple talking with the caption: 'On the contrary! I can remember exactly what I did yesterday but I haven't a clue about thirty years ago!'
- Yes very good.
- Another one was a chap in his office and in a right old mess with ink everywhere. There was another bloke coming through the door saying: 'Good lord Horsach! What are you doing?'
- Very droll.
- You two seem to be having far too much fun up here. You're not enjoying yourselves are you?
- Well dear I've read so much about enjoyment over the years that I thought I would give it a try.
- So what do you think Dad?
- Overrated.
- Your father was clearing out the attic the other day and found your old action men. Aren't they supposed to be valuable these days?
- Some are Mum but generally only those that have been kept in pristine condition in their boxes. I would imagine mine look like they have just come back from a double shift at the Somme! Not worth a great deal so keep them for the grandchildren.
- They are in a state now you come to mention it, most are walking wounded but enough of this idle chatter! I'm going to water the front garden before the council come out in their canoes to enforce the hose-pipe ban.
- I thought that there was not going to be one this year Pops?

- Pure propaganda! They are just waiting for my azaleas to start coming through.
- See you in a bit.
- He also found some old records.
- Really? Like what?
- There was a Scooby Doo single, a Wombles single, that ABBA album we bought you for your sixth birthday and a nursery rhymes album that I had forgotten about.
- Nursery rhymes? That is a new one on me. Does it contain the perennial classic about mutilating disabled animals?
- I beg your pardon?
- Three Blind Mice.
- Of course! I suppose it is really isn't it.
- It is amazing the things they get children to sing about. Take the one about the joys of infectious and deadly diseases.
- Ring-a-Ring of Roses? Yes it is odd isn't it but it was lovely seeing all of your old toys and things again I am glad we never threw them out.
- Do not start on the: 'All my fledglings have flown!' speech please.
- I wasn't going to.
- Of course not. How are my siblings? I have not heard anything for a while.
- You're all just like your father hopeless at keeping in touch.
- But anyway how are they all?
- James is doing very well as ever, publishing more papers than ever and your father still goes into the university from time to time to help with his research. Marie seems fine although that mother of hers is an interfering witch but she hasn't got her claws into Alexandra anymore. I was so relieved when they moved.
- Definitely silver-lining time was it not?
- Oh yes. But they seem very happy although they don't know when they'll be able to come over next and I get too tired going there. But there we are. I don't hear much from Susanah as she is always so busy with that job of hers but the kids seem all right though a touch precocious.
- That is American children for you. Liz sounded like Shirley Temple the last time I spoke to her, or should I say the last time she talked at me.
- They don't understand our accents and she is only four. And Luke is going from strength to strength in the cut-and-thrust world of estate agency and growing bigger by the day.
- How much does he weigh now?
- Nineteen stones.
- Good God! Six feet one and nineteen stone he must frighten people into buying property. How is that son of his?
- He hasn't seen him since Christmas. That Joan is a *bitch*!
- I hope you are not swearing in front of the children Mary!
- Bitch isn't swearing.
Well that's that done. Bloody slugs have been at the busy lizzies again.
- Joseph really! It's no wonder your children are so uncouth.
- Was I an uncouth youth Mother dearest?
- You all were when I wasn't there.
- How on earth would you know?
- I know everything, I am your Mother.
- She who must be feared and approached with caution! That's about right, isn't it No.1?
- If you are ready to join us Joseph I shall serve dinner.

- Do what you like.
- He's so rude! Back in a min.
- We were just talking about my fellow siblings.
- Idle shower! Yes James is getting on very well and he's just been invited onto the editorial board of some journal which is apparently quite a coup and has now published the same amount of papers that I did although he cheats of course, it doesn't count if they're combined authors.
- I hear you are still helping with his research?
- One does what one can when one can be bothered.
- Here you are gentlemen, dinner is served.
- Thanks Mum.
- Thank you missis.
- Seeing as how you are getting waitress service I ought to get a tip.
- Would you like a tip Mum? Never play leapfrog with a unicorn!
- Very amusing. Stop giggling Joseph you'll only encourage him. Do you want any salt or heaven forbid, ketchup?
- Dear Mother I have never had salt with my food and I stopped gorging on ketchup some years ago thank you although another bottle of rouge would not go amiss. Cheeky little turps is it not? Lingering after-burn and so on.
- I'll just get some. Do you need a drink Father?
- I'm fine thank you. So to what do we owe the pleasure of your company tonight No. 1?
- Can I wait until Mum gets back so I can tell you both?
- If you must. Have you given up on your old trick of playing us off against one another?
- I never thought you realised.
- Oh yes you were very good at it though at one point I thought: 'Oh God don't let him become a politician!'
- I could never be one of those as I just cannot lie convincingly plus I am not nearly greedy enough.
- They are all gluttonous bastards aren't they.
- I heard that Joseph!
- Oh roll on the winter when one has a hint of privacy. Would you sit down Mother for goodness sake. Thank you. You don't have to impress anyone with your hostess skills tonight just enjoy the results of your labours for once.
- Hear, hear.
- So come on Jude what is it? Spit it out man.
- Well the leg is not getting any better and I doubt it ever will.
- Have you seen anyone?
- You know my opinion of quacks Mum, I tend to avoid the useless fools.
- You ought to see someone. If I sort it out will you go?
- Of course that would be extremely kind. But anyway the flat is becoming impossible to manage as I cannot handle the stairs or clean the place and I was wondering...
- You want to come home? Of course you can, can't he Joe?
- Absolutely not! Of course you can. I could do with a bit of company when your mother is gallivanting around the town.
- I do not gallivant.
- What would you call it then?
- I am merely interacting with the community but yes, would the back room be all right for you?

61

- Has it not got a fancy name?
- No. The only room guests stay in is the Constable Room other than that it's my room, Joe's room and so on.
- How very bizarre.
- When are you thinking of...
- Darkening our door again No. 1?
- So kindly put dear Father. Well I am selling the flat and we complete on the 18th I think.
- That's a shame. Can't you rent it out or something?
- No Mum I cannot. My finances are a little complicated at the moment and I will not bore you with the details but my only option is to sell. I did offer it to Luke first but apparently it was a little beneath him as studio flats are not en vogue currently.
- You'll need to clear your junk out of the back room then Joseph.
- It is not *junk* it is years of scientific journals.
- You've been meaning to sort it out for months.
- Merely because I have been meaning to do something it does not follow that I had the slightest intention of actually doing it.
- I do not want to cause any trouble.
- That would be a first No. 1.
- Harsh but fair I feel mon pere.
- You're not on a poetry kick again are you?
- No, no I never got further than: 'Our love was like a rotting rose'.
- Good.
- Actually Jude you could even be useful.
- Warning bells, warning bells! Whatever do you mean Mother? I have survived being virtually useless for years.
- You see we are thinking of getting a computer.
- Well what they call computers these days. A real computer takes up a large house and needs three days to work out two plus two! Isn't that right No. 1?
- In the Fifties Dad, yes. What sort of computer and what does it have to do with me?
- Well it's from those Space Continuum people with Internet and so on. I don't know ask your father.
- I don't have the first idea either but you might.
- I am not sure Pops. I can use computers to a degree which is probably the wrong word to use at the moment.
- No-one has forgotten that you are the only member of this family not to have one No. 1. but you are used to modern computers and if we get one with all the whistles and bells you would be able to make the thing work wouldn't you?
- Possibly given time. All modern computers need is a little bit of knowledge and a lot of logic. They are not easy but neither are they hard.
- Well that's settled then. We'll buy the damn thing and you can work out what the hell one is supposed to do with it.
- Joseph I do wish you would temper your language.
- If I cannot swear in front of my eldest son who the buggery can I swear in front of? Expletives are no fun by yourself.
- Hang on folks, why are you getting this thing and what do you want it to do?
- The idea is that your father can communicate with James and Susanah with the what's it called?
- You are going to get a moped, sruf the fishing net and send fe mails are you?

- Send females where?
- Wherever you like Pops.
- That's the idea plus your mother can do fancy invitations for those alleged parties she keeps throwing when I'm trying to sleep.
- This isn't Spain, you know. We do not have siestas in this country.
- Damn shame if you ask me. We're supposed to be European these days aren't we? Why can't we be as lazy as the wops?
- Honestly Dad you cannot say that anymore.
- What? Wops? What the hell else do you call them? Lousy pilots they were. I tell you they start at Dover and hanging's too good for them!
- So why is there a photograph of you hugging a Latin-looking chap and a Negro?
- They were chemists and that transcends you know. But enough of this maudlin talk if we buy one of these confusers can you work it for us?
- If I cannot I know a man that can teach me, will that do?
- Good enough for me. What about you Mother?
- Wonderful. I am already looking forward to having you home Jude.
- Thank you Mum. There is one small thing.
- What's that son?
- Well it would not surprise you to know that I am in rather a lot of pain?
- Carry on.
- The only effective means of pain control I have found so far is smoking cannabis and I would need to smoke it whilst living here. I do not want to delve into the seedy world of emotional blackmail so...
- Oh stop it No. 1. I have read so many reports of the benefits of cannabis. It works for you does it?
- You would not believe how much Dad.
- Then it isn't a worry. Would you agree Mary?
- But it is illegal.
- Yes I know Mum but the truth is that it should not be. It is not the case that there *might* be reasons to decriminalise or whatever, the simple fact is that there is no way in the *world* that it should be illegal in the first place.
- But then why is it?
- Absurd politics. The Hemp plant is a veritable gift from God it has so many uses, you can make material that feels like linen but is stronger than cotton, you can make scaffolding that is half as light but twice as strong as the stuff we currently use, you can make rope from it, you can get oil from it, the list is endless. It is the most wonderful plant in fact the American Bill of Rights is written on Hemp paper.
- Really?
- Yes Dad also President Johnson was quoted as saying: 'A man can do far worse than planting an acre of Hemp on his land.' Cannabis has been used for curative purposes for 5,000 years that is documented and God knows how long before that.
- Yes son but why is it illegal?
- The two main reasons are the fact that you can get oil from hemp and you can smoke it. When corporations in America were becoming really powerful in the twenties, the oil and tobacco industries realised that something that anyone could grow in their gardens would swiftly become something of a threat to their profits. So their lobbies, and we all know how altruistic the tobacco and oil lobbies are, put pressure on the American government to make

hemp illegal. They won and the rest of the world followed suit. That is the only reason why cannabis is illegal.
- That is quite ridiculous.
- It is that simple Dad.
- So why are there so many arguments against it?
- Ignorance and gluttony Mum. Because enough time has past for people to forget the real reasons behind the criminalisation of what should now be part of the organic, alternative medicine scene all that most people know is the original propaganda, that it is a *drug*. Plus there are now a lot more industries that would be under pressure from widespread hemp farming. Hemp is just one of the modern threats to the lobbies that made it become illegal in the first place and as much as we would like to believe in democracy politicians do not listen to the electorate, they only listen to big business. Big business does not want people growing hemp and not buying their products.
- But Jude cannabis leads onto hard drugs, so we are told.
- Absolutely not. The drug itself does not lead to other drugs but the culture does. The hardest thing is to find your first dealer and that can take a long time. Once you have found your chap who can get you some weed he can also get you whatever else you are curious about or he knows a man that can. I have never known a female dealer for some reason. These people that say users are after a 'bigger hit' are so *ignorant* it is quite shocking.
- So you are saying that if cannabis were to be legalised it would reduce drug abuse?
- Almost certainly Dad. There is nothing wrong with cannabis. Do you know how many people in this country died of cannabis abuse last year?
- I'll guess none.
- Bang on and the year before?
- Very similar.
- And so on. How many violent crimes were put down to cannabis abuse?
- Still the same figure I would imagine.
- Absolutely but how many disabled people in constant pain like myself did it help last year?
- Thousands?
- Which is not enough. I have tried innumerous pain killers that did not work very well and have really pleasant side-effects like all of your hair falls out and you cannot drink. The whole situation is farcical and yet what do politicians do? They churn out the same ignorant and facile claptrap leaving us to carry on suffering with the potential of being branded criminals.
- If you need to smoke the stuff to ease your discomfort that is perfectly all right, isn't it Mary?
- Does it really help that much?
- I promise you Mum. I have tried everything else and there just is not anything as good, reliable and with no side effects that the body does not develop a tolerance to. You probably know that alcohol is kicked out of one's system as soon as possible?
- One milligram an hour.
- Thanks Dad. You never know when a chemist will come in useful do you? Other drugs are similar and they stay in one's body for a day or so. With sports drug testing they look for the breakdown products that might still be around. But do you know how long THC, the actual chemical in cannabis stays in the bloodstream?
- No I do not.
- Sixteen weeks Dad on average.
- *Sixteen weeks?*

64

- That is right but do you know why? Because it is *not* a poison! Everything else from nicotine to heroin is poisonous and the body gets rid of them all as soon as possible. With cannabis there is no need since it is good for you. The only ill effects come from smoking it with tobacco and they are minimal. In fact all drugs should be legalised.
- You are just being stupid now.
- Thank you mother I shall rush to you for my testimonials.
- But you are being completely extreme! You can't just legalise all drugs.
- I would have to agree with your mother Jude.
- All right. There are very good reasons for cannabis to be legalised immediately and none whatsoever to keep it illegal but it might seem a gross extrapolation to then include all drugs in the same arena. After all when people say: 'He's on drugs.' that is about as definitive as saying: 'He's religious.' Both expressions are pretty much meaningless.
- Being religious isn't meaningless.
- I know Mum but that expression is. Being religious covers all aspects from the bloke who sort of believes in something to Muslim extremists who blow up aeroplanes. There are so many drugs out there now to lump them all together is ridiculous. The point is that their being illegal simply does not work. The system is wrong and needs changing. The trouble is that current efforts to keep young people from trying drugs is naive and patronising and I should know. The leaflets and so on that are given to increasingly younger schoolchildren give information that usually exaggerated about the harmful effects but they do not even touch upon why people actually take the damn things.
- And why do they?
- Because they are *great*! The one thing other than being illegal that all drugs have in common is that when you are taking them you feel fantastic and forget *all* your problems. So when youngsters have read the anti-drug literature and then try them there is no correlation between what they have read and the reality of the situation: 'Once again the government has lied to us!' is what everyone thinks. The current anti-drugs policy is a complete waste of money and it achieves nothing except disenchantment and cynicism.
- Are you saying that drugs, the greatest modern evil as it's been called are: 'Great'?
- Absolutely. That is why people take them. Most drugs are naturally occurring, organic is the modern term I believe.
- Complete misuse of the word!
- You are becoming predictable Dad.
- Hah!
- Cannabis, opiates and cocaine can all be grown very easily and have only been made illegal this century for very spurious reasons. You could buy cocaine in Harrods until 1922. Cannabis we have covered and opiates are the most wonderful pain killers although heroin easily becomes an obnoxious drug and is more deadly than a swim in a shark tank. More modern drugs like ecstasy and acid were developed for medical reasons but because the law says that a drug is made illegal if it can be used for pleasure rather than medical purposes, in other words if it is fun then ban it. Because of this they too have been made illicit.
- Is that the law?
- Almost verbatim. Ecstasy was developed as a slimming drug that did not make one depressed as amphetamines tend to. Then it became apparent that people liked taking it anyway so it was criminalised. Most of these drugs have tremendous benefits. Ecstasy was directly linked to a massive reduction in football hooliganism in the early nineties and is one of the reasons why so many young people today are so fit looking. The club scene which is fuelled by such drugs is the most energetic work out one can have. Cocaine gives one

enormous confidence and should be used to treat depression and insecurity and low-dosage speed can be bought at pharmacies and is prescribed for weight loss.
- But why then are drugs blamed for so many deaths and crimes?
- It is all an exaggeration. The fact is that peanuts kill more people a year than all illegal drugs.
- Peanuts?
- Sure. People being allergic, choking and so on. Thousands die each year and as for drug deaths compared to road deaths they are in different leagues. It is *hugely* exaggerated. The crime levels are simply because the drugs trade is controlled by gangsters who make enormous profits. To feed the habit which is very expensive with any drug other than cannabis, people turn to crime. Remember drugs help you forget your problems so the people most in need of this are at the lower end of society. They are poorer and far more vulnerable to addiction than most.
- But people do get addicted?
- Of course but that is down to human gluttony and lack of accurate information. It is instinctive to do something that is enjoyable and drugs are great so the urge to overdo it is immense. It is pure greed and it does wreck lives but that is down to them being illegal and there being a drug culture controlled by criminals. Every time you hear of a drugs bust the quantities sound enormous do they not?
- It's always tons of stuff worth millions.
- That is right and how is the market affected? It is not particularly because the stuff is so ubiquitous. Ninety-five per cent of thirty year olds in this country have taken cannabis it is *everywhere*! The system needs changing because it simply *does not work*. The potential for legalising intelligently is enormous but no politician has the courage to do anything about but the first thing to do is to stop calling people like me who use a naturally occurring plant as an effective painkiller, criminals!
- That annoys you, doesn't it son?
- Any M.P. who is against the *immediate* legalisation of cannabis for any purpose, is a buffoon, a cad, a bounder, a simpleton, an ignoramus, a muppet, a muffin, a kumquat, an imbecile, a moron, a dunce, a plank, a dullard, an idiot, a nonce, a prat, a twat, a twit, a twet, a twut, a twot, a pillock, a wazack and an unmitigated fool.
- Not your favourite people then?
- Any M.P. who is against the *immediate* legalisation of cannabis is a foolish, blinkered, naive, ignorant, self-opinionated, unaware, out-of-touch, weak, easily-led, gutless, ludicrous, farcical, ridiculous, stupid and laughable piece of evolutionary detritus.
- I think you have made your point admirably.
- I can't agree with everything that you have said Jude but you are welcome home and you may smoke whatever you need to smoke.
- Thank you Mum.
- Now if you'll excuse me I have to practice for Sunday.
- A big do at the church?
- No I am just being professional.
- I shall say goodbye before I go Mum. Thank you for dinner it was lovely.
- My pleasure.

- Are you sure you do not mind me coming back Dad?
- Yes, if only to have a more regular swimming partner but don't change the subject. Although your impassioned speech was very laudable one gets the impression that you were an avid cannabis and other things probably, user before your accident?

- Oh sure. The thing is though Dad that cannabis is fantastic stuff that does a lot of people a great deal of good whilst doing very little in the way of harm.
- But what does it actually do to you?
- Do you mean scientifically?
- What a wonderful word! Yes that is exactly what I mean.
- You know that there are inhibitor cells in the brain?
- Yes they flank the neurones, two inhibitors to each neurone and they stop extraneous information clogging up the brain.
- Dems de ones. Well cannabis make them less effective so that more information than normal reaches the brain. For example one can feel the colours of the music.
- Sweetly put but how does that help pain relief?
- I am not entirely sure but it seems as though you are able to really concentrate on something specific and remain unaware of other messages from the body unless it is urgent. If one is stoned and one suddenly realises a pee is required one is standing by the loo for a good ten minutes!
- That happens to me anyway. There doesn't seem to be the slightest reason for cannabis to be illegal except for politics which is absurd. Do you think they ever will make it legal again, I take it that is the point?
- I am not with you?
- From what you are saying cannabis has been growing happily since time immemorial, been used by Homo Erectus since we discovered fire, grown for its benefits by farmers for centuries and made illegal seventy years ago for no apparent reason. Or have I got it wrong?
- Wonderfully summarised Pops I can see you were paying attention in this lecture.
- Cute, very cute.
- But to be honest Dad I think it will be decades before a politician comes along who has the balls to even try and legalise any currently illegal drug. The silly thing is that the main problems of drug abuse and it is the abuse that is the problem, have already been solved.
- Oh yes?
- Every pharmaceutical company that exists have created pills that can give you the same 'buzz' as any street drug.
- Really?
- Oh yes. This is the real gluttony that exists. Users are foolish to be greedy for the hit that does them in but there are so many companies that would survive and get into new markets if legalisation occurred. The trouble is that they would rather the status quo remained very quo to make more money, the shareholders come first you know.
- I don't follow.
- These pills have been developed. Some tobacco companies have even developed cannabis cigarettes but they have *only* been developed. To go into full production would require an enormous investment that would probably put the companies concerned in the red for a year or two since there would be no way of estimating the market as it is completely untried. Because all of these companies have shareholders they would simply not do it and continue to pressure the government not to legalise anything. These people make more money than they know what to do with, avoiding clichés like the plague but that is more important than the genuine misery that exists on the streets of every country in this world! That is what I call gluttony. I rest my case.
- I think you ought to, it's looking decidedly knackered from where I'm sitting. But as much fun as this is it's getting on to be way past my bedtime. Would you like a lift back to your flat?

67

- It is all right Dad I shall call a taxi.
- I'll do that for you. Stay there and drink your rouge.
- Thanks Pops.

- It is on the way she said. Would you like a little story afore ye go?
- I would love a funny story.
- Don't get your hopes up I mentioned nothing about humour. They were talking about what's his name on the wireless the other day. Don Snow? No, Damon Chill? No, David Frost? That's the chap and about how he has meet so many politicians throughout the years he now has enormous influence. The story goes that some young reporter was sent to interview Sir David and arrived at his office. D.F. was on the 'phone and waved the young chap into a chair. 'Yes of course.' he was saying, 'And to you. And love to the children. Oh I should think so. Absolutely. Always a pleasure Butros Butros!'
- What did the reporter say: 'Who was that then?'.
- Very good. They didn't mention that oddly enough. That rude horn beeping could well be your taxi.
- Jude? Your taxi's here.
- Confirmation from the catholic how appropriate. Good to see you boy. Swimming on Sunday?
- Yes why not, other than a blinding hangover.
- Not my problem. See you then.
- 'Bye Dad. 'Bye Mum. Thank you.

Tuesday 8th June: A DEAL WITH GOD.

I awoke to that slow, cold, horrible realisation that every alcoholic knows and dreads. I had wet the bed. I do not know how or why - sometimes it just seems to happen. Normally it happens when I have been feeling good about something and it sort of drags me back to my level. Just above excrement. Thanks.

So another Tuesday morning. The world is quite glorious at half past three. The sun is fighting from the depths of the sea, showering glints and shards of light across my window. The rising sun has always been associated with optimism. Optimism is the only thing available at this time of the morning but there is precious little of it for me. God this life is shyte.

I doubt that most people have the slightest idea how I feel at the moment. I cannot lie down as my mattress is drying. I cannot sit down as I have nothing to sit upon other than the floor. There is nothing to watch as I gave my T.V. to Thomas yesterday. Early morning wireless is people fighting tiredness with enforced humour and I am simply not in the mood. Do I pretend it is the morning and have a coffee? Do I pretend it is the night and open a bottle of rouge? Did philosophers have lives?

The day is a yawning chasm. Hours and hours of unfulfilled boredom and pain to somehow make tolerable. At least I have a sea-view. Somehow that helps. No it does not. Why does self-disgust reach a pinnacle during the hours when there is no-one to talk to? I would not even try as I know that they are all asleep. How nice for them.

So I can return to my parents' house. Redmond Grange Hospice for the Virtually Useless. Another example of my failure in life. For thirteen years I have tried to be independent. Why did I fail? I have tried to be hardworking and diligent as I was taught to be but it has come to nothing. At school they gave us these psychometric tests to help us decide what we should be in life. They always told me that I could be whatever I wanted. I have never known what I wanted to be, anything other than what I have become.

You can always tell people who have never known insomnia or depression. They have a sparkle in their eyes that you envy and disparage: 'Just wait until life hits them!' you think and somehow feel superior. The poor bastards is how I view babies. It is odd the way that people look at babies. 'Oh!', they say, 'I'll bet he'll be a footballer/ballet dancer/athlete.' They never say: 'He'll grow up to be a burden on the welfare state'. I doubt anyone said that about me. The sad thing is they would have been right.

What is the point? As I trundle through life becoming more of a burden upon the people I love why do I bother at all? It would be far more 'cost-effective' to just stop right now. I used to dive competitively and I live in a third-floor flat. One decent dive and I cannot bother anyone anymore. It is too tempting but it would be too selfish. For some reason people love me. I have not the slightest inkling why. To me I am pathetic, dispisable and obvious. Or am I just tolerated? I have not the faintest idea.

Should I just join the long list of my friends who have died in wasteful circumstances? I still miss them all. Dear Peter. I shall always remember him in his Land Rover. Driving along one day we saw a hearse, bereft of coffin and he started singing at the top of his voice: 'I, ain't got no body!' He was such an inspiration. Then he died virtually overnight. The grief was palpable in everyone. I have never known so many grown men cry including myself. When is it in life that one stops giving and starts taking? I have not the smallest notion.

It is strange when the only reason to carry on living is to not hurt people by killing oneself. I can only guess how my suicide would affect my parents. They would never forgive themselves for their lack of guilt. They gave me everything they could and I wasted it. They would never see it like that but the strength to just carry on is so tiring. Why do I have to? It would be so nice to say goodbye to the world in general and just bugger off to wherever. Adieu, farewell and ciao. I shall see you somewhere better.

Not an option unless I was feeling really selfish but how do I stop this pain? This gnawing, nagging pain that invades my formerly good and fit body, that colours every part and every movement of my life. So I drink too much - so would you if every movement made you want to shout in agony. These people that are against euthanasia do not know what the *fuck* they are talking about! If there were a debate and I was speaking I would hobble, hobble, hobble to the lectern. I would talk about unending pain. I would talk about the fact that comfort does not exist anymore. Standing, sitting, lying they all hurt. I would mention that a good night's sleep is now a distant dream and beds are to be feared. I would talk about how horrible it is to be a burden upon everyone. How foul it is to be patronised by everyone. 'Excuse me, but I am merely disabled. I am not deaf, I am not stupid. I said quite clearly twenty Marlboro please. Would you stop *pushing me*!' Everyone seems disappointed that I do not go into town anymore. They have no idea how horrible it is to scramble onto a bus and everyone just stares.

I would talk about how life is only sacred to those that have hope or something to look forward to. I can honestly say that everything good that was going to happen to me has done so. What genuine happiness have I got left? Nothing. From now on there is only pain and physical disintegration. I shall send you a postcard! Now love can only exist for me hand in hand with sympathy. How foul! It is very hard to get across just how miserable life is when disabled. Someone said the other day: 'You have good days and bad days?' and I replied: 'There is no such thing as a good day anymore.' But how are they expected to know. Quite honestly I am glad. I would not inflict this on anyone, not even that unmitigated shit of a solicitor. I do not know how God can.

Back to the debate. I would mention quite strongly the desperation of family and friends who just want their loved one at peace, to have no more pain. Like most things that one is impassioned about I probably would not get across what I wanted to but I would do my best to secure for everyone like me the right to one's own life. Or death. What is so *fucking* special about life anyway? Why should we desperately cling onto it? Personally I cannot bloody stand it! But I would end my speech and hobble, hobble, hobble back to my uncomfortable seat. Then my opponent would stand up and confident stride, confident stride, confident stride his way to the lectern.

He would say things like: 'Sanctity of life!', 'Moral society!', 'Start of the slippery slope!' and other things that would show he does not know what the *hell* he is talking about. He certainly would not touch upon desperate love. As my father says: 'There are none so adamant as those that have not thought it through!' How anyone has the gall to stop someone from killing themselves. The vicious, arrogant, ignorant *fuckwits*! Lovely thoughts for four in the morning.

It is going to be a lovely day. The sun is a veritable fireball, spilling glorious colour into otherwise lacklustre clouds that tumble across the horizon before my kitchen window. Night wins - rouge it is. The only people to worry about health are the healthy. Have a body that hates you and alcohol, and other things become long lost friends. There was a wonderful Peanuts cartoon where Charlie Brown was being coached in American football. The coach said: 'To be a good footballer your mind and your body have to be in perfect harmony.' Charlie Brown said: 'My mind and my body hate each other!' Glorious.

He always was a hero of mine. The way he just accepted life was inspirational and the ever-present threat of happiness from 'the little red-haired girl' is a concept that keeps us all going. Love is out there somewhere. A bit like 'the truth'. Why do people strive for 'the truth'? It is rarely any help at all.

It always amuses me when people talk about 'killing the planet'. We are destroying our own environment at a pace that has always stopped me from having children but we are *not* killing the world! That sun has risen above that horizon for billions of years and will continue doing so long after we have destroyed ourselves through greed and ignorance. In a few million years time the earth will be ruled by a master-race descended from scorpions and cockroaches. My father, being a chemist first heard of global warming and ozone depletion in the Sixties. They warned the politicians then. What happened? Nothing! What will politics ever do for us? *Nothing!* The cockroaches will probably make a far better job of things. Pleasant thought is it not?

Why is it that every train of thought leads to depressing conclusions? Is that why everyone is so unhappy these days? You can see it on every bus, every train, every tube. I have a reason to be unhappy so why do I spend my time cheering everyone up? Why do these walkies not realise how much they have and just enjoy it? It is only when you have so few pleasures left that you realise how much you have wasted? It is now quarter past four in the morning and I am not fighting my way out of this depression very well.

What is the point? Why do I bother? Some misguided sense of loyalty probably. Whatever exists beyond this life simply has to be better. Even if it is nothing at least it would be a decent sleep - a forgotten luxury. People tell me about their fear of anaesthesia but personally I love it. It is the best sleep available and if one does not wake up - ah well there you go. Literally!. It would be *bliss*. Unfortunately I keep waking up. Bugger!

The trouble is trying to deal with this disability. Everyone is so shocked despite the fact that I have been telling them all for the past seven years that it was going to happen. They are all so into dealing with the implications in their own lives that there is no emotion left for me. I am the one suffering but they are the ones 'getting over it'. Selfish arseholes the lot of them! They can *walk*. It has been a revelation to me the number of friends I have lost through this. They try and make me feel as if I have let them down in some way. It is not my fault! I do not want this either! Do you think for a moment that this is *fun*?

When I was first in plaster, some nine years ago I had this overwhelming urge to pass the crutches on to someone else. 'I have had my turn and now it is yours'. Unfortunately there was not that choice. What bugged me then and really annoys me now is the same questions and comments over, and over, and over... 'What have you done to your leg?', 'Is it getting better?',

71

'Have you tried acupuncture?'. *Fucking acupuncture?* Considering I have had untold osteosurgeons scratching their collective heads for the past nine years I think I am slightly out of the acupuncture catchment area. I know they mean well but it does not help and anyone that thinks they are being funny and original calling me: 'Hop-along!' discovers the wrath of Moses.

But people do say the most ridiculous and stupid things. I worked in a pub many years ago and it was a standard joke that people would ask about my name. 'Is it short for Julian?' they would nose. 'No!' I would rebut, 'It is long for Ju! Such an unpleasant monosyllable for a name.' The other option would be to say: 'No it is short for July. You see my parents named us all, I have three brothers after the months we were born in. There is Dessi, December, Gus, August and Toby, October. We are all just grateful that we were not born in April or May!' We laughed all the way to casualty and I am not talking about the program.

I know that I should be grateful that I have a home to return to but it is so galling to admit that I have completely cocked-up this independence thing. I started off well, I left school at seventeen and got a job selling jeans. It was fun. Leaving school was fun too as it was under something of a cloud. I am sure that I am the only person from that particular private school to have had a peroxide Mohican! My poor parents, how they suffered. They had to give up all those wine and cheese parties.

Mind you James was worse although he always managed to get away with things being a scholar and so on. I shall never forget that Christmas lunch two years ago when James and his family were over. Mum was telling the story of how embarrassed she was when James was caught with a dirt mag in a maths class. Because he was a scholar and so on the headmaster gave him a small punishment and Mum a hard time! The poor thing had to go to the school and collect the offending article. Just as she was getting to the point of the story, her acute shame James roared with laughter saying: 'I'll never forget seeing you *scuttling* out of the side entrance with a copy of 'Screw' hanging out of your handbag!' How we laughed. This is why I cannot kill myself. What would I do to my family? It does not bear contemplating.

This is too hard to cope with. I might have been expecting this for seven years but I certainly did not expect it to happen overnight. A bit like the Spanish Inquisition. Trust the Spanish to mess up religion! Mind you they cannot even make a decent cup of tea and the food's a bit greasy so they say. That Saturday morning when I woke up with a monster hangover and my leg simply did not move. Not at all! I stayed in all day trying to move my toes and ankle. Nothing. 'It will be all right in the morning.' I told myself with a brave smile. That was two months ago. I had come *so* close to getting the paper started. That would have meant fifty people a year no longer being long-term unemployed but now I am. Ironic don't you think?

I am going nowhere fast here. Time to roll something relaxing and see if sleep is a complete impossibility today.

* * *

I managed to get some sleep, rolled up in my duvet on the floor. I woke chewing carpet which considering I have not been able to vacuum for over a month is not a particularly good idea. I can see the social workers shuddering. What is the time? Half past nine - thank God for that!

72

At least the rest of the world is awake too. Time for a cigarette. From down here my flat looks really grotty all of a sudden. Cobwebs everywhere and in need of redecoration. It is hard to see the Hunting Lodge like this after so much effort and so many good memories. This is the only home that I have ever had but now it is just a grubby shambles with my life collected in bin bags, boxes and bits. Time for a bath. The mattress is drying out quite well the poor thing. Sorry.

One of the hardest things is that there is no dignity being like this. Every movement is ungainly and ugly. Everyone stands by wincing slightly and wondering if they should offer some assistance. I must remind them of the frailty of humanity. The first time I was in hospital someone said that you leave your dignity at the door and they were absolutely right. It is an unfortunate consequence of doctors and nurses having to distance themselves from the pain going on around them that they seem rude and indifferent. It was in hospital that I relearned the art of crying or is that sobbing? Is there anything worse than not being able to move, being in excruciating pain and knowing that the next injection is over an hour away? Difficult to say - I am very familiar with Dante and his levels.

Thank God that Paul was in hospital too although that sounds a little unkind. I wonder where he is now? I have not seen him in *years*. He was so funny. Paul had broken his leg and sprained an ankle falling off some scaffolding the silly sod. He arrived in the same ward two days after me brandishing a wheelchair. He managed to customise it to make it faster and even stole a wing mirror from somewhere! His favourite trick was to run nurses over so that they landed in his lap, the dreadful man. You would see him scoot off after one and then hear a shriek, an outraged shout and a slap! He would come wheeling back to the day-room with a red hand mark and a huge grin on his face. He would be done for sexual harassment these days and I am surprised he got away with it then.

One day some nurses were cleaning my wounds when one of them lifted the leg badly and the ends of the bits of bone rubbed together - that made me shout. One of them rushed off and returned with the gas and air which is *lovely* stuff. They were just finishing off when an alarm sounded and they all disappeared leaving the cylinders next to my bed. I gave Paul a shout, he came skidding in saw the situation and closed the curtains. We were on the stuff for three quarters of an hour! It was *wonderful*. The nurses were not impressed however and would not wheel me back to the day-room for a smoke. One claimed I would explode! Doubtful.

That first time in hospital was a very odd mixture of extremes. It was either stabbing agony or hysterical laughter. Fortunately I had lots of visitors and the folks came every day armed with a paper and some sandwiches since you could not eat the hospital food even when drugged right up. I lost four stones in two weeks - there's an effective diet for you! A bit extreme though. Someone was kind enough to bring me a spliff one day. What a combination - pethadine and cannabis! I was on cotton wool clouds for hours. Whoever it was smoked menthol cigarettes so it was like getting stoned on toothpaste! Needs must when the Devil's nicked your bike. I think I must have left my dignity there as I certainly have not had much since.

Oddly enough the last time I saw Paul was a year after my accident when he bought the bike from me, I think it was two hundred pounds or something silly. The irony was that little Boozy was absolutely fine after the crash although a commercial right-off because all the little bits of plastic - the fairing I believe - had been damaged. The actual structure of the thing was sound and it had just been sitting in a garage all year. I was just out of plaster and hobbling about on Moses. You see everyone thinks that Moses is new on the scene - au contraire. I have had Moses for ten years! I liberated him from the hospital after a previous and no so damaging accident. I had five in six months you know, all on Monday nights wearing the same clothes - very spooky. You would have thought I would have stopped. Twenty-twenty hindsight.

So Paul met me at the garage and Boozy was wheeled out. We had a look over and started her up - first time that's my girl! Paul looked at me and said: 'There's only one person to test drive her.' and threw me the keys. I could not walk without Moses and did not have my glasses with me, I have the visual capability of a bat without the compensating sonar but I could not resist. He said: 'Just take her for a spin round the block.' so I drove to Lewes and back taking an hour or so. Paul knew I would be back as he had Moses. It was a ridiculous and stupid thing to do and I loved it.

I really did love that bike although not in the Biblical sense. More in the way one loved Felicity Kendal-Cake in the Seventies. Whizzing around the Downs of an early morning going fast enough to only hear the rushing wind was the closest to flying that I have ever known. She could manage between eighty-five and ninety which are suitable speeds for spinning around country lanes I think you will find. I had wanted a bike since I was knee-high and those months were the best of my life. The first time Mum saw Boozy she said: 'All my nightmares come true!' She never has expanded on her prophetic skills. I have heard that there is a new medium on the sea-front called Madame Zanussi. Apparently it is the appliance of seance! Pitiful gag.

Why do people not realise that pity is the most destructive emotion? When that is all you can feel emanating from people it drains all of one's self esteem - a very important and rare commodity for us disabled types. Indifference is easy - a break from the pitying eyes and the patronising phrases. Life is completely different like this because disability changes and affects everything. Now I know about bigotry and prejudice, about being seen as an outsider and dangerously different. I am a limping example of how bloody life can be but no-one wants to be reminded. I never encounter indifference really it is better described as denial. If I were a horse they would have put me down long ago. They do not know how lucky they are, horses.

If one is hungry one can dream of food. If one is thirsty one can dream of water. Homeless - shelter. When one is disabled that is it mate! There is no hope just an empty box and life. 'Why don't you take up a hobby?' they say. 'Fuck off!' I reply. Walkies want cripples to have something in their lives to ease their own guilt: 'At least he has something to occupy himself with.' they twitter. When one is completely useless one is not wanted around. The disabled should be not seen and not heard. We are an eyesore cluttering up the world of the beautiful and able. So sorry to spoil your view! The only way around it is to magnify the personality and become 'an eccentric'. People like eccentrics - they are funny although the comment is always: 'He' s so funny it's shame he's a cripple!' One cannot escape from it.

Who the *fuck* is bothering me? Well they can just *bugger off*! Hang on it might be Mags.
- Hello?
- JUDE!
- Hiya our kid. How you doing?

74

- You sound awful. Are you O.K.?
- I am fine really. Just hung over and at a bit of a low ebb. Do not worry, I shall be all right tomorrow.
- You poor thing. Would you like a quick one to cheer you up?
- Do you want to rephrase that?
- Oops! No wonder I'm always getting into trouble. Anyway I've just got this thing through on the Internet about the things kids put in their R.E. exams.
- Religious Entertainment?
- That's the one. One child answered the question: 'Who was Noah's wife' with: 'Joan of Arc!'
- That is very funny.
- Jude you sound really down.
- I am just having a Shelly moment.
- What's that? Something to do with the old T.V. program?
- No! I am a cancerian am I not? I mean I am staying in my shell, i.e. my flat and I shall read poetry. A little Bisch would go down well at the moment. I am sorry Honey but I am not really up to conversation right now. When is your date with Satan's accountant?
- You are terrible! It's tomorrow night.
- Well give me a call tomorrow and in the meantime get some work done you lazybones.
- All right but *you* give *me* a call if you like. I'll leave the machine off.
- Thank you. Speak to you tomorrow. Love you.
- Love you too.

* * *

Good old Mags. No condescension from her thank God. Without my family, good friends, cannabis and alcohol life really would be totally unbearable. And antacid tablets of course. It is people like Mags caring about me that arrests suicide. They comprise a distinct silver lining but it is definitely a Shelly day today. I cannot bear the thought of anyone looking at me or my having to be funny. The only way to keep friendships alive is to pretend that I am really not all that bothered and not talk about it. No-one likes a whinger. Certainly not me. Of course the down side is that everyone, well most then bother me with their transitory and decidedly solvable problems. It does drive me up the wall! They have no idea just how much bravery I have to muster to merely limp out of my front door. Well today they can all go and *swivel*! I am going nowhere although staying here is not much of an alternative. Another bottle of rouge and a book I feel. Something comforting - ah John Mortimer.

* * *

I do love Paradise Postponed if only for the Simeon dressed as Santa story! It makes me laugh *every* time. Why does every book have to involve love in some way? Every film has to have a 'love interest'. What are people like me who are desperately interested in love but with no chance supposed to do? Dribble? What chance have I ever got of achieving that joyous harmony? Fucking *none*! It is hard to be someone that everyone else insists on apologising for. I dislike the adjective 'tragic' and object to other people's stories of how unkind and ironic life can be. I cannot remember where the quote comes from, I think it must have been a dreadful T.V. program about something dismal but the quote is: 'Well life's just bloody isn't it?' Something like that.

75

I used to be so proud of myself before the accident. Fourteen stones with a twenty-eight inch waist. Of course I used to show off shamelessly by sauntering into pubs wearing a vest and shorts, revelling in the stares of women. They still stare of course but it is not quite the same. It is hard to let go of palpable admiration. It was rather pleasant. It used to be great fun being a builder. People would criticise and say: 'With twelve O Levels and five A levels, what are you doing being a builder?' My reply: 'Qualifications increase the horizons of one's choices. I refuse to look down on an occupation that I enjoy merely because you do.' That won me a lot of friends the snotty bastards!

But it was fun. There was a brickie I knew called Peter. The last I heard of him was that he was inside after holding up an all night chemist with a water pistol! Another practical joke gone wrong. It was Peter who first made the phrase 'larger than life' make sense. I remember working on a site with him where there was a bakery next door that sold tea and coffee first thing. He used to go in at seven in the morning and demand from the still sleep-ridden staff: 'A tea and some of your stale cakes please.' They would reply: 'We don't sell stale cakes.' 'You fucking did yesterday!' he would grin. Terrible man.

At that site there was a topping out party one day and Peter insisted that four of us should be well-oiled in time for the celebrations. We repaired to a suitably unobvious pub at lunch or dinner time as it is known. It was a large enough site that one could be lost for an hour or so. We returned in time for the celebrations on the roof and I got chatting to a 'suit', as you do. It transpired that he had a great sense of humour and we spent a few minutes discussing Chaucer. Then the Mayor and dignitaries arrived with a lot of women who had clearly watched too many eighties American soap operas, the Mayor laid the final tile and the party started. That is when it all went marrow-shaped.

Peter decided that he should have shoulder-pads too and disappeared, to reappear with plastic bags shoved into his jumper that lifted it up nicely to reveal his hairy beer-gut! Tom started a food-fight with our bosses that caught the Mayor in a crossfire and I must admit responsibility for a mini-pizza in the Mayoress's cleavage! Paul was completely sozzled and was caught relieving himself in a stairwell as the Mayor was being toured around the site and poor old Tom just threw up in the punch! That brought proceedings to a premature end and we were almost certainly going to be sacked.

It turned out that the 'suit' I had been talking to was the head of the main contractors and insisted that we were retained. 'I like those boys.' he said, 'A topping-out party isn't any fun without some high spirits!' he told our bosses. Even so we found ourselves on blocks for the duration. God they were heavy. Thank goodness for memories they can always bring a smile to my face although it is draining to know that they can never happen again. Bollocks!

At that point I had no trouble meeting women who became lovers. How does the song go? 'I've had many lovers, some were handsome, but none were plain. My good fortune, I suppose.' but that is the end of that now. I saw a film many years ago. I was staying with a friend, we would have been about thirteen and were watching BBC 2 late one night hoping for a naughty French film, like you do. Instead we got a morbid French film. It was set in the Second World War. A pilot had baled out and was floundering around the French countryside when he came across a farmhouse which he approached cautiously. There were a pair of stable doors the upper part of which was open with a beautiful French girl, framed and smiling. The pilot came forward and she opened the bottom door to reveal that she only had one leg. The pilot was sent sprawling and retching back to the woods. Whimp! Disability is just *ugly*. Fancying disabled people is perversion. To fantasise about being a lover again is ridiculous and unhelpful. False hopes are soul-destroying.

But at least I have known love and have had a very full life. That is more than a lot of people although I should have travelled more. I have had some great times. Looking through old photographs it would appear that my life has been a succession of parties. It was only a few months ago that I was told I am the perfect party guest as I will always ensure background laughter! That was very sweet of Sam. I wonder where he is? I have lost far too many friends. I could do with their company now.

I shall never forget the time I was re-laying Peter Dickerson's crazy paving. It is amazing how useful building skills are. During that first period of enforced unemployment due to the terrible advice of a corrupt solicitor I managed to earn a few beer tokens wielding a trowel. Peter's paving was coming up like shoots in Spring and I reckoned it was a week's work. His patio was at the top of a very steep, twenty yard drive but was reasonably flat with a slight camber. I laid the slabs on a good six and one wet bed, very carefully mixing the colours and sizes of the slabs for the ultimate aesthetic experience. I had just finished that part and was planning the grouting when Peter insisted it was: 'Time for a little something!' which translated as: 'Just gone midday and I'm thirsty!' We went to the pub and refreshed ourselves.

When we returned a little unsteadily at four Peter suggested I tried the: 'Continental method dear boy!' which involves doing a dry mix, sweeping it into the gaps and then adding water gently. I did as I was asked and within half an hour there was the almost finished crazy-paving. Peter grabbed the hose-pipe and instructed me to: 'Stand back!' At this point I became a little concerned since delicately adding the water had been the expression used. Hose-pipes had not been mentioned. Peter blasted the hose on and six buckets of mortar raced across the patio and down the drive ending up as an impromptu speed bump just by his front gate. My carefully arranged paving was now a uniform grey. 'Sorry dear boy.' he said, eyes twinkling. 'Shall we return to the pub? Less dangerous there!' God I miss him!

Now of course I am unemployed *and* disabled which equates to completely fucking *useless*. No beer tokens to be earned this time round doing odd jobs for friends so I have penury to look forward to as well - how *wonderful* for me! Of course I actually tell people that I am retired. 'Retired?' they say. 'Oh yes it always was my intention to retire before thirty.' I rejoin. 'You're not only thirty?' they say, incredulity all over their boats. 'No.' I sigh, 'I am twenty-nine.' I just do not look or sound it. Do I?

Obviously all of the compensation money has long gone spent on forgotten pleasures and lent to friends who are incapable of paying me back. Thomas did not even mention the two thousand he owes as he told me his troubles and took my possessions. Thanks! The irony is I should have got a lot more but I had a 'bent brief'. He was charming and funny and we even had drinks together: 'Jude my old mate!' he used to say, 'What can I get you?' I sent him a get-well card when he had his back operation. Little did I know that he had done a deal with the insurance company and was ruining my case. Six years to develop a case that would not stand up in court. How can anyone do that to another human being? The level of cynical avarice is mind-blowing. Now I cannot even afford the medical treatment I need to stave off paraplegia and he drives a British Racing Green Jaguar.

That fucking surgeon was just as bad, they were in it together. I never needed that operation on my knee they just made a couple of thousand each out of me. No-one has ever been able to explain why it was done. The knee has been worse ever since and now hardly works at all. Apparently he is now in trouble for performing female circumcisions. What a *sick* individual!

As for the insurance company how can anyone be that cold, cynical and utterly heartless? What a bunch unmitigated *bastards*! I hope they all *rot* in hell!

God knows what I did to deserve being exploited in that fashion. One can only suppose that it is similar to the reason for climbing Everest - because it is there. Why do so many solicitors, surgeons, barristers, insurance salespeople and so on rip people off? Because they can! These people are worse than fascists and thugs as those fools are just angry and vicious. These people *smile* as they stab you in the back. I will not even kill insects myself, even wasps. Spiders are welcome to use the bathroom facilities as long as they stick to the rota. I treat insects better than crooked professionals treat people! I once tried having spider plants in my sitting room but I kept on finding them in the bath!

Bloody crying fits. It has only happened once in public but I think I got away with it! It is a horrible feeling to suddenly start crying for no, or no decent reason. I hear a mildly touching story and start sobbing. It is pathetic but fits in well with the new look. A fate-imposed makeover. It is not even worth thinking what my future holds as it is a dark tunnel of pseudo-bravery over hardship. Any light at the end will be an oncoming train. This is why I rant and rave about modern life to my friends it is simply my personal vicarious catharsis. When I slate politicians and demand equality I am only saying that I hate my life but no-one wants to listen to *that* conversation piece so I must always improvise and be analogous.

This is no good. It is three in the afternoon and I am emotionally painting myself into a corner. It is time to roll about three baseball bats and seek coma status. The mattress is dry now so I have somewhere to lie down.

* * *

Oh God. Consciousness. It is dark. Where am I? Oh *bugger*. Ten in the, evening? It must be it is dark. Cigarette. That is it - I am having a Shelly day and generally feeling like something Fate has stepped in and is currently rubbing off against a particularly painful piece of kerbing. I need a pee. Oh yeah! It is all coming back. **OW!** Why does every single part of my body *fucking hurt so much*? Bloody stupid question you know why.

Right - what is the situation? Two spliffs, excellent. Dribble of wine, not so good. Hang on. Ah two cases left. I love France! It is just so much more civilised in comparison to this dump. Of course getting there will not be easy anymore. All those stairs with people pushing even though they are not going to get anywhere faster. Having to go onto the deck just to have a cigarette. All those stares - it would be a nightmare. Oh *fuck* it! How many pleasures in life are left? A seat, a smoke, a drink and some music - who could want more? Hah!

78

It is odd you know that it was so long ago that I was healthy and not in pain I really cannot remember what it was like. It must have been great! I know that I was probably rather vain about my physique but does that now mean that I have to be a skinny cripple with a gut? Now I that cannot exercise at all that is what will happen. It is not what I want particularly.

I have felt sort of odd, not in more pain just a nagging feeling somewhere. I have gone through life refusing to give up and always looking for a solution which is why my situation is so frustrating. When I was in publicity - 'The Devil's Own Propaganda!' - I was known as: 'The man that can.' There must be a way out of this. There is always a solution as I have told numerous sales trainees. I don't know, me trying to be a salesman - 'The Devil's Own Sideline!' It is something I said to someone recently. That is it! 'Not without divine intervention.' Who on *earth* did I say that to? It is quite profound.

I know what is bothering me - that bloody happy-clappy church I was at yesterday giving blood. Too many memories. You see I was a happy-clappy for four years during my teens. Being brought up a catholic meant that God was always there somehow and non-existence was a startling new topic years later. But then I left and have been agnostic ever since.

When I was seventeen I was deeply unhappy about many things, your standard teenage angst although at the time it felt as if the world was going to end. To have those simple troubles now! But I will not bore you with the details. There was a leader, as they called them at the church who was supposed to be a mentor to me. I arranged to meet him and poured out my lost and lonely soul to him whilst sobbing uncontrollably so that I did not notice him looking at his watch. I finished, mopping my tear and snot-ridden face with my school tie and he said: 'I did some sermons on this sort of thing a few months ago. You can buy the tapes at the church. See you later. Oh and clear up before you go, won't you.' I do not use this word often but he was a *cunt*! I have not believed in a god of any sort since. There's a surprise!

But that was one man in one church and there is only supposed to be one god! That did not help particularly. Do you not hate it when you make a really bold comment that does not actually mean much? Everyone just looks at you. Anyway there was a strange feeling, a vibe if you will in that building yesterday. A sort of happiness in the air, a lightness of spirit that one does not find elsewhere. In more conventional churches there is a atmosphere of worship and quiet, desperate prayer but this was different. Dare one say a feeling of *joy*? I would not know of course.

Last Christmas when James was over we had a very drunken conversation where he spoke of returning to Christianity. I was shocked as he has been agnostic longer than I have and he knows all about my feelings. I went through a period insisting that if God did exist He must be the most vicious, ironic *bastard* due to the unfortunate circumstances of mine and others' lives. I have mellowed now. Honestly!

James studies the molecular set-up of compounds and so on, the very building blocks of life to re-mint a cliché. He said that the more he saw, the more there seemed to be a guiding hand as it were. I called him an innocent fool as I have called the occasional Christian gung-ho enough to try and convert me over the years. Poor things! They were not to know that I have read the whole Bible, listened to a sermon a week for ten years and normally o'erbrim with bitterness as far as religion and life generally are concerned. I hope that I never destroyed anyone's faith. I do not think so.

But if James is thinking along those lines... hmm. Time for that second join and a bit of thinking that is not suicidal. They were a great band were Suicidal Tendencies. I wonder whatever happened to them?

* * *

So the only option left is to get healed somehow. How would one go about that? I suppose I could pray. I have not prayed in, twelve years so I am probably a bit rusty.
- Hello God. Are you there?
- *MIGHT BE.*
- Does one just still pray or do I need your e mail number?
- *IT IS - GOD@HEAV.CO.CLOUD - MICROSOFT NICKED THE ADDRESS I ACTUALLY WANTED! YOU MAY JUST PRAY IF YOU WANT.*
- I do not need retuning or anything? Do I need to adjust my wavelength or something?
- *JUST PRAY.*
- Right then. Well I would like to be healed please! The thing is that it would have to be quite a spectacular sort of healing because I am rather rubber-ducked (I had best not swear). So really it is everything from my neck down including my spine, hip girdle and right leg. In fact while you are about it why not just make back to how I was before the accident. You remember fourteen stone of fitness?
- *I REMEMBER.*
- Well just like that would be very nice. You see the only parts of my body that do work properly are my head and my genitalia which is very frustrating! They are always arguing about who should be doing the thinking. Honestly you would not believe...
- *YOU WOULD BE SURPRISED WHAT I BELIEVE.*
- No doubt. So quite a big miracle then. I had better give you something in return. It is a bit insulting to go with the: 'Heal me and I'll believe!' line is it not? It used to *really* annoy me when I was a God-botherer, if you'll excuse the expression when people would say: 'Show me a miracle and I'll believe!' Honestly people are *so* cynical these days. It must be a bit better than that. I know I shall dedicate the rest of my life to Your service. Yes that is a decent deal. After all even going to church every day is better than this. There You go then, if You will heal me Lord I shall dedicate the rest of my life to Your service.
- *VERY GENEROUS.*
-I thought so and I do not mind what, You just let me know. Priest, missionary to darkest Africa (if one is still allowed to say that), or even a monk although I would not actually chose that one myself. Not a habit I want to get into! But whatever You think is appropriate. Right let us get some structure, a time frame to this. If I go to Your happy-clappy church on Sunday, this Sunday at four in the afternoon for their weekly shindig that would be a good start. Better to go to a church that actually believes in healing unlike my Mother's church that just believes in guilt and embarrassment. I shall sit through it and only have a couple of ciggie breaks, you know in the 'nothing much is happening' bits. Do I have to give some money at the offering or whatever it is called?
- *I SHOULDN'T WORRY.*

- Thank You I am a bit skint! So I shall sit through it, I shall even join in with any songs I know and at the end they are bound to have an 'any new people come to the reception' bit are they not?
- *BOUND TO.*
- That is what I thought. If I go along to that and ask if there is someone known to have the Gift of Healing because I would like a word with him or her, that would be a good move and then I get healed and dedicate my life to God. There is bound to be someone there to run through a few options in that direction.
- *BOUND TO.*
- Bound to. And that is that - no more disability. Is there anything else I should do?
- *YOUR PORN.*
- Ah right yes. Not good that is it? All right I have been meaning to anyway so I shall throw my porn out first thing in the morning. It shall be a declaration of my, Faith. That's the word! Actually it would ease my conscience to get rid of those things. Do not get me wrong it is only a couple of magazines, I do not have an Indonesian sex-slave tied up in the cupboard unlike some. Yes that is a good idea. Out with the porn. What else?
- *YOUR DRUGS.*
- Oh that is a touch harsh. My attitude has always been that Jesus did not touch on the subject but I suppose that if I were not in constant pain anymore I would not need to smoke dope and I would be *buzzing* with the Holy Spirit so I would not require cocaine anymore. I do not take anything else.
- *THAT'S THE IDEA.*
- What about smoking and drinking? Would that not be overdoing the miracling a bit? Instantly becoming a non-smoking teetotaller? After all Jesus did turn water into wine at that wedding. No wonder the disciples followed Him everywhere, that was *some* party-piece. I would throw a party every week just so that He could do it and if I used sparkling water He could make champagne! How about if I drink more reasonably, say twenty units a week instead of a day and aim to give up smoking in the near future?
- *THAT - IS A COMPROMISE.*
-Well yes but any deal has to have an element of compromise. So far I am doing all the giving. You have my life, my porn and my illicit habits. All I have got is an occasional pint and smoke.
-*PLUS YOU WOULD HAVE BEEN HEALED.*
- Oh yes. Sorry.
- *THAT IS ALL RIGHT.*
- But I see your point. I ought to give you something in return for the odd cough and drag I might have. What would be appropriate! I know, I shall keep Moses even though I do not need him anymore. That would work really well as the perfect evangelical starting line. 'Why do you carry a stick when you're not disabled?' 'Ah this is to remind me that I have been healed by a merciful God!' and so on. Good idea, I like that. I would make quite an imposing figure striding about twirling my stick. Can one get majorette lessons?
- *WHAT?*
- Sorry I forgot myself for a moment there. How rude! Anything else? What about the tattoo I am thinking about?
- *TATTOO?*
- Sure. I am thinking about getting... Hang on you are supposed to be omni-knowing or whatever the word is?

- OMNISCIENT. YES I KNOW, BUT IT IS RATHER INTRUSIVE LOOKING INTO PEOPLE'S MINDS ALL THE TIME AND IT CAN BE QUITE REPULSIVE! I WOULD RATHER YOU JUST TOLD ME RATHER THAN MY DELVING INTO THE SWEATY RECESSES OF YOUR CRANIUM. THAT IS THE CONCEPT OF PRAYER! AS A SYSTEM IT HAS WORKED RATHER WELL FOR A NUMBER OF YEARS. YES, YOUR TATTOO. WHAT ABOUT IT?

- Would it still be all right to have it done? After all it is a protest against unchristian behaviour such as greed, avarice, consumerism, commercialism and so on. Just in case people do not notice Moses they might notice the tattoo and that would be the evangelical lead-in?

- IF YOU MUST.

- Oh absolutely it is a *great* idea. A sort of Christian branding! It is quite poetic really. I think we have covered everything have we not?

- SEX.

- Oh yes please! Sorry. Are You referring to my reasonably long list of girlfriends? I have lost count. I think it is about fifty?

- DO NOT ASK ME, I HAVE LOST COUNT!

- Now there is a fact for the C.V.

- IT IS NOT A LAUGHING MATTER! I CREATED MARRIAGE FOR A REASON. GRANTED THE ORIGINAL REASON HAS NO RELEVANCE ANY MORE BUT I STILL LIKE THE IDEA.

- Hey I am with You on that one. I definitely think that thirty is a good age to settle down and accept some responsibility. No more debauched nights and loose women for me (damn I am giving away too much here!)

- PARDON?

- Nothing. No I need a good, Christian wife with whom to share the joy and wonder of my healing and conversion. Actually You know what would be really sweet? If a young female member of the church had a dream or vision or something the night before, the Saturday. If she saw me in a dream and she turned out to be the healing person or whatever and then we fall in love. Now would that not be romantic?

- IT SOUNDS APPALLING SOPPY TO ME. I USED TO BE A VENGEFUL GOD OF WAR YOU KNOW, BEFORE I RETIRED AND THE BOY TOOK OVER THE FAMILY BUSINESS. I HATE ALL THESE MODERN METHODS. HONESTLY THE SONGS THEY SING THESE DAYS! IT IS JUST NOISE YOU KNOW. GIVE ME A GOOD HYMN ANY DAY, PREFERABLY SUNDAY.

- But you would agree to a nice Christian wife?

- IT SOUNDS IDEAL. A DISTINCT CHANGE FOR THE BETTER.

- My old girlfriends were all right. In fact they were all lovely it was me that always messed things up but not any more. I shall be a changed man in many ways. Dedicated to the service of God. A clean, upright, respectable pillock of the community! This is a bit reminiscent of that old pope joke. Do You know the one... Or maybe not.

- I MIGHT BE THE WRONG PERSON TO TELL.

-You have a point. Right what else needs sorting out? I might as well return to the folks still. Well I have sold the flat so I need somewhere to live anyway plus it will keep me out of trouble. I can still go to pubs but I would not drink so much and I would be evangelical: 'God is like a pint of beer!' and so on. If I lose friends because of my new faith I shall just have to cope with it. I am bound to make new friends at church although I hope they are a little more interesting than last time I was a Charismatic and if I see that Ken Wise he shall feel the wr... my Christian forgiveness. *Hey* I am getting the swing of this! It might actually be quite fun to be a Christian again. What should I do as far as the dedication bit goes? I have a few skills now and was working with long-term unemployed types so maybe I can carry on with that.

Actually the best I could do is use my publicity and P.R. ability. I still have all of my media contacts and a genuine miracle with the romance part would be all over the local press and would probably go national. With the stick and tattoo it would be the type of story that daytime television *loves*. I would be on Runch and Jude in weeks! I could grow my hair and dress eccentrically and they would *adore* me! Plus we are coming up to the millennium so a bit of positive P.R. for Christianity would work wonders. Seeing as how I would have all the energy that I used to I could do a heavy workload and just talk about the beauty of a simple and loving Faith. It would be *fantastic*! A hint of John the Baptist about it really. Mass baptisms in the sea. This is such a good idea as my mate Percy Percy always says: 'Nothing can go wrong!'

But what if it does not work? That would mean that I could not believe in anything anymore. A one way ticket to Agnostia. That would be rather bleak. I have no safety net on this deal but I have a deal and it is going to work isn't it?

- I said: 'Isn't it'?

-Hello? Jude to God, Jude to God? Is anybody out there? Only two hours of rouge left. Repeat, only two hours of rouge left.

Oh *bugger*! That would be the faith bit then.

Wednesday 9th June: **LUST**

I had a lovely day for once! Do not snigger 'tis true - well as good as life can get these days. It started off badly, awake at half past six with no television to watch, no sofa to sit on and running low on painkillers plus there was a nagging feeling that I had forgotten something, something important. God knows what. What the hell was I doing last night?

The morning drifted on and I once again demonstrated the realities of getting on in years as I could not bear Wireless 1 and tuned to Wireless 2. Unfortunately I rather enjoyed it whilst drinking far too much coffee and waiting for a time when opening a bottle of rouge would not leave me panging with guilt. Then the day changed completely.

At half past ten the buzzer sounded and against my better judgement I answered. It was Mags armed with breakfast! We had a long chat with lots of hugs before repairing to the Carpenter's Rest. Mags went shopping at one point and Thaddeo turned up. I gave him the biggest admonition he is ever likely to get and I hope it has done him some good.

Later Mags and I shared a baseball bat and she returned to London hopefully happier than when she arrived. Feeling rather good about myself -why not it does not happen often - I crashed out with no problem at all. I am sure there is something I should remember.

* * *

- Yes?
- Jude it's me.
- Mags my favourite lunatic! Come on up.

- Hello sweetie. Big hug! What a fantastic surprise, are you all right?
- I'm O.K. but you sounded so miserable yesterday that I had to see you. Jude your flies are undone.
- Sorry kid. Look when you buzzed I was naked so think yourself lucky. Come on in. What have you got there?
- Breakfast, one bottle of pink shampoo, I know it's your favourite and some chocolate. What has happened to your lovely flat? Oh Jude!
- It is a bit denuded is it not. Well Thomas came round the other day to take the bed apart since there is no way I could do that and in a fit of generosity I asked if he wanted anything. Since I am going back to Redmond Grange I am not going to need a lot of the stuff that I have accumulated so he took the television, the microwave, the sofa and some old clothes.
- Oh no! Not your wonderful sofa. I loved that sofa.
- All gone but to a good cause I think. Never mind grab a corner of mattress, I shall get some milk to have with the chocolate before champersing and you can tell me what is up. How is that for a cunning plan?
- Very cunning indeed Baldnut.
- Do not mock the afflicted.
- Let's see the spot then.
- Just there.
- God it's huge! That one is going to explode.
- Yuck!

84

- I hate seeing you like this, how is the leg.
- Useless, painful and boring but do not change the subject. Has something happened with this Magnus muffin?
- We're going for a meal tonight. Have you had the tattoo done yet?
- Not as yet no. It does remind me of the story about the skinhead who injured his hand whilst using a chain saw and for the rest of his life had 'LOVE' and 'HAT' on his knuckles! But you are digesting, you have a date with the muffin Magnus. *Excellent*! What is the problem?
- I don't know Jude. I just wanted to talk to you so I took the day off and came down.
- And why not? You have not thrown a sickie have you, you bad, bad person? Did I ever tell you how I earned the nickname King Sickie while I was at the college?
- No?
- Well you remember I was getting all that grief last Autumn?
- Yeah from that bloody secretary.
- That is right and I was feeling very fed up. Anyhow I had to have a bit of minor surgery behind my ear to get rid of an abscess but we will not stray into the details.
- Thank you.
- So I ended up with six stitches behind my ear and as I walked home from the hospital I noted with interest that the weather was somewhat Mork and Mindy and decided to take a few days off for some deep sea drinking. The next day I rang my boss, Nicky with the best excuse you have ever heard.
- Go on?
- 'Nicky.' I said, 'I am very sorry but I have had a bit of an accident. Last night, walking home in the wind, out of nowhere I was hit on the back of the head by a roof tile that must have become loose!'
- No!
- Oh yes! 'Oh you poor thing!' said the boss, 'Are you all right?' 'Well I had to go to hospital. I have got six stitches and a hint of concussion and I have been told to take a couple of days off.'
- Did she fall for it?
- Hook , liar and stinker. I took six days off and went back the day before the stitches were due out to establish my credentials. Then I claimed to still be a little 'woozy' and took another two days! When I told the few trusted people there about it they christened me King Sickie. Let us face it if one is going to take time off one must do it convincingly. No-one but no-one is impressed by 'food poisoning' anymore.
- You're mad!
- Only for you sweetie but let us open the bubbly. That is for you, that is for me, to your future happiness as God knows you have earned it.
- Thanks.
- And here's to someone appropriate. The late and dear Diana.
- To Diana? Why her?
- She was almost as lovely as you.
- You're so nice to me but don't you think everyone overdid it a bit when she died? I mean London stank of rotting flowers for days.
- She was very misunderstood.
- By the Royal family?
- No by her fans. She hated the publicity she got but her fans wanted more and more. *They* created the paparazzi that made her miserable but I do not think it was just Diana, I think it was a catharsis for the whole nation to say how lousy life is. Her death was so ironic,

unpleasant and horrible that it shocked the hell out of everyone. Suddenly she embodied everyone's personal misery whatever it might be. The entire nation spent a week saying: 'God life is bloody lousy!' and then got on with their lousy lives.
- That sort of makes sense.
- I had a similar thing when a mate of mine died a year or so ago. Peter Dickerson his name was and a lovely man. He had been in the R.A.F. in the fifties, a bit like my Dad and was great fun. He looked just like James Robertson Justice, loved a pint or several and was so funny he was great. Then he died suddenly of cancer. Taken in one night, dead the next. I went to his funeral a few days later and just could not stop crying. The silly thing was that I had not taken any tissues with me and by the end of the service I looked like I had been run over by a gang of snails! Anyway I am sure that Peter's funeral was the catalyst for me getting a lot of grief out of my system and I certainly felt better afterwards although I still miss him terribly.
- I remember you talking about him. He was the one with the classic cars wasn't he?
- That's the chap but I think it was like that for many people when Diana died, bless her soul. So what about this Magnus then? Oh did I tell you I heard a great one the other day?
- No?
- What is the translation into English of Magnus Magnuson?
- Tell me?
- Robert Robinson!
- That was terrible. I'll have to tell him that.
- Good idea. Always check out as soon as possible if a man has got a sense of humour or not. It is a bit like testing your tyre pressures before a long drive.
- That's another reason for coming here Jude, some advice. It's been so long since I've had a first date I feel like it's my first ever first date.
- Advice according to the Book of Jude? Not a problem. First thing is to just enjoy yourself. Do not feel guilty about this bloke spending money on and generally spoiling you because it will feed his ego if you are obviously having a good time. But always remember men are only after one thing.
- You mean sex?
- Of course. It is the raison d'être for every male with a very few exceptions. It is why men want to earn lots of money, have flash cars, wear expensive perfume and designer clothes, show off in female company and so on. They think it makes them more attractive and therefore getting laid will be easier. It is completely true that men think about sex all the time.
- I knew it was. Every seven seconds or something isn't it?
- On a cold day. Do you remember my mate John you met a while back?
- Bald guy with the uneven sideburns?
- That is the fella. Anyway he once gave a running commentary on his thoughts at work: 'Oh God work. Oh there's Sarah sex, sex, tits, sex, cars, sex, tits, oh she's got a nice, legs, arses, sex, work, sex, lunch, sex.' and so on! That is what it is like I promise you.
- You're not making me feel any better.
- Ah but forewarned is four-legged or something. Just always bear it in mind. What a man has to show you is that although he is up to his ears with lust, fizzing with hormones as it has been put, he can still respect you and act in a civilised fashion. Men are always ready for sex, except at half past ten on a Saturday evening with no warning but it does takes a while for most women. There is no point going into the details of why this is, it just is most of the time. A man that recognises this fact is halfway to being worthwhile. It is a good idea not to trust men until they have shown otherwise as it will save you a lot of hurt.
- That's very cynical.

- Possibly but I am a man, I know men and I am *very* protective towards you. If you hear alarm bells ringing when you are talking to some bloke make your excuses and go because female intuition does exist and is normally accurate.
- What should I look out for?
- No breasts and an arrogant manner.
- No seriously.
- All sorts of things. The trouble is that most men have not come to terms with themselves and are constantly trying to be something they are not. Crippling insecurity is not just for women you know. Men who are reconciled to themselves and do not need to prove anything make the best partners for that simple reason. When you meet a man who has not come to grips with himself, if you'll excuse the expression, you are not off to a promising start but some specifics to watch out for are men who roll up the sleeves of their jackets.
- Why?
- Because they are making out they are better built than they really are. Do not trust a man with hair over his ears, not long hair that happens to cover them but someone who has it cut to deliberately be over his ears. The police say that ears are the only feature that cannot be changed by cosmetic surgery and criminals have been caught by their ear prints you know. It is a sign of dishonesty.
- You're being silly now.
- A hint, possibly but as the mummy tiger said to the baby tiger: 'It's a jungle out there!' Men with silly facial hair are to be avoided too, like those boy bands that start their career looking sweet so that teenage girls scream at them but as soon as the second album comes along they want to be 'taken seriously' and have ridiculous goatee beards and tattoos. What *are* they doing? Young men with goatees are trying to look older and old men with them younger but both trying to be something that they are not. As for moustaches that is matter of taste, almost literally.
- Yuck!
- Indeed. Men who swear in front of you just after meeting and say something facile like: 'Excuse my French.' to try and make light of their foul manners are to be ignored. Yes everyone swears to an extent but most women are offended by it to some level and to blithely ignore the fact is crass and ignorant. Obviously men who drink too much. You know the true definition of alcoholism?
- What's that then?
- For each person it is the same: 'Anyone who drinks more than I do!'
- Very profound I don't think.
- Did I tell you about my mate that went to an A.A. meeting?
- No?
- My old friend Simon who does seem to spend most of his waking hours half-cut but one evening he plucked up the courage and went to a meeting at a school along the London Road. He got there a little early, found the room and sat down. Over the subsequent minutes the room started to fill up with housewives or women who looked like housewives, who were trying not to look at him. Eventually this chap in a corduroy jacket with leather elbow patches came in, sat down cross-legged and said: 'Right. Who wants to start?' Simon decided to get it over and done with, rose shakily to his feet and announced: 'Hello. My name is Simon. I am gay and an alcoholic!' and the room went silent. The chap at the front coughed nervously and said: 'Er... This is A Level Spanish. You want room 2c along the corridor!'
- Oh no! The poor man! What did he do?

- Well what else could he do except find the nearest boozer and get trashed the silly old sod! Anyway where were we? Oh yes men who do not manage to get their belts through all the loops in their trousers.
- What?
- Men to be avoided. The ones who are crumpled looking and wear chinos but always miss one of the loops around the back because they obviously cannot handle life without their mothers and will be lazy, messy and unable to cook. Actually that is a serious point Honey if a man cannot stop talking about his mother run as far and fast as your little legs will carry you.
- Really?
- Absolutely. Real, decent men will treat you like I do, as though you are my sister and with respect, charm, un-feigned interest, humour and with no sense of rushing or exaggerated patience. They should treat you like a sister until you do not want them to anymore and then they should act as *they* would like *their* little sister's boyfriend to treat *her*. Does that make the slightest sense?
- It's lovely.
- Like most situations with new people be cynical but do not be surprised if someone does turn out to be lovely. I sincerely doubt that this Magnus geezer is anywhere near being worthy of you but he might be. Love does exist but just remember that there is still untold amounts of social sexism around and there are a lot of men who will lie about all sorts of things just to get a 'shag'. Do not forget that men have an expression that goes: 'You don't look at the mantelpiece when you're poking the fire!' referring to not so pretty women. It is not fair but that is how the world is at the moment and although it is a vast improvement on not so recently, there is still a long way to go.
- Should I tell him about Josh and Danny?
- That is a hard one. No absolutely not.
- Why not?
- Well first off what the God's whiskers has it got to do with him? There is no reason in the world for him to have any right to your past.
- But wouldn't it be dishonest not to tell him?
- No of course not. People have this big hang up about honesty, it is one of the favourite soap lines is it not it: 'I'll 'ave to tell'im!' What *rubbish*! Sharing your life with someone does not mean that they own you. If there is something in the past that you want to stay there that is utterly your privilege. Anyway you do not like talking about them do you?
- I don't mind with you, but no I don't.
- Then you have no reason to. Anyway if he does not have the wherewithal to regale you with erudite conversation then you are wasting your time and should order a double helping of dessert immediately. Another thing being that men do not like is women with 'baggage' as it is put, which translates as: 'A woman that has been abused by a man previously and who, understandably takes a while to trust a new one.' Some men feel vicariously uncomfortable in that situation. But the last and most important thing to watch out for is accountants that have handbags. Oops!
- You rotten sod!
- The fact is I am unable tell you if this bloke is all right or not. He might turn up on his white charger, armour newly polished and whisk you off to the Maldives or somewhere but if he does give me a call so that I can give you my duty free order. You have got to scout him out and then we can all go for a drink and put him through the Krypton Factor.
- But it might be love?

- I do not know Mags. Personally I am *so* looking forward to you being in a happy relationship and talking about getting married, worrying if you should ask Mr. R. to give you away. I do not think this is the guy but I do think you have every chance of meeting someone who could be. Do you remember David Niven?
- Of course, he was lovely.
- Smashing he was, smashing but he was married twice, both times having met the ladies concerned only a week before.
- One week?
- Yes I think so. Love at first sight and total devotion. Wonderful example.
- But he divorced the first one?
- No she died in a terrible accident. They were throwing a party and were playing hide and seek. His wife went to go down a back stairway and fell down because she did not switch the lights on. Absolutely tragic and the poor man was devastated but a little while later he fell in love again, became man and wife within days and she, years later was his widow.
- So what you're saying is be wary but be open?
- Well *that* is open to misinterpretation but yes. Look for your own David Niven, charming, amusing, gentle but still dashing, unpredictable and exciting and above all *not* a chauvinist.
- God it's a bloody minefield!
- Yes isn't it just but worth it in the end I think you shall find. Because you see my dearest Mags you have a wonderful personality, a veritable one woman dance groove party, you are sharp as a scalpel and highly professional and you are utterly beautiful so you absolutely deserve to be happy. Let us drink to that. Cheers. There are two main things to remember. Never opt for second best, if he is not good enough do not make excuses for him. This is the age of social freedoms which means you have choice and it is as acceptable to wait for however long until you are ready as it is to jump into bed on the first date. It is your freedom so never be talked out of it.
- Thank you Jude I knew you were the one to talk to. Right this flat is starting to get me down. I've got the day off and a gram of charlie so what we gonna' do?
- Buzz: 'Redmond - Drinkers College Dublin.' ' I know the answer Jeremy, take a couple of lines and a taxi to the Carpenter's Rest.' 'Well done Drinkers, here are your bonus questions.' I'll get the mirror. My defunct gold card is over there. Did I tell you I got caught having a sniff just t'other day.
- Oh no! You're not in trouble are you?
- No it was only Chris and Noel in the Carpenter's. When I say it was the other day it must have been a few months ago because the leg had not packed up by then. It was a Friday night and my old mate Samuel was down from the smoke. We meet in the Rest at about six and were well in session mood. I had taken a line a bit earlier on, it was left over from some press party and I suggested having a line to Samuel who is not backward about coming forward in these sorts of situations. We repaired to the gents cubicle and I had cut two generous lines when the main door opened and Noel said: 'Jude are you in there?'
- Oh dear. What did you do?
- Well I was coked up to my eyeballs so I came out of the cubicle and started to tell them my life story when suddenly Samuel flew out of the cubicle, said: 'See you in the Battle.' and ran out! I apologised to them both, promised I would never, ever do it again and went and joined Samuel in the Battle of the Nile over the road. He was looking very smug since he had an excuse for taking both lines and I had to get the gear off him to have one myself. Good night though.
- Were you forgiven then?

- Oh yes. Fortunately I have done them both favours in the past so I just went in the next afternoon, reiterated my humble apologies and had a few pints. It has not been mentioned since. Oh yes it has, I had forgotten. A load of us were sitting at the bar chatting about a week later and were talking about champagne for some obscure reason. Chris said something like: 'What's the best thing to have with champagne?' and I said: 'A couple of lines of...' he said: 'Don't!' and I said: 'Shakespeare!' Caught him out beautifully. Right are you finished? Let's get a cab and get pissed!

* * *

- ... So you are saying that this poor woman was sacked because she was pregnant and her so called friend grassed her up as t'were? Thanks mate keep the change. The rotten hatechildren and the utter cow. Hello Peter what a surprise.
- Oh hello Jude. I would like to say that it is an unalloyed pleasure to see you but I've given up lying for Lent.
- It isn't Lent.
- I simply must get a new calendar.
- Peter this is Magdalene known as Mags, my cousin. Mags this is Peter known as: 'Hurry up will you I'm dying of thirst!'
- Oh very whimsical. Hello Magdalene, what a beautiful name in fact you are simply far too lovely to be related to Quasi here. Actually Jude there is something I've been meaning to tell you.
- Warning bells, warning bells. Yes Peter?
- Well you know your hair is a little longer and sort of brushed away from your rapidly growing forehead?
- I am very aware of my own hair situation thank you very much.
- Ah but I don't think you are dear heart because in this light it looks well, ginger.
- *Ginger*! I thought I was going *grey*. Mags, Mags this is very important! Stop giggling, really. No stop laughing this is very serious. Now stop the hysteria, there is nothing funny about the present situation. You cad Peter! Mags stop laughing and tell me it is not true.
- I'm sorry Jude he's right.
- You will both forgive me if I sit down for a moment. How cruel can life be? Well don't just stand there man get me a pint, this is an emergency. Mags will you *stop laughing*! What do you want a spritzer? All right here is some money if you could carry them over. I am going to sit down and sulk.

- There you are. He's lovely isn't he?
- Peter? Yes he is a damn good friend. You know if I was still able-bodied I would leap up those stairs a la mountain goat and dampen my hair down. Honestly, *ginger*!
- I still love you.
- Thank God, a reason to carry on through the slings and arrows of outrageous fortune. Mind you it is very fitting is it not. I am now the complete anti-hero, the ultimate antithesis of the before and after photographs.
- What do you mean?
- In the space of ten years I have gone from a fourteen stone, twenty-eight inch waist hod-carrier with a seemingly all year tan, to a ten stone, ginger, cripple. All I need now are some black N.H.S. glasses to complete the make over. 'Banish able-bodied misery with your new Ronco R.T.A. Kit, available at all good D.I.Y. stores!'

90

- Are you feeling sorry for yourself?
- Absolutely! Well wouldn't you?
- It must be hard for you, it must be hard for everyone around you I hate seeing you like this. The way you used to stride around in those smart suits you had, turning heads wherever you went.
- I still turn heads but they tend to turn back again fairly quickly these days. The funny thing is that I knew this was going to happen so although it is not easy, it is a lot less hard for me than everyone else. I have noticed that my older friends have been able to deal with it and treat me exactly the same as before but the younger ones, like the crowd in here cannot even look me in the eye all of a sudden.
- Really?
- Unfortunately so. In fact a week after Chris caught me with the coke we were having a late night drink and chat in here. He was asking me something like why I was so hedonistic so I told him about the accident, about having a degenerative condition and about having been told I would be in a wheelchair before I turn forty. Hence I do, or did tend to live life for the moment. He thought I was joking but I said: 'No mate I am not winding you up. There is more than a strong possibility that one day I shall turn up in here with a slight reduction in the number of my limbs.'
- What did he say?
- Oh he made the normal noises about how sad it was and would I please stop taking cocaine on his premises. Then when I hobbled in here with Moses for the first time he asked what was wrong and I said something like: 'Remember the conversation we had? Well it is happening.' He has hardly spoken to me since.
- That's a shame.
- Yes I did not expect to lose friends just because I am suddenly disabled. Strange world. The weirdest one is John, not Andy's dad the other one.
- Bald guy, uneven sideburns?
- Yes him. He had a major go at me one evening, has refused to speak to me since and has completely blanked me about four times now. We had been friends for seven years but no longer apparently but this conversation is getting me down and you have reminded me of a terrible joke you clever thing.
- How terrible?
- Absolutely awful in fact it is verging on being sick and depraved.
- Sounds promising.
- A woman has just given birth and the doctors have taken the baby away. After a few minutes a very grim faced doc. came in and said: 'Mrs. Jones, we've got a thing going on. Sorry wrong script! Mrs. Jones I have good news and bad news.' 'Oh doctor what's the bad news?' 'Your baby is ginger.' 'Oh no!' she wailed with anguish, 'But what could be the good news?' 'He was stillborn Mrs., Mrs. Jones!'
- That's horrible!
- Ah but if I am now ginger I am allowed to mock myself.
- If you're starting on your rotten jokes then I'm going to go shopping. You'll be all right here won't you?
- Desert me in my hour of need would you, you heartless woman! Go on then bugger off shopping. Here, this is the pub's number to give me a call on your way back and there will be a fresh spritzer waiting for you so you can just sit and rant.
- I never rant!
- Sorry I meant to say enthuse. Have fun.

91

- See you later.

* * *

- Hello mate. I thought you'd be in here.
- You presume too much Thaddeo. What may I do for you, you dreadful man.
- What do you mean presume? You're always in here!
- Well you see there is a gap in the time, space continuum just outside my front door and every time I go through it I land up at this very bar. It is most traumatic and disturbing so I have to have a beer. It is a unique phenomenon you know.
- Yeah sure. Is that a spot on your neck?
- Indeed how *kind* of you to notice. I have been growing it especially in your honour.
- O.K. Anyway I've got a bit of money through from some old royalties and I thought that I owe you a few drinks so what are you having?
- A great time, thank you thank you for asking! Just tell Peter: 'A pint for Jude' and he will know what to do.
- O.K. mate. Back in a sec.

- There you go Jude. I was feeling a little bit guilty about all the drinks you've bought for the three of us so it's my turn to spoil you.
- If I were to be pedantic the three of you owe me more than a few drinkies do you not? About two grand if I recall?
- Yeah I know. We'll pay it back sometime.
- I sincerely doubt it but do not worry. Money is not the greatest of my current concerns but what is happening with the paper at the moment? Have you been in touch with Sam?
- You know we don't trust him. Tom knows someone that used to work for him and he says Jones is a complete bastard.
- So ten months of extremely hard work goes down the proverbial because some little twit has a grudge against his former employer from whom he probably stole anyway. God's zimmer frame are you mad man? He would be working *with* us on an equal basis with us maintaining editorial control. I just do not understand what the problem is with you people.
- It isn't down the drain, we're on-line line now although the content is more arts based.
- That is *really* what this town needs is it not? Another arts media thing.
- Actually Thom was wondering if you'd like to write some stuff for us.
- You can tell Thom: 'I doubt it'. I am a journalist not a web page designer. Anyway it is not my problem anymore and I refuse to get wound up over it. Give me some good news mate.
- Oh yeah Aaron and Lucy are getting married, we're having the stag do in Amsterdam and you're invited.
- Getting married that is wonderful. I thought it was about time he took her up the aisle, if you'll pardon the expression! I do not think however that a trip to Amsterdam is quite on the menu for myself although thank you for the kind offer.
- Oh go on. Why not?
- I just would not want to Thaddeo so leave it at that. I have no intention of giving you the chance of 'getting a girl for my crippled mate'. However I would love to come to the reception or whatever so when is it?
- They haven't decided yet.

- Oh of course, always sort out the stag do before getting bogged down in the catering arrangements! Makes sense to me. Would you give them my congratulations for me, they are a spectacular couple.
- Yeah Aaron's a lucky guy. Maybe someday I'll find the right woman for me.
- Get out of here Thaddeo. Aaron's luck, as you put it is mainly him being a thinking and sorted human being who has a relationship with a similar human being based on mutual love, respect and understanding. You however are a paid up and practising chauvinist who will never find the 'right woman' until you completely overhaul your attitudes.
- Steady on Jude I'm no sexist.
- Oh really? How many innocents are you currently stringing along?
- Only two! It was one last week but I meet Evie on Friday and she doesn't have anywhere to stay so she's at the flat.
- Evie? Lovely name. How old is she and does she know about the other one, there is so little point in trying to remember the names of all your 'birds'.
- She's sixteen and she knows but Ruth doesn't.
- Well Thaddeo I think that is definitely Quod Erat Demonstrandum. Your attitude to women can only be described as utterly abysmal.
- It wasn't my fault, she insisted on getting into bed so what could I do.
- Get some reality into your head would you! What you do Thaddeo is you are charming to men, I must admit to liking you but with women you are charming and very flirtatious and the less experienced, sixteen year olds for example fall for it and you take advantage of them. Women are more romantically minded than men and these poor things you pick up think you are glamorous, put you on a pedestal and develop a crush. You then stamp and trample all over their dreams and innocence. Do you never feel guilty about the hurt you have caused in the female community?
- You're being out of order Jude.
- I can assure you that my renowned impression of a telephone box bears no resemblance to my current actions. No mate this is the best advice you are going to get in a while. Do you know what sexism is Thaddeo?
- Yeah. 'Course I do.
- Do expound.
- Well it's when you knock 'em around and everything isn't it?
- A mere subsection of the enormous problem old chap. I shall tell you what sexism is Thaddeo. It is the fact that the only people to talk about sexism are women so that the constant and consistent response from men is: 'Yeah, yeah, yeah. Stop whingeing.' It is also the fact that as soon as a man, me for example starts to talk to another man, you for instance about sexism and women's rights the other man, that is you remember gets very uncomfortable, are you not?
- Well you're talking bollocks.
- Now there's an image, small hairy testicles flying from my mouth willy-nilly! You are feeling uncomfortable because you are unable to have a relationship with a woman based on respect and trust and you *know* it is wrong. Whether it is hatred, fear or whatever I do not know but equality is nowhere near your mind and thoughts. You know what I do not understand about you Thaddeo?
- No what?
- Well you are coloured are you not? Is that the term you prefer?
- Whatever, yeah coloured'll do.

93

- You hate it when you are patronised, insulted or even threatened because of your skin colour do you not? So why do you treat women the way you hate to be treated yourself? I do not get it.
- That's an exaggeration, I don't treat women like that.
- Look there is more to racism than shouting: 'Nigger!' and there is more to sexism than hitting your girlfriend. Every day the vast majority of women in this country suffer prejudice and stress simply because of their gender. In the office, in the pub, on public transport even just walking down the street. Every day they have to put up with that sort of, well crap is the only word for it. The very existence of blonde/Essex girl jokes are a testament to men's attitudes and women suffer at the hands of people like you who do not even realise that they are doing anything wrong.
- I don't think I am. Look if you whistle at a bird, O.K. woman it's a compliment right?
- The difference between a compliment and an insult is not how it is intended but how it is received. When the majority of women say that they do not like it then stop doing it. The answer to your question is: 'No!' and no you cannot cite any case where a woman has whistled at you.
- But that's sexism in itself.
- Oh sure. There is a certain amount of what they call negative sexism where men have the hard time. Advertisements on the television portray all men as stupid, unable to do the smallest household chore and only interested in lager and football. That is sexist! A definition of political correctness is: 'Men are wrong, women are right and gays get the benefit of the doubt!' but this is a drop in the sexism ocean. I would wager that every woman in this pub could quote you a personal example of blatant sexism that has occurred in the last week, every single one.
- And I'm supposed to feel guilty am I?
- At the moment, yes but we are only talking about attitudes and they are the easiest things to change. The really silly thing is that you are actually missing out my friend. The definition of a civilised society is one where women play an equal role. Feminine qualities are compassion, communication, understanding and tolerance, qualities that equate to 'civilised'. Male input is aggression, ignorance and intolerance which equates to 'anarchy', the opposite of civilisation. Equality is about recognising these differences and pooling resources either as a society or as individuals. At the moment your perspective is very close to those dreadful Islamic states that completely subjugate women.
- But that's their culture.
- *So*? Slavery used to be part of *ours*! Unfortunately their culture is actually a major humanitarian issue but that is a surface judgement, I do not know enough about it really although there is definitely a correlation between societies that are completely male orientated and outrageous human rights violations, to put it politely.
- I'm not that bad come on. Why are you giving me such a hard time?
- It is the carrot and stick scenario my friend.
- What?
- Well as you pointed out I have been giving you a hard time but I am now going to give you the best piece of advice that you have ever had. Why do you not drop your 'conquer and discard' mentality and try love for once?
- What do you mean?
- Correct me if I am wrong but whenever you are with a woman you are constantly thinking: 'I could do better.'?
- Well, yeah I suppose.

- The point is Thaddeo that all women are beautiful in their own right. The way to enjoy that beauty is to find it by having a relationship that is based on mutual respect and trust because that, if you are compatible soon becomes love which normally comes with happiness as standard. There is more to women than just lust. There is love which involves lust, companionship, respect, trust and so on. Try it Thaddeo it might be the best move you have ever made.

- You have gone all quiet on me old chap.
- I'm thinking about what you said.
- Put it this way Thaddeo. Basic journalism, according to C.P. Scott is to report both sides of any situation to produce a balanced account right?
- Yeah of course.
- Well so far on the subject of relationships you have only investigated the male side of the story. What I am suggesting is that you look into female attitudes to provide yourself with a balanced viewpoint. Aaron covered both sides and he will soon be getting married. Think about it my friend.
- Yeah. I think I will.
- Jude? Telephone.
- Thanks Peter is it Mags?
- Yes.
- Then do me a spritzer and tell her I shall see her when she gets here. Right Thaddeo my friend now is your chance to treat a woman with respect. My cousin is just about to arrive and if you even start to flirt with her you will feel the wrath of Moses. I shall become a lapsed pacifist for five minutes, no paci, all fist! Am I making myself abundantly clear?
- Yeah all right mate. Calm down.
- Mags dearest! Get yourself round that spritzer and meet my former colleague Thaddeo who is a reformed dreadful man. Thaddeo this is my cousin Magdalene.
- Hi Thaddeo.
- Hello Mags. Jude? What did you mean by the: 'Wrath of Moses'?
- Oh that's the name of my walking stick. I am a firm believer that inanimate objects that one relies upon should have names and be treated with tender, loving care.
- He loves his stick don't you Jude.
- Indeed did I tell you? His name was completely justified last week.
- No what happened?
- Well I had just been to my chiropractor, the lovely Debbie who likes to play the castanets with my back and the general plan was to hobble down here afterwards as is my wont of an afternoon. Unfortunately it started to rain and I did not have any option but to keep going. I was keeping my eyes on the ground as some of those paving slabs are treacherous in the rain and did not realise I was walking into a Jude trap.
- What was it?
- Well one of those furniture shops up the road had had a delivery of wood and I looked up to find myself between two piles of logs, both covered with tarpaulins that were at an angle so that there was not enough room for me to get past. The tarps were in the way. I was standing there, getting extremely damp and wondering what to do when there was a gust of wind and the tarpaulins shimmered off the ground leaving enough room for me to get through! It was *amazing*!
- Really?

- Absolutely true Thaddeo. Ask Mags, I see absolutely no point in lying and Moses did his stuff or is that staff?
- I'll say.
- Is that a hint of an accent Magdalene?
- Yes we're both part Irish.
- Really? I love the Irish.
- You have never mentioned *that* before dear Thaddeo. Have you ever been to Dublin?
- No I haven't.
- You would love it, would he not Mags? It is funny you mentioning going to Amsterdam for your stag do because when I was best man, contradiction in terms I know for my friend Matthew I opted for Dublin. I definitely think it was the best choice.
- You went mad over there didn't you?
- I would not say mad, dearest Mags but there was a lot of deep sea drinking going on! There are two things I shall always remember. On the Sunday we were kicked out of the hotel bar at holy hour, actually two hours when the men folk are supposed to go home for their Sunday dinner. Obviously we wanted to carry on Guinness tasting and Uncle Jon, one of my lunatic Irish uncles knew a place up the road. Eight of us piled into his knackered old Sierra, I think I was on the roof and we drove to a small B & B near Finglas. Jon said: 'Leave this to me!' and we shuffled into this small, quiet lobby not at all sure what was going on. Jon exchanged nods with the chap at the desk and went to a small door in the corner. When he opened it the amount of smoke, music and sounds of drunken shouting that came spilling out were amazing but then disappeared again when the door shut! It was *unbelievable*! Then we went in. The place was huge and packed with families watching football and we had a wonderful time. It is a grand place is Dublin
- It sounds it. What was the other memory then?
- Oh yes the morning that we were coming home. You see Matthew and I were staying with Jon and Martha and Matthew was in little Anna's room. Martha took a cup of coffee into the room at an ungodly hour on the Monday morning and said: 'Wake up Matt it's tomorrow!' and you have never seen someone leap out of bed so quick!
- I've always found Irish people to be great fun.
- What was that comment Jude? The little old guy?
- Oh yes, you will like this one mate. Some local English television company were doing a documentary on Dublin and they had this smarmy looking guy in O' Connell Street interviewing passers by. He stopped a little old boy, gave him the spiel and asked: 'Have you lived in Dublin all of your life?' and the old boy looked him straight in the eye and replied: ' Not yet no!'
- Really? That's fantastic!
- There are lots of them. Mags you tell him about that time you went to the off licence.
- Oh yeah. I was over around Christmas a couple of years ago and on the way back from town one day we stopped off to stock up on essentials. Bottles of anything do not last long chez Redmond. This offie was huge and stacked to the roof but in the middle of all of this booze there was one shelf containing only corn flakes.
- Corn flakes?
- Yeah believe it or not. Anyway I got my vodka and so on, took it to the counter and gave the man my plastic. He had an old fashioned swipe machine and something wrong with his hands that made it difficult for him and I was feeling quite embarrassed. To break the tension I asked: 'Why do you sell corn flakes?' He looked me straight in the eye and said: 'So people can come in and buy them!' You see Irish people aren't thick, they just think more logically.

- I think you must be right. Anyway Jude, Mags I'm off.
- Good to see you Thaddeo. Thanks for the drinks.
- No problem.
- Nice meeting you. 'Bye.

- Who was that?
- One of the guys from the paper. He was in charge of advertising.
- He was the one not bringing in enough money?
- Harsh but fair. Anyway what have you bought?
- Your birthday present.
- Oh let's have a look?
- No! Not until your birthday.
- But that is *ages* away.
- You'll just have to wait. Anyway what were you two talking about it looked very heavy.
- I was showing Thaddeo the error of his ways. You know it is interesting that a lot of older people go on about how words have been stolen for dubious purposes. They say that the word 'gay' has lost it's beauty or whatever although I think it is highly appropriate myself but the other one they quote is 'chauvinist' since they claim it is used incorrectly.
- What's it supposed to mean then?
- A chauvinist is someone that is *too* proud of their country. It is similar to xenophobia in a way but that is why it is the perfect word for men like Thaddeo. He is similar to the people that use terms like 'Paki' and so on in that he has a terrible attitude towards women.
- I hope you put him right.
- I doubt it but you never know.
- Why are you so understanding? All my girlfriends think you're lovely, sort of one of the girls.
- Because I believe in all levels of equality and the funny thing is that it is more fun to respect and get on with women than it is to fear and distrust them. I find that in all relationships and what you sow is what you reap most of the time. Plus of course, I subscribe to Cosofmepelican Magazine which is always quite an eye opener. It is true what the chap says in that song you know: 'Do not read beauty magazines; they will only make you feel ugly.' I am a man who is ugly anyway but I feel positively *deformed* after flicking through Cosofme! Mind you I shall never actually understand you lot.
- What do you mean?
- Well I do not think that the sexes are supposed to completely understand each other. It would take away the mystique. When I am with you and your friends I feel a bit like Davey Atombomb with the gorillas. I know it is not the best analogy in the world but it does sum it up. I feel accepted and tolerated but I do not know what the hell is going on and it could turn nasty at any moment.
- Gorillas! I'll tell Mary you called her a gorilla.
- Oh please don't.
- You like her don't you?
- I think she is absolutely lovely and I would much rather you told her that to be honest. But as I was saying before you threatened to slander me to the woman I would like to meet again, there are intrinsic differences between the genders but that is no reason for one to look down on the other. We are all equal and all different but it is about time I got off the soap box and I keep forgetting to ask. How are things on the job front?
- Oh I didn't tell you I've got an interview next week for a really good job.

- Wow!
- Yeah it could be great. You know how much I enjoyed that marketing post last year?
- The one you got sacked from because of that dreadful woman? Honestly some women give women a bad name.
- She was an absolute witch but anyway this one is like that but more so. It'll involve P.R. and everything. Honestly I was starting to think: 'Who should I fuck to get a decent job!' I was getting that desperate! This one sounds perfect, I just hope I'm good enough.
- Of course you are. If they do not employ you within seconds of you walking in the room then they are wrong! I mean it Honey that stuff you did for the drama school last year was *wonderful*. You have a great eye and a natural sense of style with regard to layout and colour, you are a wizard on the ol' confuser plus you are one of the best communicators I know. I do not know how you do it.
- You can use a computer perfectly well.
- I can hammer out an article in Worm or whatever and print it out but that is the extent of my abilities. I thought spreadsheets are what posh people take on picnics and a web site is the corner of the flat that I cannot get to with my duster! In fact a few months ago someone asked what my e mail address was but I did not have any cards on me and he seemed very bemused when I said: 'I'm not sure. Some strange and jumbled collection of letters as far as I can make out!' That is what they are, are they not? You chaps that can make confusers do tricks, roll over and take the dog for a walk and so on, you are like magicians to me.
- Don't be so silly it's easy but what are *you* going to do with yourself now?
- I think I shall become an alcoholic.
- What do you mean become?
- Everyone says that.
- Then maybe you should start listening to them.
- Possibly but I have come up with an idea. You know when you are at a boring dinner party and wish you could think of something to liven it up? Well I am compiling a list of party games, for example Things People Would Never Say. I say something and you have to guess who would never say it. Right: 'No thank you lady, I am a married man.'?
- Don't know.
- Clint Clingon of course! How about: 'Hasn't she got intelligent eyes.'?
- Any tabloid reader but don't change the subject, you are drinking too much.
- Yes I know. As you pointed out there is not a great deal else for me to do at the moment but things will get better when I move back to Redmond Grange. Sitting around in the Hunting Lodge is so depressing. It is the only place that has ever been *my home*, you know and look at it now. It is a mess! I do not even have anywhere to sit down. Anyway one cannot just stop being a hedonist overnight you know. I am still living for the moment.
- Even if it kills you?
- That is a long way off yet. I see no point in frustrating the best part of my life to elongate the worst and I would understand not drinking, not smoking, eating properly and regular exercise if it made you immortal but it don't. Did I ever tell you the Jim Fix story?
- Jim Fix? Don't you mean Jimmie Saville you always get your names wrong.
- No, no Jim Fix was this cove in the States who in the late seventies made jogging the fad that it was. You remember when everyone went jogging mad?
- Yeah sure.
- Well Jim Fix was one of the forerunners, if you'll excuse the pun. Anyway he dropped dead of a heart attack, aged fifty-two whilst out, guess what?
- Jogging!

- Absolutely. Well the story goes that in heaven one afternoon Yul Brinner was holding court with a group, you know that Yul was not only spectacularly beautiful he was also a major party animal. So there Yul was saying: 'So we were at this party right. Some of the women were just about clothed I think. There was champagne everywhere and the mirrors stretched from here to right over there and were loaded with charlie and, oh look everyone here's Jim Fix. Come on in Jim, welcome to heaven. This is Caligula, this is Rasputin, that's Machiavelli, this is Byron, here's Casanova, he's Catullus, anyway you'll get to know them all soon enough. So what did you do with your life Jim?' 'Well I ate muesli and ran a lot.' 'Right. That's very nice. So we were at this party and the mirrors were enormous...' and that, my dearest Mags is my philosophy on life.
- Just take it easy Jude. You worry me.
- If you want to worry about me then you will have to get in the queue. Do not concern yourself, as soon as I am reinstalled at Redmond Grange I shall straighten out a bit but for now, more fun! What would you say to repairing to the Hunting Lodge for a couple of batons and a bottle of Chateau Eurotunnel?
- I'd say: 'I'll order the taxi.'
- *Splendide*!

* * *

- I did not get the chance to tell Thaddeo about my trip to Trinity, have I told you that one.
- I get the feeling I'm going to hear it Jude.
- You can always tell me to shut up if you like. Anyway a toast, what would be appropriate? I know, to the great women of history Boedicea, Cleopatra, Joan of Arc, Elizabeth I, Victoria, Amelia Earhart, Amy Johnson,
- Emily Pankhurst, Germaine Greer, Madonna, Cher,
- But we do not include Mrs. Butcher.
- Absolutely not. Cheers.
- Cheers but I was telling you about Trinity. It was around four years ago and little Anna was thirteen I think so that is about right. I was staying with Jon and Martha and one day I mentioned to Martha that although I was thoroughly enjoying seeing the insides of lots of boozers my visits could have a little more in the way of culture about them. She suggested that I go to Trinity the following morning with Anna and her friend Jem, also thirteen. They were both very much into Take Smack or whatever they were called at the time and staying in her room was eerie because her walls were covered in posters so that you could feel all these eyes looking at you when you tried to sleep. It was a good thing I was smashed all the time.
- I stayed in her room once and it really freaked me out.
- So the next day the three of us got the bus into town, myself with hangover and the other two with far too much energy. They were on the top deck of the bus eyeing up every young man they could see: 'Look at the arse on that!' they kept shouting, it was a nightmare! Eventually we got to Trinity and paid for the tour. Our tour guide was obviously a very avuncular student from England: 'On our rrrright we have.' and so on. He was also very obviously gay and took quite a shine to me. The girls picked up on this and decided to, very kindly protect me which involved running straight up to the poor chap every time he stopped and eyeballing him from about a foot away.
- They are very funny those two.
- Quite hysterical. So we did the tour and ended up seated in a room with our guide wondering if we had any questions. Some Americans asked something as did one of the cyclopses.

- The what?
- Japanese tourists. They always wander around with their cameras up against their faces so they look as if they only have one huge eye! Anyway there we were and Anna started tugging at my shirt wanting a question to ask. You know that there is a Henry Moore sculpture in one of the quads?
- Oh yes.
- Well as you know it is absolutely *filthy*! There is no way in the world that it is anything other than a penis in a vagina so I suggested to Anna that she asked the nice man what it meant.
- You didn't?
- Oh yes. The poor man, having a thirteen year old girl asking him to explain a heavily erotic work of art.
- What did he do?
- Other than going extremely red he mumbled through a speech about how art meant different things to different people. A few more tourists asked some banal questions and he recovered his composure, to remint a cliché but then Anna demanded that I ask him a question. At that point I just wanted to find the nearest pint of Liffy Water so I stuck my flipper in the air and your man eventually ran out of sensible looking interlocutors and guardedly said: 'You have a question?' 'Yes.' I replied. 'My French au pair is lousy in bed so should I fake my orgasms?'
- No! What happened?
- He very sensibly walked off. The rest of the crowd muttered : 'What did he say?' and I dragged the girls to the nearest boozer. That was the end to any cultural sight-seeing in Dublin. Right get your laughing gear around that one and I shall stick some music on.
- Oh please if only to get that bloody music in the cab out of my head.
- What? Good old Seal Club Heaven or whatever their name is?
- That's actually quite sick you know but yeah them. Bloody kids' music!
- It is sort of Co-ed Power is it not but why is it that everyone wants to lambaste groups like them, Stairs, the Herb Women and Besmirched or whatever? And what ever happened to Cunning Stunt?
- Who?
- There was band called Cunning Stunt a few years ago but they never sold any records. Apparently D.J.s were too scared to announce the name. Anyway there is nothing wrong with kid's bands as not only are they harmless but they also perform a valuable service.
- What *are* you talking about?
- Well bands like that are very accessible which is why young children like them. They are the first point of contact for youngsters and they help start a lifelong love of music. As everyone matures they get into different types of music, let us face it there are lots out there and people can find their own niche. But everyone needs a way in as t'were and at least these bands have a clean image and can string a sentence together. Come on we listened to some old tut when we were young although ABBA are now deemed to be classic artists of course.
- It's still crap whatever you say.
- Certainly it is not my pint of ale as I prefer something a little more pretentious in my dotage and I am getting old you know. I was listening to Wireless 1 t'other day, wincing slightly and they were shouting about millennium anthems or something. You know: 'THE SONGS THAT CHANGED *YOUR* LIFE!' and so on. 'What a good idea.' I thought and things like Baker Street and Stairway to Heaven started edging their way into my cranium. Then the wireless started to suggest some ideas. Not only did I hate all of their choices but they were all at least ten years younger than my favourite songs! What it is to be past it.

- Yeah but the majority of modern pop is just noise these days. Why *do* people listen to dance music in their cars? At least we have got years of decent music to choose from.
- Oh sure. My main problem is that I cannot afford to buy all the C.D.s I want but I still like these new bands. There is nothing wrong with them leaping about the place and being generally energetic whilst wearing revealing clothing. It keeps this dirty old man happy if a little frustrated.
- How is the love life at the moment?
- Hah! Non existent and likely to remain so.
- Have you heard from Ruth at all?
- The last time we spoke she was decidedly brusque to put it mildly and that was ages ago. That relationship is well and truly over unfortunately.
- No-one on the horizon?
- Well there is a scrumptious barmaid in one of the pubs in town.
- You and your barmaids!
- But they are *wonderful* people if not my favourite people in the world especially when they are like Solly.
- Solly?
- Yes why not. Stop giggling, she is bright and funny and great company plus she is rather beautiful being an actress between gigs apparently.
- I cannot believe you fall for those lines.
- She *might* be! I am certainly perfectly willing to give her the benefit of the doubt but yes there is no fool like an old fool, avoiding clichés like the plague.
- Is she very beautiful?
- Oh yes, very Celtic looking. Auburn hair cascading to her slim waist.
- Yuck!
- A face of character and strength surrounding twinkling sapphire eyes.
- Yuck, yuck!
- A willowy yet strong figure with a navel-ring that shows just how flat her stomach is.
- You *dirty* old man!
- Dirty old men need love too! If you were going to be so unpleasant why did you ask me?
- I'm sorry. So when are you going to ask her out?
- You have *got* to be joking.
- Why not? You get on don't you?
- We get on famously, we do crosswords together, I have lent her a book and so on but I cannot ask her out. You walkies think *you* are scared of rejection.
- Walkies?
- My little derogatory term for you able-bodied types. You see when *you* get turned down you can stride away with dignity but that option is not available to us cripples you know. The fact is that there are two main reasons for attraction, beauty and wealth. Everything else, personality, sense of humour et cetera are merely subsections. As a disabled person by definition I am poor and ugly.
- Stop sounding so full of self pity I think you're lovely.
- I know I am feeling sorry for myself but I have to face facts. I used to be attractive you know. About fifteen years ago I was fed up of people calling me: 'Pretty-boy.' which is hard to believe now is it not? These days people just look away when they see me. I look ugly to myself and I simply would not believe anyone trying to telling me any different.
- You're lovely to me. Give me a hug.

101

- Thank you Mags. Having you around really helps and fortunately I have enough friends so I can cope with the stares and embarrassment of intolerable walkies but as far as love goes I do not think I should hold my breath. In fact I am thinking of availing myself of some professional women.
- You mean *prostitutes*! Are you mad?
- There is nothing wrong with prostitutes! They are an underrated and very important sector of society and should be given a lot more praise for their brave and vital work. Did you know that there is a local by-law that allows a prostitute to have a glass of water in a pub as long as she does not tout for business. She cannot mention the phrase: 'Big boy!' but you can say: 'How's tricks?'
- Very funny but you can't say that whores are an important sector of society.
- No I am serious Mags. I would guesstimate that every professional lady in this country stops about ten rapes a week if not more. You women simply do not realise the power of the male sex-drive and how ruinous frustration can be. There was one woman being interviewed the other day claiming that: 'Men say they think about sex a lot but women think about it too. Why just the other day I had a sexual fantasy!' Just the other day! For men it is just the other millisecond!
- But you wouldn't really go to one would you?
- There are three things stopping me, lack of money, the stigma and not knowing what could happen. This is another area where our so-called government are wholly blinkered and stupid. It is the exact opposite of: 'If it ain't bust don't fix it.' because it is *so* obvious that the current system of soliciting being illegal is farcical. If it were legalised the government could kill two birds with one stone, if you'll pardon the horrendous pun.
- How so? This is good stuff isn't it?
- Oh yes only the best. Well if it were legalised it would free up currently wasted police time plus imagine the amount of tax that prostitutes do not pay each year. What we should have is government controlled brothels in every town, there are plenty of empty buildings around, with security guards and panic buttons to protect the women themselves. Plus you could have counsellors and doctors and an open-minded, non-denominational priest would not go amiss. Proper sanitation to protect everyone from disease and the whole thing would make a tidy profit. Give it a generation and the stigma would go for both the ladies and their clients plus there would be other benefits.
- Like what?
- This is where I start sounding slightly contentious. You see there is a part of me that feels sorry for paedophiles. The trouble is that people cannot help what turns them on. I am lucky as I am aroused by naked women which is perfectly acceptable in our still prudish and moralistic society but God's joke on the world was to create seven sexualities and tell us there are only two, it is very confusing. So if in all your brothels around the country there were some young-looking, slim women who shaved and wore school uniforms or whatever how many children would be safer?
- Contentious isn't the word! It wouldn't work, it's too simplistic.
- Well the system does not work *at all* at the moment so something has to be done to protect everyone involved and stop gangsters making money. The point is to drop all of the puritanical attitudes based upon dubious religious dogma which no-one believes in anymore and *do* something! When a good idea is developed by intelligent and freethinking types all sorts of benefits can come about. It strikes me that currently a lot of women suffer because of the hypocrisy of men.
- Well that's true enough.

- Why is it that a woman in the public eye who keeps her clothes on is deemed intelligent and taken as seriously as people will allow but a woman who takes her clothes off is stupid? It is pure prejudice! And it is not just in magazines and newspapers. In an office environment a young women walks a minefield as you know. If you sleep with a colleague you're 'easy' or 'a slut', if you turn someone down you're 'frigid', and heaven forbid you actually wear what you would like to wear! Women get all the flak for men's complete inability to realise what equality is.

- I get really annoyed when that happens but it is everywhere. You even get judges saying that a woman deserved to get raped because of what she was wearing. It's *disgusting*!

- It is quite outrageous. Rape is the most horrendous of crimes and it has a ten per cent clear up rate which most of the time can be attributed to deep-rooted misogyny in the police, the prosecution service and the whole criminal system. 'She was asking for it!' the destructive hatechildren say! Of course the situation is not helped by women making it up.

- Oh come on! How often does that actually happen?

- It happened to me.

- You're joking! When? What happened? Did you?

- We did not even *have* sex! She did not even take her *clothes* off! It was all very odd. I meet this girl at a club, got chatting and so on and she invited me back to her place. She was a work colleague of Zak's who is a mate of mine. I went back with her, she took off her shoes and got into bed. I went to find the bathroom to clean my teeth and so on and when I returned she was snoring away happily. I squeezed into bed as there was nowhere else and fell asleep. In the morning I had a cup of coffee and she made it plain I was not wanted around so I left. That was the Sunday.

- What happened?

- On the Monday she went into work and told her friends that I had raped her. One of them knew my address, I was picked up and spent two very uncomfortable hours in an interview room. The police went to interview her and fortunately she recanted and they let me go. That was it.

- You must have been furious.

- Not really. Apparently she was having a bad time and was very depressed. People do strange things when they are depressed but every *that* scenario happens it probably means that ten legitimate cases do not even get to court and how many lives are ruined? It is an horrific crime that is not taken seriously enough and anything to reduce the amount of untapped male lust out there has got to be a good thing.

- I suppose you agree with porn as well then?

- You have touched upon my greatest shame, my major act of hypocrisy.

- You haven't?

- I am afraid so and I hang my head in shame and self-disgust.

- I really wouldn't have thought of you having, those things. Can I have a look?

- I would really appreciate it if you didn't actually. I would not be able to look you in the face again.

- Oh all right then.

- Thank you. I could try and justify myself by saying that they were always around at school, I had a good public school education me you know. If you had a copy of something squalid it was enormous dorm-cred. Believe me at school pornography was hard currency, if you'll excuse the expression. For most men being able to just walk into a shop and buy one was incredible and most do at some point but one is supposed to grow out of them. I could also say that I always seem to buy them when I am absolutely blasted, I used to wake up in the morning

103

with a hangover and a copy of something vulgar in my briefcase but that is no excuse as I do not throw them away and I know that I am contributing to an industry that exploits women. It is out and out double standards on my part. One of the few good things about my disability is that I cannot get that pissed anymore and I do not saunter past newsagents on my way home.
- What do you think of the women that do it?
- What do I think? There is very little to go on other than they are very beautiful. As I said there is no correlation between intelligence and clothing removal and they do tend to be just pictures really. One would like to think that models generally are quite intelligent with a smattering of degrees in their sorority. What would be fantastic would be if a glamour model turned out to have a beautiful soul voice and recorded a wonderful album.
- Unlikely.
- I doubt that they would be allowed to. If soap stars have a hard time turning to music what chance have models? But I could not look down on them. If they want to use their looks to make a living why should they not? Jesus said use your talents and in today's sexist parlance that is *exactly* what they do. Anyway I have been a far worse member of society than any glamour model. It was not so long ago I was a drug dealer.
- You weren't!
- Sure about five years ago. It was only grass to mates to pay for my own but I could still have 'gone down' I believe is the expression. I also worked a stripogram once.
- I don't believe you.
- 'Tis true! For about a month just before Christmas a few years ago. Actually it was quite funny. It was when I was vaguely healthy again after all of the operations but I was not in the best frame of mind. I was signing on and drinking far too much so I worked 'cash dans mitt' for this agency and did one or two a night during the week and three at weekends. I was the best Tarzan they ever had apparently. Stop laughing it is true!
- I just can't imagine you in a loincloth.
- Probably a good thing. I was about two stone heavier then. My first one was in a hotel function room and I was so nervous as I had to walk between all these people with my loincloth and two G-strings.
- Two?
- Oh yes, you could not be too careful! It definitely felt like vicarious revenge some nights. I had one loose one that I could lose if things became nasty and one that was *soldered* on! Anyway I must tell you about my debut. I walked in with plan A being to pick up whoever I was for but was then confronted with a sumo wrestler in a polka dot dress! Plan B, give her a hug so I asked her for her name: 'Dot.' she replied. I asked if the occasion was her birthday but it transpired it was her leaving do. I inquired for whom she worked and she said: 'The D.S.S. What's your name again?' 'Tarzan will do!' I quickly rejoined and got on with the act.
- Why?
- Well I was working cash in hand wasn't I! So I started my little routine which involved bananas and whipped cream, working towards the grand finale when I would whip her the appropriate number of times, one for each decade she had worked there or whatever. I did resist the temptation to inflict pain. Suddenly I realised that I had left my whip in the car as there is only so much you can pack into a loincloth you know and with this enormous woman bent over a chair I decided the only thing to do was to come clean with the audience. 'Sorry folks.' I said, 'I seem to have mislaid my whip!' Then a voice came from the back of the hall shouting: 'Here you go mate, borrow mine!' and this whip sailed over the heads of the crowd and landed at my feet. Trying very hard not to be completely nonplussed at the turn of events I

finished off the routine, posed for a couple of photographs that would never appear on a mantelpiece and got the hell out of there! Very bizarre.
- Oh my God! You never fail to surprise me Jude. How many did you do?
- I do not know since I was blind drunk for most of them. It became a vicious circle of drinking to handle it and having to do it to afford the drink which is why I could not condemn glamour models. All these things are a slippery slope where one finds oneself saying: 'I'll only do topless.' and with all the pressures it does not take long before one is doing all sorts of things. I did one job for a gay couple involving coat hangers would you believe! It is amazing what you end up agreeing to if the price is right.
- So what made you stop?
- Oh God that was a nightmare. I had got involved in a charity pub crawl, like you do although I have not a clue what it was for, which involved me shaving my hair off for some reason. When my boss saw me he was furious: 'You're no fucking good for Tarzan now are you?' he shouted. It was a good thing I was bigger than him, he was not happy. Another advantage that women do not have. Then a couple of days later he rang up being nice again because he had had an idea. I went round to see him and he had my new outfit.
- What was it?
- An enormous bonnet, a white towel and a safety pin you could fence with! 'Jude.' he announced proudly, 'You're going to be this agency's first babygram!' and gave me a big smile.
- A babygram?
- That is right though he still wanted me to do the routine with the bananas, whipped cream and the whip. He talked me into it and I went to a job that night in one of the night-clubs on the sea front. Because he never supplied a minder I always preferred night-clubs as the doormen are normally very pleasant and one feels safer. Some of the parties I performed at got a bit iffy. The trouble with this particular job was that I did not know the scenario. It was a hen do, no problem but the groom-to-be was an unpleasant mixture of jealousy and violence. Instead of having a stag do he was following the hen party round to check up or something I suppose. I turned up at the club and was pointed towards the bride-to-be. I came within a few feet of her and this wild-eyed bloke appeared from nowhere shouting : 'I'M GONNA KILL YOU, YOU BASTARD!!'
- God how scary!
- Fortunately I was suitably attired for dealing with surprises! Even more fortunate was a doorman got between us and stopped the bloke but he was fighting to get over the bouncer's shoulder calling me everything under several suns. There I was dressed in a Florence Nightingale hat and a nappy wondering: 'What *are* you doing?' They kicked the guy out and the lady was very apologetic and paid me anyway though I do hope she did not actually marry the vicious fool and that was the end of my stripogram career which is why I sympathise with models and so on. I know how it feels to be merely an object of lust.
- Did you get paid much?
- Not really. You could say I went for a thong!
- That was awful. Does nothing ordinary ever happen to you?
- It does not feel like it sometimes but I consider myself lucky to have had such an interesting life.
- That's one way of putting it. What's the time? Shit I'd better catch that train.
- There is a taxi rank just down the road. You will forgive me if I do not accompany you down the stairs but I do not think that movement is an immediate option. Do not worry about tonight

just be yourself, enjoy it and do not believe a word he says! Do not forget your bag. Call me when you want since I shall leave the answer machine off.
- Lovely to see you Jude.
- And you Honey. *Big* hug! Go catch your train.

Thursday 10th June: **ANGER**

This has to be as low as I can go. To wake up on the bathroom floor in a pool of vomit is as close to the end as I can cope with. What the hell happened yesterday? I think it is vomit, the redness could be rouge or blood. I filled up the bath and just clambered in. I shall have to find some energy from somewhere before clearing up this horrible mess.

My mind is torn between feeling utterly bloody about myself and remembering a great day with Mags. It seems to be another world sitting in the sun, laughing, joking and drinking. Was it L.P. Hartley who said: 'The past is another country, they do things differently there'? I cannot remember. *Pathetic.*

Suddenly I knew what I had forgotten yesterday - I did a deal with God the other night! I am going to be healed on Sunday! And there is Puffin's party on Saturday for a final fling! All I have to do is think of a costume and throw away some porn, I was supposed to do that yesterday. And try and keep this side of insanity. A deal with God? *Are you mad?* Oh well I do not suppose the porn matters as I have not looked at it in months anyway. Out of the bath, find some cleaning jollop and a bin-liner. Oh I seem to have found some energy from somewhere! I might even eat something today.

What are the chances of being healed? More than my surviving for much longer like this. This is my reality - welcome to Hopelessnesville, population millions. I can even pretend I am a Christian in the build up. It might be amusing if nothing else.

Further inspection revealed a nasty cut by my left eye. Moses was not in the bathroom so I must have forgotten that I cannot walk. What a spooning muffin! I have lost count of my drinking scars - they are everywhere. It is difficult adjusting to this new loss of balance as my head feels fine but I cannot walk. Odd and annoying.

Mags rang early on the poor thing. The accountant has shown himself to be just that. I think that she is all right but I might have to visit to make sure. Peter was more acerbic than ever and drove me to a haircut. The hairdresser was very pleasant but I think I overwhelmed him - we Christians do that you know! I saw Jamie and had a good chat, he always survives and is quite inspirational really. My old boss Nicky showed up to apologise! She is so unhappy the poor love but hopefully my counsel has helped. I did Mags a small favour this evening which I enjoyed no end and it certainly cheered her up. What a day! I am determined to wake in bed unscathed and dry tomorrow. I must talk to someone about my deal with God. What on *earth* is happening to me?

* * *

- Hello?
- Oh Jude.
- Mags! What's wrong? What is it Honey? Are you all right?
- I'm fine. I'm O.K.
- Where are you? Are you safe?
- Yes I'm at home. I've 'phoned in sick and they understand.
- Sweetie have you got a drink and so on?

- Yeah.
- Then relax, breathe a big sigh and start at the beginning. Big brother is here and I shall sort it out. What happened? Is it Magnus? Do I need to kneecap him?
- Oh no. Well, possibly.
- Take it from the top my heart. You were to meet in the pub.
- Well he was actually waiting outside the pub and said that we had better get going. He said that we were going to a place in Richmond and then managed to get lost!
- Oh no!
- I wanted to correct him as I know the way like the back of my drinking hand but I thought it best not to say anything. Eventually we got there and it was all very posh and the waiters ignored him. It took him twenty minutes to get a drink and I can't talk without a drink in my hand and I didn't want to smoke too much as my throat was so dry. We were sat there in an awkward silence waiting to be noticed. It was awful!
- Not a good start?
- Oh Jude. Why do these things happen to me?
- Because you are too good for this grot-hole of a world and the inadequate people within it but carry on.
- Well I did as you said and ordered a nice wine and something expensive, I didn't bother with a starter. He managed to find his voice and started chatting about his horse and then how he never got over being adopted!
- Adopted! *What*?
- He talked for hours about the hardships of being adopted.
- When are people going to realise that *everyone* has had a hard childhood of some description. Honestly the way they harp on about how others tried to help but did not quite succeed is more like Eric Idle than anything to be taken seriously. Harbouring festering hatreds is so pointless. Just get on with life that is what I say.
- Well I didn't want to hear all of that crap and that was the trouble. I was ignoring him and drinking too much.
- What happened Mags?
- I don't know Jude. I woke up at his place.
- What did he do? I am going to come up and *kill* the bastard!
- No Jude nothing happened. I was fully dressed when I woke up.
- Are you sure? I shall rip his bollocks off if he laid a finger on you!
- Honestly Jude *nothing happened* I just crashed out there. Calm down I'm all right. That's not what went wrong.
- What did go wrong Hun?
- Well I woke up and he was sitting at the end of the bed in his dressing gown eating cereal. I said hello but he was just staring at me as if I was an animal at the zoo or something. Then he got dressed and told me to let myself out before leaving himself.
- Is that all he said?
- That's it. Anyway I started to get myself together, you know find my shoes and such when the 'phone rang.
- You didn't?
- Of course I did it's an instinct. It was his girlfriend.
- Oh Mags. He has a girlfriend? He did not tell you? The lying toe-rag!
- No. He didn't.
- Do not cry Honey. It is not your fault that he is an arsehole.
- I just feel so *fucking*...

- I know, I know. Do you want me to come up?
- No. I'll be fine.
- I can drop everything even though I have a packed schedule of drinking to attend to?
- No really Jude. I think I just want to be alone.
- A Shelly moment Greta?
- That's right.
- Listen to me for a second. This situation *has* a silver lining. You now know that this guy is the muffin we thought he was, right?
- I suppose so.
- You have found out in record time, one week d'accord?
- Yes.
- And now you have a great excuse to go to the pub and get trashed with lots of sympathy. Is Mary working today?
- I think so.
- You go and find her and get trounced whilst slating men generally. Understood?
- I think I will.
- Get angry for a bit but then let yourself calm down. Go and have a boo if you want but do not let this prat ruin more than one day of your life.
- Thanks Jude. You're always there for me.
- And always will be. Now go get pissed!
- Yes Sir!
- I hope you are saluting. I shall call you later. *I* love you and *my* opinion is far more important than any slimy accountant's.
- Love you too. Speak to you later.
- 'Bye Honey and give my best to Mary.

* * *

- Ah bon jour Peter mein freund. Comme es da? You did not know I was fluent in Esperanto did you?
- I'm still not convinced.
- Unos pintos del Harveys tavarick.
- Oh give over Jude! I get enough of you being indecipherable most evenings.
- Sorry. I was just trying to be, upbeat. It is one of my many hidden talents you know.
- So well hidden they can now be considered lost.
- Consider me outrageously flattered. It is rather quiet for a Thursday afternoon.
- Jude we don't officially open for another ten minutes but it isn't worth the sulking to make you wait. But now that you are here I can insult you to warm me up for the other daily annoyances that insist upon being called 'regulars'. A little long in the sun yesterday? It's very sweet. What with your ginger hair and that glistening spot of yours you are one big walking clash. Where *are* my Wayfarers?
- You are more waspish than normal. Why so angry?
- Oh no reason. Hangover and generally intolerant as is my wont of a working day. Is that a cut by your eye?
- Yes I inadvertently took a leaf from your beer-sodden book yesterday. I think that I went to be sick but fell over and hit my head on the loo. The consequences I shall leave to your hard-bitten, veteran experience.

109

- Oh dear. I don't know if I would have liked to have witnessed that or not. What made you ill? Not a normal occurrence is it?
- Far from it. It must have been too much sun yesterday although that smacks of an alcoholic's excuse. The reason I was ill is quite simply from drinking far too much.
- Your honesty is underwhelming. Your life is something of a soap opera is it not?
- Do not talk to me about soap operas, they are the methadone of the masses.
- Do I feel a soapbox moment coming on?
- Well honestly it winds me up. One of the last features I did for the paper was about the changes being made in education. In my research I meet a lot of very hardworking and almost idealistic teachers and groups dedicated to improving educational standards. That lot work hard as teachers do all over the country. Then what happens? Children go home to switch on the brain-sucker and watch soaps where their heroes and role-models can hardly string a sentence together! What is the point of trying to enthuse youngsters about the joys of knowledge when the people that actually listen to only say: 'D'ya knaw wha' I mean?' or: 'Wha's goin' on?'
- You're just being a snob.
- Possibly but I happen to think that is a correlation between education and quality of life that soaps are trying to belie. The vast majority of soap characters, I would not know about the actors themselves, are ignorant, stupid, angry and aggressive. No wonder children are confused these days as the information they receive every day is completely conflicting. The essence of soaps is a combination of anger and revenge that is extremely dangerous and has enormous impact on our society. The television has more import in people's lives than any other medium and these are the things that most people watch, full of anger, bitterness and bigotry.
- Oh come on Jude. It's harmless pap.
- Oh no they are not. Children are parked in front of these things because they are deemed to be safe. Idiots keep whining on that children should be protected from swearing and sex, what *balderdash*! Every child knows every swearword that there is and they will need to know about sex in the very near future. Is there a correlation between children being shielded from practical sex and the high teenage pregnancy rate, the fact that every glossy magazine has to put: 'This Season's Sex Tips' on their covers and not to mention the soaring divorce rate? I think that there might be! What children really need protection from is bitchiness, cynicism, prejudice, violence, sexism, selfishness, bullying, ignorance, anger, aggression and every base human emotion. In other words a *mild* soap story line! These things are ruining our society. They are conditioning everyone, especially children that it is all right to be selfish and vicious.
- And that is ruining modern society?
- Of course it is. You hear the expressions everyday: 'Clear the air!', 'Sorted!' and 'You're out of order!', it is pure Soapese. The amount of angst in every episode is extraordinary and just propagates a system of ignorance, anger and unpleasant, selfish behaviour. *These* are things that you would never hear in a soap opera: 'I'm terribly sorry!', 'I seem to be completely in the wrong and apologise unreservedly!' and 'I think you'll find that this is a very happy pub!' There is no chance is there? Soap operas promote insular thinking and stop people enriching their *own* lives with their *own* thoughts and actions. They are living vicarious and unstimulated lives. Life on the edge; of the sofa! The trouble is that children believe what they are told unquestioningly. They might say: 'Why?' a lot but they always believe the answers. We are raising a generation that actually thinks that is how people behave in a civilised community.
- You can hardly call any soap an example of a civilised society.

110

- Exactly. Everyone that watches soaps will never realise the real truth. Anger, revenge and violence can never resolve problems, they only make them far worse. The only way to resolve human difficulties is through forgiveness and gentle communication. Many years ago when there were only two soaps...
- And Lego looked like Lego.
- ... only two soaps, a charming tale of country folk and a charming tale of northern folk was the time when Morecambe and Wise shared a bed in their stripy pyjamas and no-one thought it odd! The other day I was introduced to a four year old girl by her mother and she ran away. The explanation: 'It must be all the things I have told her about strange men!'
- It might just be good taste on the part of the little girl. I would run away from you if I could.
- I think that it illustrates the soap opera world we now have. Progress apparently.
- Some people don't understand diplomacy; you have to beat it into them!
- What has that got to do with anything?
- Nothing at all. It is just that you are simpering on too much again and I felt like saying it. It is a good quote don't you think?
- Viv Stanshall.
- Indeed. Very impressive.
- I am a great fan. In fact a toast to the late and great. Cheers.
- Yes cheers. I know what you are going on about Jude but the fact is people like soap operas. By presenting obnoxious, fictitious characters to the fools who watch T.V. rather than use their lives, it makes them feel better about themselves. I believe it is called aversion therapy.
- But that should stop people from watching television.
- Like most therapies it hasn't been thought through. Something you should know all about Rufus.
- Thank you. Talking of diplomacy did you hear the story of the British diplomat at Christmas?
- Go on, I prefer your dreadful stories to your preaching.
- It was coming up to Crimble a few years ago and a notice had just gone out to all diplomats and so on not to except overly lavish presents as there had been problems the previous year.
- Problems?
- The usual bribery and corruption. That day a British Ambassador received a call from a Reuters journo who asked what he would like for Christmas. The diplomat, with memo in mind replied that a small tin of crystallised fruits would be ideal.
- A man after my own modest heart.
- Indeed. The next day there a story in the press about what world leaders wanted for Christmas. The U.S. Secretary wanted: 'World Peace!', the Russian Envoy hoped for: 'An End to War!', the Chinese Attaché was striving for: 'An End to all Disease!' but the British Ambassador...
- Wanted a small tin of crystallised fruits. Very good Ginger.
- I do wish you would not mock me so.
- That wish will never be granted Duracell.
- *That is it*! I am going to get a haircut.
- See you soon Carrot-top. Get them to give you a shave while you're there, your beard is ginger too!

* * *

- Good afternoon sir. What can I do for you?

111

- A number two please. I have been accused of being ginger so extreme measures are called for.
- Personally I find that very insulting. Haven't you noticed the colour of my hair?
- Of course, it is a delightful shade of auburn.
- You think I'm gay don't you?
- No. I just want to get my hair cut and so have walked in here. So far you seem to be very pleasant and amusing and I only want a number two. I do not care what your sexual proclivities are just do not make me look stupid, please.
- I think you have had a head start!
- Very good! That was funny! My name is Jude how do you do?
- I'm Barney.
- Really?
- Yes I know! Does it bother you my standing here? You know, with direct eye contact because most people are used to seeing me in the mirror. If I stand here to talk to them they get all fidgety.
- That is because you look different.
- Do I?
- Everyone does. Very few people have symmetrical faces so away from the mirror you look different all of a sudden and it unsettles everyone. Most people do not even know what they actually look like because photographs are a mirror image and two-dimensional, videos and so on are grainy and: 'They add at least ten pounds you know!' so most people have no idea. That is why there are so insecure.
- I always thought, are you sure you want a number two? that it was insecurity that made people so angry.
- Very possibly but there is too much anger around these days for that to be the only explanation. There is air rage, road rage, trolley rage, the list is endless. It is only a matter of time before we have 'Petunia Rage'. What fascinates me is this air rage. A few years ago it only happened very occasionally but now they are hushing up the real figures.
- Really?
- Oh God yes! It is becoming a real problem but do you know why? Because people cannot smoke! The sort of people that do smoke are far more likely to be worried about flying to start with and then they are told that they cannot smoke in the airport except at the bar. So we have untold numbers of irritated smokers draining pints and chain-smoking. Then there is all of the rigmarole of getting to the damn plane, duty frees: 'Why the hell can we buy them but not smoke them?', passports, the right departure gate, boarding cards, the late people: 'Will I get a decent seat?' and so on. By the time you finally sit on the plane and they announce that it will be delayed for an hour you could *really* do with a smoke but you cannot *for ten hours*! They wonder why air rage has increased! It has foxed me Holmes.
- I hear that they are now offering nicotine patches.
- Why? Why do they just not let us smoke again? Everyone would be happier. Come on let us be reasonable what non-smoker has ever suffered in the way that smokers do every single day? Let them be told that they are pariahs all the time and see how they like it! It is not surprising that anger is such a feature of modern life. One thing that I do not understand is that you know that people in Mediterranean countries live longer than say, British people?
- Yeah. It's something to do with their diet isn't it?
- I would imagine that their diet is part of the equation but they all smoke like troopers! Almost everyone from those countries smokes like the proverbial roof decoration.
- But isn't it the olive oil or something that makes them live longer?

112

- According to the advertising. I am sure that there are a lot of elements to the reason but how can smoking be as dangerous as people make out if large numbers of chain-smokers can live longer than non-smokers merely because of their diet? I am dying for one actually. All this talking about smoking.

- You can smoke in here if you like.

- Oh thank you, that is extremely kind.

- Jodie! Can I have an ashtray here please.

- Thank you Jodie. Barney do you know why there is so much anger? It is not just the trivial things like lousy holidays it is at the very roots of the system. It is about justice. Great Britain is famed for its sense of decency and 'fair play' so what about Stephen Lawrence? A young man was attacked by a gang of racist thugs and killed. What happened? The police refused to believe that it was a racist crime and dropped it, no doubt in favour of traffic duty. His family were not convinced and started amassing very obvious evidence. The story then dragged on for quite a while because the media and the police were indifferent and it was only the Big Issue that kept with the story. Finally it became clear that a group of vicious young fascists who train with knifes were responsible but they had already been tried and found not-guilty. Now they are unable to find jobs and that is the *extent* of their punishment.

- It was quite horrible and still is.

- Indeed. It was only the other week that someone was fined for spitting on the memorial plaque. Why so angry? Coloured people, Negroes and Asians only comprise five per cent of our population.

- Five per cent! Is that all?

- Yes according to the Guardian but they are hated so much. Why? That is one end of the legal system, no justice for the murdered black man but the other day a man shot dead a burglar and is being tried. This poor chap was retired and lived in a remote cottage far from alleged civilisation. He knew the statistics as we all do, every day we hear of a vulnerable person being attacked, robbed, hurt or even killed. Where this chap lived it would take the police far too long to reach him in an emergency even if he actually got to a 'phone so he got a shotgun. It must have eased his insomnia somewhat. Then it happened and there were two of them. He fired. One burglar died. Good riddance I say! Now this poor chap is being prosecuted. The system is unworkable from the roots because innocents receive no justice, the system is designed to protect the guilty.

- This all sounds very bleak. What is one supposed to do?

- Well speaking as someone who has been very hard done by the system I am going to church on Sunday.

- Church?

- Yes. I am going to ask them to heal me.

- Good idea.

- Can you think of anything else to do?

- What happened? To your leg I mean?

- Do not ask. Would you like a big clue? Every disabled person's least favourite topic of conversation is their disability. I would rather talk about nuclear holocaust but I know what it is like to be a victim as the Lawrences have been, as every victim of greed, stupidity and anger have been. I ask: 'What the hell has happened? Why is it that an innocent person, any innocent person is always at risk in this allegedly civilised society?' So I am going to church on Sunday. Christianity is the last bastion of decency. Have you finished without wanting to sound rude?

- I finished cutting your hair twenty minutes ago Jude.

- Thank you. It looks short and not particularly ginger. Now I can scare small children again! How much do I owe you?
- Six pounds mate. Hang on..
- Oh pteuh! keep it! Thank you Barney and I hope see you again. I am always available in the Carpenter's Rest if you fancy a pint.
- I might take you up on that.

* * *

- Oh look at her!
- I think you will find that the ginger jokes are somewhat out of place all of a sudden.
- You're just a closet ginger now are you?
- You cad and bounder, I am undone. Do not just stand there gawking I require a pint forthwith and immediately please.
- Why are you looking so pleased with yourself?
- I have just used a barber for his ultimate purpose and it was highly cathartic.
- What do you mean?
- I spouted at him for about half an hour on my tallest soapbox. It was *marvellous*!
- Does that mean the rest of us are safe from your spleen for a while?
- You are safe from the whole of my digestive system, vestigial or otherwise.
- The spleen isn't vestigial.
- I never hinted that it might be.
- Oh oh! The brain is staggering into action. Alert the media!
- Hark at her, I knew 'er when she was a wrestler!
- Please don't be cheerful Jude, I couldn't stand it. *Please* do not be cheerful. After all this is a serious drinking establishment.
- Then you should have barred me years ago.
- It has been an ongoing oversight but I can dream.
- I am sure you can. Normally about Brad Pitt I would wager.
- *Don't*! I'll only dribble in my Stella. You know suddenly you remind me of someone that I just can't place. That's it, Yoda! With no hair, a walking stick and let's face it your ears are not small young Jude, you're only the wrong colour.
- Peter?
- Yes Jude?
- You. Are. A. GENIUS! I have been wracking my brain for a suitable person to go as to a fancy-dress party this weekend and you have solved the problem. Yoda! Of course it is *perfect*! Thank you mate.
- Oh God what have I done? I have made a monster.
- Not at all. I use to go to fancy-dress parties as Jimmy Bond in my D.J. with a water pistol and it was great fun but now I have a new persona. Cheers my friend, I owe you one. To the late and great Graham Chapman! Did I ever tell you about the time a had a major haircut?
- No? More major than that one?
- Relatively speaking yes. It was a few years ago when I was doing a lot of sailing and had not had a trim, excuse the pun, for a couple of years. Cascading it was, very Rapunzel. All blonde from the salt and sun and pleasantly ringletted. I decided to get rid of it one day, long hair can be *so* annoying and went to a barbers. When it was my turn I stood up, took off my glasses with a flourish, pulled out the ponytail holder thingie and shook my spilling locks down my back. The barber said: 'But miss Jones, you're beautiful!' It was a very special moment.

114

- I can imagine. Did you pull then?
- No. The other amusing time was the haircut before last done by my dear friend Linsey who now lives in France I think. He had been cutting my hair for a while and I decided I wanted something different as one does from time to time.
- I tend to leave my mange pretty much as it is.
- You have a lack of options certainly. So I said to Linsey: 'I would like something different. I want to make a statement!' and he said: 'A statement like: "I am nearly thirty, I am going bald, I am going grey but I don't give a damn!" That sort of thing?' 'No.' I replied, 'I was thinking more: "Nice for the summer" actually!'
- He had obviously became far too familiar.
- It gets better. 'What were you thinking of then?' he inquired, 'Oh, I do not know' I shrugged nonchalantly, 'Something a little George Clooney?' 'George Clooney sir? Certainly sir. We'll do the haircut down here then you can go upstairs for the plastic surgery!'
- It must have been very tempting for him. Honestly Jude you're about as George Clooney as I am Shirley Temple.
- The voice is uncannily reminiscent.
- Oh thank you. She is still *such* an inspiration.
- There is another hairdressers story that is rather good.
- Oh one more if you must.
- This one is good I promise. A chap had just sat down and a lady hairdresser was in attendance. Under the gown his hands started moving in an unusual fashion that would suggest he might be playing with himself.
- Not that an unusual fashion then.
- Certainly. Anyway this hairdresser immediately plumped for that assessment and brained him with a hairdryer yelling: 'You dirty bastard!' Once splayed and unconscious across the floor it became apparent that he had, in fact been cleaning his glasses!
- Oh dear, oh dear. A suable matter then?
- I would not know. Is it relevant?
- It would just round the story off in a professional manner.
- Professional? Me? Hah! But it is strange the way that people are quite willing to believe the worst of any situation. I suppose that is why smear and innuendo are enough to ruin a career, fanned and whipped up by the salacious and hypocritical parts of the media. Why do they do it? It only spreads hatred.
- But it sells newspapers.
- That is not a good enough reason for causing so much destruction. You know having spent large and dull tracts of my life unemployed, I am not unfamiliar with daytime T.V.
- You're not alone there.
- That early morning stuff strikes me as merely a forum for people to vent their anger and aggression against whomever they feel like. People getting into rages about the most trivial of matters and once again it is deemed all right for children to watch. What *is* going on?
- It would seem that there are a lot of very unhappy people out there.
- No joking! As for the American ones where they all scream and swear and come to blows, is that really entertainment? It just seems to stir up hatred and resentment for no apparent purpose other than to incite normal people to shout at their televisions. I have no concept of how anyone can enjoys those things as there is nothing to relate to.
- Oh I don't know. I imagine it would be rather fun to rail some fool who thinks aspirin should be banned which is their general level.
- I know but then there is the *nice* daytime T.V. like Runch and Jude.

- Dicky and Dumpling?
- Ouch. You bitch!
- I know.
- But they are lovely and she has lost a little weight you know! That is another very salient point. These people present a magazine program designed to help and inform and they do it very well. It is as close to community television as you can get. It is certainly better than those consumer programs that simply want to criticise everyone and everything so why is it that the press and population want to knock them down? Why is it that every time a pleasant and able person becomes famous it is knifes out as far as the tabloid writers and readers are concerned?
- It sells newspapers.
- Foul is it not? One can almost see why the Nazis indulged in book-burning. I would join in with some tabloid-burning especially if we also barbecued some Jilly Bowman books at the same time.
- Not a fan?
- Of course not although rumour has it that it is actually his wife that writes the damn things.
- Really?
- So the story goes. But with a few exceptions I could not enjoy myself because someone else is being slated for no reason.
- What about Sandy Meddlesome?
- He deserves it. The man is almost certainly on the wrong side of the thin, completely legal line and he should be treated as any other criminal suspect. His uncovering was done through proper, investigative journalism not hate-inspired bitchiness. It is a different scenario.
- I suppose so.
- But the gutter press are also responsible for much more on a social level. It is not just celebrities that they attack. What is the main reason for the failure of Care in the Community other than lack of funds et cetera, et cetera?
- Go on shock me!
- Because the press have whipped up suspicion toward the mentally ill by finding isolated stories about violent schizophrenics. Occurrences like that are so unusual that they are statistically insignificant but the tabloids have created a society where no-one trusts anyone who appears not to be normal. Hence the majority of these mentally unwell people have very little in the way of human contact and being constantly spurned is hardly beneficial for an unwell mind. There is far too much ignorance about mental illness because it is just that you know, *illness*. It is as easy to catch a mind-affecting disease as it is the 'flu, if not easier. It can and does happen to anyone. People should be finding out about it rather than just being fearful, angry and aggressive. Why are you looking at me like that?
- I am wondering if I could light a swan match against your head!
- Pay attention boy! I was just moving on to a subject that must be dear to your heart.
- Very little is dear to my heart young Jude. Too many cynical years to return from the Dark Side.
- Rather melodramatic even for you but I was coming on to education. As an educated man I would trust that it is an important topic for you?
- Oh sure. When I gaze back through the mists of time to a place where a cap and sloppy socks were de rigeur and my mother was not ashamed of me. Oh happy days!
- One of the recurrent things that many people say is that the greatest problem in today's society is ignorance. Therefore the solution *must* be education. I am convinced that anger and violence stem from not being able to express oneself verbally or because one does not understand what is going on. The answer to both is to be educated and informed. Currently

116

there is not enough quality education getting to large groups within our culture. There is also, still the unfortunate attitude that leads to people being branded 'swots' or 'boffins' or whatever insults are en vogue at present.

- I think you are being a little simplistic Jude.

- Not at all. When there is trouble in here what is the best way to calm it down? Sensible communication from someone who can express themselves well. It is an antidote. Personally I enjoy being educated. I love to mess around with words, be involved in discussions about philosophy, politics, history, science and so on. Is it wrong of me to enjoy knowledge? Am I a bad person for having had an education? Is it elitist of me to prefer an educational T.V. program to a soap opera? Am I mad?

- No, no, no, just snotty and almost certainly.

- How very reassuring but it is a pleasure to watch quiz shows and know a good percentage of the answers. I would like more people to have that pleasure. For example this is a question from a quiz the other day that you do not know the answer to but you will be able to make an educated guess.

- Go on?

- Which American state was named in honour of Elizabeth I?

- Hmm. Virginia?

- Absolutely! I can remember being enthused about knowledge by a succession of teachers and my parents and I am *extremely* grateful. It is a joy! One understands more jokes, more of what is going on in the world and more of the pleasures in life. By understanding cultures different to one's own, one can relate to and enjoy many more of the world's people. I have meet people from all over the gaff and am immediately able to converse on all manner of interesting topics. It is great to anticipate new friends rather than be fearful and angry about 'strangers'.

- The: 'You're not from round here?' syndrome?

- Very much so. Would the world be a far happier place with more education, hence understanding, and knowledge, hence positive communication?

- What's so funny 'bout peace love and understanding?

- Great song! But yes exactly. Ignorance leads from frustration to anger and to violence. It is so much more fun to be a pacifist. I do not even kill insects you know. In fact I do not believe in killing anything for no good reason.

- But you are not a vegetarian?

- No I am an omnivore. It is a natural phenomenon that species prey upon one another so I do not feel that I am doing anything wrong. Nature is a vicious place and even some plants are aggressive. The point is *for no reason*. Killing spiders because they happen to be in the bath? Killing wasps because they *might* sting you? It is horrible! Let them live!

- So if I gave you a big knife and put you in a field of sheep or something you would kill one?

- In Theoryland yes although someone would have to hold one down, otherwise I would be hobbling after them for days. Also could it be another animal? I do not want to be done for sheep-worrying again.

- Sheep-worrying? Again?

- Yes it was a terrible night. But when in Wales...

- I'll have to try that one on Jeremy.

- It is a strange name for a Welshman is Jeremy or is that xenophobic or something?

- No more than your previous sentence.

- I was given a caution, nothing more! If people do not want to eat meat that is absolutely their prerogative but it is a bit like religion. Vegetarianism has been institutionalised with all of the dogma and intolerance that goes along with religion. More anger and ignorance unfortunately.
- Dogma rather than dog-meat one would have thought.
- Oh dear!
- Venison too?
- Go and serve someone.
- Release! Freedom from the dreaded Carpenter's Sage!

* * *

- Hello Jude.
- Good lord! 'Tis Nicky. How are you? You do look a little fatigued. Sit down and have a drink for goodness sake. What would you like?
- A large G and T please.
- Certainly. Peter? Can we have a large G and T please?
- It would have to be very large for both of you.
- Please excuse our host Nicky he is a little odd.
- Coming from you that is quite an insult Jude.
- Good! You deserve it! Anyway Nicky how are you and what are you doing in here?
- Better for this and I came to find you.
- What is happening Nicky? You look like and have the vibe of an extremely unhappy person.
- It has just been awful since you went. Everyone else has gone, I have half a department left. The mad season is almost upon us and I don't know where the banners are. It is all getting too much.
- Do not upset yourself. You are in the boozer so nothing bad can happen to you here. That is why men love pubs so much, there is no danger. Enjoy your drink! The shyte will stay where it is until you return. Let me tell you a joke, I know you like my jokes.
- I've missed them actually.
- Thank you. Talking about drinking I saw my doctor the other day. He did the examination and so on then said: 'The best thing you can do is give up smoking and drinking.' 'O.K.' I replied, 'What is the second best thing I can do?'
- That's very silly.
- I know but it gets the giggling going does it not? I have always wondered, whilst we are on the topic if you had a female doctor who was something of a feminist would you call her Ds.?
- I don't know.
- These are the things that whirl around my head at four in the morning when I should be sleeping.
- I've got terrible insomnia at the moment.
- Only think pleasant thoughts! You are in the boozer and there are *rules* you know. Anyway playing misery one-upmanship is utterly pointless and I always win.
- What's wrong with your leg?
- It is painful and boring and I demand another topic of conversation immediately! I was telling you jokes if you recall. Funnily enough you have just reminded me of the one joke that is actually mine own, all the rest are nicked you know. Was it Shaw that wrote: 'Sir. Thank you for your manuscript, it was both original and amusing. Unfortunately the parts that were amusing were not original and the parts that were original were certainly not amusing!'?
- I'm not sure. It might be.

118

- Anyhow my one joke. It was when I was studying a couple of A Levels at the college but I had not been to lectures for a month or so, far too much drinking to do I would imagine. I walked into a psychology lecture after my absence and Judith said: 'Ah, Jude. I thought you had left the fold?' 'No.' I retorted, 'Just the crease!'
- That's very good.
- Thank you. We have not had a toast as yet, how very remiss. To the late and great Sir Mike.
- Who?
- Sir Michael Hordern. Cheers.
- Cheers. He was one of my favourites.
- Right then Nicky, now that you are a little cheered why were you looking for me?
- Oh. I wanted to apologise.
- Apologise? For forcing me out of my job with atrocious internal political manoeuvring that made my life miserable for two months and then dropping your support of the paper so that I never managed to get it off the ground?
- Ah, well, yes.
- Do not worry, it is not a problem. I forgive you unreservedly and these things happen.
- You don't mind?
- Of course I *minded*! I was furious at the time but there you go. Life's just bloody! But I bear no ill will toward you and I thank you for your apology. I apologise for not being aware enough of the political shenanigans that were going on. I should have realised exactly what was happening and been more aware of the strain and pressure that you were under. Essentially you just took it out on me. People do that sort of thing. Do not worry Nicky. Expunge any feeling of guilt about what happened but may I give you some advice?
- Of course.
- Leave.
- Leave?
- Not here and now! Leave the job! Give it up, vamoose, scram, be gone, be hence, jack it in and do it no longer. Leave the job Nicky before you *really* become depressed.
- I can't leave just like that.
- Au contraire my erstwhile boss. Not only can you but you should forthwith and immediately. You do not need the money, it is making you miserable and there is plenty you would rather be doing. Hand in your notice and go sick for the month. If you need to you, you can go to your doctor and tell him that the job is making you ill. That way the corporation will still have to pay you. Makes sense. Those hatechildren are ruining your life so you owe them no loyalty. Take your life back from the people that are making it a living hell and start being happy again. Take up a hobby. Write a book, it cannot be that hard!
- I don't know.
- Do not faff about woman! Swap anger and misery for leisure and contentment. Take it from the man that knows, I should have retired years ago. Would you like another large one, if you'll pardon the expression?
- No. I must get back.
- If you left the job you would never have to say that again. You have my number? Call if you would like a chat or find me here most days.
- Thank you Jude. 'Bye.
- Laters.

- Who was that? Not your normal sort of companion.

119

- That was my old boss Peter. Poor thing she is so miserable mind you that is because she is absolutely useless at the job. Why do people have such a hard time admitting to things that they are bad at? It just leads to frustration, anger and other unpleasantness.
- So what are you bad at?
- I am *hopeless* at Tupperware parties.
- That's another good excuse not to invite you somewhere.
- Charmed.

* * *

- OW! I *do* wish you would not do that.
- 'Ello darlin'. How's it going? You're ready for another one? Yes please Peter? Two more of them.
- Thank you Jamie dear chap. Always a pleasure though I do wish you would not tickle me. I jump right out of my skin.
- And lose all of your hair too by the look of things. That is some spot you've been cultivating. Can I squeeze it?
- No you *cannot* get off! Thank you. Yes it is for the local agricultural show this year. My Father grows tomatoes and I grow pussy spots.
- You're in with a good chance of winning then! How's it going anyway?
- Steadily down the drain.
- Situation normal then. Fuck me what a morning, bloody amateurs. Heard a great joke though.
- Up to your normal impeccable standard?
- It's a blinder! The Liverpool head coach is travelling across Europe seeking out new talent.
- And new civilisations?
- That's the idea. He's in Bosnia where they're playing round the mine fields and he sees this young lad that has the gift! He's a *natural*, running rings round everyone else. Ah cheers. Who to today then?
- The late and great Dermot may I suggest?
- Good one. 'What would you say to a nice cup of tea Father Jack?'
- 'Feck off cup!'
- Classic! Cheers.
- Cheers.
- Yeah so he spots this young lad who is brilliant and brings him over to Liverpool, starts him off in the second team in a friendly, score line: Liverpool 15, losers nil and your lad has scored all the goals. So they put him in the first team that Saturday. He scores a hatrick against Arsenal or whatever, the kid is a *genius*. Anyway he plays the season and Liverpool win every game with this kiddie scoring like anything and then there's the F.A. Cup against Manchester United.
- I can see why you like this joke.
- It's probably the only way it'll ever happen. So Wembley Stadium with the world watching and he scores four goals to bring the Cup back to Anfield where it belongs. He gets home at the end of the remarkable day and rings his mum. 'Hello mum.' he says, 'I've had a great day. I've won the Cup for Liverpool. How are you?' 'Well done son. I'm proud of you but we're not very well. Your father was mugged and beaten up this morning and is in the hospital. Your sister went to visit and got raped and she's in the hospital too. Your brother went to see them both and got stabbed and I was shot at visiting all of them!' 'Mum!' he says, 'That's terrible.

In many ways I blame myself.' 'So you should!' she shouts, '*We* never wanted to live in Liverpool!'
- Wow! Only a Scouser could get away with that one.
- Of course. 'Calm down, calm down!'.
- So what happened this morning?
- Oh it's a new magazine being produced by some fucking do-gooders up the road. You know the type that help young offenders to re-offend or whatever.
- You know that they do very good work with those that have not had the same luck in life as we have had.
- Yeah yeah. Your trouble Jude is that you have always been a soft touch. That's why you are always getting shafted. How much are you owed now?
- It is about twenty thousand I think, including the five hundred that you owe.
- Yeah but I'm going to pay you back.
- That is what they all say dear heart.
- Yeah but I will.
- Only when you can mate. I do not need it at the moment and you have small mouths to feed. Anyway you were telling me about the do-gooders.
- Oh yeah. There's this stupid bloody woman in charge who doesn't know the first thing about printing. I saw her a month ago to work out the time frame and all the rest of it and do you know what she said to me?
- No?
- I was introduced to her as a print broker and she said: 'So you help to destroy rain forests?' so I said: 'Not unless they have found a way to make paper from fucking hardwood!'. I mean the fucking stupid things people say! Anyway I told her to put the thing on a zip disc in Quark Express, like you do. I go to pick it up this morning and looks O.K. I get it to the printers and we try and open in up. No joy. 'What the fuck is wrong with the thing!' is phrase of the moment. Then it struck me that she has done it in P.C. rather than Mac hasn't she.
- Oh no!
- Where's the only printer that can handle P.C. stuff?
- Worthing?
- Yeah fucking Worthing but I had to get it done. We can't let the kiddies down can we? Even if they are all qualified stereo thieves.
- Your heart is bigger than you make out my friend. You are a soft touch yourself.
- You tell anyone that and I'll break your other fucking leg.
- Talking of magazines I have had that idea we always talk about.
- The one that will make us rich?
- That is the one. It will take some time and research but I think it will be worth it. We produce a magazine called something like: 'Crawling Vaguely Home' and it will be full of the stuff that we talk about in pubs. Things like witty stories and jokes, advice for hangover cures, information on different beers and so on. Essentially it will be packed with the sort of content that pub-goers enjoy and share.
- What about some birds?
- I take it you are referring to the non-feathered type? We could have artistic photographs of women taken by women. That would be interesting would it not?
- Sounds like a load of bollocks to me.
- Don't call us we'll call you? Just an idea. How is your leg at the moment Jamie?
- Painful and boring. You know the score.
- Indeed. Life six, cripples nil.

- Don't call me a cripple you cripple. Go on sup up. It's your round.
- My turn for a joke.
- Go on then. I'm calming down nicely. Another pint of anaesthetic and I might even laugh for you.
- Oh joy, oh rapture. There is an express train that goes from Dublin to Belfast, the name of which escapes me at this moment.
- I know the one.
- Anyway one day there was a group of lads going from carriage to carriage shouting: 'Is there a priest on the train? We need a priest!' but not being able to find one. They get to the final carriage and are getting a little desperate. 'For goodness sake we need a priest. Is there a Father on the train?' At the end of the last carriage a thin little man stands up and rather nervously and said: 'I am a Methodist Minister. Can I help in some way?' 'Have you got a corkscrew Father? We've been trying to open this bottle of wine for ages!'
- Do Catholic priest always have corkscrews then?
- Irish ones do. It is traditional.
- What's the score in Northern Ireland at the moment?
- Pretty dodgy I am afraid to say. Bloody politicians messing around with rhetoric and the two sides winding each other up with marches and beatings and so on. If it does not work this time God knows what will happen.
- Why can't they just grow up and sort themselves out? Nobody actually likes losing members of their family.
- It has been going on too long. It is a bit like what the Nazis did.
- The Nazis? What the fuck are you talking about?
- One of the first things that those hatechildren did was to start teaching the children that Jews were responsible for all of Germany's problems so that by the late Thirties there were a large number of young and passionately patriotic people that actually believed all of that. This is why the concentration and extermination camps *could* happen. They actually *believed* that the Jews were evil.
- And?
- The same is true in Northern Ireland. For generations parents have been telling their children: 'Don't trust the Proddies!' and 'Don't trust the Catholics!' so consequently most people actually believe there is something wrong with the other side. Children believe what they are told unquestioningly. One has to make a major mental effort to break down the prejudices learnt at the knee. It is called indoctrination and it has been used for many nefarious purposes over the years.
- Conspiracy theory time.
- Not at all. It is entirely logical. Do not forget that they constantly reinforce their bigotries on both sides, what with all the marches and celebrating ancient battles and past disgraces on the part of the Brits. It just goes on and on because no-one has the nerve to break the cycle of hate and revenge or rather none of the politicians have. The ordinary people have known that it is all stupidity for some time but these damned politicians and leaders just keep on stirring up the hatred and look what happens.
- Not very optimistic.
- How can one be. There seems to be little room for forgiveness in all of the angst because that is the only way to end anger and violence, forgiveness. It is not just in that scenario either one can see it everywhere. In a way the same is true of England and Germany but the difference is that our situation has had what I believe they call closure. There was a definitive end to the

122

situation and forgiveness was allowed in. Now we are allies although some ignorant people still try and stir up trouble.

- 'Two world wars and one world cup, do da, do da!'
- Tunefully put but did that make sense?
- As much as you ever do Jude.
- There was some injustice done in Northern Ireland in the late Sixties and Seventies and the anger spilled over but nothing was done. Now all that exists is anger and until forgiveness and understanding show their rather lovely heads that is all there will ever be.
- You always know how to cheer me up! Another?
- Oh yes. I was talking to Peter earlier about soap operas and how destructive they are but I saw a thing the other night, what is he called?
- Who? I thought you didn't watch T.V. except for the news and the Simpsons?
- I thought that I would watch this because I like the books. You know the policeman with the Jag? Moose! That is it, Inspector Moose but there was a lovely quote. Old Moosey boy had annoyed a woman by being sexist and patronising and she reacted somewhat. He said: 'To have upset you was as unforgivable as it was unintentional. I apologise unreservedly.' Is that not lovely?
- I don't remember hearing that or anything like it in a soap.
- My point entirely. But that is the best way to deal with anger, apologise and forgive.
- Yeah but what if it was not your fault?
- Does it matter? What are words other than communication? An apology costs nothing.
- Except pride.
- Which is a sin and also very stupid actually. 'Is it true that all politicians are abnormally stupid Mr. Member?' 'Sorry I didn't understand the question!'
- They should repeat those.
- Oh yes. Do you remember that secretary, Bella?
- How on earth could I forget the stupid bitch!
- It was not really her fault. I should have been more aware of her insecurities.
- Hard to tell when you've just met someone.
- True but I should have been more thoughtful. What happened to Bella is exactly what I am on about. She started to hate me for her own personal reasons and it started the cycle. She used to hide important files and not pass on messages and so on. I ignored it, and her really so it just got worse and worse until she started trying to get me sacked.
- Very nearly succeeding.
- I know, that is still a bad memory those bloody people! The sad thing was Bella was the one suffering the most. Her hatred consumed her and made her miserable. She put on weight and her skin exploded with all the self-created stress. Even though I did apologise to her it was too late by that point and she ended up leaving of her own volition. It was very sad but I hope she is happy now.
- What's she doing?
- I am not sure. I think she is working abroad.
- You managed to drive her out of the country?
- It would appear so. Oh well.
- So what are you going to do with yourself now then?
- I am moving back to Redmond Grange soon, probably next week.
- With your folks? You get on don't you?
- Sure, well you have met them.
- Oh yeah. They seemed real nice.

- They are and we get on as famously as the Stooges.
- But what are you going to do with your time? You could be Social Secretary for the Waifs and Strays Guild?
- No I shall leave that in your capable hands. I thought I could write a compendium of party games.
- Like the bar room olympics?
- Not quite so strenuous and a little more pretentious. For example: 'Defining laughs', the game where you have to quote a funny, or otherwise to be honest, line from a film and we have to guess it. For example: 'I am a Red Sea pedestrian?'
- Life of Brian, easy. 'One move and the nigger gets it?'
- Blazing saddles. 'Looks like it was a bad week to give up glue-sniffing?'
- Airplane. Jude considering we have the same taste in films we could be going on like this forever.
- Needs work does it not? I am something of a learner. Oh that reminds me of a great story.
- Make it quick I've got to go soon.
- Oh sure. Scenario, female learner driver at a busy T junction with tailback growing.
- Oh oh!
- Now do not be sexist! The reference to gender was merely information to help with the mental picture. Anyroad, if you'll pardon the pun, there she was, all nerves and the drivers behind have started to become a little impatient with horns beginning to sound. About four cars back was a police car and when the shouts and jeers started to turn abusive they switched on their tannoy thingie: 'Would everyone calm down! We were all learners once and you are not helping the situation. Please show a little patience. Thank you.' The other drivers calmed down. A few moments later a gap appeared in the traffic and the hapless learner took off the hand brake and, stalled. Unfortunately the coppers had not switched off the tannoy and it boomed across the area: 'What's the stupid cow doing now?'
- Nice one. What was that bit of graffiti: 'If pigs could fly Scotland Yard would be London's fourth airport!'
- Now, now. Those gentlemen in blue are the upholders of our peace and safety.
- Yeah. Silly thing to say to a Mickey Mouser. Right! I have children to beat and it is my turn this evening! I'll catch you later.
- Cheers Jamie. Give my love to all.

* * *

- Still here Jude? I thought that I had had the pleasure of the last of your company for this afternoon.
- That is what I would call a velvet glove.
- Whatever do you mean?
- How you managed to say something very rude in a very polite fashion.
- Jude are you pissed?
- I should hope so with the amount of alcohol that I have consumed this very day. Either that or I shall demand a refund!
- Keep your voice down you fool.
- No Peter seriously, I have learned a veritable truth today.
- Oh God! Are on insisting upon mounting that overused soapbox of yours?
- You may mock, you may pooh-pooh and filibuster but I, Jude of the Clan of Redmond have today discovered the secret of Green my Lord. What the hell I am talking about?

124

- It is a frequent visitor to my brain that particular question.
- For some reason every conversation that I have indulged in today has been about anger and there is anger everywhere. Take a specimen human being and call him Duncan. Duncan awakes far earlier than he would actually like to but he has a job to go to and those bills do not pay themselves. Would that be 'duvet rage'? Because of the fact that he has to rise earlier than he would like to he leaves it to the last minute to get up but then something always goes wrong and our Duncan is always behind schedule. Is that 'razor rage'? He then jumps into the car and speeds to work which is our archetypal 'road rage'. Then he has a horrible day at the office, 'photocopier rage'? Then it is back home with a hint more 'road rage': 'OH, COME ON!' then he sits down to relax. The news is 'stupid-bloody-politicians rage'? Quiz shows are 'Joe Public rage'? Soap operas, 'other-fictional-person rage'? When is anyone supposed to relax?
- In the pub?
- Well indeed but what is the regular pub-going population? Minimal! People seem to spend the majority of their lives in situations that wind them up. Then they go on holiday to relax. Delays at the airport and problems at the hotel: 'The brochure never mentioned THIS!', return at boiling point and then people wonder at the rising violent crime figures. These rising figures are not the crimes we fear, muggings and aggravated burglaries, it is ordinary people being wound up in pubs and bars and so on just *snapping*. They have simply had enough and anger spills. It all becomes very ugly very quickly.
- So what is the answer oh sage?
- It strikes me that the opposite of anger is forgiveness.
- Forgiveness?
- Sure. If you forgive someone something you cannot be angry anymore. The best way to forgive someone is to relate to them. The best way to relate to someone is to understand them. The best way to understand someone is to know something about them. The best way to know something about *everyone* is to be educated and knowledgeable about every culture on the planet. The opposite of anger is knowledge.
- You have just disproved yourself in one paragraph.
- That is what happens when you ask old and cynical drunks deep questions.
- Are you going to go home now Jude?
- Would you be kind enough to ring the chauffeur please Peter?
- Do you have the twenty pound deposit?

* * *

- Hello.
- JUDE!
- Good evening Mags my *favourite* person. How are you feeling?
- Drunk.
- Good. Anything else?
- Sort of angry and a bit deflated.
- Did you have a good day with Mary?
- Yes, she's lovely and she likes *you*.
- I shall have to visit very soon but go on, let us have a summary of the day?
- Not much really. We just decided that all men are bastards, except you, and none are worth the aggravation. SO BOLLOCKS TO ALL OF THEM! except you.
- How very prosaic, I am honoured and privileged but do not give up on everyone just because of one spooning muffin.

125

- Where did you get that expression from?
- Spooning muffin? It is an phrase coined by a friend of mine, John.
- Bald bloke with uneven sideburns?
- God's Lupins no! I said a *friend*. I think you have met John E. Vangelis.
- I've got all of his records!
- Very good! You are obviously feeling better and you will feel a lot happier in the morning. Would you like a silly joke to end the day laughing?
- Yes please.
- Picture if you will a wild west saloon.
- Sounds exciting.
- The Sheriff walks in and announces: 'Has anyone here seen Brown Paper Bob?' 'Why no Sheriff.' they reply en masse, 'Why Sheriff we don't even know what he looks like?' 'You can't miss Brown Paper Bob.' says the Sheriff sternly, 'He's got a brown paper hat. He's got a brown paper shirt. He's got a brown paper waistcoat, brown paper pants, brown paper chaps and brown paper boots.' 'We'll look out for him Sheriff.' they chorus with community spirit. 'What's he wanted for Sheriff?' 'Rustling!'
- That's very silly. Thank you. Look Jude would you do me a favour?
- Of course Sweetie, just say what.
- Well I want to get some revenge on the toad Magnus.
- Revenge is not a good thing you know. I know you are angry but let it go. Revenge never achieves anything and just makes everything worse. Just see him for what he is, a spooning muffin and remember that you did nothing wrong. He *lied* to you.
- He didn't lie he just didn't mention the fact that he had a girlfriend.
- He was dishonest and was found out. Has he been in touch at all?
- No and that's why I want revenge. He hasn't even had the decency to apologise. All I have had is indifference.
- What would you like me to do?
- If I give you his 'phone number would you call him and insult him?
- You want me to ring the toad Magnus and insult him?
- That's it.
- And is that it? You are not going to want him kneecapped or anything?
- No a small Jude insult will do very nicely. Then ring me back and tell me what happened?
- I shall take his telephone number, ring him, insult him and then call you to tell you what happened.

* * *

- Hello?
- Oh good evening. Is that Magnus Farquar?
- Yes, it is he.
- Oh good. You are a proud, envious, gluttonous, lust-driven, anger-inspiring, covetous, sloth-ridden piece of evolutionary detritus.
- *Really?*
- Good evening.

* * *

- Hello Mags?

126

- JUDE!
- Who have you been talking to all this time?
- HIM!
- Him?
- He rang up as soon as you put the 'phone down on him. You were supposed to leave a message on his *voice-mail*!
- Oops. What did he say?
- He wanted to know who I had ringing him to 'fucking insult him?'
- He was rude to you?
- He called you an arsehole.
- Are you all right? Did he scare you?
- No I scared him. I told him you are one of my cousins who runs a debt collection agency and wanted to have him kneecapped but I persuaded you not to as long as he leaves me alone!
- Brilliant! That is real thinking on the feet stuff. No wonder you are a media professional.
- I feel really funny. What did you say to him?
- I asked if it were him and he replied to the affirmative, what a horrible voice!
- It is rather annoying I must admit.
- Grating I would call it. He sounds like one of those incredibly pompous critics like the ones who said the Fast Show was no good.
- Bloody idiots. Get on with the story!
- Sorry. Anyway I said: 'Good. You are a proud, envious, gluttonous, lust-driven, anger-inspiring, covetous, sloth-ridden piece of evolutionary detritus!' and then I wished him a good evening and put the 'phone down.
- What did he say?
- He squeaked: 'Really?' at the end. I doubt that this has happened to him before but he called you straight away?
- It must have been the first thing he did.
- Well that shows us something. Obviously he does not have one friend who would do a silly gag like that to him. If I received a call like that the list of suspects would be huge.
- Me too. Anyway thank you for doing that. When he 'phoned he was rather unpleasant in a way that made me feel sorry for him. He *is* a spooning muffin.
- Would that have been a better insult?
- No. I love what you said to him. That's the deadly sins isn't it?
- Indeed, I thought I would put the fear of God into him. It was Moses' idea.
- You're mad!
- So they say but all are yet to prove it. The main thing is that are you feeling better?
- I feel O.K. just worn out really.
- Good. You shall get an excellent night's kip then?
- I hope so. You don't think I've done something wrong do you?
- Au contraire Cherie. You have acted with the innate dignity and grace that makes everyone jealous of you. You have done nothing to feel remotely bad about in fact you have done the fool a favour if he has the sense to realise.
- What do you mean?
- You have taught him some valuable lessons in life. Firstly no-one deserves to be treated the way he did you and I know *exactly* what he was doing. Obviously things are not going well with the current girlfriend so he thought he would 'line the next one up'.
- Really?

- Men do it all the time Honey but this time he has not got away with it. He has lost a ravishing girl, that's you and has been insulted like he has never been insulted before. I would wager that he is now very angry. The lesson he has to learn is that his anger is the direct result of his own actions and the only person he can genuinely feel anger towards is himself. Will he realise this?
- I shouldn't have thought so, he's a right arrogant bastard.
- So you said. The thing is people have to realise that anger and revenge lead to nothing but trouble and hardship as any soap opera can show you. To enjoy life is to forgive otherwise your anger will destroy your happiness. I hope that you do not feel angry toward him anymore?
- I just think he's a sad twat.
- Admirably put. Would you like my little story of gentle revenge from a few years ago?
- After this I'm going to bed.
- Certainly. It has been a day has it not?
- Oh yes but let's end it with a laugh. You tell me your story.
- When I first started sailing it was in an Etchell 22 with Seamus O' Hooligan and Huff down in Cowes. These boats are three man jobbies and any more or less would get you disqualified in a race. We went down for a weekend regatta and Seamus had invited a friend along so we would be one man too many but we never won anyway so it did not matter. When we got down to the quay another boat was a man short and Seamus offered my services to them.
- You sound like his slave.
- Not really. I was not overly happy but it was experience so I went out for the three races that day with these two very posh blokes, Simon and Andy. They were a bit dull but what did I care, I was out sailing and in a more competitive boat than I was used to. The races went well and we came eighth, fourth and third out of fourteen in a very tough fleet.
- Where did Seamus come?
- Fourteenth, fourteenth and: 'Sod this, anyone fancy a pint!'
- He went to the pub while you were still racing?
- That was another bad point to the afternoon but let me continue. We were coming back in after the races and I inquired if Simon and Andy were staying in town. The skipper Simon was, in a pub that I knew served a very decent pint of Old Speckled Hen which is one of my favourites and I mentioned this to him. No real reaction.
- Isn't it traditional to buy your crew a drink?
- It is highly traditional to get them hog-whimperingly drunk but some people just do not respect tradition! So we had tidied up the boat and so on and were walking up to this pub. Just outside Simon thanked me sketchily and went off. I then had to find Seamus and Huff who were already half-cut and finding my story of woe highly amusing. I was *furious*.
- I'm not surprised but yachties aren't normally like that are they?
- First I have come across. So that was the Saturday. On the Sunday Seamus' mate had gone home and the guy from the other boat had shown up. Everyone was happy. I bade a good morning to Simon who studiously ignored me. Charming! By this time my anger had gone and I just thought he was...
- A spooning muffin!
- In one. We went out and raced. There were only two and we came last in both. As we were returning to the Quay I noticed something. You see Etchells do not have an engine so one has to sail them back to the quay and at that wharf they used to line up the boats bow to stern. As we were drifting towards the quay we were told to moor up alongside Simon's boat and he was on the stern, taking off his oilskins. As we approached Seamus shouted: 'Fend off!' but I

thought better of it and we collided with a reasonable, though not dangerous thud. Simon overbalanced and fell right in!

- No?

- Oh yes. He surfaced, spluttering rather unpleasant water to see me standing over him. 'Hello Simon.' I said, 'You see this is what happens. You don't buy me a drink, you end up in the drink!'. With that I walked off.

- You are *outrageous*!

- I have my moments but are you sure that you are feeling better now?

- Yes Jude. Thank you.

- It is my pleasure, honour and privilege to serve my lady.

- Lunatic! I'll give you a call.

- I am counting the seconds. Sleep well. Love you.

- Love you too.

Friday 11th June: COVETOUSNESS

I woke up in bed as dry as a dry thing and without too much of a hangover. Everything else hurts like billio as normal but I am being healed in a couple of days so why worry? I seem to have unearthed a mote of hope from somewhere but I do not want to dwell on it. False hopes are soul-destroying you know.

I spent the morning with a bottle of rouge doing the last of the packing. It is amazing the small amount of belongings I have. Take away the records, the bed and my clothes and there is precious little else. I never had any desire to posses things purely for decoration or whatever as I would always prefer to spend money on having fun or helping others. Beautiful things should be on public display. Sanctimonious git!

I went to the Temple Bar to catch up with my good friend Jim and had a chat with the lovely Solly. I do not think I impressed her particularly but skint cripples are not that impressive. When I am healed I shall stride in there and sweep her off her feet although I am supposed to have a nice Christian wife am I not? It was part of the deal. I could convert her! With my miracle and new body I am sure that I could convince her after a time. Or even a few times if possible. This train of thought is leading straight to Frustration Junction.

Jim was as funny as ever and his poetry sheets seem to be getting off the ground. I hope he will be all right soon and he is something of a survivor. Why have all the Irish people I have ever meet been wonderful? Hitler tried to create a master race but the Irish seem to have unlocked the secrets of life. Well most of them. Bloody politicians!

I found a tattooist and had the thing done at last. He was a delightful chap and strangely spiritual. He wants me to show it to him when it is healed. I shall have to write that down somewhere so that I do not forget. I would not want to let him down.

I got home quite early for a change and spent a mellow night in the company of T.H.C. and friends. What splendid company they are! Mags had left a message on the machine. I should really get one that does not cut people off in their prime. Tomorrow I must get my costume sorted for the party. It is a shame that I cannot afford any cocaine but there you go. The perfect way not to get addicted but I do not think it will catch on. You could not sell the joys of being poor to anyone even though it is almost always better than being rich. Why do they all look so miserable and shallow? I shall ask God on Sunday. How do you know when sanity fails? We should have a little light on our heads as an indication.

It is a good thing that I only say to people a fraction of what actually goes on in my head.

* * *

- Good morning Solly.
- Hello Jude. I haven't seen you in a while.
- Oh you know people to do, places to meet and things to be. Or something like that.
- You sound pissed already.

130

- Au contraire dear Solly I am extraordinarily sober and would like to enlist your support to rectify matters forthwith and immediately.
- A pint of Harveys?
- What an excellent idea. I can well believe that we have already hit upon a solution to the problem.
- There you are.
- God bless you.
- But I didn't sneeze! That's a painful looking spot you have there.
- I can assure you that this is no spot. It is in fact the very latest in communications technology. Some people have their satellite dishes, some even have their little black boxes whereas I have this remarkable device that means all I have to do is place this finger into a T.V. socket and have instant access to eleventy-three channels of absolute tut from all around the world.
- Does it work?
- I do not know, there has not been anything on that I have wanted to watch as yet.
- You are silly. When did you have your hair cut?
- Yesterday. Do you like it?
- I'd love to feel it. Bend over. Oh that's lovely. It's very soft.
- I am sure that this is someone's fantasy.
- What shampoo do you use?
- Strangeways special, one of those wash and that is it jobbies. What do you get if you cross Vidal Baboon with an obese and obnoxious comedian?
- I don't know?
- Wash and f*** off!
- I like that. That's very funny.
- The new shampoo for new age travellers?
- Don't know?
- Go and wash!
- You are silly.
- Stick to what you are good at that is what I say. Cheers. Up with temperance and down with strong drink.
- That can hardly be your philosophy.
- I assure you Miss that rarely a drop touches my lips.
- No you swallow too quickly.
- I am undone. You know that there is a conspiracy theory about shampoos?
- Really?
- Well a few years ago everyone just used shampoo and had perfectly lovely hair. Then we were told that we needed this conditioner as well and people duly went and bought the stuff. *Then* they tell us that they have managed to squeeze both shampoo and conditioner into one bottle but it is very expensive. Nonetheless everyone buys it and says: 'How marvellous. I only need to take one bottle into the shower!' It strikes me that we have been conned, it is all the same stuff.
- That's very cynical.
- Ah but I am an old cynic you know Solly. Anyway how are things with you? Any big parts on the horizon, if you'll excuse the expression?
- No not really but I have joined a Shakespeare group in London on Sundays. It's great fun and very useful to meet other actors and gain experience.
- Fabulous.

131

- Oh it is. We discuss everything about the parts and do role-playing around the characters, it's very releasing.
- Oh good.
- And we talk about how the real people must have felt in those circumstances and we all end up crying and hugging each other.
- Sounds marvellous.
- Oh it is Jude, it is and I've joined a performing arts group.
- What dancing and stuff?
- No! It is Visual Performing Arts.
- I do apologise, what *was* I thinking?
- We are doing a project entitled: 'The Dance of the Seven Vales of Tears'.
- There's a thing, in the words of Barbara Hershey.
- Who was she?
- The actress in the first King Kong film I believe.
- Oh. That's a bit rude isn't it?
- That depends upon what your imagination came up with.
- That's very silly. How are you Jude?
- Oh the usual. Ducking and diving, hopping and limping. You do not want to buy a flat do you? It is something of a budgerigar?
- A budgerigar?
- Going cheap.
- I don't think so! You're selling yours are you?
- Indeed that is the plan of action. There are too many stairs and I cannot handle the cleaning anymore so the Hunting Lodge has to go.
- Where are you going to live then?
- I am moving back to my folks to become a resident at Redmond Grange Hospice for the Virtually Useless. We are going to enjoy our dotages together.
- What do they do?
- My father is a retired Molecular Chemist and my mother, the Dragon is a music teacher.
- Really?
- Which bit?
- Your mother is a music teacher? What does she teach?
- Singing and music theory.
- Really?
- Indeed. A very good one by all accounts, she is also known as the Nightingale.
- I could do with some singing lessons so do you think she could teach me?
- I would imagine she would be delighted and her rates are very reasonable as she teaches from home.
- Oh I couldn't have you in the house when I'm singing.
- Oh?
- It would be too embarrassing.
- Ah.
- That sounds wonderful.
- Would you like the number and I can mention to her that you are interested. She also runs the choir at the local church which is apparently very good practice.
- I've got my Shakespeare on Sundays.
- Never mind, just an idea.
- It's so cathartic that I would simply *die* if I missed a session.

- Well we cannot have you dying on us can we? Who would pour the beer quite as beautifully? Talking of which.

- Another one?

- What a good idea. You see I would be lost without you.

- There you are. I would have to save some money to afford lessons. Maybe when I win the lottery I could start.

- Here is the number but I would not rely on the lottery if I were you. They say that there is as much chance of ringing a random London number and getting the Queen as there is winning the lottery. Interestingly enough that happened to a friend of mine.

- What did?

- He was ringing someone in London, got the wrong number and a voice not dissimilar to her Maj answered it.

- What did she say?

- 'I think one has the wrong number!'

- Really?

- Who cares it is a good story but doing the lottery is such a waste of money because not only do you have to beat enormous odds to win the thing you then have be one of the very few lottery or pools winners to actually be happy. You must have seen those documentaries about lottery winners who say that it has ruined their lives?

- No.

- Only about ten per cent of people who win large amounts of money are actually happy as a result. I would rather be poor and happy.

- I'd rather be rich.

- That is very much your prerogative but the problem with being rich is that there must be an element of guilt involved. If one has enough money to waste on designer dresses and so on and one hears the news about another humanitarian disaster in Africa or wherever it must bring some reaction. When it becomes apparent that the clothes one is planning to wear to a premiere or something would keep the population of a village alive for a year where they are currently dying there must be a feeling of guilt somewhere.

- I don't think about those things.

- Ah that is the other option.

- But the lottery gives money to good causes.

- That is the 'spin' as it is called these days. I like the idea of giving people money to throw a party and so on but they give very little away in what is known as 'real terms'. Why people do not give the money they spend on the lottery each week to charity I have no idea. If they really want to support good causes it would cut out the middle man. Saying that doing the lottery is all right is the utter antithesis of Christianity. You spend your pound or whatever of which a few pence might do some good in the world and hope to win lots of money that most have no intention of spending on anyone other than their immediate circle. That is giving little, hoping to gain a lot. Christianity was about giving as much as possible but expecting nothing in return.

- But hardly any of the money you give to charity actually goes to the causes does it?

- That dear Solly is an absolute lie propagated by the selfish and covetous. In fact the average is eighty-seven pence in the pound given to charity goes to the appropriate cause. How much do you spend on the lottery a week?

- Ten pounds.

- That is about a dozen clean wells a month.

- Oh. I suppose you are against lottery money going to the arts?

133

- Not at all. That is absolutely wonderful! The arts bring entertainment and happiness in this seven vales of tears and I love those new statues and so on.

- But everyone hates them.

- They are the artistic statement that this generation is making. Could you imagine trying to build St. Paul's Cathedral today? It simply would not happen. When it was built it nearly bankrupted the country and many people were killed in the construction. You would have every do-gooder against it backed up by the tabloids and it would *have* to be stopped. So instead we can have statues that people hate as our statement for generations to come.

- I never thought of it like that but the lottery does bring hope to people.

- Sure and then it brings crushing despair. There was a documentary about a woman who was addicted to the lottery. This poor lady did not have much going for her in life as she was rather unattractive, very poor and not particularly well educated. Some might even assume her to be stupid. Every week she spends all her money on the lottery and is being sued because she sold all the furniture in her rented, furnished flat. Her local shopkeeper had barred her from buying Moments or whatever they are called and she is anorexic because she does not spend enough money on food.

- This sounds very grim.

- It is. The documentary followed her for the week and she does not have a very pleasant life but the thing that keeps her going is: 'It might be me!' On the Saturday she sat in front of the T.V. on the floor with all of her tickets spread out in front of her and too excited to even speak. Then the draw. She did not even win a tenner. Her face was the ultimate picture of collapsed hope and utter despair but through her streaming tears she managed to whisper: 'There's always Wednesday.' How many people are there like her that are emotionally and spiritually tortured twice a week?

- I don't know.

- Hard to say is it not but do you know the really sad thing about her situation?

- No?

- If she did win she would be prey to all of the vultures out there and everyone would look down on her because she would be a: 'Stupid lottery winner.' in their snotty eyes. *She* would not be invited to any premieres. Who would actually want to win the lottery? Knowing that their new-found wealth was based on others' misery but they keep on trying do they not. It is pure covetousness.

- I wouldn't want to win millions, a few thousand would do.

- Really? Tell me something Solly. There is an attitude that women are generally after a man's money and any attractive woman is considered to be a potential gold-digger. This is why men try and be flash and look rich to try and attract women. Did you know that people even have fake mobile 'phones.

- Really?

- Absolutely. There is a story of a chap who walked into a posh restaurant talking loudly into his mobile, something like: 'Sell coffee! Buy pork-bellies!' but then suddenly the 'phone rang! He was laughed out of the restaurant!

- What an arsehole!

- Indeed. Would you say that you might marry for money?

- Yes I would. Obviously it would be better if he was nice or even lovable but it probably wouldn't matter if he wasn't as I would just go shopping all the time.

- How interesting. I have always thought that love and laughter would provide a lot more happiness than a wardrobe of expensive dresses that annoy you so much you only wear them once. Is it foolish of me to think that one's soul is more important that money and looks?

- No just naive.
- Naive? There is an Oscar Wilde quote that might be relevant here. He was chatting with a lady and asked: 'Would you sleep with me for a pound?' 'No!' she replied rather outraged. 'Would you sleep with me for a million pounds?' he continued. 'Yes.' she rejoined after thinking about it briefly. 'But would you sleep with me for ten pounds?' he persisted and she lost her temper saying: 'Sir! What do you think I am?' 'Madame.' he said sternly, 'We have ascertained what you are now we are merely haggling!'
- Ah more customers, excuse me Jude.
- Certainly.

* * *

- Hello Jude.
- Jim! How are you my friend?
- Grand thank you. Actually I'm completely pissed off but I hate complaining.
- Rather dull is it not? A Stella for you?
- That would be very kind.
- Brisk trade today?
- It's never brisk by the theatre there. It is about as brisk as a tortoise with heartburn.
- Now there is an image! Still how is the poetry coming along?
- Very well but very slowly. I am amazed at the time it takes people to do the very little that you are relying on them to do.
- I know mate. What was it, a year ago when you started on the project I was very tempted to tell you how inefficient and unprofessional the majority of working people are but I did not want to put you off. I hope that that was not patronising?
- Of course not. I'm glad you didn't tell me so that I have been able to find out myself. People do have strange attitudes don't they?
- All these people that have stable jobs, nice homes and enough money to go out at weekends but who say: 'I don't get paid enough to work hard!' Yes they have a slanted angle on life.
- They seem to do O.K. from where I'm standing which is on a street in the rain most of the time.
- That will not be for much longer mate now that you are very close to being a poet for a living.
- Thanks to you.
- Not at all! It is you that has done all of the hard work. You took the courses, you wrote the poetry...
- And you got me on the courses and found me a illustrator that you bullied into not charging me.
- He claims to be a socialist so it is only right that he 'donates his services' is the expression I think but come on Jim, all the credit goes to you. Actually I am being very ulterior you know?
- Oh yes and how's that then?
- Well I have latched on to a modern ironic poet that I feel will make a major impact and you are using your abilities and technology to be successful. It is all very impressive Jim. Getting your poetry on the fishing net through a poster company is a stroke of genius. It is only a matter of time now. How is the more traditional approach going?
- That is what has been pissing me off! I gave a few hundred of the posters to the manager of the bar two weeks ago and they are still in his office.

135

- Not the best place for public viewing.
- The display boards are still being sorted out so it'll be a couple of weeks or so yet.
- I heard a very silly gag the other day?
- Is it a paddy one?
- Indeed.
- Good!
- An Air Lingus flight is coming into Berlin or wherever and the control tower comes through: 'Hello flight AL302, please confirm current height and position?' 'I'm six foot in my socks and I'm sitting at the front!'
- I nearly spat my beer out!
- Oh do not do that! 'Burgle my home, steal my girlfriend and run me over but do not spill my beer!'
- My thoughts entirely. No Jude I think that with a bit of luck I should be off the Issue in a month or so.
- That's wonderful news Jim. Pass on the pitch! How many more have made use of the initiative?
- How many vendors? About six were going to but you know what their lives are like. It's very hard for them to get it together to survive a college course even if it is for free but I think a young girl is now on a photography course and doing all right.
- Fantastic.
- Oh it is Jude. It's just a shame more people didn't use your initiative, if you'll pardon the joke. Although the Issue has helped me a lot it I will not miss all of those rude people on the street.
- It amazes me how anyone could be so rude! All of those people that call your colleagues a nuisance and aggressive really ought to have a close look at themselves. I wonder if all of them spent eight hours in the pouring rain with people either ignoring them, being rude to them or the occasional decent human patronising them merely to earn less than a tenner, their opinions might alter a little?
- Oh they would all right but it'll never happen. There will always be people like them and people like me but fortunately there will always be people like you and Jamie and Diz. I feel that there is balance in the world.
- Balance! Then what is imbalance like?
- It's when you fall over, normally drunk!
- I walked right into that one didn't I?
- You did right enough.
- How do you cope with all of the rude people?
- I feel sorry for them.
- Really?
- Well you see they all look so unhappy. Here I am with nothing except a thin chance of getting a little bit of money to get my own place or something and they have got all that they need and more but are miserable. It's very sad.
- That is very profound mate and I think you are right. The ultimate example was poor old Diana who had everything worldly that one can think of and she was incredibly unhappy apparently but no-one seems to notice this do they? They are so proud of themselves are rich people and I have not a clue why. I know one couple that are self-made, wealthy and lovely, intelligent and funny but they do seem to be the exception. The reason why that film Trading Places was so good it that it is utterly believable, it does not take much to make money if you

are wealthy and a bully which is the American system and why they are the world's biggest superpower. They are rich and bullies and the secular world is their oyster.

- But are futures are clams!

- Great song! It is very hard to think of any occasion when money has inspired beauty or creativity and I would wager that it is actually the reverse. Money stifles creativity. People are amazed that Van Gogh only sold one painting in his life time.

- Who was that to?

- His brother so it does not really count. I would say that because money never came into the equation he is arguably the world's greatest artist. There is a wonderful Johnny Peel quote that goes something like: 'Their first album was written over five years in a bed sit in Lambeth and was inspired. Their second album was made in three months in a studio in Miami and everyone wonders how they lost the common touch!' How many businesses that have wonderful ideas still manage to fail? Because they are not fiscal sharks and go bust. Most small businesses go bust because large corporations do not pay them on time. Covetousness destroys creativity.

- So if I became rich my poetry would suffer?

- I would think that your poetry would shrivel up and die. I honestly think you are better off than most people mate. I had money for a while and thought that I was happy but it was actually a nightmare. Suddenly I did not know who my real friends were and the woman I met was very beautiful and utterly mercenary sowing doubt and suspicion amongst my old friends: 'You can't trust him, he ripped off a friend of mine!' It was horrible.

- Did she stay around when the money ran out?

- Of course not. It was all very prodigal son really but now I know that I can trust everyone that I get on with because I have nothing to take. I would not say I am happy particularly but my human trust account has a very healthy balance. Funnily enough she was one of those people that always slates beggars and vendors: 'Oh they're so rude!' she would protest, 'And some of them are not real beggars you know!' I never asked her what her definition of a beggar exactly was. To me they are people that stand on the street begging for money but she wanted references to prove that they were really poor before gracing them with a pound coin and looking smug.

- What was someone like you doing with someone like that?

- She was beautiful and I was innocent of the ways of the Dark Side. It is funny I was skint for six years and you know what it is like, counting up one's pennies on a Wednesday to see if one can afford some milk. According to the world that should make me miserable but my memories of the time are all laughter and parties. What really made me unhappy was the whole litigation process because it is ran by the most foul and covetous pieces of *scum* that ever slimed across the world! Everyone was just out for the money and they all got some. I was sent to surgeons that would give me a cursory examination and then write what they wanted to write. The insurance company's bloke would use lots of long words and say that I could still be a hod-carrier and the solicitor's chap would say that I was about to collapse in a heap. None of them actually gave me a complete prognosis and I used to have to point out things to them.

- You're joking?

- Not at all. Everyone I went to see in Harley Street that cost a Third World economy a millisecond was absolutely hopeless. They are lazy, covetous charlatans to a man and should all be shot.

- That's rather extreme for you.

- I know but it is very hard to forgive some people. I know that about twenty so-called professionals made a lot of money being incompetent and greedy whilst at best doing me no good and at worst doing me actual harm. They are all part of the world of litigation which is hell on earth.

- Really? There's a mate of mine whose livelihood is litigation and he spends all of his time suing people.

- God's briefcase how bizarre. Mind you the reason I suffered so much was through ignorance and naivety as I had no idea just how unpleasant and aggressive the whole thing was. If I had another accident I would not sue.

- You're joking!

- No. It would achieve nothing. If I had spent my time after all of my operations when I could walk all right rebuilding my life instead of being persuaded by crooks to lie for money, those times would have been a lot more pleasant. Humanity has been dealing with suffering and loss for thousands of years and so I was able to cope with the pain and so on it was the utter callousness of the compensation process that really made me depressed. Things would have been a lot different if I had not have bothered.

- Ah but Jude it was all part of the life process. I am ten years older than you but come to you for advice. You have seen and done so much that you will always give good counsel and you seem to understand the difference between right and wrong.

- That is only because we are both poor and our lives are full of the simple things. This is what happens to governments. Before the election they talk about 'ethical' foreign policy but as soon as they get into power the mandarins tell them about the politics and job losses and how it will affect the economy and all of a sudden Indonesia has lots of British fighters to help play 'totalitarian state'. Rich people are all scared of us poor types you know. They all must shake if one says: 'Marie Antoinette!' in a stern voice. As soon as people have money they feel compelled to lock themselves away from the rest of the world and security and privacy become watchwords. It is all very odd.

- They don't like us do they? I think we do make them feel guilty.

- I think they inhabit another world that is full of solicitors, cronies and con-men. They have a different morality. It is fine for them to buy cocaine by the truckload but the poor smack-head that nicks their car stereo should be locked-up to protect society. Then they want us to like them and buy their glossy magazines that are designed to show us how inferior we are to them simply because *we* do not know *them*.

- I think they all should read the Issue. It is not a case of real life or any of those other things it's just that they should realise what is going on with the world and how hypocritical their actions actually are.

- You know the film Rope?

- Hitchcock?

- That is the chap. It is a deeper two Ronnies and Basil Fawlty number. The arrogant pseudo-intellectual that orchestrates the murder represents rich people, how can anyone justify spending so much money on a dress that will be worn for one evening when the same amount of money would keep untold villages across the world away from crisis for months. The victim was we poor types because of their covetousness innocent people are killed every day and Jimmy Stewart's attitude is that of the majority of rich people, apathy and cynical arguments.

- Jude now don't get me wrong but you are moving back to your parents who are very middle class.

- My folks are middle-class and I am a middle class socialist because of my parents. They came from nothing fifty years ago and have toiled ever since to achieve what they have which is a large house with no mortgage that can accommodate a large family near a park in a fairly ordinary town. Because of this I should feel guilty? Because I believe in Socialism and I am not 'one of the workers'? Prejudice is so endemic now. Apparently you have to be fat to be stout these days. Everyone is trying to pretend that they are not as greedy, avaricious, mercenary and covetous as they really are and that is where prejudice and hypocrisy come in. That is why they do not buy the Big Issue, *naturally darling*!

- How can someone give to a charity that helps Africans but turn their noses up at vendors who are just as much in need?
- They only like their suffering on T.V. or the occasional article in their magazines between the 'shampoo of the month' and 'a lovely little restaurant in Knightsbridge'. Real life smells and they cannot relate to it. It must be frightening for the poor loves.
- People in this country don't understand money properly. In Cork there are rich and poor like anywhere else but money is only money and no-one is starving to pay for someone else's car. I knew two fellas that were horse traders in Cork and they could spend an evening selling the same horse back and forth and both would make a profit by the end of the evening! You try explaining that to a clever accountant but I know who the clever ones are, the ones laughing and drinking.
- That is wonderful!
- You would love Cork Jude. The Guinness is the best in the world and no-one really cares about anything else except that, Cork Gin and the crack.
- It sounds perfect. A few years ago a mate of mine was travelling through the Cork countryside when his car broke down. Fortunately he could see a telephone box down the road that seemed to have a few buildings scattered around it. He walked to it and opened the door to reveal an old wind-up 'phone.
- The ones with the little handles?
- That's the fella. So he picked it up, gave it a wind and got through to the operator. He said that his car has broken down a few yards up the road and the operator said: 'Right the best thing you can do is to go to the pub. If you turn around you will see the pub behind you, the Grave Diggers and by the bar is a fella named Connor. Buy him a drink and he'll have a look at your car.' My mate was amazed at this apparent technology in an unusual place and asked the operator how she knew where he was. 'Oh it's easy!' she says, 'Can you see the big building next to the pub? Look at the third floor window and that's my hand waving at you!'
- They think that Irish people are stupid, all of them that aren't as happy as we are.
- They would be wrong. It is a major case of people not believing something despite enormous evidence to support it. Irish people are stupid and money makes you happy, *right*! It strikes me that every new pop star or actor is seen being interviewed for the first time full of optimism and hope, quietly determined to be successful and happy but it is never more than two years before they give an expose on how horrible it all is and how their lives have been ruined by the media. It happens time and time again and as soon as they are off to rehab along comes another young hopeful with sparkling eyes and an uncongested nose to fill the gap and keep the cycle turning.
- I would say that they were the stupid ones.
- One thing that the whole compensation process showed me is the disgusting things that people will do for money. The perennial question of 'how much to take your clothes off?' is the tip of the proverbial polar bear's home. The level of dishonesty on all sides during these cases is staggering. I ended up not sure about anything that might or might not have happened because I was fed so many lies. What people do not realise is the damage that it does to their consciences, compensation money is smeared with blood. When they stoop to that level of

139

base dishonesty it changes their lives for ever. We have created a society of revenge that is utterly destructive. When something bad happens people want compensation, someone to blame and obvious but bearable symptoms. Why? I can tell you that money does not improve an injured life and trying to put figures on injuries and emotional trauma et cetera are pointless. Everyone would be far happier to recover as much as possible with no ulterior motive for not doing so and getting on with their lives. The only people to win are the solicitors and the insurance companies and an ordinary non-mercenary person will be made far worse off in terms of their lives by the whole process.

- But when something bad happens don't people need help?
- When has a solicitor actually *helped* anyone? Why is the wonderful N.H.S. in so much trouble? Because too many doctors and surgeons are tied up doing meaningless reports on people who want some money for nothing. Instead of solicitors and surgeons screwing the system for thousands a day the money should be put into a trust that gives victims ongoing support as it is needed. Cut out the crooked middlemen!
- They are right bastards aren't they?
- Unmitigated. The suffering they cause is immeasurable in fact that is it! I have made up my mind! I am going to get a tattoo done.
- A tattoo?
- That is right. I am going to have a bar code tattooed on my left hand as my little protest against all of these bloody people that ruin our lives and justify their inexcusable actions with phrases like: 'More cost effective.' and 'Improved profitability.' Just because everyone else has fallen for the scam it does not mean that I have to. They came very close to ruining my life.
- Are you sure that they haven't?
- How do you mean Jim?
- Well since you became disabled you have changed you know. There is a lot of anger in you and you're not looking at all well. I bet you don't eat properly.
- I keep dribbling and missing my mouth all together.
- An eating problem?
- That was a great film but I do have a drinking problem, two hands but only one mouth it is *very* frustrating!
- Seriously though are you sure you're all right? How are you getting by at the moment?
- A freak of luck in a time of need. Up until this point in time I have only ever won two things, a box of cigars when I was seven and an Outward Bound course but that changed just recently. There is a pub near me that does a draw on a Sunday night. Through the week people buy groups of ninety-nine numbers for a pound each and on the Sunday at five o' clock they do the draw and the winning number gets forty-nine quid.
- What about the other money?
- Twenty-five goes to the R.N.L.I. and twenty-five goes into a safety deposit box. If you are there when you win the draw you are given a choice of ten envelopes with keys in and if your key opens the box you get the money inside.
- Very clever.
- Sunday afternoon trade has picked up somewhat, well from a quarter to five at any rate. People are so transparent in their covetousness. Anyway about a week before my leg gave up I was passing by at about three and went in for a jar. I was chatting to people when Naomi, the Landlady hassled me into buying some of the remaining numbers so I bought four and asked her to pick the numbers for me. When the draw happened I was chatting away and Naomi had

to say: 'Jude it's you!' as she gave me the forty-nine pounds. Of course I had to get everyone a drink.
- Of course. Churlish not to.
- Then I had to select an envelope. A weedy little key was produced and I did not rate my chances. In the absolute hush the key was inserted in the lock and with a click and a thunk it opened. I looked at the poster with the accumulator figure written on it and nearly fainted.
- How much was it?
- One thousand, one hundred and twenty-five pounds!
- Good God!
- Absolutely! I could not *believe* it but that is now what is keeping me in beer and chocolate and why I do not mind buying you a couple of pints.
- You must have a guardian angel!
- I really do not think so unless he is the patron saint of walking sticks!
- Good for you. Right a quick joke before I get back, those things don't sell themselves you know! This fella goes to a brothel as he's feeling a little, itchy shall we say. He walks in and says to the Madame: 'I'd be needing a little refreshment. What can you do for fifty pee?' 'Fifty pence!' she squawks, 'You cheap bastard! For fifty pee you can go around the back and have a wank!' 'Oh right.' says your man and leaves looking a little disappointed. Five minutes later he walks back in and says: 'That was great, who do I pay!'
- I like that. Jim! As ever it has been a pleasure and the best of Irish luck with the poetry.
- Thank you Jude for everything. Have a pleasant day.

- That was a bit intense.
- Oh hello Solly, yes I suppose it was.
- You are a bit though aren't you? Did you say you were getting a tattoo done? A bar code?
- That is right on my left hand.
- I can see what you mean but it is a little extreme.
- Most things of meaning are. Right then thank you as ever Solly and I shall see you soon. Time to find a tattooist.
- Lets have a feel of your hair before you go.
- Oh that is nice. I shall fall asleep in the chair if you are not careful. See you later.

* * *

- Good afternoon.
- All right mate. What can I do for you?
- I would like a bar-code tattooed on my left hand please.
- Sorry mate. Don't do bar-codes.
- Oh how disappointing! Is there any particular reason?
- 'Cos I don't want to and it's my shop!
- Sounds perfectly reasonable. Good day to you.
- Fucking weirdo.

- Good afternoon.
- Hello there.
- Do you do bar-codes? The gentleman up the road seems a little reluctant.
- Yes we do bar-codes. Where did you want it done?
- On my left hand please.

141

- On your hand? Are you sure?
- Absolutely positive thank you.
- Have you had tattoos before?
- Indeed and I am still in possession of eight. Like this.
- O.K. Are you sure you want it on your hand?
- Indeed if you are willing to do it for me?
- As long as you are completely sure. A tattoo on the hand can make life difficult. Only if you are sure?
- I am determined actually.
- Fine. I shall do you a bar-code on your left hand.
- Fabulous. My name is Jude how do you do?
- Hi Jude, I'm Jesus. Please come this way.
- Thank you Jesus.
- Sit down here. Are you comfortable? Good. Let's have a look at your hand. Good shape, this will work well. What numbers would you like?
- I have written them down for you, here.
- Thank you. Are they significant?
- They are my parents' dates of birth.
- That is impressive. It really expands the irony of the statement, I take it this is a statement?
- Bold and true.
- Good, that is important in life. The figures from history that everyone loves and looks up to are the bold and true ones like Robin Hood, King Arthur, my namesake or even Churchill. It is a good model to have in life.
- Is that a South American accent I can hear?
- Very good. Yes I am from Columbia originally. It is a very popular name in that part of the world.
- What is?
- Ha, ha, ha. You are a funny man Jude but if you want a good bar-code on your hand and not one that will make you feel seasick you had better cut down on the irony and humour! Just fermez la bouche and listen to Jesus. Ha, ha, ha! Your face! But seriously do not crack jokes.
- Silence it is then.
- I would imagine that you don't like talking about your disability? Look, I was *joking*. You can talk as much as you like just don't move. I would rather you say yes than nod your head O.K.?
- Yes Jesus.
- You are a funny man Jude. Why does someone like you have so many angry tattoos and want me to add to the list? Why the anger Jude?
- I am not angry I gave up that a long time ago. I am just tired, exhausted and utterly wearied by this thing called life. You asked me three times if I was sure about this tattoo did you not?
- I did.
- May I tell you why I am having it done?
- Sure I'm not going anywhere!
- True. People are going to ask about it are they not?
- Bound to.
- In fact it is so obvious and meant to be meaningful that *everyone* will ask about it.
- Bound to.
- Would you stop saying that please?
- Sorry.

- S'all right. When they ask I shall probably give them a glib reply like: 'It is a protest against capitalism, consumerism and the genuinely mercenary hearts of the people that control our lives!' I might be bold enough to say that.
- Might be.

- That's an interesting look! Please continue Jude.
- Thank you. I might say that or I might say something completely flippant like: 'Isn't it pretty? Does it make my bum look big?'
- Jude I told you do *not* make me laugh. These lines are supposed to be straight and your veins are already reminding me of the Nile Delta which does not make my task any easier. Stop making me laugh O.K.?
- Sorry mate. What I was getting to in my circuitous fashion is what actually made me decide to have this done. Would you like to hear?
- Go on. It is always interesting to hear the 'whys?'
- Right. As you can see I am disabled. This is due to an R.T.A. that occurred nine years ago and left me with a degenerative condition that I cannot hide from the world anymore. That is how my life is currently.
- I am suitably sorry for you.
- Thank you. I have always known that this 'end is nigh' situation as t'were was going to happen at some point which is why I had insurance on my credit cards and loan. That does not sound shocking does it? It is perfectly normal to have those things in today's society is it not? As it happened I had four cards, a loan, an overdraft and a mortgage. But they talked me into it you see! All those envelopes covered in promises and one thinks: 'Oh what's inside, what's inside? It's a 7.3 something or other and it's a *gold one*. And no-one is here to ask if I can have it or not. It's mine all mine!'
- Plastic pleasure hmm?
- Isn't it just. One can say to oneself: 'Of course you can darling! You deserve it!' all the time, it is *wonderful*. So I had insurance on all of them, the: 'In case you leave work for medical reasons.' policy that gave me peace of mind.
- Rack up the debts without bothering your conscience?
- You have seen straight through my cunning plan, I am undone. It was not like that. I am owed money by friends that has always exceeded the amount that I owe. Somewhat naive though.
- It happens all the time.
- So in March I needed to make use of my insurance policies that I had been dutifully paying each month but I received a reply so swift that it cut right through all of those 'three days to clear' arguments one always receives. They told me that I was not covered because this is a 'pre-existing condition' apparently and they want their money back.
- What are you going to do?
- Well thank God I have parents to go back to and I can sell my flat. I have thirteen grand's worth of equity that can cover the mortgage and then throw something to the vultures to keep them from snapping at my heels, mixing my metaphors like the plague. The fact is that if it were not for my parents I would be out on the street in fact if it was not for my parents I would be dead. This tattoo asks the question: 'What sort of world is it where this can happen to an innocent like me and in fact does happen every single day to someone at some level but the majority of people are more interested in a young woman's breasts?' An interesting question would you not say?
- Would you like an honest answer?

143

- Yes please Jesus. You are about to make me feel very small are you not?
- In this country you have compensation, credit for most and things like It Girls. Jude can you explain to me what the concept of It Girls is all about?
- Certainly. They are beautiful young women whose families are extremely wealthy so that they can do whatever they want, whenever they like. Literally.
- Literally? They could have a man killed?
- Of course! When we live in a world where people have been killed for fifty quid girls like Laura Farmer-Pathos-Blenkinshop could have killed any critic she wanted. It amazes me that she has not thought of it. Too much shopping to do one would suppose but that is a tad extreme and not particularly helpful. Essentially they are famous for being rich and famous but are despised by the people that they are trying to impress because everyone knows that their lives are utterly meaningless.
- I thought so. No we don't have them in our country.
- Would you like to borrow some? I am sure we would not miss a couple.
- You have a wicked sense of humour Jude.
- Oh it is merely a hint of persiflage.
- I know.
- But it is quite incredible that these people exist who have enough time and money to do incredible things but all they ever do buy clothes and drugs.
- What would you do with that much money?
- I would spend time finding small local ventures that just need a little bit of money, something like a couple of grand and *give* it to them so that they do not need to go crawling to a bank. To get a loan these days one has to prove that one does not actually need one! For example I would set up a local weekly paper that only used long-term unemployed people who wanted to get into media. They would be on courses at the local college, live education it is known as. They would be getting their qualifications in journalism, photography, design or whatever whilst working on a real paper that only subscribed to the journalist principles of C.P. Scott.
- Are you local?
- Very funny but that is what I would do. Plus I would hire a firm of private detectives to find all of my old friends and throw the biggest party you have ever seen although it would be a decidedly sweet and sour moment as a lot of my friends would now be dead. I seem to get on with people that have quiet, desperate humour and run on self-destruct mode. Another thing would be to advertise or something for all disabled people to ring a free phone number and then buy them the one thing that would make their lives easier. A car, a microwave, a hamster whatever. That would be fun. I would love to see their faces.
- That is interesting Jude. My country is very different you know. Half of it is completely controlled by the people that make money from the It Girls and their hobbies. The government tries to do something about this but they are out-manned and out-armed by the gangsters. So now the good ol' U.S. of A. are lending a hand. Of course they do not want anyone to know this because it is too reminiscent of Vietnam plus of course they do not actually want to get rid of the gangsters as they comprise a large industry that oils many a politician's rhetoric. So the killings go on day after day after day. They killed my family you know?
- Really? I am truly sorry.
- I was in America studying for my degree when our village was wiped out although I do not know which side did the wiping. I lost my parents my brother and my two little sisters.
- That is a terrible tragedy Jesus. I have two brothers and a sister.
- Do you? Cherish them, they are assets to your life. Everyday in my country children are shot and killed for no reason other than to impress or assist the people with money but mine is only

144

one country in a very large world and you have problems with the money people in your country. There are terrible problems in every country.

- It is a horrible world.

- It used to be beautiful. Let me tell you something. There is a European company that makes coffee and chocolate and other goods. It is very large and profitable.

- I know the one.

- A few years ago they launched a very large advertising campaign in Africa pushing their powdered baby milk. Unfortunately our African brothers and sisters are not so wise to the wiles of advertising and believed all of the pictures of happily bouncing babies that they suddenly saw everywhere and do you know what they did? Instead of giving their babies their perfectly healthy breast milk they used what little money they had to buy the powdered stuff believing that they would raise strong, healthy children but that did not happen. They used water that had not been sterilised to make the milk and typhoid, dysentery and many other diseases spread across the continent. The infant mortality rate went through the mud roof simply because an already prosperous company wanted to make more money from poor people.

- That is quite horrific.

- It is one example of the developed world-wide trend of covetousness, one of many sins that engulfs the world. Do you like coffee?

- Of a morning.

- Buy a brand called Cafe Direct.

- May I ask why?

- Because the coffee comes directly from the people that grow it so they are not defrauded by the middle men. Why it is that you westerners believe you have the right to ruin thousands of lives a day in the Third World I do not know. But you do it. Have you heard of Jubilee 2000?

- Wiping out third world debt? Yes I think it is very important.

- Do you know how much it would actually cost the taxpayers in your country if British debts were repaid by British taxpayers rather than the countries themselves?

- No?

- Four pounds a year.

- Is that all? Good Lord! So they must be going to do it?

- I severely doubt it but it shows you something else doesn't it? All of the populations of Third World countries cannot afford a few pounds a year each to clear the debts themselves while the people that run these countries have learned from their developed world peers and swan around in Rolls Royces surrounded by security guards.

- They tend to live the high life do they not?

- They shall meet their maker. You see Jude there are many terrible things done in this world but one of the worst is that you are all being lied to.

- We are?

- Yes. People talk about countries becoming democratic and this is not true. Democracy does not work and never really has. If it did you would have more than a quarter of your population turning up to vote. The political system that is sweeping the world is capitalism. Capitalism has only two rules, make money and do not care about who suffers because of your actions. It is a horrible system and the vast majority strive, suffer and perish under its yoke. Love of money is the root of all evil you know.

- So they say. What do you think about all of this G.M. hoo-ha?

- It is a very good example of how the masses might suffer to make the rich richer. There is enough good land and food on this planet to feed everyone but that would not make large

145

companies enough money so they play about with nature to produce a seed that can resist their pesticides so that it is deemed to be better that natural seed. But the most cynical thing about this modified seed is that the plant itself will be sterile therefore every farmer has to buy the same grain from the same company every year. They will be trapped into doing so and that makes the shareholders happy. 'Who cares about the fact that it could turn out to be dangerous for the majority, this is *capitalism* for goodness sake!'

- But it will probably happen?

- It will happen because the people with power want it to happen. Genetically modified food is just one example of that capitalistic trend. Take the Euro for example. No-one actually knows if joining the Euro will be beneficial to ordinary people but you can be sure that it will be very good news for the few that are insisting you join it. The wants, not needs of the powerful and rich few are far more important than the genuine needs of the many. That is capitalism and it is ever growing. Now hospitals are businesses, schools are business and even churches are now businesses and a business can be defined as: 'The balance sheets are more important than the people.' Children will be taught how to invest their pocket money when it would be more beneficial to teach them sign language. Covetousness not communication is the basis of the curriculum.

- Capitalism is man's exploitation of man whereas Communism is the exact opposite?

- That is very clever but do you remember the comparison a little later in that book?

- The one directly comparing Communism and Christianity?

- That's the one.

- But that argument does not work. Heaven was compared to the fact that in Communist Russia the children of parents who had been good workers were given educational advantages but that in itself is immediately against equality and therefore not true Communism.

- True but it is the start of the process that eventually leads to all being equally educated. Communism never really got off the ground and capitalism has better P.R. and spin doctors.

- Spin doctors? I thought that was a modern phenomenon?

- Not at all. People in power have paid others to lie for them for centuries it is nothing new. What you should be asking yourself is why your new government has more of that accursed species than any previous government?

- Yes that is interesting is it not. Old Johnny Minor had about seven personal spin doctors but *Tony* has about seventy I think. Why would you say that is?

- Well work it out. Spin doctors are essentially professional liars so if there are more of them it follows that there is more to lie about.

- Computers, G.M. foods, hospitals, education, transport, foreign policy, Europe, Northern Ireland, spying in general, the police...

- That is some collection of lies. Spin doctors make sure that the lies get into the tabloids and onto the lowest common denominator television programs so that the majority of the population do not know what is really happening. That is why it is very sinister that there is no hard-hitting political satire in this country anymore. That wonderful traditional started by That Was the Week That Was, through Not the Nine O' Clock News to Spitting Image has disappeared. Is it because of hushed conversations in wine bars between spin doctors and T.V. officials? Who knows but they are all propagating mass ignorance. Most people haven't even heard of East Timor at the moment but they will.

- It is shocking what is going on there.

- It is merely capitalism in action. You know that film Alien where it leaps out of stomachs?

- Yes.

146

- That is what capitalism does to small developing countries. It sucks them in, develops its strength and then explodes killing the original host. The trouble with capitalism is that it fools you all. You were talking about your problem with the credit cards. Would you like some advice on that?
- Yes please Jesus.
- Get yourself a lawyer on legal aid and say that you were miss-sold the insurance.
- I tend to avoid lawyers myself.
- Why?
- Well the one I had for my litigation took money from the insurance company and ruined my case. They are not my favourite species but I shall take the advice since I have not got a clue how to sort this out.
- You were betrayed for money?
- Indeed.
- He is obviously a good capitalist, an excellent temple trader.
- You know what amazed me about the whole credit card situation?
- Go on Jude.
- How horrible the people that I talked to were. It completely threw me when I said: 'I am terribly sorry that my insurance does not cover me but I am now disabled and on income support and shall be for the rest of my life. I have no way of paying you back.' and their reply was: 'We don't care. We want our money back!' The thing is that it is not their money, it is the company's money. It does not affect their wage packets in the slightest so why are they so unpleasant to a human being because of this concept called money?
- That is their faith and reason to live. It is more important to them to impress their bosses with the hope of promotion and more money so they treat the less fortunate in a disgusting fashion. It is a shame that the majority of lives are purely about making money. Most people have nothing else in their lives than the pursuit of money labelled in the advertising as pleasure. One receives pleasure from *people* not objects and things yet they do not see the evil of money. Of your friends that owe you how many have you lost touch with?
- Six.
- In how many cases of friends or couples falling out is it over money?
- About ninety per cent I would hazard.
- Who knows but think about it. If money no longer existed how many less arguments would there be in the world? It would be a world where everyone has what they need.
- That sounds like socialism: 'From each their ability, to each their needs.'
- Indeed. That is another system that died a premature death. It is always a shame.
- But money will always exist because everyone is so covetous.
- As each man must die so must his creations. There will come a time when money no longer exists because it is merely a concept. That is being shown at the moment. Time was when a country's wealth was determined by the amount of gold that it had in the bank but now that is only a small and quite unimportant element. They will be selling gold soon and the price will drop. Now a country's wealth is based on things like market trends and so on that are completely conceptual. It is getting to the point where money will not actually exist at all.
- It will be replaced?
- With credit and only the people with power will know that.
- What can be done?
- The only way is to abolish money. It does not make the world turn round or the sun rise in the mornings.
- That was a tautology.

147

- You are a very clever man Jude.
- Thank you but I am not as clever as you. I do not even have a degree.
- I have two. Would you like one?
- If only life was that easy.
- You are not surprised that I have two degrees? Everyone else is.
- I am not everyone else and nor is anyone else. People should be taken as found without resorting to prejudice. You are obviously very intelligent and as far as I am aware coming from Columbia and having tattoos does not affect the brain in any way.
- Very true. You are an unusual young man Jude. You have not asked me the question that everyone asks me.
- What question is that then? I am not very good at being obvious, Jude the Obtuse one might say.
- Everyone asks me if I am a Christian.
- Do they? Oh. Are you?
- Yes.
- Good for you it is a pleasant faith.

- Is that all you want to say Jude? Normally people ask me lots of questions because of my namesake.
- Well I do not actually believe in your namesake and I am more interested in hearing about Columbia.
- You are a strange man Jude. You are publicly defiling yourself in a very artistic and ironic fashion and your reason? Hatred of covetousness and gluttony and all of the other sins. Some might say that you are being very Christian but you are obviously an agnostic.
- This is true but it might not be soon.
- Oh?
- I have done a deal with God you know.
- Have you now?
- Yes. This Sunday I am going to an evangelical church and I am going to ask them to heal me. Last Tuesday night I got very stoned you see and had an interesting conversation with the Big Boss during which I promised that if I am healed I shall dedicate the rest of my life to His service. In two days time I am going to the church to be healed. This time nest week I could be an able-bodied Christian.
- That will work then. Right I have finished.
- It looks wonderful.
- Yes I am very pleased with it. Will you come in and show me when it is healed?
- Of course.
- Now treatment. You will need to buy some Preparation H from the chemist. It is normally used for piles but it is perfect for tattoos in delicate places like the back of one's hand. Just smear some on twice a day until the scab has gone.
- Will it be all right until tomorrow as I will not be able to get to a chemist today?
- Oh yes. Have a little faith.
- Thank you. How much do I owe you although that is a strange question after our conversation.
- Thirty pounds please Jude.
- Have thirty-five.
- No. The price is thirty pounds and your needs are greater than mine.
- Are you sure?

148

- Yes and you don't need to ask me three times! You will come back and show me?
- Of course Jesus I would not let you down. Thank you very much for my tattoo and a pleasant afternoon. You know I expected it to be a lot more painful. See you in a couple of weeks.
- Good luck with your deal.

* * *

- JUDE! IT'S MAGS. JUDE ARE YOU THERE? PICK UP THE 'PHONE PICK UP THE 'PHONE. OH *BUGGER*! I just thought that I would tell you some gossip about the spooning muffin that I heard in this wine bar I was at with some friends yesterday after they called round at the house and had a smoke. Apparently his mum used to be a...

149

Saturday June 12th: **SLOTH**

I woke up dry and horny. I think I was dreaming of Solly. I wonder if that is short for something? Frustration, frustration, frustration. I could write a book on it! I had a Chinese lover once - the strange thing was that half an hour after sex I felt horny again!

What a day! I was on the go *all* the time. First Mags rang up which was good news as she is back on an even keel now. I must go and see her soon. Then I had to go to the chemist which was amusing and then to a costume shop for my outfit. They are strange places those. There was a man returning a lot of outfits saying: 'We seem to have lost a sombrero!' *Nutters*!

I got to the Carpenter's at about one to meet Andy who had also 'phoned and his dad John turned up. We had quite a heavy conversation after Andy left that I hope left us both feeling better. Will there ever be a day when someone is not miserable about something? Probably not.

I had to rush home to put my make up on for Puffin's party! Unfortunately my flat is now green everywhere - that is going to help sell it! The ears were a little tricky but I managed and the costume went down very well.

What a party! I must have fallen in love at least three times and I heard some very cheering news. I got home when I did and fell asleep dreaming of being healed and beautiful women. Tomorrow is H day.

* * *

- JUDE!
- Mags my sweetest angel! How are you feeling?
- I'm fine Jude, much better.
- That is bound to be the most fantastic news of the day.
- Other than your bloody answer machine cutting out when I'm about to tell you some juicy gossip.
- I know I am sorry Honey. I really should get one that does not do that but there again I am no gossip. All right what is the news?
- Well apparently his mother was a prostitute which is why he is so hung up about being adopted.
- The *poor* man! Life can be so cruel.
- You feel sorry for him?
- Of course I do! He blew his one chance with a gorgeous creature like you and he is ashamed of his heritage. The poor chap. It is all very well for us to discuss the pros and cons of prostitution, if you'll excuse the pun, but to find out that one's own mother has been a professional lady must come as quite a shock. I hope he has the emotional strength to deal with it and forgive her.
- You're being very generous to the toad Magnus.
- Well he did not do you any damage did he?
- No I just missed a day's work and woke up with a hangover. I suppose you're right.
- How are you feeling in yourself now?
- Absolutely fine if a little, what's the word?

150

- Anticlimactical?

- That's the one. I'm just wondering if it's worth bothering with men at all.

- Of *course* it is! Love is the most beautiful thing in the world when it actually is love. I heard a definition of love the other day that I thought was rather good; unconditional, positive regard. Do you like that?

- Say it again?

- Unconditional, positive regard. That is the sort of love that babies have for their parents which is why parents of new-borns are always so uplifted because they are loved whatever they do. It is a wonderful feeling. You see, my dearest Mags you are in the most empowered situation due to your efforts and bravery over the past few years.

- Am I?

- Absolutely! You are now completely self-sufficient. You are a whizz at D.I.Y., you can cook very well and you have a high-flying career. The only things you actually need a man for are fun, love and babies if you want them.

- Yuck! No thanks.

- Well just the first two then but you have all the time to find the right man and I think that you will.

- But it is so much effort.

- Oh do not be so lazy. Having men take you to dinner and try to impress you is hardly a Herculean task is it now?

- I suppose not.

- Remember that we now live in a society of choice. It is absolutely your choice and prerogative when you decide to sleep with a man again. It could be hours after meeting him or months. You should enjoy the near-equality that you now have but not revenge.

- You've already told me that.

- Have I?

- Yes on Wednesday.

- I do apologise. It is one of the disadvantages of being an old soak. Sometimes I repeat myself, other times I say the same thing more than once and I even have conversations that are pure reiteration. Does it show?

- You are completely mad Jude!

- I think you will actually find that in the scheme of things I am only just into eccentric territory as far as your archetypal, classic Jude is concerned.

- You're an archetypal Jude are you? Who are you going to betray?

- Just myself Honey, just myself. But we are talking about you and your finding true love and happiness.

- Some chance. I haven't even seen anyone I fancy in ages.

- That is because you had a type of man that turned you on and the two of that type that you had relationships with let you down badly. Psychologically that is very confusing but you must keep trying because it is worth it and I want you to find the right man so that I can be your best man.

- Girls don't have best men silly.

- *Doh*! Shall I give you a clue? Real love is when your partner has foibles that amuse you. If he has bad habits that drive you up the wall then something is not right and always listen to your friends because they can see it when it happens. When one is infatuated it is like being in a mist that starts off very exciting and intriguing but all your friends are shouting for you to watch out. As one carries on through the mist doubts and fears start to creep in until suddenly

151

it clears and one finds oneself on the edge of a cliff! The sort of cliff that is not singing: 'Living doll!'
- That's a bit frightening.
- That is what happens when you are with the wrong fella. You keep looking out for your David Niven. Actually I had a thought the other day that I thought you would like.
- What's that then?
- How important humour is to every aspect of a relationship. If one has laughter then difficulties are kept at bay. A laugh a day keeps divorce away one might say.
- Stop it!
- Sorry. But think of it this way. If one asked a widow to talk about her husband most would start crying but Mrs. Morecambe, for example would be smiling and laughing through the tears. Does that make any sense?
- Sort of.
- When troubles occur in a relationship the easy option is to get angry and fight but if one sees the other point of view and the humour of the situation it is a lot easier to resolve the problem. I suppose that is what these people mean when they say that one has to work at a relationship.
- I've always wondered what they meant by that.
- I assume that they mean one has to actually bother, care and put some effort in to understanding one's partner.
- That can be difficult.
- Certainly. It is a lot harder to be faithful than it is to indulge in infidelity. It is also a lot easier for men to be aggressive, threatening and violent to women than it is to communicate effectively.
- Tell me about it.
- I know Honey. You were very brave during an incredibly difficult time of your life but you did the right thing, you left the vicious hatechild. If every woman in the country signed a pact with each other so that at the first hint of violence or infidelity they would walk out without another word, things would be very different would they not?
- Yeah but it will never happen as you're always going to have some silly tart saying: 'But I love 'im!'
- It is sloth my heart. If women spent as much time looking out for each other as they do worry about their make up I feel you would all be a lot happier.
- You've never done any of that have you Jude?
- Any of what?
- Violence or infidelity?
- Good Lord no although I did once try sleeping around but I got it all wrong.
- What do you mean?
- I slept with the same woman in seven different beds in one week!
- I think you got the wrong end of the Moses on that one!
- Very good! Ho-ly Mos-es, King of the wild frontier. I think I got that one a bit wrong as well!
- Just a little bit. Nice voice though, you should sing more.
- Thank you, I shall have to serenade you one evening!
- I'd better get some work done.
- I believe that is the basis of your contract.
- I must come down soon.
- Or I up?
- We'll sort something out.

- How is the job going?
- *Brilliant*! I'll tell you when I see you. Thank you for all of your help this week Jude I don't know what I would have done without you.
- It is my pleasure and honour now get to work woman! Love you.
- Love you too.

* * *

- Hello Peter old chap how the devil are you?
- Oh *God* look who's turned up. We had a lovely Judeless day in here yesterday and now you have to spoil it all by showing up now.
- You missed me really did you not?
- Jude the only time that I might ever miss you, I would curse my bad aim and eyesight. I suppose you want to raid the Harveys barrel?
- If you would be so kind.
- Don't think politeness can get you anywhere.
- Are you all right? You seem a tad more unpleasant than usual?
- I'm fine it's just that being rude is easier than being polite. How are you though, you're looking a trifle peaky this morning?
- I am all right mate thank you.
- We were a hint worried when you didn't turn up yesterday. I know there isn't a contract that orders you to come here every day but you are considered part of the fixtures and fittings.
- Oh Peter I am touched.
- That was very apparent within the first five minutes of meeting you! Have you been vandalising yourself again?
- Do you like my new tattoo? I think it works rather well don't you think?
- Is this your protest against capitalism? I'll bet Bobby Styles is quaking in his virtual boots. You are looking like a walking battlefield at the moment with your spot and tattoos. Let's have a look. What are the numbers?
- My parents' dates of birth.
- Oh very ironic! What do you think it would come up as in a supermarket?
- I would hope that it would be a crate of beer and a carton of Marlboro.
- Knowing you it is probably a bumper pack of nappies.
- I have thought of that and they would not be unuseful I can assure you.
- Why?
- With the number of my friends that have babies, what did you think that I meant?
- I wouldn't like to say.
- Or I could sew them all together to make a novelty duvet.
- It would be rather noisy though. I suppose you want another?
- A pint of pain killer please landlord. Are you having one?
- No thanks Jude I'm feeling a little rough. I think I ate something that's disagreeing with me.
- What did your stomach just say? 'Oh no you haven't!'
- Oh very amusing. That was an old Viz cartoon wasn't it?
- It is amazing to think now that I bought the first copy of that by post in what, '87 I think.
- You are getting old.
- I think my favourite Viz joke was the spoof advert for toilet tissue.
- Go on, I know you're dying to tell me.

- Well they had the puppies leaping about and the caption was: 'Spandex - soft on your bum and your fingers don't come through!' Having been in advertising and had to think up the lies for rubbish products that line rather tickled me.
- Yes. I've found a new shop up the road that sells the most marvellous cards. There is a series that you would like.
- Really?
- They involve Moses you see.
- Is that the one: 'What do you mean muddy?'
- That's it, you've seen them?
- Seen them, liked them, bought them. They also have a good range of Far Side cards as well which I love.
- My favourite is the two deer chatting and one of them has a target on his chest with the caption: 'Bummer of a birthmark Hal!'
- It is brilliant is it not? My fave is the one set in a packed circus tent with a dog on a unicycle on the high wire with a cat in his mouth and juggling.
- I haven't seen that one what's the caption?
- 'Above the hushed crowd Rex went through his act with style and aplomb but at the back of his mind there was one nagging doubt; he was an old dog and this was a new trick!'
- Wonderful. Oh here comes the Friday lunch crowd. I wonder which bank's canteen is bereft of boring bastards this week?

* * *

- Hello Jude.
- Andy! You look worn out as ever have you been working too hard again?
- Eighteen hour day yesterday.
- You poor love. Sit your weary self down and have a pint of something restorative. You work far too hard for your own good which is something of a novelty in this day and age. Far too many people are very good at talking and absolutely hopeless at doing.
- Yeah I know. John's coming down in a bit.
- Yes? How marvellous, I do like your Dad. How is he doing?
- I don't know. His Mum died a month ago...
- I know mate.
- And he hasn't reacted as yet. He just seems to be...
- Stoic?
- Yeah stoic about the whole thing. And he's drinking way too much. He keeps ringing me up when he's pissed and I don't want to talk to him when he's out of his head, it winds me up.
- He is obviously in pain. Here let me bring a smile to your face with a joke that I thought was rather appropriate to your situation.
- What situation is that then?
- You and your dear lady wife.
- You've never liked her much have you?
- She got on perfectly well with David Atombomb!
- Ha, ha! You know what I mean.
- I think that you will find that most of your friends would be happy to get on with Deborah if it was not for the fact that she hates all of us. But anyway here is the joke. I do not mean to wind you up as you put it.
- O.K. Jude.

154

- Imagine if you will a small boy who woke up of a morning and went into his parents' bedroom only to see them making love quite noisily and so he left discretely. At breakfast a little later he asked his dad: 'What were you and mummy doing this morning?' 'Ah.' said the father, 'You see son your mother wants you to have a little brother or sister to keep you company so this morning you saw us making a baby.'

- Perfectly reasonable.

- Indeed. However the next morning the little boy again went into his parents' room but this time he witnessed fellatio in full swing and was somewhat confused. At breakfast your boy quizzed his dad once more but this time the father looked a little sombre: 'Son.' he said, 'Yesterday I lied to you. When I said that your mother wanted you to have a new sibling that was incorrect. What she actually wants is a new B.M.W.!'

- Very droll but what has that got to do with my marital situation?

- Well you are a hint under the thumb is I believe the expression. I do not want to be rude or anything my friend but people do giggle at you, openly.

- At least I *am* married Jude. Some might say that you are a touch on the shelf now?

- Ouch! What a horrible expression! Surely it is never too late for love but I have done you a favour you know?

- Oh yeah what's that then?

- I have never done my favourite couple wind-up on you because I know it would lead to divorce.

- What are you talking about?

- The best way to get a couple going is if you are having a drink, a meal or whatever when the lady goes to the loo and then returns after a time you say to the partner: 'Go on! Say to her face what you were just telling me!'

- That is *nasty*!

- I know which is why I would never do it to you. Deborah would never believe either of us that it was a wind-up.

- She's not that bad.

- I know mate, you love each other and that is all that counts. After all you are a father now with another on the way which does take priority over drinking partners, much as I miss your regular company. However I do feel it was rather harsh saying that I was on the shelf. I have plenty of time to find a woman that has the tolerance required to put up with me.

- You're not that bad.

- Thank you kind sir, I shall rush to you for my next testimonial. At least I have had love in my life which is more than a lot of people in this world can say. I shall never forget the first time I saw a woman climax in my arms, it was almost a spiritual experience.

- It is rather marvellous isn't it. It sort of makes the whole thing make sense.

- Deep brother, deep. The thing that I do not understand is why good sex is apparently still so elusive for the general populus? Every week there is another magazine headlining: 'Twenty top tips for sex!' and you see all of these sad people buying it and hoping for clues. Considering that mankind has been having sex since it existed one would have thought that the majority should actually have some idea by now would one not?

- One certainly would. I don't understand either.

- One can only presume that people are too lazy or preoccupied to actually talk to each other and find out what the other wants. Or of course the majority of men are too lazy to bother about good, prolonged sex. It is odd the way that being slothful actually restricts the enjoyment one can get from life. I do think that it is a major problem in these times. Certainly

155

if ignorance is one of the main faults in society then it is sloth that is holding up change. People simply seem too lazy to get an educated perspective.

- Ignorance is everywhere I agree. I was at the supermarket the other day and there was a problem with the tills so that they couldn't do the automated bit. I had two tins of baby food and the girl at the checkout had to use a calculator to work out how much I owed them! Then I discovered an old fiver in my wallet and I made a comment about the Battle of Waterloo but she said: 'Yes, poor king Harold. An arrow right in the eye!'.

- Amazing! It comes back to the old adage that a little bit of knowledge is a dangerous thing. You know all of this hoo-ha about global warming?

- Sure.

- These experts come out and say that actually it will mean a temperature increase of about two degrees so there is not much to worry about but it seems to me that the best analogy for what is happening is a duvet.

- A duvet?

- Sure. The ozone layer does a lot of good things but it acts like a duvet to the planet so ozone depletion means that the duvet is getting thinner which results in warmer summers and colder winters. This is what we are experiencing, more extreme weather all year so that the average over the year will not change much.

- So the Summers are hotter and the Winters are colder and the mean doesn't change much. That makes sense. Why haven't I heard that before?

- God knows. People do not seem to bother to *think* these days which is why it is such a pain being like this. No-one actually thinks about what they say so they all say the same things. There is no thought about what is an appropriate topic of conversation.

- Do you get a lot of that?

- All the time mate. Only last week I was having a pint and I put my foot up on a seat because it swells up less when horizontal. This woman asked me to take my foot off the chair and how rude I was doing it.

- What did you say?

- I kept my temper if that is what you are implying and I merely informed the lady that I was disabled and pointed out that as a human being I was slightly more important than an inanimate object. She was very embarrassed: 'Oh I'm sorry I didn't realise...'

- It must be annoying.

- One gets used to all sorts of things. Have you heard of middle-class malnutrition?

- No what's that?

- It is a horrible example of the a little bit of knowledge situation. Apparently parents have heard a meagre morsel about nutrition from daytime T.V. and so on and are eating healthily themselves but they are also forcing their children to eat low fat, vegetarian diets which is of course very bad for them. Growing children need lots of fats and sugars et cetera plus if a child is brought up as a vegetarian he or she will never be able to eat meat since the appropriate enzymes are never developed. So all across the country children are suffering from stunted growth and in extreme cases brain deformation because their parents are essentially starving them.

- Really? Deborah's a veggie and we have been discussing this.

- If people want to be vegetarian that is very much their choice and right but it is absolutely wrong to rob children of choice and endanger their health. An individual's rights are slightly more important than those of animals. The fact is that parents know more about soft furnishings than nutrition because they are too damn slothful to find out. It is absolutely *scandalous*!

156

- Is that true? If you don't feed children meat they will never be able to eat it?
- They can eat it but they will not be able to digest it and it will make them rather ill as will the inevitable lack of essential amino acids. One must give them meat until they can make a choice for themselves as adults. What amazes me is parents saying that they are concerned about their children's diet but then take them to macslimes! What *are* they doing?
- They're pretty horrible aren't they?
- They are absolute rubbish! I am not a fan of food generally but I would never eat one of *those* things. I would have to be so drunk to even contemplate eating a burger that I would not be able to walk into the place! Everyone knows that they are foul and also that the company itself does not do a great deal of good for the environment but instead of people boycotting those disgusting pseudo-restaurants, as they should, they take their children there! Are they *mad*? No they are just lazy because it is easier to give in to a sulking child that has been brainwashed with advertising than it is to teach them about proper food and nutrition.
- I will certainly never take Henry there.
- Do you know an interesting fact?
- Plenty thank you but I think you are about to tell me a new one.
- Now there is propellor-head logic for you! Did you know that the only survivor of the Massacre of Glencoe was Ronald McDonald?
- No!
- Absolutely true. Mind you it is not surprising, they must have burst out laughing when they saw him: 'Leave the clown alone! Put the clown *down*!'
- Have you ever had a burger?
- Once many years ago. I was twelve I think and in a choir that was on an exchange trip to North America.
- You were on a choir trip? You are so middle class.
- I know but I am not ashamed. Was it John Fowles who said: 'The middle classes have been distinguishable throughout history as the only class to despise themselves.'?
- I don't know.
- I think so but I refuse to be ashamed because I am middle class and I firmly believe that everyone has the right to the privileges I enjoyed. A good education and worldly experience are fundamental to quality of life for everyone and that is why I am a middle class socialist. Anyway we were on a choir trip and were driving from Seattle to Vancouver which is a *beautiful* part of the world and I was in the front seat of a minibus admiring the views. The American chap driving the thing suddenly said: 'Here we are, the golden arches!' and I thought he was referring to a landmark of some description. What a *disappointment*!
- I can imagine.
- It is an interesting example of the way that advertising does affect us. Twenty boys aged from nine to thirteen who had never heard of macslimes were ushered into the place and burgers, fries and cokes were placed in front of us with the surrounding adults expecting us to be joyous or something. In reality we gingerly opened the cartons and were utterly *appalled* at the contents. If I recall only one of us ate the whole thing and his party piece was drinking ink! The rest of us were hungry until dinner. It is only the hype that makes children want to go to these places.
- And the bribery of toys.
- Absolutely it is very cynical. But so many parents are simply not informed about anything. Take dyslexia for example. How many children these days are labelled dyslexic?
- Thousands and lots of adults claim to be as well.

- I am very dubious about the whole thing. You see if I were nine years old *now* I would be called dyslexic.
- Really?
- Oh yes. At that age I could not spell at all in fact I had a little book with 'sepling' written on it! There are people with genuine dyslexia but for most of the people it is just laziness. My English teacher at the time told me to read and read and then read some more and once I had done that to do some reading. 'It doesn't matter what.' he said, 'Just read!' and I did. After six years of reading all the time I could spell reasonably well.
- How did you achieve that?
- Well I find it very hard to work with phonetics so I memorise words in their entirety. If I have seen a word I can spell it if not I cannot.
- That must have been interesting as a journalist.
- Thank the Lord for spell-checks! This is why I used to make a big deal about the difference between spell-checking and proof-reading and how one should do both. Most people are just lazy about it and only do one but it seems that labelling someone as dyslexic just gives them an excuse to go through life admitting to not being able to spell properly. What is the point of that? I overcame the problem through hard work over a long period which seems to be rather out of fashion these days.
- You do come out with some wild theories Jude. Dyslexics are just lazy?
- Utterly slothful! No not really but I do think there is a great deal of room for a lot more effort on the part of many. You see making an effort in life improves the quality no end. You have been working incredibly hard for about four years now?
- Five.
- And look at what you have, a lovely house, a thriving business and no financial worries for your family. You work so hard that Deborah does not have to.
- She might work part-time again.
- But she has the *choice* not to due to your hard work. If you had been slothful where would you be now?
- Fucked.
- Exactly.
- Did you hear about the dyslexic diabolist?
- Sold his soul to Santa!
- Do you know every joke Jude?
- It feels that way sometimes. There are a few dyslexic gags are there not? The same diabolist went to a toga party as a goat, the dyslexic pimp bought a warehouse and dyslexics of the world should untie but my favourite is the dyslexic skiers.
- Go on?
- Well they were having a ski but wanted to be a little more adventurous so they headed for the slalom. At the top they got into something of a discussion over whether they should zig-zag down the slope or zag-zig.
- It must have been very confusing.
- Certainly. After a while another chap wondered past and they enlisted his assistance: 'Were both dyslexic.' they said, 'We don't know if we should zig-zag or zag-zig down the slope?' 'Don't look at me.' the chap replied, 'I'm a tobboganist.' 'Oh!' they responded, 'Well while you're here can we have twenty Marlboro and a box of matches?'
- That's brilliant.
- It is a fave of mine but why do people not put more effort into their own lives? Sloth is so counterproductive. Take phobias for example, lots of people are scared of all sorts of things

like 'planes, spiders, snakes, you name it but very few do anything about it and so spend their whole lives with an irrational fear. Some spend a lot of money on quack treatment which essentially involves someone telling them how ridiculous their fear is but most do nothing: 'I can't go and see my son in America because I am scared of flying.'
- These fears are genuine though.
- Oh I know I used to have a phobia that was terrifying.
- What was that then?
- Think about it. You know my history and you remember your stag do when I refused to go go-carting?
- Sure. Do you mean you were scared of driving?
- I was scared of cars, highly nervous when in one and petrified of driving itself bearing in mind that I could not drive at that point as I had only had one driving lesson in a car.
- But you drive now.
- Well I cannot now unless it is an automatic but yes I learned how to drive three years ago, I overcame my phobia.
- How?
- I had driving lessons, this is not rocket science you know! The first one I had I was shaking and sweating like you would not believe and I had to tell the instructor why I had turned the colour of snow but he was very understanding and I passed my test three months later.
- First time?
- It was, yes. I have never actually liked driving and I certainly do not miss it now but I overcame my fears to an extent were they stopped frustrating my life. People who say: 'I can't do that I'm scared.' are just putting obstacles in front of themselves. Get over it and stop making excuses for underachieving! Did I ever tell you about my first driving lesson?
- No?
- It was quite hysterical. I was seventeen and something of a muffin to be honest. This chap turned up in an old Metro and we drove down to the sea front. Because I had been driving bikes I knew about gears and so on and I quickly picked up how to change gears and use the clutch et cetera. Unfortunately I picked it up a little too quickly and within a few minutes we were speeding along the sea front. Then a police car hoved into view and we were pulled over.
- You were done for speeding in your first lesson?
- No but the instructor was, being legally in charge of the vehicle. It did not endear me to him particularly. Then we went to a car park along the road and he told me to try a three point turn. I threw the car around the gravel for a few moments before proudly announcing: 'Did it in two!' He was not impressed and decided to give me a real driving experience, down to the pier.
- That's a busy road for your first lesson!
- I know but at that age I was fearless and it was quite fun until I got to the traffic lights. Because I had been used to bikes I completely forgot about the hand brake and the car started rolling forward. The instructor panicked and yelled: 'Quick the hand brake the hand brake!' and I pulled the thing right out of the floor! At this point his nerve failed entirely and I had to drive round the corner to park. He said: 'Look I have a wife and two children. I never want you in my car again!' That was the end of my driving lessons at that point in time.
- Only you Jude. That could only happen to you.
- I know. I sometimes feel very alone in the world like the old expression of the only boy marching in step. Do you think about modern issues and wonder what the hell is going on? Like the new things being put on the school curriculum. Children are now going to be taught how to best use their pocket money would you credit? I am not that old but when I was a child

159

your parents taught you that, in fact your parents taught you as much as you learned at school. What has happened?

- You obviously have a theory?

- One can only assume that parents now just plonk their kids in front of the T.V., a computer game or something instead of communicating with them so that not only are modern children being denied as much in the way of knowledge as we had but they are also being spoon-fed the rubbish and propaganda that streams from the goggle box merely because their parents are being slothful.

- You're a bit intense today Jude.

- Well it annoys me that most people cannot be bothered to enrich their own lives. You see it does affect things. In this country we are always short of blood donors as only five per cent of the population give blood regularly which I find absolutely *inexcusable*. Do you give blood?

- No I'm anaemic.

- That is fair enough, a lot of people are not allowed to but why do more people not give blood? It *does* save lives. What possible reason can anyone have for not giving blood? A reasonable excuse does not exist.

- Some people are scared of needles.

- Hah! That is possibly the most *pathetic* excuse in the world! Are you trying to tell me that some people are refusing to help save lives because they are *scared of needles?* What is going on inside their heads? Apart from anything else I have donated ten times now and I have never even seen a needle. There is a tiny amount of discomfort...

- You might feel a bit of a prick?

- So what's new? And it takes about half an hour every sixteen weeks but people just cannot be bothered can they? It is utter sloth and others suffer as a result.

- So the world's problems are down to laziness?

- It is not quite that simple. A lot of problems are caused by sloth but the reason nothing is done about *all* the planet's problems is completely down to apathy and inertia. No-one wants to know but the silly thing is that when ones does actually make an effort it really helps. You know that I have done a lot of public speaking in my time? Well I never get nervous until about five minute before the actual speaking. People who have something along those lines like an interview or whatever spend the week beforehand worrying about it. What a waste of time! I spend that week running through the whole thing in my head and planning it completely in case something should go wrong so that when it comes to the moment I am slightly nervous but very confident and generally do rather well. Or did until recently. Does that make sense?

- Of course but people don't do that as they always leave everything until the last moment and then panic. You would call that sloth I presume? Look John's coming now so do what you do best and cheer the old bastard up.

- I shall endeavour my friend.

- Hello boys how are we?

- I'm O.K. John.

- Great thanks mate. Can I assume that you are in need of liquid refreshment?

- Absolutely Jude. What's the wine like in here?

- The rouge is perfectly quaffable and the blanc I would not know about as I never touch the stuff.

- Really? Why's that?

- For some reason it gives me chronic indigestion which is never a good drinking companion.

- I'll have a glass of rouge then please Jude.

- Peter? Can we have a bucket of the red kerosene? You will need to be careful John, if you spill that stuff it tends to eat through the floor.
- Sounds like the sort of stuff I like. What's that on your hand Jude?
- My new tattoo that your observant son has completely failed to notice.
- Oh yeah? What's that all about then?
- It is a little protest against rich and greedy people but let me tell you what happened this morning. Apparently the best thing for treating new tattoos is to smear them with this stuff called Preparation H.
- That's for piles isn't it?
- Indeed John, in your maturity you are obviously far more familiar with that condition than we mere whipper snappers.
- It has been a while since I whipped a snap or snapped a whip.
- They make them too well these days! Anyway I went to the chemist along the road from me this morning to buy some. My local chemist is more like a library than a shop it is so quiet and my walking in halved the average age! I went to the counter to ask for some Preparation H and the lady asked if I would prefer ointment or a suppository. I opted for the ointment to which she replied: 'Yes it is a bit more comfortable isn't it.'
- She didn't realise?
- Why should she? I paid for the stuff after thanking the nice lady and sat down on the seats that are there for people awaiting their prescriptions next to a little old lady. You know when you know everyone is watching you whilst pretending not to?
- All the time Jude.
- Well I knew that everyone in the shop was watching me as I took the tube from the box and made a hole in the top of it. The tension was palpable and the little old lady was shifting nervously away from me. I put a big dollop of the stuff on my right index finger and carefully replaced the tube in its box. No-one had said a word or even breathed for three minutes. I then rubbed the ointment into the tattoo and left the shop thanking them for their kind help. For some reason they all were leaning on surfaces and breathing out in a relieved fashion. I wonder why?
- You are a piss-taking bastard Jude.
- You should have taken your trousers off as well!
- I think that might have been overdoing it John. I could have cause a heart attack!
- Upsetting old ladies should be against the law.
- Au contraire dear Andy it is a marvellous spectator sport. But talking of stories have you heard about the Waifs and Strays Christmas Do two years ago John?
- Do you have to Jude?
- Andy, did you not say that your Father might need cheering up? What better way to achieve that end than to humiliate you in front of him?
- Oh go on then.
- What's the Waifs and Strays Christmas Do?
- It is a party organised in here by my good friend Jamie the printer.
- Jamie the nutter more like.
- Now, now Andy he is a damn good friend. I do not know about you John but to me a mellowed, salt of the earth Scouser with a colourful history makes a very good drinking partner and general mate.
- He does sound interesting.
- Interesting! He's a nutter.

- He is one of those people whose presence ensures that any party will not be quiet John. One of my favourite stories of him was time in Fecamp before he met his 'Alleged Dear Lady Wife Whose Name Currently Escapes Me' as he calls her when he was determined to get laid, for want of a more erudite expression.
- You are making yourself abundantly clear Jude.
- Thank you John. He had tried quite a few ladies when he turned his attention to one that was a police woman. He had just started on his charming patter when she said: 'Look Jamie, I've already got one c*** in my knickers I don't need you there too!'
- Excellent!
- He is quite a character although of course more settled now. Every year he organises a party in here for anyone who is self or unemployed since they do not get their own Christmas parties. We have a few drinkies, then lunch and everyone has to do a party piece whilst wearing the Antlers of Mirth.
- Which are?
- A pair of silly party antlers with flashing lights. Andy was invited but could not come although he did manage to pop in for a drink at about four in the afternoon on his way back from shopping. We were having a good chat and I insisted that he have another beer. For some reason which I have forgotten he was wearing the antlers. Suddenly Deborah burst through the doors and although she is only a petite woman it was like Moses, the real Moses and the Red Sea as everyone was diving out of her way she looked so angry. Andy was standing at the far end of the bar head down, antlers drooping as she stormed up to him and in a voice of thunder demanded: 'What the *hell* do you think you are doing?' Poor Andy did not have a chance to reply before she bellowed: 'Come home now!' and *threw* the antlers across the pub. In absolute silence Andy traipsed after her with hung head and we all looked on in utter disbelief.
- Did that actually happen Andrew?
- Yes John. Thank you for that Jude.
- My pleasure Andy. John seems remarkably cheered now.
- I haven't laughed so much in ages. What were you two talking about it seemed very intense?
- We were discussing the amount of laziness and sloth that one encounters almost everywhere these days.
- Ah sloth, it's a deadly sin you know?
- Indeed.
- I would blame it upon a lack of education myself.
- Would you mate?
- Oh God, they're both off!
- Somewhat uncharitable Andy since I am sure your father has insight into the situation.
- Well it struck me the other day how there does seem to be a reduction in the levels of basic education that I am sure is not down to the teachers themselves. The other thing I have noticed is the level of pseudo-education that exists. People claim to have knowledge that they don't actually have.
- Like film experts?
- What do you mean Jude?
- Well John, one often hears or sees people that are very knowledgeable about films which is one way to sound intelligent without actually having any in depth knowledge on topics other than films.
- That is intellectual snobbery Jude.
- Good! Because Andy if there are not people like me saying that situations like this are quasi-education then it will be accepted. To find a middle path one has to see two extremes.

162

What I mean is that it is perfectly feasible to have no standard education other than watching films and sound knowledgeable because one can glean all sorts of bits of information from that medium without knowing anything in depth about the subject concerned. One could claim to be knowledgeable about the history of the American Indians whereas in fact there has never been a Hollywood film that comes anywhere close to the reality of that horrific scenario. It is virtual knowledge in today's parlance.

- What you are saying is that when one is knowledgeable generally then one already knows about the content of an historical film rather than the other way around?
- Precisely John. I can honestly say that I do not understand the current teaching practices. Why do children need to be taught how to use computers?
- Why do children need to learn how to use computers?
- Congratulations Andy you have won today's Mynah Bird Impersonation Contest! Yes that is what I said.
- But why do you say it Jude?
- Two reasons. I have been lucky enough to have had a good education as a result of which I have only needed an hour's tuition in I.T. to use a computer with no problem. It strikes me that it is neither easy nor hard but simply a small amount of knowledge and then progression through logic. Secondly the more advanced computers become the easier it is to use and understand them so why do we need to teach children how to use computers? It seems that it is the easy option for teachers who have little control in the classroom and we are back to sloth again.
- It's not as simple as that Jude.
- Of course it is Andy, the majority of things in life are simple once the politics and claptrap have been removed. We seem to have a cycle of covetousness and sloth. Parents will work all hours of the day to afford a large home and all the gadgets money can buy which means that they have little time for their children. So they go and buy a computer with all the whistles and bells to give the child a parent substitute as far as learning is concerned because mummy and daddy are out earning money to pay for all this or too knackered and uninterested when they get home. What *utter* stupidity!
- So what would you suggest instead Jude?
- Well John it would appear that technology is progress but whether it is toward good or bad it is hard to tell. The constant complaint of the police is that criminals are using technology to outwit them. Certainly when one has football hooliganism being organised over the Internet something has gone horribly wrong. I do think that being surrounded by electronic distractions does not help a child's development in any way. How many children would nowadays think that a thesaurus was a type of dinosaur?
- Possibly quite a few.
- The original idea of computers and so on was to increase efficiency and productivity but how often have you *actually* seen that? If anything our technological world is far more inefficient than ever. They call it computer error but in fact it is human sloth and indifference. How many 'phone calls and different data centres does one have to go through to sort out a simple error on a credit card bill? Through the Internet we have access to all sorts of knowledge and information but it has actually helped the pornography industry far more than most. Paedophiles now have a way of organising and distributing material and as for organised crime the mind boggles. But everyone just sits and lets all of this happen as long as it does not affect *them* too much. If you are talking of deadly sins sloth is by far the worst.
- Actually Jude it is pride that is the main deadly sin.

- Not any more John. There is much in this world that can be categorised as pride and envy and so on but the single reason that these can carry on unscathed is because no-one can be bothered to stand up and say anything. The world is full of clever people clinging on to stupid ideas. But do you know why? Why is it that the insult of this generation is: 'Get a life'? Because most people do not have lives. They get up, they go to work, they come home and eat, they watch T.V., they have a row and they go to bed. At the weekend they do what the T.V. has been telling them to do all week whether it is D.I.Y., cooking, watching football with the lads or going shopping. If they are lucky they will actually communicate and make love once a month which is also how often he and she do not worry about money. Where is the joy, the spontaneity, the laughter, the love, the expression, the freedom, the giving, the energy, the drive and the reason for living in the first place? No-one has to think for themselves anymore so they do not bother. 'Banish individuality misery with the all new Ronco Virtual Life. Never again will you have the burdensome task of thinking for yourself - all your thoughts are supplied.' You say that pride is the worst of the seven deadly sins. Rubbish! It is *sloth*. Why is America allowed to bully the rest of the world, why are politicians allowed to be exploitative liars, why are soap operas allowed to spread their malicious poison, why are the rich allowed to squander money that could save lives, why are women highly unlikely to receive anything like justice if they are raped, why is it that the levels of education across the world are consistently falling, why is it that the money a big corporation deems to be its own is more important that any human life, why does everyone think that everyone else is better off than they are, why is it that some countries have a fifty per cent obesity problem whilst others starve, why is there so much violence and why is it that this world is such an *unpleasant* place all of a sudden? Because no-one can be arsed to do anything about it! As we approach the millennium, the eclipse and Nostradamus' deadline and everyone is whispering: 'Armageddon!' can no-one see that we are approaching an oblivion of our own creation that *nobody* is doing anything about? The world will go out, not with a bang but with the whimper of sloth.
- There's too much apathy in the world but who cares!
- I hope that you do not expect me to laugh at that Andy?
- Maybe not but I need to get going.
- Thanks for the drink mate, I hope to see you soon.
- Give me a call later Andrew.
- Will do John. See you Jude.

* * *

- He is a fine man is Andy, you must be very proud.
- Oh I am, I am and of his sister too.
- But you feel that they do not look up to you in the same way that you looked up to your parents.
- No I don't.
- I am sorry about your Mum John. There is only one thing harder than losing one's parents.
- What's that?
- Losing one's children. To have a child die is possibly the most meaningless and destructive thing that can happen to a human being. How are you feeling mate?
- Empty.
- But you have so much John.

- I have lost the people that I loved and respected most in the world and I have no idea what to do with myself.
- Other than getting trashed all of the time?
- Other than getting trashed all of the time but can you blame me? *You?*
- Not in the slightest. I have skimmed the surface of hypocrisy in the name of caring or so they say. Tell me about them John, tell me about your parents.
- It's very hard to.
- Would you like to though? Think about it John.

- Yes I would.
- I tell you what. You know the old joke about the guy that says: 'Do you know the way to Milton Keynes?' and the answer is: 'No, but you start and I'll hum along!', you know that joke?
- Yes of course.
- Well mate we shall do it like that. If talk about my parents and you join in and take over all right? I shall tell you a funny story about them because it is their humour and their open-mindedness that make my folks so fab. Years ago, when I was about ten years old I went for my first meal in a restaurant.
- Jude you're starting to sound poor! Do we need a fiddle?
- No mate not at all, we were not poor we were middle class. I went to public school! Even more middle class I was expelled but that is another story. You see John my parents sent four children through public school education by supplementing their incomes at every possible opportunity. When I was very young life was glorious. My Father was a research chemist in Leicester and my Mother was an up and coming musician. There was not much money but who cared? By the time I was ten I had three siblings and the house was full of lodgers and foreign students to raise money for our education as my parents had decided that the best gift that they could give to their children was the best education that money could buy. So instead of having the latest fashions we had music lessons. Instead of having a new, shiny B.M.X. I had extra lessons in the subjects I was weak on and my cousin's old Chopper, if you'll pardon the expression!
- Consider yourself pardoned.
- 'Consider yourself, one of the fam-il-ly!' How much more middle-class can a joke be? But I was saying.
- I do apologise.
- Think nothing of it dear sir. Instead of having family holiday to Majorca we had choir trips to America while the folks stayed home and took another foreign student in for a few weeks. Especially during the Summer our house would be full of people from *all over* the place. No-one watched television because there was too much going on and there was a park opposite for goodness sake! It was Summer and the world was waiting for us. Can you imagine trying to teach German exchange students Cricket?
- Good God man! You'll give me a heart attack.
- Exactly! I had the most wonderful childhood and upbringing that any man could ever ask for. How many people do you know that can say that without irony? That is why the middle classes feel guilty.
- You were going to tell me a story.
- Oh yes sorry. When I was ten or so I was taken out to dinner for the first time by the parents of my best friend at school. They were also lovely as it happens. They had money but they were very generous and took me on holidays, to restaurants all the time, to the theatre you

165

name it: 'Taxis all the way Professor 'Iggins!' So I came back from this Chinese meal that I had been out on, at which a lifelong love affair with Barbecue Spare Ribs was first consummated and after a couple of days I asked my Mother why our food was not a little more, well spicy?
- Wasn't it?
- When one is cooking on average for ten people a day whilst working full time as a social worker the food tends to be nutritious and stolid. Spaghetti Bolognese was the highlight of the week! Anyway she gave me a withering look and said: 'Your Father doesn't like spicy food!' and that was that. But a few years ago I was having a beer on the patio with Dad and he was reminiscing on his time in the R.A.F.
- When was he in the R.A.F.?
- During the War. He flew Catalinas for Coastal Command. Anyhow he was based in Jordan I think and was part of the Jordan Waddi Walkers club.
- The what?
- The Jordan Waddi Walkers Club. Waddis, or is that Waddies are rivers that are dry in the Summer and rivers in the Winters so during the Summer they used to walk along these things. It was like hiking but you can never get lost. Look people did this sort of shyte in the Forties as they did not have television to ruin their lives! Dad was recounting this wonderful story about one of their trips when he said: 'There was this wonderful little village just to the North of somewhere or other where I had the best curry of my life!' and suddenly my mind clicked to the previous memory. I said to Dad: 'Hold on there Bald Eagle! Mum told me that you do not like spicy food?' and he said: 'I love it but your mother won't cook it for me!'
- That is priceless! So what happened?
- I called Mum onto the patio which quickly became a stage for my best Poirot impersonation and from then on Mum makes Dad curries. Ironically, even though Mum does not like curry her Chicken Gubbins is fantastic. You must come round and try some. Come on John what about your folks?
- Well. We lived in Manchester. My father was a window cleaner, although in the Second World War he was in the Fire Brigade because he didn't want to kill anyone but he did want to help.
- What a brave man.
- I know. He was awarded a medal you know but didn't collect it. He said that the service was full of utter shits that were actually cowards. One time when he was in Southampton his life was only saved by an abandoned raft that drifted past on the river when he had been cut off by the fire. But it is not just that he was a hero, both of my parents came from nothing and they gave up everything to give me a chance in life. My school friends were going to go into the family businesses and so on but they wanted me to do better so I ended up in Oxford doing a degree because they themselves had had nothing all of their lives in order to help me. And what have I done?
- John, John. Come here mate, it's all right.
- I'm sorry Jude.
- Don't be. You are only being human.
- Sometimes I don't know why I bother at all.
- John snap out of it now! *You* have everything to live for. One's parents dying puts live into a completely different perspective but it does not mean that your life is over. John, you have two fantastic children, you have a beautiful grandson with another one on the way, you have an incredibly successful career that is so important that you cannot even talk about it and most of all you have a delightful personality that only brings happiness to the people you meet.

- I suppose so.
- There is *no* supposing about it! You know we talked about clever people holding onto stupid ideas? Well that is what you are currently doing. Life is not perfect but then it never is but there is *always* a reason to live.
- You know for the last two years my Mother didn't even recognise me. Some days I was an auntie, other days I was my Father who died fifteen years ago and often I was one of many cousins.
- Did she ever realise that it was you?
- Yes and she used to bollock me.
- The sign of a proud parent! A friend of mine lost her parents about a year ago and I was talking to her recently. She said it was a definition of adulthood as you no longer have someone to look up to. Now you are the senior member of the family and it is hard to adjust but you *must*. Your children are young and still do not realise what you have done for them. Andy will, now that he is a father himself but it takes time. It is a strange foible of human nature that it takes so long for us to realise how wonderful our parents are although in these times many parents are not. But yours were, mine are and Andy will keep up the tradition. Come here John do not be embarrassed. All of these bright young things have yet to encounter what you are dealing with, thank God.
- I'm all right Jude, thank you.
- The old crying fits? I know how you feel.
- Do you?
- No but I can relate to how you feel better than most. Individual grief is exactly that and I would not patronise you for a minute since my parents are both alive and I have no idea what it might be like to lose them. But I do know loss very well and I can also recognise a suicidal at twenty paces. It was that word you used: 'Empty.'
- I have tried suicide you know.
- What happened?
- Once I tried an overdose of Aspirin and another time I threw myself under a bus. I was too pissed and missed it completely only managing to annoy a taxi driver.
- You spooning muffin! Honestly John it is almost impossible to kill oneself with Aspirin as you will throw them up before they can kill you and to miss a bus! Thank God you did not succeed because you would have damaged your family terribly.
- I know. It is rather pathetic isn't it.
- Not at all. Pain of that intensity is never pathetic whatever the cause. Fortunately one tends to be an amateur at suicide by definition. John there are two reasons not to kill oneself.
- What are those then?
- Firstly all of the people that love you whether you have met them or not yet because, my friend there are a number of people out there that have yet to have the pleasure of John E. Vangelis and will know and love you in your future. Secondly there is always someone in more pain than you and if they can cope with it so can *you*! It always annoyed me my first time in hospital when I was not dealing with the situation very well.
- When was this?
- 1990. My life was in pieces around me, I had just turned twenty-one and had rather a bad attitude that wound up the nurses somewhat. They always said: 'There's people worse off than you!' and I thought: 'How is the concept of someone that I shall never even meet, that is in some way worse off than me supposed to help my pain and frustration in the slightest?' although I never said it. *That* was not very helpful but the extension of that, how *that person* survives is quite inspiring. The strength is within you to get over this John and *you will*.

- Thank you Jude. You have a reputation of being an angry young man you know and I can see why they say that so I didn't expect this much empathy.

- I only create things to talk about to avoid talking about my condition. The more contentious I am the less words like: 'Cripple.' pop up. I know that I get carried away but there you go, I have not lost any friends yet. Yes I have.

- You don't like talking about your disability?

- It is not that so much that as I become very wound up telling people who have no experience of what I am talking about.

- So how would you describe being disabled? I feel that we have something in common i.e. recent loss. Possibly I might understand.

- Thank you John. You actually want to hear this do you? All right. Being disabled is the most *fucking horrible* thing that has ever happened to me and I have had a shitty live by *anyone's* standards. I do not know how to handle this. I have always been able to deal with whatever has happened in my life until now. You see John your situation is very rough and your emotions are haywire but I can tell you that you *will* get over it. In a years time you will still miss your parents but you will have survived and life goes on. That is not the case for me. There is no getting over disability it is just there *all* of the time. This pain will never go away. It can only get worse until I am no longer able to live without constant medical supervision as I will almost certainly end up paraplegic within the next decade. I know that there are amazing people like Stephen Hawking who have made good things come of their condition but dear Stephen was never a builder and everything that I have ever tried to do has ended in failure even when I was able-bodied. What can I do now? Nothing except be a burden upon those that love me. My life has as much point as a fly caught between double glazing. I shall buzz meaninglessly for a while and just die and I wish it would hurry up. This is why I said all of those things to you John, I can see *your* life has meaning. Just think what your death would do to your children and grandchildren. Even if your only reason for living for a while was to build up an education fund or something for them your existence has meaning and potential.

- What would your parents do if you killed yourself?

- It would kill them. You have hit upon the red traffic light of my personal journey. I would never do it to them and my moving back there is going to reinforce the decision but my Father is seventy-five and my Mother is fifty-five. I do not have long to wait.

- But what about all of the other people that love you?

- I am lucky enough to have many friends and my funeral would be very sad but they would all recover once they realised that death was what I wanted most in life. My brothers and sister would hardly even recognise me now and I would disgust them as much as I disgust myself.

- What do you mean disgust?

- Well look at me John. The fact that I used to be considered handsome is nothing really to do with it but I am now grotesque. Is this the face of a twenty-nine year old?

- You're twenty-nine?

- Exactly! My right leg is atrophying while my right arm become disproportionally large due to Moses here. As time goes on I am becoming stooped and malformed. All I need is a couple of bolts in my neck or some bells to swing on because both of those stories are very accurate about people's reactions to ugliness. What can I achieve in life now? Nothing except for the world record in pathos.

- Have *you* tried suicide?

- I do not want to sound rude John but if I tried I would succeed. Everything that I have put my hand to in life I have been very good at.

- But you said that you always failed?

168

- I said that everything that I have tried to do has failed but that has generally been because of others although that does sound very arrogant. The fact is John that I cannot deal with this pain much longer.
- Do you take pain killers?
- Hah! They are as much use as an ashtray on a motorbike. The only things that give me any release are cannabis and alcohol which make me a criminal and a lush. God this world is so *fucking horrible*. I just want to get off. I was going to kill myself once back in '93 I think. You see a drawback of using alcohol as pain relief is that every now and then I drink myself into a coma and wake up in a soggy bed. This particular morning there was a girl in the bed as well that had appeared from somewhere. I certainly did not remember meeting her. She left fairly swiftly which was a shame because she seemed bright and beautiful, a combination that always brings pleasure. I never even remembered her name.
- If she had been really nice she would have stayed.
- You believe that as much as I do, not at all. She was being very sensible and I would not hang around with me. At the time I lived in a second floor flat in an Edwardian building so that my windows were about forty feet from the ground. I took a bottle of whisky and some ciggies and sat out on a windowsill planning to dive off when I had finished the bottle.
- What happened?
- My friend Zak rang up. I did not answer it but the machine kicked in. He was worried and it made me come back in.
- Thank goodness.
- Possibly. I often wish that I had not changed my mind as everyone's hurt would have subsided by now.
- You can't think like that Jude there must be something we can do?
- We?
- Yes we. Those who care about you and do not want you to die. Has Andy ever told you what you did for him?
- Did for him? You mean the money I lent him? He is the only one to have paid me back you know.
- No when you two first met. He had just discovered that he was epileptic, he had split up with the girlfriend, his mother didn't want him living with her so he came to me and he didn't know what to do with his life. Then he met you and your friends and six years down the line, well look at him. That is thanks to you.
- I never realised.
- Thank you for helping my son through the worst period of his life Jude.
- My pleasure.
- Now *you* come here, bloody crying fits.
- *Fucking* crying fits!
- Are you two all right?
- We are fine thanks Peter. A couple of little tears wanted to see the world but have now given it up as a bad idea.
- O.K. Jude? Do you want another drink gentlemen?
- Same again please Peter. Look Jude you must have plenty of reasons to keep going?
- You seem to have produced one from up your sleeve. It is a funny old life. Just when I am as low as low can be something really cheers me up. Thank you John E. Vangelis.
- My pleasure Jude.
- Look John if you feel near it again you call me. If I feel close again I shall call you and you repeat that story about my folks. What do you say?

- I say a deal!
- Then let us have a toast to life for a change. Cheers John it has been inspirational to talk to you.
- Cheers Jude likewise.
- Do you know that there is a special toast for the Queen Mother, bless 'er?
- No?
- It goes: 'Hip Hip, Replacement!'
- It like it. Hip Hip, replacement!
- It was very odd that you should use the word: 'Deal.'
- Why?
- Well I have done, or am going to do something very strange.
- What?
- On Sunday I am going to that happy-clappy church up the road and ask to be healed. It is one of those classic scenarios that in utter desperation I turn to religion.
- What made you think of that?
- I do not know. I was very stoned when the idea came to me but I am going to that church tomorrow.
- Is tomorrow important?
- Yes it is part of the deal.
- The deal?
- It is a long story but I must go tomorrow because I could not cope with another week like this. John I am really sorry but I have to go now.
- What time is the service?
- Four in the afternoon.
- Would you like a couple of beers first?
- That sounds like a very good idea to me thank you John. About midday?
- I shall see you then. Will you be all right tonight?
- Yes I have a party to go to and I still manage to find them very distracting.
- Enjoy it. See you tomorrow.
- Sleep well my friend.

* * *

- Hmmm good evening dear sir.
- 'Evening. Somewhere near the Dagoba system I would presume!
- Indeed, the top of Church Street to be precise.
- On your way to a fancy dress party?
- No a funeral.
- Funny man huh? Would you like to hear a joke?
- Nothing would give me more pleasure.
- There's this farmer right? He's a cattle farmer and one morning he wakes up and there's been the most fucking awful frost. He throws on his clothes and rushes out to his field. All of 'is cows are frozen solid, stiff as boards they are. He runs back to the 'ouse and rings 'is vet. 'All of me cows have frozen fucking solid!' he says. The vet says: 'Don't you worry son. I know just the person for your little problem. I'll send 'em round.' The farmer waits outside for a while worrying like fuck about 'is cows. Eventually this little old lady turns up and asks what the problem is. 'It's me cows!' says the farmer, 'They're frozen solid!' Your little old lady says: 'This is not a problem. Take me to the field.' So the farmer takes the lady down to

'is field and shows 'er the cows. She goes up to each one in turn and sort of lays 'er 'ands on 'em and one by one they come round and they're all O.K. When she's done the last one she comes back to the farmer who's gob-smacked and 'e says: 'Thank you so much you've saved me cows. Haven't I seen you on the telly?' 'You might of done.' she says coyly. 'So what's your name then?' asks the farmer. 'Thora Hurd!' she says.
- That is very funny I like it.
- Here you are mate, I take it it's the one with the lights outside.
- Thank you sir.
- Thanks mate that's five pound ten please.
- Take six mate. Right let us *party*.

- Good evening gentlemen does anyone know where Philip is?
- In the kitchen mate. Through there.
- I am indebted.
- UNCLE PUFFIN, as a penguin?
- Hello little one. No I am The Penguin you know, Batman.
- Was he not a man who *looked* like a penguin rather than just a whopping great penguin?
- I don't know as I've never seen the film but I think this works?
- Ah yes of course it does. What was I thinking of? Who are the young people in the front room?
- They're friends of Cain's I think. They're feeling a little left out because they're not in fancy dress.
- Serves them right. If they had put a little effort in rather than be slothful they would be a-mingling now would they not?
- Self-inflicted?
- No-*ho-ho* sympathy! I must say you are very convincing as a, sorry The Penguin.
- Do you like it? Guess what?
- I do not know?
- I'm naked underneath.
- Ah. Are you now? Could we keep that particular piece of information unproven for the moment and quite far beyond?
- I think that it would be wise.
- Surely that more in the line of an owl Puffin, sorry The Penguin.
- You're getting me all confused. I don't know if I am flying or swimming. That reminds me of a joke little one.
- Go on?
- A chap is walking around town and suddenly he realises that he is being followed by a herd of penguins.
- A herd?
- A group?
- A flock?
- A gathering of penguins. They won't go away and just keep following him everywhere. Eventually he gets fed up, finds a policeman and says: 'Excuse me officer, what should I do with these penguins?' and the nice policeman replies: 'Take them to the zoo.' 'Thank you very much.' your man says and off he goes. The next day the same policeman sees the same man with the same penguins but this time they are all wearing sunglasses with rolled-up towels under their little flippers. The policeman stops the chap to enquire: 'Didn't you take those

171

penguins to the zoo yesterday?' 'Oh yes.' retorts the man, 'We had a great time thank you so today I'm taking them to the beach!'
- That is wonderful Puffin, wonderful. Tell me are there prizes?
- Yes there are first and second prizes. First prize is a big bag of sweets which has been won by my little boy and the second prize is a bottle of malt that I have won. In the best traditions of competitions this is completely rigged and utterly nepotistic.
- It would be foolish to try otherwise.
- I know. Well have you brought anything?
- Indeed sir. I feel that with parties one should always bring an approximation of how much one plans to drink so have three bottles of Chateau Eurotunnel.
- Thank you little one I shall gag on that later. I have a little something for you.
- For me?
- Yes for you. Here you are it'll help keep you upright for a while.
- Thanks Philip this is *really* kind.
- Just don't snort it all at once!
- Where is the nearest gents?
- Well there's one right at the top of the house up five sets of stairs.
- Oh no!
- Although you could use the one just here but I do want to see you struggle up those stairs in fact would you mind an audience and I could get my camera?
- You rotten lovechild!
- After you have powdered your nose go and mingle in the garden.
- Certainement monsieur.

- Wotcha Yoda.
- Hmmm Zorro it be. How are you mate?
- I'm a bit tired actually Yoda.
- You should catch some Zs then! Where is the booze?
- On the table over there.
- Thank you kind bandit.

- Ladies do you mind if I join you?
- Of course not Yoda.
- There seems to be a lack of seats and I am in need. May I be rude enough to inquire who you have come as since I am nothing of a film buff.
- We're Patsy and Edwina.
- Of course you are, how stupid of me, I wish I were dead! You have caught them to a tee.
- You're very good as Yoda. Can I feel your ears?
- That is a perfectly reasonable place to start.
- Ugh yuck, they're all rubbery.
- Very perceptive dear Patsy and far too expensive as well, one could almost say it was daylight rubbery! Tell me how do you know Uncle Puffin?
- Uncle Puffin?
- Philip.
- Oh we're friends of Anne from college. Why is he called Uncle Puffin?
- Well it started off when he was doing some work for Percy Percy, have you met him?
- No. Percy Percy?

172

- Indeed, a fine chap. Percy had an office at the top of a converted Victorian house that was, and still is of course absolutely enormous and every time Philip came to see him he was out of breath by the top of the stairs so he was called Puffin.
- Oh puffing!
- Exactly Eddie if I may be so bold. Then when I was working at the college he did some design work for us and every time he turned up at reception he would ask the ladies there if they would fetch me as my: 'Uncle Puffin was awaiting.' I am an honorary nephew apparently.
- You used to work at the college? What's your name?
- Jude Redmond a delight to meet you.
- You're Jude Redmond? I'm Beth, the Big Issue girl your scheme helped.
- Oh right. Jim was telling me about you the other day.
- Ditty Jim? Yes he's lovely isn't he. It's wonderful now, I'm sharing a flat with Gabby and Anne and I'm on the course and I haven't been this happy in years. Can I have a hug? Thank you so much.
- It is my pleasure entirely. By the by my doctor insists that I have a hug every ten minutes so can I rely on you for this evening? But seriously that is fantastic news Beth, congratulations. Having been involved I know how much work you must have put in and I hope that you are suitably smug about your achievement. Well done Eddie! Excuse me if I revert to your character names as unfortunately names tend to go in one large, pointy, green ear and out of the other to fall uselessly on the floor. It is lovely to meet you Beth and I wish you all of the luck that you deserve.
- Thank you Yoda. Jude.
- Hmmm my pleasure it is. Actually you have reminded me of a story which was one of the funniest things anyone has ever said about me if I may be permitted to regale you?
- Hmmm go ahead Yoda.
- No it needs to be back of the throat love, back of the throat, from the diaphragm although this is far too early in the conversation to mention contraception. Hmmm like that.
- Hmmm?
- Much better. The scenario was that I was the best man, contradiction in terms I know at a wedding in Northern Ireland and we decided to stop off at my uncle's in Dublin on the way. There were four of us I think and with my mad, beer monster uncle we had quite a session over three days. On the last evening we travelled to Burren which was the place in the North and I was looking a trifle rough, four days of growth, hair a little longer than this, biker's jacket, old jeans and tee shirt and stinking of alcohol. Then I was introduced to the Mother of the Bride who looked a hint concerned as I mumbled: 'Hello.' and went to find the beer. She turned to Hannah and said: '*That's* the *best man*?'
- She wasn't impressed then?
- My dear Patsy she was as impressed as the Queen when someone farts. Hannah tried to calm her down with: 'He'll look better in his suit Mum.' and other platitudes. On the day of the wedding I had shaved, was wearing the monkey suit and looking quite dashing in a hung over fashion and when Ruby saw me she breathed a sigh of relief and exclaimed: 'Doesn't he clean up well!'
- Really?
- Oh she was a delightful woman who raised twelve children would you believe and still did not look a day over thirty. Actually that *was* funny. We were chatting about the family one night just before going over and Hannah mentioned that all of the children's birthdays fell in August. I did some mental arithmetic and asked: 'So what happens in November?' to which

she immediately replied: 'It's their wedding anniversary!' They were a good Irish family! Who is that over there?

- That's Anne's little brother. He's an Ewok.

- An Ewok! That is not an Ewok!

- Shush he might hear you.

- But this is an outrage! He is wearing the bottom half of a dog with a Wookie's head stuck on top! He has not nearly enough fur!

- Shush Jude!

- But this is terrible! I demand a retrial! The bag of sweets is rightly mine!

- Your costume isn't that brilliant and Yoda didn't smoke.

- I can assure you my dear Eddie that between takes he was in his little trailer, more of a kennel really, puffing away like a good 'un reading the Guardian.

- You're very eccentric aren't you?

- Eccentric? Ich? Good Enoch's donkey woman do I look the sort of bluff cove who would indulge in the general skulduggery of pretending to be anything other than absolutely normal? Oops me ear's fallen off!

- You're mad Yoda!

- Would you like to know the secret of being eccentric?

- Yes please Master Yoda?

- Hmmm the secret I shall tell. All you do is say the first thing that comes into your head after checking that it is not offensive or rude. So one says things like: 'Good morning Mrs. Fotheringill would your budgie like some Kippers? They are fresh in from Guatemala and recommended by the Duchess herself!' and the bus driver gives one a very odd look! It whiles away the hours most commodiously.

- It's not a lot of use though is it?

- Why should it be? Does everything now have to be useful, cost-effective and energy-saving? What it does mean though is that one is practised and able to speak in very long sentences that are not rushed but relaxed and natural whilst still holding a perfectly rational topic that is quite undisturbed amongst the rattle and hum and general kerfuffle quite frankly of the completely irrelevant, meaningless but strangely charming words that flow unhindered from me gob. It can be quite a boon at interviews.

- Hello.

- God's whiskers it is an Ewok! Good evening young bear, I suppose. Are you having as splendid an evening as I?

- Yes thank you.

- I must say and I think the ladies here will back me up that you are utterly convincing as an Ewok, would you not concur ladies?

- Oh yes.

- In fact that is the most convincing Ewok outfit that I have seen all day! The prize is yours I would wager.

- What's wrong with your leg?

- My leg? Well it does not move below my knee so I cannot walk without my stick.

- How did that happen?

- I used to have a motorbike, you know what a motorbike is? One night a man in a car did not see me on my bike and knocked me off which damaged my leg very badly so that now it does not work any more and so the moral of the story is?

- Don't have a motorbike?

- No have a bike if you like and be careful on it. No the moral is expect life to go horribly wrong just when you think everything is all right.
- Jude! You can't say that to a young child.
- It is the best advice you can give to anyone but anyway Mr. Ewok it has been an honour to meet you.
- Bye-bye Yoda.
- How kind of you to notice.
- Jude you shouldn't have said that.
- What advice would you give to a small child Eddie?
- I don't know. We're going to get some food, do you want anything Jude?
- No thank you but if you could track down another bottle of rouge I would love you forever.
- See you later.

- Ah it is Percy Percy as, Percy Percy!
- Hello boy. How you doing?
- Oh you know ducking and diving, hopping and limping.
- Thanks for the contact with that reporter it worked out well.
- Oh good.
- Old Puffin knows how to throw a party doesn't he?
- So that it lands bang in the middle of happyland. He is *such* a good bloke, there is not a bad Adam in his botty!
- Now there's a thought! I heard a great joke for you. This bloke dies and goes to Heaven. St. Peter is showing him around and they pass a bloody great room full of clocks, enormous it was. Your man asks what it is and St. Pete replies: 'This is where everyones' lives are measured. We used to do it with hourglasses but we updated recently. Everyone's life is shown here.' The chap is standing watching all of this in wonder when he suddenly notices one of the clocks jumps half an hour ahead and he asks St. Pete why. 'Well you know that Onanism is a sin? Every time someone relieves themselves they lose half an hour of their allotted span.' This fascinates the man and he asks to see where his old mates' clocks are. Pete shows him and he stands there for a bit watching: 'Oh there goes Puffin!' and so on. Suddenly he notices that there is one missing and asks: 'Where's Jude's clock then?' 'Oh.' says St. Peter, 'We use it in the office as a fan!'
- Thank you so much.
- I thought you'd like it. Have you heard any good ones lately?
- No, no jokes but did I ever tell you about the worst blow-job I ever had?
- No?
- It was fantastic!
- Very good.
- Here you are Yoda.
- Hmmm grateful I am dear Eddie. By the by this is Percy Percy, Percy meet Eddie a Lord Snowden of the future.
- Hello Eddie what are you doing with a loser like this?
- Nothing at the moment I'm going to eat. Excuse me, see you Jude.
- 'Bye Beth.
- She's far too young for you.
- Dirty old men need love too!
- That's a good one. Remind me to mention it to my wife. I'm following that arse to the food, see you later Yoda.

- Hmmm again until we meet.

- Jude you're alone.
- Your powers of observation never cease to amaze me Jeremy.
- Seriously Jude I need your advice. Why are you laughing?
- Sorry Jeremy, sorry. You cannot see the humour in the situation?
- No I need some advice.
- Who have you come dressed as?
- Luke Skywalker.
- And you want some advice from...
- Oh. I see what you mean.
- What is on your mind my friend? Problems with Mia?
- Yeah. She's being very distant and I don't know what's wrong with her, she won't talk to me.
- Is there anything going on like life decisions or something?
- She was talking to a friend about moving to London.
- Ah and she has not talked to you about it yet?
- She said it wasn't important. Jude you're the only one of my friends that she respects.
- Mia respects me?
- She says you're the only one with a brain over his shoulders.
- How flattering.
- Would you talk to her Jude, tonight?
- Of course but in a while, she is watching us. No do not look you muffin! I shall tell you a joke so we look natural or as natural as Luke Skywalker and Yoda can look at a barbecue! You will like this one. A young couple fell in love at first sight and after a week or so of talking sweet nothings got married and go on honeymoon to a posh hotel somewhere. On the first day they were relaxing by the pool and your man said: 'Darling? I'm just going for a swim.' He walked to the diving boards, selected the tallest and climbed it, executed a perfect triple back somersault, swam ten lengths in a perfect and very fast crawl before leaping out at the end. Everyone around the pool was suitably impressed including his new wife.
- As you would be.
- Indeed. He sat back down next to her and said: 'Darling. We met and fell in love but we don't know everything about each other. I used to be an Olympic swimmer but I didn't want to tell you as I wanted you to love me for who I am. Can you understand?' 'Of course I understand darling.' she said. 'Now it is my turn for a swim.' and she got up, headed for the same diving board, performed a perfect triple back somersault with twist and whizzed through twenty lengths in a perfect freestyle before leaping from the pool so quickly that she was not even wet. The audience around the pool gave her mild applause as she returned to her amazed husband. 'Darling!' he said, 'There is obviously much about you that I don't know about. Were you an Olympic swimmer as well?' 'No.' she replied with a smile, 'I was a hooker in Venice!'
- That's very funny Jude. You will talk to her won't you?
- Of course my friend. Now tinker off and enjoy the party.

- Hello mate.
- Ah ha it is, well, in the words of the late and great Arthur Negus: 'It could be Louis XIV.'
- No you fool I am a Musketeer.

176

- *You?* Firstly do not call Yoda a fool as the wisdom of the universe is contained in this little green head and secondly you look more of a Mouseketeer. We shall call you Pathos.
- You rotten sod. How's the leg?
- Useless, painful and boring. How is business?
- Well as long as you keep drinking in my pubs I have nothing to worry about! Have you heard this one? A horse walks into a pub and the barman says?
- 'Why the long face?' Let me tell you a little secret Pathy if I may? At the last Waifs and Strays Do, before you bought the Carpenter's my party piece was to do the A to Z of animals in pubs jokes.
- Really Jude? Can you remember them?
- That is a tall order in the words of Christopher Lee's tailor but I shall try. An Aardvark walks into a pub and the barman says: 'Why the long face!' A Boar walks in and asks for food: 'As long as you don't make a pig out of your self!' A Camel: 'Why so sad?' 'I've got the hump!' A Dromedary: 'I'm twice as peeved as him!' An Elephant is there when the 'phone rings: 'If that's a trunk call it's for me!' A Fox: 'You're looking a bit hounded!' A Giraffe walks into a pub and says: 'OUCH!' A Halibut: 'Better line them up, this one drinks like a fish!' An Impala asks for a Babycham : 'They're a little deer I'm afraid!' A Jaguar saunters in and asks for a German larger: 'I thought you were quintessentially British?' 'No that's Daimlers!' A Kiwi walks in: 'We don't serve your type in here, we all know you're a fruit!' A Lobster walks in: 'I shouldn't serve you after last night, drinking too much and giving it all of that!' A Monkey: 'Out for a swinging night sir?' A Nest: 'Has anyone seen my bird!' An Owl: 'Just an orange juice please, I'm flying.' 'Very wise sir!' A Penguin: 'Have you seen my brother?' 'I don't know sir, what does he look like!' A Quail: 'Don't look so frightened!' A Rabbit: 'I'd like a real ale with lots of hops!' A Snail: 'We don't see much of you sir, you should come out of your shell a bit more!' Closely followed by a Tortoise: 'I'll have a sloe gin please!' An Ursa walks in:
- An Ursa?
- Another name for a bear, I was getting a little desperate at this point. An Ursa walks in and says: 'I'd like a, a, a,' 'Why the big paws!' A Viper slithers in and asks for a snakebite: 'Do it yourself!' A Wolf: 'Just a pint please.' 'Aren't you hungry sir!' A Xylophone: 'Get out you're not an animal!' A Yak: 'Just don't start talking, you make me sick!' And finally a Zebra: 'Why the long face!'
- Very impressive Jude.
- Thank you kind sir. Are you going to come to this year's?
- Would I be invited?
- Well you are self employed are you not so you fit the requirements. All you need is a party piece.
- I could bring my guitar.
- Oh God preserve us from frustrated guitarists!
- I'm not bad actually.
- Of course you can bring your guitar Pathy.
- Don't call me that.
- Sorry Path.
- You'll end up barred if you're not careful!
- You will end up with a large dip in profits and there is another pub over the road. Anyway it is better than being called Penfold!
- Only kidding Jude.
- I know mate.

- Right I'm going to get some food, do you want anything?
- Could you liberate a bottle of rouge for me?
- No problem.
- Thanks Pathos.

- Hello Jude.
- Mia what can I say? You are looking even more beautiful this evening than normal. Your pulchritude leaves me breathless and weak.
- You look an absolute green mess.
- Mia my angel of the dusk your honesty is underwhelming, please delight me with your company for a moment.
- May I sit down?
- Please justify that piece of plastic's role in our world.
- I must say Jude that you are the most charming man I have ever met.
- No, no, no Mia my Venus, your resplendence merely brings out the Keats in me.
- You were talking to Jeremy.
- Yes.
- What about?
- I was telling him a joke Monsignor.
- Jude I am not fucking around. What did Jeremy talk to you about?
- How soon you were going to dump him.
- What?
- Look Mia if you do not want to fuck around as you so delightfully put it, Wordsworth I am sure, then it has to work both ways. If you want to use up my time then it is an end to pleasantries. You are becoming very career minded and you are wondering if dearest Jeremy, whom you love will be an asset or a liability when you start earning more money than he does?
- I see Jude that you are now so arrogant you think you know how everyone else thinks?
- Ironically Mia you have helped me to cut to the chase. Yes I do know what you are thinking because stereotyping has become a self-fulfilling prophecy. Psychologists have been trying to find evidence to support stereotyping for decades and they cannot but what is happening now is that people are becoming stereotypical of their own violation and the whole Astrology culture is gaining momentum.
- You're saying I am obvious?
- No, if you would listen Mia I am saying the reverse. I want to have a bet with you. I shall bet my stick Moses against, what do you bet?
- Your walking stick?
- Yes it is a reflection upon my certainty of winning. Without Moses I cannot walk. What do you bet? I shall make life easier for you, say a fine Rioja.
- But what is the bet about?
- I shall tell you that when we have sorted out terms. I bet Moses against a bottle of Red Faustino V, what do you say? You can reject now or after you hear the bet?
- O.K. then Jude. What is the bet?
- I bet I can give you the name of a character from a film that you immediately recognise, you might even giggle but you will not know the name of the actor? You see I have already given you a clue.
- O.K. then I accept your bet.
- Cato.

- You *bastard* Jude.
- The answer is Burt Kwouk. I can also say one sentence that will immediately make you stand up in indignation: 'I completely agree with fox hunting in fact they should breed them especially, like grouse.'
- You *double* bastard Jude!
- Hang on Mia I am telling you this for a reason and the reason is the same one that made you come over here in the first place. Sit down. Thank you. The point is my dearest Mia that ninety-nine per cent of the people that one meets are not individuals they are sheep and within five minutes of meeting most people you know *exactly* what their opinions are on *everything*. That is why most only have a few good friends that are all different to themselves. The point I am clumsily making is that you have the capacity to rise above predictability and be someone which is what you want is it not?
- Yes I do.
- Well you will Mia, you will. I may not be an expert in anything but I do know that you will become very important and successful in whatever career you chose, I would recommend something in the media. You have to decide if you want to take Jeremy with you and *only* you can decide that. Jeremy has a big heart and he is enormously loyal but he is also lazy.
- I know but I can't decide, it would mean moving and everything and I don't want to make a mistake either way.
- Be logical about the situation. Get a piece of paper, draw a line down the middle and on one side have pros and on the other cons. Write them all down and then look.
- As easy as that?
- If you are honest with yourself yes.
- That does make sense.
- Unfortunately Mia although sexism is decreasing it still exists which means that you are not allowed to have a family *and* a career and quite frankly I would not bother trying. You need to have a career to fulfil your innate abilities and if you do not for someone else's reasons you will end up bitter and frustrated. You need to decide *now* before it all gets too heavy. Jeremy knows that there is something afoot so talk to him and be as honest with him as you are being with me.
- Do you think I should?
- I know.
- Thank you Jude, I'll think about it.
- No problem. You do look ravishing tonight. How about a torrid fling?
- I don't think so Jude.
- Damn you women of taste! If you are going to talk to Jeremy I would do it sooner rather than later with the way he is attacking that bottle of Jack Daniels.
- Oh no! Thanks Jude I'll see you later.
- Au revoir dream lady.

- Hmmm it's Yoda.
- No Mark, back of the throat mate, back of the throat. Hmmm what character Mark be?
- Dow de le low dow, dow dow - squirt!
- Are you mad man? You will make my make up run!
- I thought that I would do your old trick.
- Yes thank you for reminding me of happier days. How are things in Germany mate?

179

- Fine, the wife and James are just great. This party has been something of a pain you know. Normally I have two standard costumes that I would chose from but it having to be related to films and the presence of small children has limited my range.
- What would you normally do then?
- Well I would normally wear my dressing gown, like you but with a head-dress and darkened skin. I would have a bread roll in one hand and a baby's rattle in the other to be?
- I do not know?
- Sheikh, Rattle and Roll!
- Oh yes!
- The other one would be to wear only black soaks and black gloves and wander around with my hands in the air.
- Go on?
- The five of Spades!
- Yes I can see why the children might have influenced your decision.
- Do you want the world's silliest joke?
- A rhetorical question I feel.
- This husband finds out that his wife is being unfaithful to him and, not being a man of grey areas he decides to have her killed. So he gets his Yellow Pages and looks up hit men and right at the top is: 'Artie - cheapest and most reliable hit man in town.' So he gives him a ring. 'Hello Artie here?' 'I want you to kill my wife.' 'Certainly sir. Our standard charge is a pound and I will need a time, location and a description.' 'She'll be at Strangeways doing the shopping at ten o' clock this Wednesday, I'll make sure she wears a red dress.'
- Very efficient.
- Of course. So Artie goes to the supermarket and hides in the frozen peas. A little while later a lady in a red dress opens it up, he leaps out and throttles her to death. Pleased with a good day's work he starts to leave when he notices another woman in a red dress and hides in the freezer again, this time under the pizzas. She opens the lid, he leaps out and strangles her too. He checks there are no more women in red dresses and then leaves. Do you know what it said in the local paper the next day?
- Go on?
- 'Artie chokes two for a pound at Strangeways!'
- Very good, I like it. That is very silly.
- Go on then Jude what's your latest.
- Well did you know that the Catholic Church are trying to update their image?
- Oh yeah?
- Indeed. They are trying to be more dynamic and relevant in order to attract some younger people and one of the things that they are doing to this end is offer a low-fat alternative to the host, the wafer.
- Go on?
- They are going to call it: 'I can't believe it's not Jesus!'
- Like it! That's fantastic.
- I thought that you would appreciate its finer qualities.
- Have you told Percy that one?
- No.
- Right I'm going to. See you Yoda.
- Hmmm well fare.

- Hello Jude did you miss us?

- Patsy and Eddie, I missed you inexorably and unflinchingly. I have been desolate since your departure.
- Have you ever acted Jude?
- Many years ago I trod the boards. At school like most people. Actually it was rather funny.
- Go on shock us.
- Well the first play I was in was a gentle and whimsical English comedy called Penny for a Song by someone whom I have forgotten. The main character is called Sir Timothy Bellboys and he lives on his estate in the south of England during Napoleonic times when there was a threat of invasion apparently. He has a cunning plan.
- How cunning my lord?
- Very cunning indeed Baldnut. Sir Timothy bears a striking resemblance to Napoleon himself and his scheme is that when the invasion happens he would don his costume, pretend to be the diminutive Corsican and tell the armies to return to France.
- Very cunning indeed my lord.
- Yes. To help spot the invading enemy at the first possible opportunity he has installed a servant, named Humpage in a tall tree just outside his bedroom window. All through the play Sir Tim throws the window open and yells: 'Humpage!' 'Sir?' 'Anything to report?' 'No sir!' and this happens many times. The highlight is when the local Home Guard hold manoeuvres on the beach and are mistaken for the French with hilarious consequences is I believe the parlance. Unfortunately that is not what happened at the dress rehearsal.
- What happened?
- What should have happened is that to the regular cry of: 'Anything to report?' Humpage would excitedly say: 'Yes sir, oh yes sir! There are landing craft and men, lots of men...' and so on and Sir Tim would swing into action. As it happened Sir Tim threw open his window, bellowed: 'Humpage! Anything to report?' And Humpage said: 'No sir!' The silence was breathtaking. Sir Tim busked a little and said: 'Are you sure?' 'Yes sir!' came the very unhelpful reply. 'Take another look.' urged Sir Timothy, 'Are you sure that there aren't any landing craft at this stage of the play?' and finally Humpage caught on. You know what they say about dress rehearsals?
- No?
- They are just before the first night normally.
- So what part did you play Jude?
- My part? Well you must remember that I was twelve years old at the time and was not singing bass if you understand? There was the part of Lamprett who was Timothy's eccentric brother and he had a wife named Hester. I was their very charming daughter named Dorcas.
- Dorcas? You?
- You must remember that this is an all boys boarding school, well all boys until the sixth form. We had to play women and girls in the best Shakespearean traditions I can assure you.
- Did you have a nice dress?
- You may mock and giggle. Actually I had a very pleasant dress, resplendent in lilac I recall but it was very problematic on the first night.
- Oh no! What happened?
- My entrance was delightful. I would appear at the right wings and perform gentle ballet movements across the stage before realising I am being watched by another character Edward to whom I chat for a while before leaving to rustle up some food for him. Unfortunately I had not realised that my dress had split from the neck down to my coccyx. The first I knew was Edward covering the view of my behind as I left the stage with him lisping: 'Oh you have got kinky pants on!' It was a good thing I had, otherwise we would have lost our PG certificate.

The poor lady in charge of costumes had to stitch me back up in record time as I pondered on why there had been so many laughs during my opening scene! The rest went smoothly thank God.

- Dorcas!
- You may laugh at my expense you horrible creatures. The funny thing was that the play was being reviewed for the college magazine by my house master who said that my performance was: 'Too coquettish!' How on earth can a twelve year old in drag be 'coquettish'? That was twisted.
- Was that it?
- God's roll-up no, that was merely the start of my glittering thespian career. The next year they did a version of Anhouilh's Becket in which I was all of the bit parts, pageboy and messenger and all of that. I had a notable scene where I run in to tell the king about Becket's entrance to Canterbury after his banishment to France. There were two problems with that scene. Firstly I had to say: 'Episcopal crook.' and I never could, it always came out as: 'Epa, epis, episcop..' and so on. The second problem was my shoes.
- Your shoes?
- My shoes. You see we wore our own shoes with bits of something over them, this was a school production you know and I had just got some new ones. Instead of the sturdy grip of a Clarkes' sole I had on some poncey suede things with a smooth leather sole. Consequently I ran on stage to deliver my big bit, if you'll pardon the expression, knelt down before the king and slid right off the stage disappearing into the left wings. I had to run back round the backstage to reappear a little slower. When it got to me trying to pronounce: 'Eper, epis...' the king just butted in with: 'Yes Episcopal!' It was very embarrassing.
- You just slid right off the stage?
- Indeed, apparently it looked quite graceful. The next year I was in a Midsummer Night's Dream.
- There's more?
- Loads! I was one of the Rustic Players who put on a play within a play near the end. I was Robin Starveling the tailor and played Moonshine. As part of my costume I had a dog created a la Blue Peter by someone doing Art A level and the hound was not very convincing. On the last night I could not find the damn dog and one of the stage hands gave me a panda cuddly toy as a last minute replacement. Apparently it had been a gift that evening.
- A cuddly panda?
- The very same. So I was being introduced to the on stage audience as we all were but with the Bard's lines being adjusted somewhat: 'This man with lantern, bush of thorns and cuddly panda bear. Panda bear?' said the other actor. 'Dog died!' I explained and it brought the roof down. After that I was not allowed on stage anymore so I used to build the sets instead although I do still feel the frisson of excitement when I see a cuddly toy but you probably do not want to know about that.
- Oh dear, you are funny. Jude we have to go now.
- Break my heart why don't you! Beth it has been a delight and I wish you every success. Here is my number if you ever need any help. Patsy?
- Gabby.
- Gabby what can I say? Marry me?
- Not now I have to get home.
- A tragedy in itself. It was lovely to meet you both and thank you for your glorious company.
- See you Jude.

182

- Hello little one, all alone?
- The party is diminishing somewhat.
- How's the gear?
- Ah! Uncle Charles White does not visit often unfortunately but when he does he is *most* welcome.
- It is good isn't it?
- Absolutely fabulous as my previous companions would have said.
- They were rather nice weren't they?
- They are friends of your daughters.
- Really? They get so old so young these days.
- How is business by the by?
- It will be great when I get some clients.
- You? Needing clients? No-one can do what you do with a computer, you can even get it to take the dog for a walk!
- That's only the mouse although he has to be very strong.
- I heard a lovely story about one of those computer help desks.
- Oh yes?
- This chap rang one to say that his confuser had just packed up all of a sudden. The help desk bloke ran through the options of standing on the printer and checking leads and so on but with no joy. Then he asked the chap: 'When did your computer stop working?' 'At the same time as the power cut.' was the reply.
- Oh dear.
- So the help desk chap said: 'I know what to do. Do you still have the packaging for the machine? Good I want you to put it all back in the boxes, take it to the shop where you bought it and tell them "Sorry but I am too f***ing stupid to own a computer!"'
- Really?
- Yes he was sacked.
- Oh no!
- Unfortunately so.
- What's this?
- Hello Percy, Jude was just telling me a story.
- There has to be a first time for everything don't you think Jude?
- Of course Percy.
- I was just talking to Zorro over there about ridiculous signs that we had seen. There was some place in Wales where in the middle of a field there was a sign saying: 'Do not throw stones at this sign!' I mean what is the point of that?
- It's like the: 'Ears pierced while you wait!' one that I like.
- I must say chaps that my favourite sign was one I saw in Ireland some time ago. We had stopped at a boozer for lunch and there was a sign on the door saying: 'Pint of Guinness, pie and free advice - £2' and we thought that we would give it a go. We went in and said: 'Two Guinness and pies please.' 'Certainly.' said your man and started pouring. One had to so I said: 'What is the free advice?' He looked me in the eye and said: 'Don't eat the pie!'
- Wonderful!
- That's great.
- Jude?
- 'Tis Pathos.
- I'm sharing a cab back your way with Princess Leia if you want to join us?
- Hmmm be with you I shall. Puffin thanks for a great party and the little gift.

- My pleasure little one.
- And I shall see you soon Percy.
- 'Bye boy.
- My chariot awaits.

- Oops sorry Leia I seem to be on your lacy bits.
- You are a clumsy Yoda!
- I can only apologise for my oops, Moses! *Really!*
- Your stick is rather cold.
- I am terribly sorry.
- Jude what are you doing?
- Sorry Pathos my robe is caught in the door with hilarious consequences. That's better. Are you all right Leia?
- Yes thank you. You must be Jude?
- Absolutely a delight to meet you.
- Go on then Jude tell us a joke.
- Yeah tell us a joke Jude.
- A captive audience, how wonderful. This is my favourite joke in the world. A young, high-flying executive from Budweiser managed to arrange an audience with the Pope after much negotiation. He entered the Vatican in his sharp suit and got straight down to business. ''Morning Pope.' he said with his best smile, 'I know you're a busy Pope so I'll get straight down to business.' Told you! 'We at Budweiser think, in fact we know that we can do business with you, the Vatican.' 'Go on.' said the Pope. 'We feel that working together on this project, which I shall outline in a moment will benefit both of us considerably in terms of profit and exposure.' 'Go on.' said the Pope. 'Well you know the Lord's Prayer?' 'I am aquatinted with it.' replied the Pope. 'Well you know the line: "Give us this day our daily *bread*?" we want that changed to: "Give us this day our daily *Bud*!" you see and you can imagine the impact of the advertising, holy water and so on.' 'Young man!' said the shocked Pope, 'We just can't change bits of the Bible when we feel like it!' 'Ah but there's ten billion in it for you. *Dollars*.' 'Oh!' said the Pope, 'Young man this is the Lord's Prayer, the very words of our Saviour we can't mess around with that.' 'O.K. Popey you drive a hard bargain, by the way I love the hat! Call it *twenty* billion.' The Pope was by this point looking a little rattled. 'I'll have to talk to the cardinals!' he stuttered as he left the room. He went to another room and called the cardinals to order. 'Boys, boys, let's have a little bit of hush. Now I have good news and bad news.' The cardinals immediately started chatting away again until one asked: 'What's the bad news?' 'Well.' said the Pope, 'As we all know the Hovis contract is running out!'
- That's wonderful Jude.
- You're very funny.
- Ah ha this is my domestibule, I shall alight. Thank you all for a delightful evening and I shall see you anon.
- Are you in the Carpenter's tomorrow?
- What a good idea. Straighteners at midday? See you there.

Sunday 13th June: **A DEAL WITH GOD?**

I woke up feeling as close to hell as any human being can be expected to endure. A cocaine hangover, a neck made from mouse traps and the rest of me feeling as though I had been run over. Believe me I know *that* feeling *intimately*. Oh yes and a raging erection! Why does the expression 'role reversal' come to mind?

I creaked and grunted to the bathroom where I almost screamed - the whole thing was completely *green*! Oh *those* suppressed memories! Oh fuck! And I am supposed to be going to that fucking church today! Oh fuckety fuck! And I am supposed to be meeting John. At least I shall have someone to talk to. When does one actually realise that one is mad? Face it Jude just *look* at yourself! Go back to your mattress, sit down, light a cigarette and come back to reality for a while.

You are disabled - a cripple, a Quasi, something ugly and undesirable that they have minority programmes for on BBC 2 serving eight million spastics. You threw away a perfectly good life to look 'hard' on a motorbike due to which your life has been a burden on the Welfare State ever since except for those brief periods when you were squandering your compensation money or attempting full time employment. You are sitting in a bed sit that you are having to sell because you completely screwed up your finances. Your bathroom is indescribable because you went to a party covered in green paint with the sole purpose of indulging in what is known as a 'drink and drugs cocktail' and the possibility of corrupting a young woman 'if you got lucky'. Currently you are partially green and wondering whether you should go to church and ask to be healed as part of some 'deal with God'. You spend your time being an alcoholic in various pubs that would be staggered if they knew how much you *actually* drank each and every week. You fool yourself into thinking that you help people when in reality you just preach your embittered and twisted thoughts at your friends which alienates them while you slowly kill yourself with self pity. *DO YOU THINK YOU ARE MAD?*

What the hell is going on in my head? I do not think that I can cope. It is time to break all of my golden rules.

At just past nine in the morning I had a breakfast of a very large Bloody Mary and a fat line of coke. Once the tremors had calmed down I managed to do so as well and had three baths accompanied by further Bloody Marys and Wireless 2 which was a religious program and played lots of hymns that I had not heard since I was a child. I cried gently into the tepid bath water. It killed a couple of hours.

These mornings are the worst times. Having been a tele-sales type for a few years I am now scared of the telephone even when I should be calling friends. Fortunately people still seem to call me but I cannot raise the energy to call them myself. A further example of my hypocrisy and patheticness. Is that a word? Do I *really* think that there is the slightest chance of being healed at this place? It is such an enormous concept that I cannot get my mind around it. To think that this pain and misery could all be over with the waving of a hand and a few prayers but I do know one thing - I *want* it to happen. I want to be able to walk and run again. I would love to go for a cross-country run in the pouring rain and then go to the pub! I would love for

185

women to look at me with desire again instead of pity. I would like to have a life again.

I would make a good ambassador for Christianity I feel. Apparently I have charisma and ability in public speaking which could be put to good use. I am highly practised in the fine art of talking a lot which is perfect for evangelism and if I found my former energy I would be *unstoppable*. God has definitely got Himself a good deal here. I would fulfil my part to the letter.

To be able to *walk* again. To be seen as *human* again. To be *alive* again.

Suicide is a lot like addiction. When one has been addicted to whatever it will always be there even when one is dry. It is always there at the back of the mind, a little voice saying: 'Take some it won't matter.' and it requires *such* a force of will to keep to the straight and narrow. Suicide is the same. Once you have been through it in your mind and imagined the consequences including your own funeral the thought will always be there: 'All I have to do is jump out of that window and it will all be over.' The list of people who do not want me to do that is ever growing unfortunately. Have these people not heard of emotional blackmail? That is *exactly* what they are doing. It is amazing the strength of conviction of the ignorant. Everyone who has no idea of what I go through all the time are the ones convinced that it would be wrong of me to take my own life. What the *hell* would they know about it?

Do you remember when they banned dwarf throwing a few years ago and all of the dwarfs said: 'What? You're banning my livelihood? Why? Because it degrades me? Well thanks a lot you *bastards*! What the hell am I supposed to do now? Oh you *do* want me to be a burden on the Welfare State for the rest of my life? Thanks for *nothing*!' It happens all of the time. People think that they know how someone else feels but they never do. If you are not then you do not know! It *is* that simple. It is like when greedy children force their parents into homes with ulterior kindness: 'It would be much easier for you and *we* wouldn't worry so much. It is definitely best for everyone that we turf out of your home for the last thirty years so that we can live in it and you go to where all the other old loopies go.' Everyone looks down and abuses the enfeebled. God I *hate* this world!

But if I am healed I can *be* someone again! Once more I shall be 'the man that can' and stride about town doing things. Oh bugger this, anyone fancy a pint?

* * *

- Good morning Peter how's you?
- Rough! You're looking a little green around the gills yourself, how were the tiles?
- Ho, ho, ho! Green around the gills! I suppose you think that you are being funny?
- A touch snappy this morning young Jude?
- Just thirsty Peter. Thirsty days hath September, April, June and November. All the rest are thirsty too except for him who hath home brew!
- Very lyrical for this time of a morning. What was that? Byron?
- No it came from one of my Dad's mugs.
- We were talking about good drinking quotes the other day and I thought that you of all

people must know a few?

- Well there's the Dean Martin ones.

- We know all *those*.

- I do not know who said it but one of my favourites is: 'I love going out and getting drunk on one pint, normally the fifteenth!'

- That's very good.

- And there is a good W.C. Fields one as well: 'I always carry something to drink on me in case something happens like I see a snake, which I always keep handy too!' One can picture him shaking a rubber snake at himself whilst hammering the hip flask.

- Yes what a vision. Oh did I tell you that we have a special promotion on next week?

- Oh yes?

- A free pint of Harveys, every time it's not your round! Ha ha! Your face!

- That was pure and unadulterated cruelty.

- It can't be: 'Be Nice to Jude Day.' again can it? I thought that was last month.

- You should be nice to me all the time.

- In your dreams Buster.

- Hello Jude.

- Hello Andy this is a pleasant surprise.

- John said that he was meeting you here and I thought that I would come along for a pint. I hope you don't mind?

- Of course not my friend! Pas de tout and petite pois! Take a pew and what are you having?

- I'll have a Fosters please.

- If you must. A toast I feel. To the late and great Frank Muir and Malcolm Marshall.

- Cheers. To them.

- You look as if you have been working too hard again.

- Funnily enough I crashed out for twelve hours yesterday. I do that you know, I work God knows how much for a month or so and then sleep for a day.

- If it works it works although you are one of the few people of my own generation that looks as knackered as I do. Here comes John.

- 'Morning John what are you having?

- A wonderful time thank you!

- Oh God there are two of them! Meeting up for another touching and weeping session are we gentlemen?

- Just get me a bucket of rouge thank you Peter.

- You are picking up the scheme of things very well John.

- I'm a quick learner Jude. You look *terrible*!

- Now do not beat about the bush John you say it straight out! Say exactly what you mean without fear of repercussions as I can assure you that you are amongst friends, my friend.

- I'm sorry but you do, take it from an expert! Have a shave Jude, you would feel much better for it.

- Thank you John. Harsh realities sometimes need to be spoken. Thank you for reminding me of my own sloth, motes and beams and all of that sort of thing.

- Let me cheer you up Jude. Some say that one in the hand is better than one in the bush but I say that one in Kate Bush is better than ten in the hand!

- You know Andy I shall forever be grateful that my outrageous and lunatic parents do not drink in pubs.

- No kidding, he can be a nightmare!
- Oh I don't know Andrew you seemed to rather enjoy living with me.
- You put me off red wine and curry for the rest of my life!
- Do you remember the caviar vindaloo we had?
- It was foul!
- It was foul?
- I was *so* ill!
- God's broomstick gentlemen are you mad?
- You see Jude we have eaten our way through Red Dwarf.
- Oh yes I remember the party with the lobster vindaloo, that was years ago was it not? That was before you were even going out with Deborah and you fondled her on the scaffolding if I recall Andy?
- That's my boy!
- That was still a year before she did go out with me.
- It is amazing to think that your proud wife and mother of your delightful son was once the unpopular barmaid in the boozer!
- Jude!
- I know that you don't like Deborah Jude, *but*!
- Honestly my friend ignore me. I am just jealous really. You are one of the most successful of my peers and I believe that you will be a millionaire before you are thirty-five due to your flair and ability with the fishing net and programming.
- Thank you.
- I know that Deborah will never like me but that is completely understandable because she was *right*. I spent my time and money in boozers while you were out grafting and look at the difference.
- Don't be hard on yourself Jude.
- If I am not then who shall be?
- Look I've got to go.
- I shall see you soon Andy and please give my best to your loving wife.
- See you soon Andrew.
- 'Bye.
- So Jude how are you feeling this morning?
- Bag of nerves mate, bag of nerves. I keep going from zenith to nadir as I try to contemplate being healed whilst at the same time thinking that it could never happen. I need about fifteen Valium to get down to hysterical!
- That was a bit hard on Andrew.
- I know. No excuse. How are you doing?
- A lot better than yesterday thanks to you which is why *I* am going to help *you* today. Bearing in mind what you have planned for the day I need to ask you a very pertinent question. Are you a Christian?
- No. Are you?
- Yes.
- How nice for you.
- It has its moments. Have you been one?
- Oh yes from when I was born I suppose until I was seventeen.
- What happened?

- Lots of things really. It just seemed that life was so ironic and cruel with the worst possible thing happening to the worst possible person at the worst possible time. That happened time and time again and with the difficulties of adjusting to adult life and all of the nastiness that that involves I found it impossible to believe in a god of any description, especially one that seems to have caused so much suffering over the years. Northern Ireland, the Spanish Inquisition, Henry VIII, the Borgias, Mother Theresa, the list is endless and religion generally has been used to subjugate the masses and for political shenanigans for centuries. How could God let this happen?
- A difficult theological point I agree but what do you mean Mother Theresa?
- She was evil John.
- How?
- Well she started off very nicely by helping the poor and so on but then she preached Catholicism to them, especially the part about not using contraception to ensure that she had a job for life. That woman caused *thousands* of children to be born into poverty who would have been better of not existing. As for their poor mothers it does not bear contemplating.
- I wouldn't agree with you but carry on.
- Then of course I had my accident. The irony of it was torture but the worst thing that happened was little Ruth.
- Ruth?
- Yes the most significant of my former partners. When we meet she was twenty-three and I twenty-seven. We spent the day together with a group of friends and by the end of the evening she was in my bed. What a glorious day that was. I was older, cynical and spent all of my time reading and drinking and she was impressionable, intelligent and spent her time reading. It was a house on fire situation and she gave me a level of stability that reduced the drinking and I was quite happy for a while as both legs were working quite well at the time. Then disaster, two things at once. Ruth was the youngest daughter of a catholic family that had hammered into her the importance of not getting pregnant as they did not agree with abortion. In one month her father had a heart attack and she discovered that she was pregnant, there had been one night when she changed pill brands to a cheaper one.
- What did you do?
- Nothing.
- Nothing?
- She told no-one except her G.P., not me, not her parents not even any of her dizzy friends. She went through the whole thing alone since she knew that everyone else makes the decisions as far as abortions are concerned. By that point we had split up because I knew that something was wrong but I did not have the patience to find out what. I was an absolute bastard and dumped her in her time of need.
- But she didn't tell you?
- No which made it easy for me and hell for her. The irony was to the extent that she had the abortion on a Sunday when she knew that I would be in here with Zak, laughing, drinking and joking. She became a little unbalanced at that point.
- I'm not surprised. When did you find out?
- About a year later. We bumped into each other as one does in this town, had a drink together and she told me the whole sad story. We had a cry together and ended up in my bed again. We went out together for a second time and she dropped her boyfriend to do so but she had become very unstable and something of a lush, which with my being a complete hypocrite I

189

could not stand and that time lasted a month or so. We split up in January and I have not seen her since. It was situations like Ruth's that stopped me from believing in any god.
- Did you love her?
- Desperately but I was a fool. Apart from being bright, brave and caring she was also beautiful, blonde hair, amazingly kissable face with plenty of freckles and a body one only thinks exists in magazines. It would have been a beautiful child.
- Do you still feel the same about God?
- No I have mellowed since to a point of Agnosticism. I do not bother God and vice versa.
- Until now?
- Until now. Christianity is a very pleasant faith I think rather than an religion. Religion is institutionalised faith with all of the dogma, politics and pettiness that goes along with that but the original faith is very nice. In the words of Eddie Izzard: 'Jesus was groovy!' and taught decency, tolerance, communication, understanding, pacifism, humility, altruism, loyalty and so on.
- Yes Christianity is interesting in that most other religions have sets of rules that must be obeyed: 'You will go to the temple and wail against a wall every Saturday!' or whatever. Jesus gave us guidelines in a way that is almost existential.
- I have always thought that religion is essentially us being told to fight our instincts in the name of civilisation.
- What do you mean?
- Well it is human instinct to eat and most religions involve fasting and control over diet in some way. It is instinctive to have sex and procreate and all religions have strict rules on that one and it is utterly instinctive to be aggressive and control one's territory and most religions preach peace, at least in one's own community.
- That's interesting Jude. One of my degrees is in theology you know?
- Really? I am talking to the right man then.
- A touch of serendipity one might say.
- If you like. There are nice things about Christianity like that film with the explorer chappie who finds the Holy Grail and it turns out to be very modest and unassuming which is believable because that was what Jesus was supposed to be like. In an age when women were completely subjugated He was kind and egalitarian to those around him and theologians even argue about whether He was poor or not.
- Again another tricky theological point.
- Oh I think He had some money don't you? After all He did work as a carpenter for fifteen years or so and in those times that was an important position. Jesus was middle class and it would not surprise me in the slightest if He spent those years saving up for His ministry. Why did He call a tax collector? To balance the books one would think.
- What an intriguing idea.
- That is the thing, Jesus is one of the most enduring characters from history because He was so decent, obviously not a hypocrite and seemed to inspire thousands of people to follow Him just to listen. Obviously the miracles made excellent party pieces but it was His teaching that everyone was after. Remarkable really. I actually try to live my life according to His dictates even though I have stopped believing simply because the world would be a better place if everyone lived a Christian life, or as Christian lives are supposed to be which cuts out all of those foul Americans that are in it to get rich and screw beautiful women.
- Which is understandable.

- Is it? Being an utter shyte is understandable is it? Possibly I have not mellowed that much then but the main thing about Jesus was that He advocated equality which is my bee in bonnet because I am at the bottom of the heap in this world. That is very important to me.
- Are you sure you're not a Christian?
- Positive at this moment in time. In a few hours who knows?
- How would you define equality Jude?
- That one is easy. One needs to put a bit of work into it and travel around a lot to meet lots of people because when one has met all sorts of individuals from all manner of different cultures and subcultures one suddenly realises that within every group of people, no matter what demographics one works from, every culture has complete spooning muffins and innately delightful people. Anyone's appearance, gender or religion has *nothing* to do with the person that they really are. Equality is not treating everyone the same it is realising that we are all completely different and treating everyone appropriately and with *respect*. This is why insular communities are the bastions of ignorance and bigotry.
- That's not bad.
- It works for me. It is not just Negroes or whatever it is women and the elderly and the ugly and so on. It applies to the whole of the world's population whether they are one's neighbours or across the globe. In fact one could say that equality was the antithesis of sin.
- Interesting. What would you say the definition of Christianity is then Jude?
- I would liken it to the Freudian concept of the Superego. If one sees a purse unattended that one could swipe there is a little voice saying: 'Take it, take it!' but if one is a Christian there is also a voice saying: 'Take it to the police station so that it is returned to whomever is missing it.' which is why humility and altruism are such a major part of the faith.
- That's not bad.
- I do not think that the dogma is important even to the extent of the resurrection. When the Gospels seem to be constructed around parables it is slightly possible that the whole thing is a parable. Who knows? Surely it is the faith that actually matters and things like poverty, transubstantiation, even the Christmas story, lovely as it is, do not really *matter* and are certainly not worth arguing over. I see Christianity as being like cannabis.
- Cannabis? Why?
- Well lots of people take the stuff but some prefer weed, some solid, some slate, some skunk and so on. Each person has a preference as to how they express their belief in dope and their own dealer but they are all part of the overall cannabis system. In the same way I doubt if God cares which church one goes to as long as one believes.
- Are you sure that you're not a Christian?
- Yes.
- Cock-a-doodle-doo!
- Very funny! Actually that was quite witty John.
- I think that you are a Christian you know but you don't realise it yet.
- Well now is a good time to become one. I would like to believe in a heaven where I would be able to walk again.
- Is that what you think heaven is?
- Pretty much. I know that people argue over what heaven would be like with angels, clouds and harps and so on but I feel that it is a lot more simple than that.
- Really? Go on?
- This world is a very obvious mixture of good and evil is it not? There are salient examples of

both good and bad all around us and some would even say that there is good and bad in all of us in some sort of innate fashion. Well heaven is all of those good things and hell is full of the bad things. In heaven there would be no money, no pain, no inequality, no venereal diseases and so on. All of those things are in hell with the politicians and solicitors. Heaven is an unspoilt planet full of the good things like beer, women and books but hell is full of the bad things like gangsters, fear and heroin. It would be like that terrifying Scottish film what was it called?
- Which one?
- Pigeon Fancying or something. Hell would be like that, no hope or any way out from eternal meaninglessness but in heaven you would have tigers as pets because there is no hunger in heaven so they are docile. No colds, no banks and no failure just good things and humour.
- That's very sweet.
- I still can be on occasion. Only an agnostic could think that up do you not think?
- Indeed.
- That is the trouble that a lot of people have, the faith is lovely but the religion is quite disgusting. I was taught, as a catholic child about original sin which is one of the most *foul* concepts that I have ever heard of. I could not believe in a god that had such an unfair system. Are you trying to tell me that my aborted child is now in hell?
- Actually I disproved that theory when I was at university. When a baby is in the womb it has no *opportunity* to sin and a new-born is simply using the only method of communication that is available so that its insatiable demands cannot be deemed sinful. It is only as they grow older and communicative that any child could possible sin. A baby that dies goes straight to heaven.
- Thank you John, that was actually quite beautiful. This is what I mean about the faith being great. My brother James is starting to return to some sort of belief because of his work.
- What is he?
- An X-ray Crystallographer which means that he studies the basis of compounds and so on. I am not that knowledgeable about his work unfortunately. He produced a book a few years ago and I had difficulty finding a word that I could read but there is so much around us that screams: 'Divine influence!' Why is it that the moon and earth are exactly the right size, distance apart and on orbits that produce eclipses? I do not know. When I used to sail a lot it always struck me how wonderful nature is and how easy it is to have pantheistic thoughts. I survive in many ways on humour which is a gift from God surely? He must have invented it which is why it makes me laugh when people decide to be offended by religious jokes. I am sure that He loves to hear inventive humour and I am sure that Jesus has a favourite joke.
- Go on let's have a Jude religious joke.
- I am not sure that would be completely wise at this juncture although the thing that made me laugh most recently was a joke from Red Dwarf.
- I love Red Dwarf.
- It is wonderful is it not? There was a news broadcast or something which said that the first page of the Bible had been found on Mount Ararat. It said: 'To Candy with all my love. All characters in this publication are fictitious and any resemblance to real persons, living or dead, is purely coincidental!'
- I like it.
- That was a fantastic joke although it could not just have been the first page as there would be about ten pages listing the reprints, originally published by The Sinai Press! I am sure that the

Christian God would find that hilarious and I bet He loves Life of Brian as we all do.

- Did I ever tell you about the Red Dwarf sound man that Andy and I high jacked one night?

- No?

- We were having a drink in the Hand and there was a chap sitting there by himself. You know me I just started talking to him and it transpired that he was in town for Songs of Praise the next day. We asked him what else he had worked on and he said: 'Red Dwarf.' and that was it! We took him back home, fed him lobster curry and lager and made him watch lots of the videos. The poor man eventually staggered back to his B & B at about three in the morning! God only knows how he felt during Songs of Praise!

- How absolutely wonderful! Was he grateful?

- It was hard to tell as he was having problems with language generally when he left!

- Brilliant! But John what is the point of arguing over silly points that do not have much relevance to the actual faith? These people who insist that the Bible should be believed word for word have obviously not read the bit about women having to sacrifice two doves every period and I would bet that even if they have they do not try and enforce it! In a lot of ways the Bible is a guide to sexism and St. Paul must be the world's most widely published misogynist.

- Actually he was very progressive. As you pointed out women were treated very badly during those times to the extent that they weren't much better treated than slaves. St. Paul managed to have them accepted as equals in Christ to a very large extent. In many ways he did more for women than all of the twentieth century feminists put together.

- Not a pleasant thought. I would not be comfortable at that party! I never realised that about St. Paul but that does highlight one of the crucial things about the Bible that it should be taken in historical context.

- I think you have a point about people becoming bogged down in the minutiae, it is very much a wood for the trees situation. The important thing about Christianity is that it brings hope and meaning into people's lives.

- I could do with a little bit of hope as my reserves are running very low. One does say though that certain things are gifts from God like humour, love, beer, women and cannabis in fact all of the things that I love.

- Cannabis?

- Absolutely it is a *major* gift from God! A plant that grows naturally from which one can make rope, paper, scaffolding, clothes and so on plus it makes one feel really rather nice! Believe me mate there are a few thousands people around like me that could not cope with life without cannabis.

- What does it do for you?

- Well I would not be able to sleep without it.

- Does it help insomnia?

- Oh yes in fact have you ever met Zak's mother?

- No?

- A few years ago she was suffering with insomnia and I got some grass for her. That afternoon we all sat out in her patio and had a smoke or several. Normally she is very quiet but on this occasion she was rabbiting away like a good 'un and after a while she stood up and said: 'I don't know about you lot but I'm very hungry. This stuff doesn't seem to be working!' She has been sleeping soundly since.

- How old is she?

- In her sixties I think. It is never too late to be introduced to the joys of dope my friend in fact

193

if you are suffering from insomnia I shall come round and have a smoke with you one night if you like?

- I think I would actually. I rarely get more than four hours.

- No problem at all John, I shall get some decent grass sorted out and we can have a smoke in. When one considers that it still grows wild at the roadside in Israel it begs an interesting question does it not?

- Does it really?

- Oh yes and always has done. It would throw a little light on the Book of Revelations do you not think?

- Yes it would. So cannabis is a gift from God as are women?

- Oh absolutely! Is there anything in the world that affects a man more than a beautiful woman? Empires have been won and lost because of a wondrous face. Every day throughout the world men are making fools of themselves because of love. What is that wonderful expression, I would walk five miles on my knees over broken glass just to see her smile.

- Where does that come from?

- The heart of course! Some bloke said it in a boozer one time although he used something a little less prosaic than 'smile'.

- Ah.

- Yes do not ask. Do you know that joke about two blokes arguing in a pub about God's profession?

- No?

- One of them was an artist and insisted that God is similar: 'When you look at those perfect lines that all focus in upon that most sacred place that makes a woman a woman.' and so on. The other chap is an architect and argued God follows his calling: 'How such a fragile looking creature can withstand the agonies of childbirth.' et cetera. The barman was listening and disagreed: 'If anything God is a town planner.' he said. 'A town planner?' the artist and architect protest. 'Of course.' continued the barman, 'Who else would put a leisure centre right next to a sewage farm!'

- That's a bit naughty.

- I know! But yes the lovely things of this world are gifts from God. Why do so many Christians not drink? As I recall the first miracle was the Wedding at Cana when He turned water into wine and one finds the wine motif all the way through the Gospels. In fact the Last Supper was the first ever cocktail party.

- What?

- Think about it. Not enough to drink and feeble eaty things, it was the first cocktail party hence the joke about Judas going to the off licence as he was the only one with any money!

- That is outrageous and very funny.

- The drink is still lacking at most cocktail parties.

- I accept that your favourite things in life might be considered gifts from God as you put it but you are missing the real benefits of Christianity in that it wipes away the fear of death and gives meaning to the deaths of loved ones. It is *so* powerful in one's life not to fear death.

- As you know John I have not feared death for some time in fact I look upon death as a relief whenever it eventually becomes my turn but is not that being a bit negative about the faith?

- What do you mean?

- Well there are other benefits that enrich life rather than make fearful things less so. Surely Christianity opens up a whole new way of thinking, I mean why do people consider faiths incompatible? As far as I can remember Jesus did not touch on the subject of reincarnation for example.

- Reincarnation? That's completely unbiblical.
- Why? The theory by itself makes no sense at all. What is the point of leading a succession of lives when one cannot remember a damn thing from one to another? However if you mix that theory with the catholic one about purgatory then it might make sense.
- How?
- To atone for sins of one life one comes back as something appropriate in another. I know that it all sounds a bit Cliff Toddle but I would not be surprised if I was Judas in a former life, it certainly feels like it sometimes.
- I would sincerely doubt it Jude.
- So would I but it is a thought is it not? What about the three wise men in the Christmas story? What were they? They must have been astronomers and I would wager they were into astrology as well. Possibly there is something in it?
- I believe if there was we would know about it.
- Why? You Christians do not even know when He was actually *born*! How on earth can you be so smug about anything else?
- You have a point.
- Another thing, if you are a Christian it makes the possibility of aliens more feasible.
- Why?
- Think about it. If God made the world in six days about ten thousand years ago, according to some then what hobbies has He had to while away the hours since? Granted things here have come to a major cliff-hanger situation as far as humans are concerned but He must want to change the channel occasionally! I am convinced that He has made a myriad of worlds like ours which only begs the question of where do we fit into the scheme of things? How advanced are *we*?
- Not particularly.
- Possibly. It turns out that the world is a hint older than previous guesses by a few billion years or so and that the universe has apparently been knocking around for a few million billion years. That is a lot of leisure time for a God that makes worlds in six days so there must be other sentient worlds out there somewhere and I can prove my point.
- Go on I am very intrigued?
- The answer is macslime burgers which might sound strange but embrace the two concepts together, God and aliens. It is like in A Hitchhiker's Guide to the Galaxy when the visiting alien adopts the most common name on earth in order to fit in and becomes Ford Prefect.
- Jude that is fiction.
- I know, I know but follow the logic. What has happened is that God-fearing aliens have been visiting this planet as a matter of interest for a long time as is seen by the pyramids and Stonehenge and so on. A recent visit brought amusement to the alien fraternity as a whole after a simple misunderstanding. They arrived at the planet and made an analysis of what was the most popular food on earth and the answer was a macslime burger. At some point recently two aliens visited one of those places, bought two burgers and were highly disappointed which let us face it we *all* are. The last time I was collar-dragged into one of those dens of mediocrity I apparently acted against the norm. Having acquired the alleged 'food' I bade my diminutive companion to sit down and wait as I ascended the macstairs, entered the macgents and the maccubicle to deposit my macburger down the macloo thus cutting out the macmiddle man. I

returned to my maccompanion and having ascertained that he had indeed found his minuscule, sweatshop produced, immediately implodable plastic 'jolly toy' I deposited his macmeal in the mac-break-your-fingers-bin and we went to the pub for something to eat.

- Very wise.

- So like all of us the aliens were a little confused over the popularity of the stuff: 'If this is the most popular food on the planet why does it taste like shyte?' 'I don't know Djgfsfg we could try Chicken Tikka Masala?' 'No, no Kskegej we must not give up on our research. We must be doing something wrong. In the data banks it mentions another method of preparation called a Barbecue!' So your aliens tried to recreate the burger from the beginning of the process. They knew that burgers were made from bits of cows so they found the most cow-dense area of the planet hoping that one or two would not be missed. They beamed down to Texas and collected the needed bits, the hooves, the tail, the lips, the bollocks because yes chaps *that* is what burgers are made from! We shall not even talk about 're-claimed meat' it is so *disgusting*. 'This is the simple explanation for bovine mutilation Mully.' 'But what about the sheep that have been mutilated Scolder?' 'Maybe they are trying shepherd's pie Mully!' At which point I ought to be off.

- Would you like some moral support?

- No thank you John I had better do this alone.

- Shall I wait here for you?

- I should not worry. The service does not start for another half an hour and it is bound to go on for ever. I shall let you know.

- What are you going to do if it doesn't work?

- I shall come back here and get absolutely hog-whimperingly drunk.

- You'd do that anyway wouldn't you?

- Who knows what a merciful God has planned? The fact is John that this quite reminiscent of that old story about the two tribes on a desert island.

- What story's that then?

- It is an old mind teaser or whatever they are called. You are on a desert island and you have to get to the other side quickly as Ursula Andress is just coming back from her swim or something. On the way you come to a fork in the road and do not know which direction to take. Sitting by the fork is a member of one of the two indigenous tribes but there is a catch. One tribe only tells the truth whilst the other only ever lies and there is no way of telling them apart. What question should you ask the native who is sitting there?

- I ask which direction would he tell me to go in if he were a member of the other tribe and then take the other route?

- That's the one. Whatever happens today will give me the direction for the rest of my pitiful life because if I do not get healed I shall never be able to believe in *anything* ever again.

- That's a bit harsh isn't it?

- It is part of the deal.

- Should I say good luck?

- I would imagine: 'Mend a leg!' would be more appropriate.

- Mend a leg Jude.

- Thank you John. See you later. 'Bye Peter.

- Tara.

* * *

I hate hills! I am glad that John was around it has steadied my nerves as much as the several pints. Well I do not know *what* I am doing but I am doing it. It is odd the way I have not even contemplated not going to this church today at the appointed hour. That must say something about me although whether it is single-mindedness or bloody-mindedness is open to question.

This is one of those very deceptive streets that although one can say: 'Oh it is just down the road.' it takes one forever to get there. Where is this damn place? I can see cars pulling up and people greeting each other so it must be close. Here we are. First thing to do is sit on this little wall, have a smoke and watch all of the God-botherers. They really are a self-satisfied looking bunch of muffins. I am not ashamed of being middle class but these people flaunt it. Jesus said: Pick up thy cross and follow me.' but the only cross these people have is taking the Volvo for an M.O.T.! Why I am being instinctively antagonistic to them? Probably because they look happy and contented. I am *envious*.

By the look of things it is nearly time so put out the ciggie and get inside. For once I was not pushed as I made my way into the building. To call it a church would be stretching the imagination somewhat it is more like a leisure centre than anything. A nice lady was kind enough to point me to the lift as the meeting is on the second floor apparently. That will cut down on the cigarette breaks! I followed the slow but purposeful flow of people into the main room which was surprisingly large and buzzing with anticipation. I sat down near the entrance which had become the exit and avoided the stares which were surprisingly few. This is obviously a time to be surprised. All around me people were greeting and hugging one another and the air was vibrating with the warmth of three hundred people being nice to each other.

I had completely forgotten that feeling. Oh sure Pink Floyd at Wembley was impressive but *that* was reaction and *this* is interaction. It is amazing to be surrounded by pure and unadulterated goodwill. I should have brought a spliff. Why did I leave all of this? Oh that's right, a smug *bastard* and the lure and allure of vice. I felt that I was too innocent being a Christian. Well now I am back and not so innocent in fact I am guilty as charged with eleven other counts to be taken into consideration! I managed a rakish look over the top of my walking stick at an impressionable looking girl with a navel ring and a, good *Lord* she blushes easily! If there were a world championship in blushing she would at least get to the semi-finals! It is one of the few sports at which England could still dominate the world I feel.

Mind you the state that I must look at the moment would make a statue blush with full eye contact! It is very difficult to remove green body paint from underneath eight days of stubble and I was not shaving for *anyone* this morning. If Joanna Lovely had asked me to shave this morning the answer would still have been no! I would have shaved for a bottle of malt mainly because my hands have started to go again and I cannot *handle this*.

I'll say one thing for this church, it is good place to cry as no-one seems to notice or be bothersome. What *are* they doing? They are either praying or comparing deodorants. Their eyes have closed so it might be the deodorants. If they are that bad I had better pray too, I might look like shyte but at least I am fragrant of a June afternoon. Sure Jude, Eau de Harveys et Marlboro, *sensational darling*!

197

I think that one is being a hint superior and judgmental. The truth is that these people are happier than I have been for many years and it is annoying me for no good reason. Look on the bright side Jude, being a Christian could be fun and being healed would be *cool*. It is interesting that John is a theologian since apart from being a media superstar and giving away lots of money when I am healed I could have great theological and philosophical discussions with him. Questions like why can guide dogs be incredibly communicative using a range of senses but even though dogs have been around for millions of years they have never shown the slightest interest in being able to talk as we know it? In fact very few animals are interested in chatting and we do not have a *clue* what whales talk about. I fact I have not the faintest idea what the Welsh talk about! I like talking about stuff like that as it tends to be a lot less depressing than politics or current affairs. What isn't?

We would talk about life the universe and *everything*. If God allowed us to discover things like fossils which actually helped disprove the flood story and hence the majority of Genesis, why is it that no-one has yet been able to absolutely disprove the authenticity of the Turin Shroud although it is highly dubious because of the positions of the hand holes? But there again there is only one piece of physical evidence that the practice of crucifixion existed at all and *that* is a bent nail. Life is interesting.

There it is again that feeling which seems to live in this place, a feeling of... I do not know. These ordinary looking people that are leaping around the place and singing about: 'The blood of the lamb.' apparently, seem to have something. It must be a song about a really good Chinese meal.

But the other angle is the things that God has not let us discover or understand, like how the brain actually works which is still a major mystery to one and all as is the so-called 'secret of life' that we all search for. Except me of course. Why on earth anyone would imagine that life is so wonderful it is worth a quest for the Holy Grail to discover immortality? Eternal life on this hell hole? I would rather eat me feet! But I am becoming morose again and I should be awaiting and preparing for healing and spiritual resurrection. It might be an idea to pay attention to what is going on.

They are having a sort of personal private moment at the moment and they are speaking in tongues. Good old speaking in tongues, there is nothing quite like it to make one feel very *spiritual*. It is strange that these people believe in a God that communicates through the heart, soul and mind but they are impressed by these strange words that actually sound as if they are all reading aloud from an Israeli 'phone book!

I suppose I could get used to this again. *Just* but I am definitely not giving up drinking and smoking, talking of which it is definitely time for some fresh air. What are they up to now? Everyone is sitting down so I would not miss anything except giving them my money. I saw some buckets being produced as people reached for their pockets so now is the time to be scarce. Is there a correlation between how rich a church is and how ugly the building?

Out the door, along the corridor to the lift which is not here. *Why* do they have to have their fucking meetings on the second floor? Do they *know* how frustrating that makes life for a disabled nicotine fiend? Do they fucking *care*? I doubt it. Here is the lift, ground floor thank you, out of the lift, along another corridor past the gents, remember that, through the foyer with three strange looks to the very heavy and cumbersome doors and the little wall outside for a lung full of smoke. *Bliss*! I wonder how long I have been in there?

What the *hell* am I doing here? You want to be healed and a Christian again. Oh right.

It is a strange thing this Christianity lark. All the people in there look so smug and I would wager that they do not buy many copies of the Big Issue each week but *that* is bigotry. Think of the Christians that you have known Jude. Peter spent the last night of his life with a priest and was greatly comforted apparently. Good old Jolly John is still ferrying little old ladies to and from church in his minibus by all accounts and of all the people I have talked to this week John was the only one with a real problem and the only one to help and support me. He is a Christian. Right then back to the *fun*.

Thinking about it, which church I actually go to once healed was not discussed. Anyhow one can be a Christian on a desert island so I would not have to put up with these people. Oh come on you are being too hard on these lovely chaps, I am sure that they are delightful once one gets to know them. There must be a drinking partner in here somewhere.

What there is in here is a chap in front of me in a wheelchair. I must talk to him.
- Hello. I hope that I am not disturbing you?
- No not at all.
- Hi my name is Jude.
- I'm Chris.
- Hello Chris. Tell me are you a Christian?
- Yes Jude.
- But you are in a chair?
- I know.
- What is your prognosis if you would excuse my rudeness.
- M.S.
- Shit! That is rough.
- Yes. I have lost my business, my wife and kids and of course my mobility.
- But you are a Christian?
- Yes. Jesus has given me more in disability than I ever had in life.
- Which is what exactly?
- Love and acceptance.
- Right.
- You're not a Christian are you Jude?
- Nope.
- Jesus heals you know.
- So they say. Thank you for your time Chris and Good luck mate.
- I hope to see you again Jude.

I had to get away from him as I need to cry. It always dents the self-pity when one meets someone worse off.

Shit! What *am* I doing here? Here comes the sermon, pay attention. Blessings apparently, how *delightful*! Essentially this chap is exhorting these people to be kinder and more Christian and they are all agreeing. Why is it that he has not mention the Beatitudes and why are they all saying that they do not do what I do every day? There is something screwy going on here. In fact I do not want to listen to this and it is time for another, less rushed smoke. Door, corridor...

Smoke. God I could do with a pint or several. Right then Jude it is coming to crunch time are you ready? Well I am wearing a baggy tee shirt and shorts so that there is room to grow if I am to go back to how I was. I am here and I am putting up with a self satisfied sermon that is making me more nauseous than a school dinner. Look I am willing to do anything just *fucking heal me would you*! I cannot go on like this. The pain is too much.

Right back inside. I wonder how many of *this* lot give blood regularly? That poor chap in the wheelchair how does he cope? At least I have some level of mobility, I could not handle being in a chair. Here I am doing exactly what I detest in other people. Why is religion always associated with guilt? What do I have to feel guilty about? Lots of things.

Well it looks as if it is all over as everyone is getting up and looking relieved. I used to hate those sermons that went on for hours. I still do and that was *really* dull.

- Excuse me?
- Hello.
- Would you mind if we prayed for you?
- No go ahead.
- What's your name?
- Jude.
- Dear Jesus we thank You for Your love and kindness and the fellowship we have had today. We ask You now to look upon your friend Jude. We ask You to forgive him his sins and to show Yourself to him in all of Your glory. Take pity upon him and show him that only through You is life meaningful and joyous. We ask You to heal him of his ailments and bring him to happiness in Your glorious name. Skaravank messash belendigo meriash.
- Thank you Jesus please come to Jude.
- Dear Lord show your face and majesty to Jude. Glorienca te himinous keras.
- Thank you Jesus, thank you Jesus, thank you Jesus.

Nothing.

- How are you feeling Jude?
- I am all right thank you.
- Have a tissue.
- Thank you. How *did* you know Holmes?
- Hi Jude.
- Thank you all. Hello Chris.
- Did you enjoy the service?
- Not particularly, there are pubs open.

- I think that you will find that Jesus is more refreshing than beer.
- So you say.
- There is a welcoming meeting downstairs for first timers would you like to go?
- Yes please.
- It is just by the front door. I hope to see you again Jude.
- You never know Chris. Thank you.

Right then. Calm down and get yourself together, if you are not careful your make up will run! Go and find this meeting and someone that might heal you. Through the door, along the corridor, bloody great queue for the lifts, try the stairs, they have bannisters thank God, do not fuss just get out of my way thank you *so* much!

- Hello I'm Andy.
- Hello Andy I am Jude. Would you do me an enormous favour?
- If I can.
- Wonderful. Is there someone in the congregation or around the place somewhere that is known to have the Gift of Healing?
- I could probably find someone.
- If you would I shall be sitting over there.

If at first you do not succeed and all of that. I did feel a warmth in my leg when that lot were praying for me or is that my imagination? I wish that I could stop crying as I am getting bored with having to clean my glasses. I feel *awful*. I wish this was over with. If you are going to heal me just *fucking* hurry up all right!

- Hello Jude this is Mel and this is Stephen.
- Hello Mel and Stephen.
- Hi Jude. We are going to pray for your healing as I imagine you would like?
- Yes please Stephen.
- Before we can we need to know what is wrong with you.
- All right. Excuse me.
- That's O.K. Jude you take your time.
- From the bottom up, the bones in my foot are shot and hurt terribly, there is only ten per cent potential movement in my ankle but there is no movement below my knee and that part of my leg is dying, the ligaments in my knee are not any more, my hip girdle is knackered and painful, my spine is twisting to the right and the vertebrae are fusing and my neck is almost locked solid. Other than that I am fine!
- O.K. Jude we will pray for you. Mel here was in a wheelchair until eight months ago.
- That's right Jude, Jesus can and does heal.
- Goodo.
- Dear Jesus we ask You to take pity on Jude here. We ask You to bring Your salvation and healing upon him and take away his pain. We ask You to loosen his foot and bring back movement to his leg. We ask You to straighten his hips and his spine. We ask You to help him stand up and walk again. We banish any evil spirits within him and make him whole as You intended.

Please?

- Yes Jesus we pray that You will bring Your spirit of healing upon Jude and show him that You are a loving and healing God. Take away his disability and suffering and bring him back to the health that he used to know. Havebhosma tey manfhuatred...

Please? PLEASE!

- Gerthabdsoth hos in ferunthmapit...

Nothing.

- Well Jude God will heal you in His own time.
- Don't give up it can take a while.
- Thank you both very much.
- Goodbye Jude.
- Goodbye Jude.
- See ya.

Well that is that then. Back to the pub. I cleaned up my nose and eyes and hobbled to the exit. Hang on I have a better idea. Back to the gents, no-one around, good, into the cubicle, it is nice and clean and one big, fat line of charlie. *Fantastic*! Now it is time to go hobble, hobble, hobble! As I left the church with happy and oblivious people milling around me I realised something. Not one of those *caring* people had given me a contact number or asked me for one. *They actually did not give a damn.* Well to hell with the lot of them and life generally.

Jesus answered him, 'It is also written: "Do not put the Lord your God to the test."'
Matthew 4:7